"IN THE BEST OF THE NORAH LOFTS TRADITION OF SKILL AND EXCITEMENT"

—*Buffalo Courier Express*

✻

"A ROMANTIC NOVEL SKILLFULLY DONE . . . AN INTRIGUING TALE"

—*Fort Wayne Journal Gazette*

✻

"A MASTERFUL JOB"

—*Wilmington, Del., News*

✻

"AN IMMENSELY READABLE NOVEL"

—*New Haven Register*

✻

"A SUSPENSE-FILLED STORY"

—*Springfield Sunday News Reader*

Fawcett Crest Books
by Norah Lofts:

☐ THE DAY OF THE BUTTERFLY   24359 $2.95

☐ THE HAUNTING OF GAD'S HALL   24272 $2.25

☐ JASSY   24101 $1.95

☐ NETHERGATE   23095 $2.50

☐ SCENT OF CLOVES   22977 $2.50

☐ TO SEE A FINE LADY   22890 $2.25

NETHERGATE

Norah Lofts

FAWCETT CREST • NEW YORK

NETHERGATE

THIS BOOK CONTAINS THE COMPLETE TEXT OF
THE ORIGINAL HARDCOVER EDITION.

Published by Fawcett Crest Books, a unit of CBS Publi-
cations, the Consumer Publishing Division of CBS Inc., by
arrangement with Doubleday & Company, Inc.

ISBN: 0-449-23095-3

Printed in the United States of America

First Fawcett Crest Printing: March 1974

15   14   13   12   11   10   9   8   7   6

❖ ❖

Narrative by Martha Pratt.

(1740–1793)

Poor people don't set much store by birthdays and I never knew the day or the month when I was born. The year I can get fairly close to by reckoning back. Mother always said I was three and a bit when Tom was born, and she knew that she had him the year Top Farm changed hands and they were worried about whether the new man, Mr. Rowe, would keep Father on. Father's old master was named Mason and he's in the churchyard at Ockley, under a stone that says he died in April 1743, so Tom was born that year, we know. Whether I was born late in 1739 or early in 1740 depends on what Mother called "a bit." Not that it matters.

I was the first-born and I had advantages. Three and a bit years to grow in. Father earned sometimes eight, sometimes seven, shillings a week and a quartern loaf was ninepence even then, but Mother was young and lively; she could dig the garden behind our clod cottage so we were never short of potatoes and onions and cabbages, and she could do any job that offered, indoors or outdoors. So I had a good start. If I've told myself that once I have a thousand times.

I was three and a bit when Tom was born; three and a bit more when Mother got an outside job picking stones in a field which Mr. Rowe, who had kept Father on after all, had just brought under the plough. We took Tom with us, wrapped in a shawl and I was set to mind him, but he went to sleep and needed no minding. I remember as clear as day, looking at Mother, toiling away and thinking that I could pick stones too. So I started and when Tom woke and howled and Mother had to stop and feed him, I went on. Going home in the dusk, Mother said, "You been a real help, Martha," and I was pleased and proud. That day we'd earned sixpence. That day I started my working life.

Tom didn't have the time I did. Almost before he could walk there was a new baby, Sally; and another, Mary; then two who died and after that William and George. My poor mother just went downhill and got into a muddle that she never got out of.

Tom fell to me. I was his sister, three and a bit years older, but all my life I've felt more like a mother to him. Or perhaps, in those distant days, he was to me as dolls are to some children. I know that when I got my first *paid* job, which was rook-scaring, I took him with me. He was a pretty little boy and always so good.

When I went out to work *properly* I couldn't take him with me because my first real job, when I was eight, was in Mrs. Rowe's dairy where I scrubbed floors and shelves, and scalded pans and tools and fetched water from the pump and pounded salt. I still slept in my muddled home and whenever Mrs. Rowe, who was kind, gave me, in addition to my shilling a week, a bit of cold pudding, or stale cake, half a sausage, I'd take it home and make a little sign to Tom and give him whatever it was. Unfair to the others? Maybe. But, I still hold, sensible, since so little, divided amongst so many, would have been useless.

Then the time came when I must find a living-in job. I was twelve, Sally was eight, about ready to take over where I had begun in the dairy at Top Farm. So I went to work, odd-job girl, at the Grammar School at Baildon. To me a really wonderful job, three pounds a year and my keep.

The school needed girls quick and nimble on their feet—sixty beds to be made, sixty chamber pots to empty, sixty ewers to be filled. And all pretty briskly, because there was kitchen work as well. Youth was needed and yet youth was suspect, only plain girls could be employed there, and even then . . . My fellow toiler, Daisy, was squint-eyed, I was simply plain, but there were rules. Daisy and I had to get the beds made and the pots emptied while the boys were at their prayers; we swept and dusted the dining room and the common room while they were at lessons, and the classrooms while they had supper. We used a separate entrance; we slept in an attic on the far side of the house.

It suited me very well. I had no need of a boy, or a man in my life. I had Tom. I did resent, in a way, the fact that my wages, sent home, complete except for the times when my shoes had to be mended or renewed, must be shared by all in that cluttered cottage at Ockley. I also resented the fact that I never saw Tom. He was in Ockley, I was in Baildon, a mere five miles away but it might have been a hundred. Sam Lockey ran his carrier cart, his carrier service between the two places twice a week, but he charged a shilling, and if I went to Ockley where should I sleep? However, though I couldn't see Tom I was always on the lookout for something to send him. The boys at the school often flung quite good clothes away. I used to save whatever I could collect until I had a big bundle, because Sam Lockey had a stupid rule that you must pay sixpence a parcel whatever the size.

I was fourteen when the woman who helped the cook and did the marketing had a little accident and I was sent to do it. Things like meat and flour, sugar and oatmeal were always bought in bulk and delivered to the school, but butter and greenstuff were cheaper on the market. I was a good shopper. I walked all around the market comparing the prices and the quality before buying, and the cook was so pleased with what I took back that day that after then I always went to the market on Wednesday and Saturday. I hoped that one day I would see somebody from Ockley who perhaps had seen Tom, but somehow I never did. Still it was nice to get out twice a week and I hoped that if the cook continued to be pleased with me she might let me watch her and help her and learn something; for I could see that the only way for a girl like me to better herself and get away from the pots and the bedmaking was to become a cook. I was ambitious even in those days.

One morning when I set out with the two great baskets which, when filled, would have made a fair load for a donkey, I heard a tapping on a window. I looked and saw a little woman, beckoning. She opened the window and said she'd seen me going into the market regularly and wondered if I'd do an errand or two for her as she was getting so very lame. She asked me nicely, in a soft gentle voice, so I said I would if she didn't want anything very big or heavy, since I always came back with as much as I could carry. She only wanted a few eggs and a little tea and sugar. After that I always called at the house to ask if she wanted anything, and presently we became friends.

Her name was Miss Raker and for most of her life she had been a lady's maid. When she was past work her mistress had bought her the pretty little cottage in which she lived and pensioned her off. She asked me about my free time. It was Sunday, between dinner and supper, but I had never taken much notice of it. I had nowhere to go; the shops were all closed; the time was too short to allow me to walk to Ockley and back. I generally spent Sunday afternoon washing and mending and wishing I could read. Miss Raker asked me to tea with her and that was quite an experience. Everything, even her teacups were so pretty. It was in her cottage, so neat, so clean, so quiet, at the table spread with a white lacy cloth, that I had my first glimpse of a completely different way of life.

She talked a lot about the past. She had had an exciting life, in London, in Bath, in great houses where she had stayed with her mistress. My ambition began to shift. One Sunday I said to her, "I should like to be a lady's maid."

Miss Raker said, "You'd have a lot to learn."

"Learn me, please," I said.

"I will begin at once. I will *teach* you. You will *learn*."

She taught me for the next six years. Every Sunday afternoon, and, more often, during the school holidays since then we looked only to work—scrubbing floors and walls and benches and desks in the mornings and having the afternoons free. Miss Raker said I was very teachable, and as imitative as a monkey. She said I must learn to read and write, as well as all the other things; a lady's maid must be able to read the recipe for making a cosmetic preparation, and to write the label for it. She taught me how to wash and mend delicate fabrics, how to iron them; how to shampoo and dress a lady's hair. Some things were difficult at first because my hands were so rough from hard work, but Miss Raker made me some hand cream and gave me a pair of gloves to wear in bed.

I repaid her as well as I could, doing her shopping and later, as she grew lamer, doing cleaning work which she could no longer do easily. I chopped her kindling, split logs, carried in coal.

In all this time I went home once. Miss Raker had been ill, and every morning, before my ordinary work began at six, and every evening when I should have been having my supper, I ran to her house and did what there was to be done. When she recovered she said she wanted to give me a treat, what should it be? I spoke the dearest wish of my heart and said, "To see my brother, Tom." As soon as I had said it I knew that it sounded as though I did not care about the rest of my family. "And my parents and the rest of them," I added quickly. Miss Raker said she would hire a conveyance for me and that I must ask for a whole day off. I chose a Sunday; I was about eighteen then, so Tom would be about fifteen and out at work all week—if work was to be had. I did not realise that the man who drove the cart charged double on Sundays.

I'd been away for six years; Mary, William, and George did not recognise me; Sally was not there, she had just gone to a living-in job at Ockley Manor and Mary had started work in Mrs. Rowe's dairy. My parents both looked terribly old and kind of hopeless. There were no babies now to be cleaned up after, but the place was even more cluttered and it stank, of onions and cabbage, of boiled salt pork, and of too many people whose bodies and clothes were insufficiently washed.

My poor mother burst into tears at the sight of me—she thought I'd come home because I'd lost my job! I hastily explained that this was not so and she said, "Thank God, thank God! How we should manage without what you send, I don't know."

I knew, from doing the marketing, that prices were going up all the time, while wages were not. I still had my keep and now four pounds a year and knew perfectly well that if I asked for more I'd get the sack and my place would be filled by somebody only too willing to earn what I did.

Tom was the only one who seemed really pleased to see me for myself. He'd grown less than I had thought—far less than I had—and I realised that most of the cast-off clothes I had sent home lately had been too big for him. He was small and thin, but he still had the pretty curly hair and the long eyelashes and the sweet, gentle expression which had endeared him to me. At fifteen he was doing a man's work, but at a boy's wage, three shillings a week.

William and George, now aged ten and nine, were entirely unlike Tom, loud-voiced, rough-mannered, and Mary hated Mrs. Rowe who had always seemed kind to me and who had,

9

in fact, fitted me out with the made-over clothes which I had taken with me to Baildon. "She's allust on at me," Mary said. "I can't do nothing right for her." Mary also said, when I opened the bundle I had brought, that it was a pity I didn't work in a girl's school, then she'd have got something.

All in all a dismal visit, but Tom who, after all, was the one I had come to see, said two things which I carried away with me, like treasures.

"I've often thought, Martha, of walking in of a Sunday, just to see you, but it's a long way and hard on the boot leather."

And: "I think of you, Martha, odd times. I look at that bank with the primroses, and when there's the bluebells in Layer Wood, I call to mind how you liked them."

I called the flowers to mind, too, and how, as a little boy, he'd simply pull a flower off by its head and offer it to me; and how I had shown him how a flower should be picked, and how after a session of stone-picking or crow-scaring we'd go home with bunches of flowers into that muddly cottage with babies being sick, or dirty in the other way, and always so noisy.

I said, "Tom, I think of you, every day. You and I are going to get out of *this*." He and I were outside the cottage then, walking towards the waiting cart. "I've learned such a lot, Tom. I'm going to be a lady's maid one day. Lady's maids have a lot of influence. I'll get you a nice job. An indoor job, footman, valet." Miss Raker's talk had made me familiar with such terms and with the fact that one could still be a servant and live like a lord. Many of her stories were concerned with precedence in the housekeeper's room, or the servants' hall, and with the way in which she, "a word in her ladyship's ear was enough," had made a ploughboy a footman, a footman a butler. What she had done, surely I could do.

"We'll do it, Tom. One day," I said.

So then I was twenty and Miss Raker said, "Martha, you now know all I have to teach. I think you should begin to look about for a post. I will help you to the best of my ability. I shall begin to write around. I am positive that anyone whom I can recommend so warmly . . . But, oh dear, how I shall miss you. Still, I must not be selfish."

She said that on the Sunday. Bright and early on the Wednesday morning I knocked on her rose-arched door, awaiting her market order. I no longer cared whether what she asked me to bring was light or heavy; I was so grateful to her that if she'd asked me to fetch a ton of something, I'd have done it, bit by bit. She did not come to the door, so I knocked again, more loudly, and then used the key which she had given me that time when she was ill. She was more ill now; in fact by the time I had run full pelt to Doctor Stamper and brought him back, she was dead.

Except for those two babies who came between Mary and William and could hardly have been said to have lived at all, I had never seen anybody dead. Looking at Miss Raker, such a power in my life, lying there, gave me, not a shock exactly but a sharp realisation of how fleeting life was, even if you lived to be eighty, as she had. I also thought that now those warmly recommendatory letters would never be written. I must look about for myself.

A job as full-time lady's maid was not so easy to come by in our part of the country where the kind of life that Miss Raker described was not common. There were plenty of big houses with wealthy people living in them, comfortably but not grandly. I could have found a place in London, I suppose, if I'd known how to go about it, but then I should have been completely out of touch with Ockley and it would have cost me more than the sixpence Sam Lockey charged to send my wages and anything else I could get hold of home to Mother. So in the end I went to work for Mrs. Fanshawe at Muchanger, a big house just within reach of my house, if you walked briskly; and there for five years I combined the duties of parlourmaid and lady's maid. I used to walk home, briskly, every Sunday afternoon and I seldom went empty-handed, for I managed to get on the right side of the cook who'd give me jars of dripping, ham bones with a good deal of meat still on them, odd bits of cold meat, chicken carcases from which only the white meat had been taken. At Muchanger I earned six pounds a year and spent nothing on myself, except for shoes. Actually I was all right for clothes. Miss Raker had left everything she owned to a niece I'd never seen or even heard mentioned and she did not want her aunt's old clothes. They were all a bit small for me, but by that time I was adept at letting out and letting down and putting in gussets.

On the whole those five years were good ones. Up to a point. Sally and Mary both got married; too stupid to see what marriage and bearing children and bringing them up on a farm labourer's wage had done to Mother. William and George, between whom there was something of the same

11

kind of link as between me and Tom, had done what they always wanted to do, gone to be soldiers. There was one short time when it really looked as though we might be out of our muddle. Two men earning and Mother, though now sickly and a slattern, still able to cook. Tom filled out.

He always walked home with me on Sundays. We didn't talk much because really there wasn't much we had to say; a comment about the weather, harvest, evenings darkening or growing lighter. But there was a kind of accord. When we could see the lights in the Muchanger windows, he'd say, "Well, there you are, Martha. See you next week. Good night," and I'd say, "Good night Tom. See you next Sunday."

So from Sunday to Sunday I lived, until the Sunday when he wasn't there. I said, "Where's Tom?" And got my answer. Tom, for a week or two, had been walking out with the cowman's daughter, Emma Pledger, and the Pledgers had asked him for Sunday dinner—in our part of the country a sure sign that they approved of the match.

I said, "Oh. Where are they going to live?"

My father said, "Here." And my mother said, "There's room now. It'll be nice to have some little 'uns about the place again."

I thought: Here we go on the same old round! I swear I was not jealous, or envious. I loved Tom but I had never once entertained a wrong or unnatural thought about him. I was merely concerned with the thought that Emma Pledger would have baby after baby and end like my mother, dragged down, slatternly and with a perpetual pain in her side.

And indeed Emma, when I met her, my parents returning the gesture of offering a Sunday dinner, was very much like my mother as I could just remember her; lively and spry. I tried to think cheerfully; Emma would dig the garden as Mother had once done, she would grow potatoes, onions, cabbages, and help out, doing the odd job here and there. But presently she would have a baby, and another and another and we should be back where we were.

In thinking that I was overoptimistic. Within a year, in fact just before Emma had her first, Sally was back home. Her husband had cut his leg with a scythe and died of lockjaw. She had one child, a little girl, just on her feet, and one to come. My father said, "It's a good thing we're here or it'd be the poorhouse for Sally." My mother said what she had said about having little 'uns about. Tom said that Emma was very good natured, prepared to make room for Sally and her child. "And they'll help each other when the time comes," he said. He sounded resigned and cheerful, and inside me something withered and died. I had hoped, hoped clean up to his marriage that one day I might get a proper job, heave myself up that last step of the ladder and pull him after me. Too late now! Tom had condemned himself to the family life which, with the poor, means privation and squalor. He had also condemned me, not to privation, I ate well, and not to squalor, I lived in pleasant surroundings, but to responsibility. I must help to carry his load, because he was my brother and I loved him.

Then I had a stroke of luck. Mr. John Franklin of Nethergate went to London, fell in love and married a lady from Ireland; such a lady that although she was now married to a plain Mr., she was still Lady Rosaleen.

My goodhearted old mistress at Muchanger, who was also a great gossip, said to me one day, "I'm given to understand that Lady Rosaleen brought no maid with her from London and is looking about for one. It would be just the job for you, Martha. You are wasting your skill here, setting tables and making my twelve hairs look like two dozen. Shall I recommend you?"

I did not know quite what to say. I'd been happy with Mrs. Fanshawe who was kind and easygoing; and the cook was my friend. But Nethergate was nearer, much nearer to Ockley, and a proper, full-time lady's maid should be able to demand a better wage. I had Tom to think of.

I said, "Could you manage without me, ma'am?"

She laughed, a little harshly and said, "As one grows old, my dear, one learns how well one can manage without anything or anybody."

I thought: I couldn't manage without Tom! If anything untoward happened to Tom I should just lie down and die.

"I'm not saying," she said, "that I shan't miss you, Martha, but I think it is an opportunity that should not be missed. I will write you a letter of recommendation and you can carry it. Then if her ladyship wishes to see you, you will be there to be inspected."

So, carrying the sealed letter, I walked to Nethergate, taking the way through Layer Wood which lies like a great six-fingered hand over all our part of Suffolk. There are villages, or big houses, at each finger tip and in the spaces between the fingers, and the road winds between them, miles of it, linking Muchanger, Clevely, the three Minshams—St. Mary's, St. Faith's, and All Saints—Nettleton, Merravy, and Ockley, and all within sight of the Wood. But there are short cuts, through the trees, some wide enough to be known as "rides" and others too narrow for anything but a person on foot. When I reached Nethergate I was within fifteen minutes' walk of Ockley, by a woodland path.

I handed in my letter and was told to wait. Then I was told that her ladyship wished to see me and I was conducted into her presence.

I'd never seen such a room or such a person, both so beautiful. Muchanger was a big house but everything in it was old and dark and the rooms all of a clutter because Mrs. Fanshawe hated so much as a paper to be moved. Here everything was new and clean and bright, everything white or blue with here and there a touch of pink, an exact match for her ladyship with her white kid-glove skin, her very blue eyes, blue as a cornflower, her rose-coloured mouth.

Entering I made my bob and she said, "Good afternoon, Pratt. I understand that you are seeking employment."

"Yes, my lady."

"Your present mistress appears to think well of you. What other experience have you had?"

Question and answer. Question and answer. No question unreasonable and not a single false answer, except that when she asked why I wished to change my place I did not say, To be near Tom and get more money. I said, To improve my situation. But there was something so chilling, so nearly frightening about her that I almost hoped I *wouldn't* get the job, much as I wanted it really. Her questions stripped me down to nothing but an overambitious country girl who, because she had once known a lady's maid and helped an old, obscure woman to make her scanty toilette, had actually ventured to think that she was fit to be a lady's maid to a real lady. All my life I had been humble, but I'd been a humble person, not a humble nothing. It was not that she was unpleasant or asked a single question that any careful person would not have asked, it was just that she reduced me. Even when she asked questions which Miss Raker had made me able to answer in the right way, and I did so, not a flicker of expression crossed her face, and up to the moment when she said, "I think you may do," I had no inkling of what she was thinking. "Your free time will be on Thursday afternoon and as much of the evening as suits my convenience. Your wages will be nine pounds a year," she said. That was a full pound more than I had even hoped for, but I should not have taken the job if it hadn't been for Tom.

When I got back to Muchanger old Mrs. Fanshawe was

all agog. She asked me first whether I had obtained the post, and then said, "Now, tell me, is she as beautiful as everybody makes out? Somebody was telling me the other day that in London people used to stand on chairs just to catch sight of her."

"Her ladyship is very beautiful," I said, and tried to describe her. Then, in the way of an old, rather lonely woman who would rather gossip with her maid than stay silent, Mrs. Fanshawe rambled on about the oddity of a lady of title, so young and so beautiful, marrying Mr. Franklin, a plain country squire. "Not a penny of dowry, of course, but still one would have thought . . . Now tell me another thing. Lady Fennel told me that Mr. Franklin had had a lot of alterations made to the house, a fine new drawing room. Did you see it?"

I described the room; the curtains and upholstery all of satin, cream-coloured with garlands of embroidered rosebuds and forget-me-nots. I was rather surprised to find how well I remembered what I had seen at a time when I was ill-at-ease.

"You're a noticing girl, Martha," Mrs. Fanshawe said. I thought: Yes I am; I don't miss much, and one thing I didn't miss was the difference between her and you and I know who I'd rather work for. But there was Tom and his burden to consider. Mrs. Fanshawe gave me two guineas as a parting present and I went to work for Lady Rosaleen.

Before I had worked for Lady Rosaleen very long I thought I knew why she had chosen Mr. Franklin; he was so easygoing and so devoted to her that he let her have her own way in everything. I swear that if one night she had looked at the moon and said, "Jack, I want it," he'd have tried to get it for her and, having failed to do so, apologised for having failed.

I also knew, or guessed, why she had felt able to do without making a splendid marriage; she was so proud, she looked down on everybody from such a height that to her there was no difference between Jack Franklin and the Duke of Grafton. In fact I have heard her call the Duke an upstart. Her own father was Lord Barryfergus and he could trace his descent from some King of Ireland who'd ruled there a thousand years ago.

In addition to being the most beautiful and the most proud woman I ever knew, she was the most coldhearted. No, that is a silly thing to say, for to be coldhearted you must have a heart and she had none. She did not love Mr. Franklin, or she would have let him have his way just occasionally. (I must admit though that she managed him so cleverly that he often thought he was having his own way.) She did not love her children, both boys, John born in 1766, a year after her marriage, Alan in 1767. She saw to it that they were provided with nurses, governesses, tutors, she used the word "darling" very frequently, but she never gave one sign of real motherly feeling for them and if they did the slightest thing wrong—as children will—she visited them with that icy disapproval which was her expression of displeasure. She never scolded, or raised her voice, or frowned, but when her ladyship was displeased everybody knew. All the servants were terrified of her. So was I. There was never a moment in all my years with her when, if I'd been offered the same wage in a place as near to Ockley, I shouldn't have left her.

One instance sums up what she was like. My father became ill; something went wrong with his breathing. He was thought to be dying. I was sent for. I had to ask leave to go home, and I explained why. When I came back she never asked me was he dead, or better. In fact it took him a long time to die because in warm sunny weather he improved enough to be able to do casual jobs at hay-making and harvest time; but as soon as it was foggy, or the east wind blew, he'd be back to wheezing and choking. So the only regular wage earner was poor old Tom. "I reckon you're the best sister a chap ever had, Martha, and how we'd manage without you, I don't know," he said.

I went on spending nothing except for the making and mending of shoes: being nice to cook, frizzing her hair, making bleach water to cure her freckles, helping her to cut out and sew clothes, and in return getting stuff to take home. Lady Rosaleen often gave me things too, always in a manner that took all joy out of the gift. "I shall not be needing this any more, Pratt."

Once, coming home through Layer Wood in May, I saw the result of a freak weather change. There was a hawthorn tree in full bloom, iced all over so that it stood in a shroud of glass; it reminded me of Lady Rosaleen.

However, even self-loving, well-beloved ladies in ice-glass cases are in the end overtaken by Time. At forty her ladyship was still beautiful—in fact with those eyes, that shape of face, that proud tilt of the head she would always be beautiful, but beneath and around her eyes, at the corners of her mouth and on her throat there began that slight crumpling of the petal-like skin. I have noticed that very fine, very fair skin, the best kind to have in youth, tends to go early, as though, at the back of it all, there was some kind of justice. I was seven years older than she was, I'd worked hard all my life and I'd never used anything on my face except soap and water, but sometimes, as I did her hair or fastened a necklace, I'd see both our faces in the glass and was bound to admit that apart from my greying hair I looked younger. My skin was of the other kind, tough and firm; when it went it would go all at once and I should look like an old withered apple.

If I'd liked her the least bit, if she'd even once said or done an endearing thing, I should have felt sorry for her then. The ice-glass case split, just at one point and disbelief mingled with her dismay.

I remember the very evening that it happened.

Mr. Franklin had a dressing room adjoining her ladyship's bedroom; actually it had been his bedroom as well as dressing room, ever since Mr. Alan was born. The door between the two rooms was always open and as he dressed he'd stroll in and out. He had no valet; in fact he disapproved of them, "jackanapes waiting on jackanapes," he said. "When I can't climb into my own breeches I'll ask Pointer to shoot me." Pointer was one of his gamekeepers. On this particular evening Mr. Franklin came in and said something and her ladyship said, "Darling, is that really a good idea?" and smiled as she always did to conceal the fact that she was bent on getting her own way, once more. He said, "Well . . . maybe not," and gave her a smile, which she did not observe, for she was leaning forward, staring into her glass as though it had done something to merit her displeasure. Mr. Franklin had wandered back into his room and was ringing his bell for Page, the footman, to come and tie his cravat. (Apparently to his mind there was a difference between the helping into breeches and the tying of a cravat.)

Her ladyship said, "Come here, Pratt. Look! You must have applied that *maquillage* too heavily. It creases when I smile." To prove her point she grimaced, a smile of a kind. And there under the eyes and around the mouth, were Time's little footprints.

"I am sorry, my lady," I said.

She called, "Jack darling, I shall be at least another ten minutes. Don't wait. Go down and have a glass of wine. I'll come when I am ready."

To me she said, "Remove it. Start again. And more lightly."

She chose to assume that I was to blame. But I noticed that when the pink and white mask had been wiped away and replaced, she did not risk a test by repeating that grimace into the glass. She knew. But she had always had her way and would have it now. Even the ravages of age must be overcome. Miss Raker had told me of a preparation to renew the complexion—Fuller's earth mixed with lemon juice and spread over the face where it set into a kind of mask. Her ladyship said, "I can feel the tautness, Pratt," and for once she sounded approving. But the effect was not lasting, and presently she was sending away for stuff from London, from a quack whose motto was "Beautiful Forever."

The truth is that nobody can be, in that sense, beautiful forever, but this truth she would not accept. So we fought a losing battle; and all in secret, since Mr. Franklin must not know. It was called resting. "Jack, darling, I am going to rest for an hour."

The irony of it all was that he would never have noticed. He loved her as I loved Tom. If one of Tom's arms or legs had dropped off, or he'd lost every hair on his head, what would that have mattered to me? Love has only one eye and that eye sees what it wants to see. By this time Tom was very different from the good little boy with curly hair and long eyelashes who had followed me about as I worked the clappers to scare the crows. I had loved him then. I loved him still. Mr. Franklin had loved his Rosaleen and would have loved her still, of that I am sure, if one night every hair on her head had dropped out on her pillow. He'd have gone up to London, a place he hated, and come back with the best wig he could buy and offered it to her, as a good gun dog offers a retrieved pheasant. But she, never having known what love was, could not understand that. Like being unable to read.

Fighting this losing battle alongside her, I realised that age was catching up on me, too. I had always had splendid health and that had enabled me to do what I had done and even now I did not ail. My father had died of breathlessness, my mother of a pain in the side—at least that was all she had ever complained of. My trouble was the one that had afflicted Miss Raker, simple plain rheumatism. She'd had it in the knees, and had become lame, and so tapped on the window, and with a tap, shaped my life. With me it was in the hands. My knuckles swelled and became shiny and stiff. When I woke in the morning I had to rub my fingers together and press them back, work them, painfully, into flexibility and usefulness. My thumbs gave me most trouble. They were inclined to lie there, not knobbly or painful, but flaccid, weak, across my palms. It sometimes took me a full fifteen minutes to push and rub them into activity. Once in a while, in the early morning, I'd look at them, lying there across my palms, not hurting as my fingers did, but resigned, ready to give up and never work again. But I forced them to it. A lady's maid whose thumbs fail might as well be dead. And I could not afford either to die or to go into an almshouse, for there at Ockley was Tom, struggling bravely along.

So we came to October 1792. It was a chilly evening. Mr. John had gone out for the evening, probably to the Rossiters; it was now generally assumed that he would marry Miss Harriet Rossiter. Mr. Franklin and Lady Rosaleen, having supped alone, were in the drawing room playing some card game. Clamp the butler, Page the footman, Cook, and I had settled down cosily to our supper in the room which served both as butler's pantry and upper servants' room. The front door bell rang and Page went to answer it. When he came back he said, "It's one of those poor people from France."

Page could read and so could I, so we knew what had been going on in France; pretty shocking things three, two years back, but they seemed to have calmed down lately. "Drenched through, she looked," Page said. Another bell rang and I had no need to look out into the passage; I knew after all these years, the exact tone of her ladyship's bedroom bell. I scurried up the back stairs and there in the bedroom, before the blazing fire stood her ladyship and—it gave me quite a jolt—a young woman, so exactly like her as she had been when I first came to serve her that she might have been a younger sister, or a daughter.

Her ladyship said, "Pratt, find some nightclothes for Mademoiselle de Savigny. Yes my dear, I am attending. Your father, despite his manoeuvrings, has lost his head, but that is no reason why you should catch your death of cold. Strip off those wet clothes."

The girl said, "I was trying to tell you . . . He was always on the side of the people. He was an elected member of the National Assembly. But he would not agree that the King should be brought to trial and so they killed him."

I'm not given to easy pity, but she sounded so sad, and

looked so forlorn in her drenched, ragged clothes, that even I felt sorry for her.

Her ladyship said, "Yes. It is all most unfortunate . . . Thank you, Pratt. Now, go down and tell Effie to make up the bed in the room next to yours, and to warm it well. Tell Cook to heat a bowl of chicken broth."

The girl said, "I am not hungry, Cousin Rosaleen. I have not been able to eat since it . . . since it happened."

"Then you must be in need of sustenance. Starving yourself is quite as futile as taking your death of cold. Take off those clothes now. Pratt will bring the broth and by the time you have eaten it your room will be ready."

The choice of room told me something. At Nethergate there were several guest rooms, the beds aired regularly, ready for occupancy at a moment's notice. But the newcomer was given the room next to mine, a servant's bedroom.

Later, when she was in nightgown, dressing robe, and slippers, and had taken a few sips of soup, I took her along to the room. I saw that she was surprised to find herself in such a place. She was too miserable to care much, but she gave it a single, flashing look. No hearth, a narrow bed with a cotton cover, a corner washstand with a coarse bowl and ewer, a pewter candlestick. The handle of the warming pan was still sticking out at the side of the bed. I pulled it out and said, "The bed will be warm," and she said, "Thank you, Pratt." She had a nice voice with just that lilt to it that wasn't quite English.

I overheard everything because Lady Rosaleen and Mr. Franklin treated me as though I was a piece of furniture. Sometimes I was actually in her ladyship's room when Mr. Franklin came in for his morning visit; sometimes I was in the little room which led off it on the opposite side from his dressing room. The little room was a good place for ironing —it had a hobbed grate on which flatirons could be heated and a solid table on which I could iron or beat up emulsions; but its door sagged on its hinges and could not be fully closed.

On the morning after Mademoiselle de Savigny's arrival Mr. Franklin said, "My dear, you should have called me. I should have welcomed your cousin with open arms."

"Of course, darling. But I saw no reason to disturb your card game. And all she needed was rest. You will be able to extend your welcome when she has recovered."

"Page said something about her being in the room next

to Pratt's. Is that suitable?"

"Jack, should I have chosen it otherwise? Isabella is in a state of collapse and must keep to her bed for several days; that room is most convenient for carrying trays from the kitchen. So near the back staircase."

He said, "I'd never have thought of that."

A little later her ladyship said to me, "Pratt, could you put your hand on that black dress I had when old Miss Franklin died?"

I could indeed. I'd had my eye on it for years. So seldom worn—black did not suit her ladyship, despite her fair skin—of dark hue and solid weave, that dress would have been far more useful to me, to the family at Ockley, than many things which her ladyship so carelessly disposed of. But it had hung in the back of a closet for years. Understandable, her ladyship disliking black, she would not wish to spend money on new mourning, should the occasion arise.

"It needs very little alteration," her ladyship said when I produced the gown. "Mademoiselle de Savigny—who will be known here as Miss Isabella, you might tell everyone that—is very slight now, but she will doubtless fill out. But, come straight from France, she will feel the cold. I think the neckline should be filled in and the sleeves lengthened." For her ladyship's wear the dress had been made so that her white throat and arms were exposed and did something to combat the unbecoming colour.

I said, "With what, your ladyship?"

"A panel from the skirt."

If she'd given it to me to make over for one of Tom's family, I wouldn't have made it quite so plain and ugly. Presented with it and a set of underclothes, Miss Isabella gave it much the same look as she had given the dreary bedroom. Scorn mixed with I-must-put-up-with-it. But, wearing it, she thanked her ladyship for giving her a black dress, for having remembered that she was in mourning. Behind the thanks, the meekness, I could see, could almost smell, something neither thankful nor meek. In fact her likeness to her ladyship was not confined to their faces or their colouring; there was the way they carried their heads.

Mr. Franklin must have noticed it. One day, soon after Miss Isabella, in the ugly black dress, had begun to take meals with them, her ladyship, in the little morning talk, said:

"Jack, I am sorry. You never inflicted your family upon

me and I never had the slightest intention of inflicting mine on you. But she ran here for shelter. I could hardly deny it . . ."

He said, "My dear Rosaleen, nothing could give me more pleasure. Surely you must know that. Apart from all else, she's so like you; the spitting image of you as you were when I first set eyes on you . . ."

He meant well, he always did, but he couldn't have said a worse thing.

It was on that day that her ladyship said, "Isabella, I think you would feel better if you had some occupation. Pratt would welcome some assistance; her hands are half-crippled."

As usual she spoke as though I wasn't there, but the last words rang doom to me. I would have said that she had never noticed the state of my hands. In fact I should have said that if my face had turned black overnight, her ladyship would not have noticed so long as I was there, at the right time in the morning, with the breakfast tray, the cans of hot water for her bath, the freshly ironed underclothes. But I had deceived myself; nothing escaped her eye.

Sounding meek but looking prideful, Miss Isabella said, "But of course, Cousin Rosaleen, I shall be happy to help in any way I can."

After that we spent a lot of time together, in the oddest way. She was less help than hindrance; she'd never seen a flatiron before, and I doubt if she had ever threaded a needle. "My papa," she said, excusing her clumsiness, "was not in favour of convent schools where needlework is taught. I had a tutor . . . I am sorry, Pratt, show me again. I *am* capable of learning . . ."

She could learn; clumsy at first; not clumsy in the sense of being heavy and awkward, rather I should say helpless, slow, thinking out what to do next, and tiring very quickly. Feeling that she was about to take my place, I lost pity, pretended not to notice that she had to take both hands to heave a flatiron on or off the fire. I'd stand aside and think, young as you are, I'm worth four of you; her ladyship must *see*. And yet, even when I stopped being helpful, she always treated me as a friend, and when we sewed together in the little room talked freely. She was always saying what a good man, what a good landlord her father had been, and how the three rogues who now ruled France had used him and then betrayed him. She spoke of her homes, one in the country, one in Paris. "And now I have no home," she said. And it was true. She had no home; she had no place. She ate at the family table, it is true, but she did not belong. Mr. Franklin, a kind man, a man who would have liked a daughter, perhaps, would have made much of her, but for her ladyship.

One morning he said, "My dear, it will soon be Christmas. Don't you think Isabella should have a new frock? She can't join the festivities looking like a black crow."

"Darling, she cannot join any festivities this year. She is in mourning."

He said, "I think too much is made of it. Her father was a cantankerous fool by all accounts, but he's dead and there's nothing to be done about it. I think she needs cheering up. A pretty dress and an outing or two."

"Not this year," her ladyship said.

"Not even to the Rossiters'? They're almost family now."

That was so; Mr. John had decided upon Miss Harriet; there would be an engagement at Christmas, a wedding in June.

"Darling, try for one moment to put yourself in Isabella's place; she has had a tragic experience. What she needs now is time to recover and a little occupation to distract her mind. And—it was clever of you to think of it—a new dress. That she shall have."

That was how her ladyship managed. Never the downright contradiction; always the cool and sensible reason for everything and then she'd give way an inch and make it sound as though she'd given way altogether.

Miss Isabella did have a new dress in time for Christmas. Half mourning it was, that dead shade of purple like the plums that fall from a tree so overladen that it can't bring them all to ripeness.

There was Christmas, and the New Year, 1793. Happy New Year, everybody said. For myself I doubted it. I could feel myself being edged out. "Miss Isabella will do my hair, Pratt."

Hair styles were changing. There was no longer a need for the skill which Miss Raker had taught me; few heads were properly "dressed," nowadays. The newer, simpler styles had, like most other things, come in from France. Miss Isabella's own hair was a cap of short-cut curls which at first I thought to be like the poor, tattered clothes, part of the disguise in which she had escaped, but she said that this way of wearing the hair was the latest fashion in Paris.

If I hadn't felt her to be a threat to me, I should have felt sorry for Miss Isabella at this time. Her ladyship was never easily pleased, and always sparing of her praise, but now she

23

seemed to delight in carping. Nothing was ever quite right. Once or twice, for reasons of my own, I said, "Would you like me to take over, my lady?"

"No, Pratt. Miss Isabella must learn."

At such moments I often observed that Miss Isabella's mouth tightened as though she was keeping back words, and her eyes would flash. After all, she was Lady Rosaleen's kinswoman and probably just as proud, inside; but she was homeless and penniless, absolutely dependent—and never allowed to forget it.

The year moved along to April. There came a day when on my free afternoon I noticed that the bank of primroses which Tom had once said reminded him of me was in flower again and the leaves were green and curly on the hawthorns. At such times, in mild promising weather you tend to look ahead. I thought: If only Lady Rosaleen would deal with me as Miss Raker's lady had done with her, how happy I should be. The tiniest cottage and just enough to live on. I'd eat dry bread all the week in order to give Tom a good dinner on Sunday.

Over the years the faces in the cottage had changed, but it was still a muddle, full of hungry mouths. Tom's wife had taken my mother's place, doing a bit of cooking and not much else. My mother had been thin and Emma was fat in a flabby way, and that was about the only difference. My sister Sally, as soon as her children were big enough to go into service, had married again, not badly, an old man, a retired butcher, but she never sent a penny home despite all that Tom had done for her.

Tom and Emma had had seven children and reared four, all girls. The eldest of these was named for me, Martha, but always called Marty; and there had been a time when I had had hopes for her. She once said she'd like to be a lady's maid, like Aunt Martha, and didn't want to get married. I thought that maybe with her the pattern would be broken a bit. But I was wrong. She got married, had four children, and ended up not a widow but a deserted wife. Her husband's parents took the two boys and she arrived back at the cottage with two girls, one a toddler, the other a babe in arms. Tom, with the patience of a saint, repeated what my father had said when Sally came home—a good thing she had somewhere to turn to, otherwise it would be the poorhouse; and Emma said exactly what my mother had said—it'd be nice to have something young about the place again.

There was just no end to it. It was not a nice thought, but

24

I couldn't help remembering Miss Raker and her cat. She took it in as a kitten and thought it was a tom. In fact she called it Tommy and was glad of its company. Then it had four kittens, for which she managed to find homes; soon it had four more which nobody wanted and she asked the coalman to drown them. And then one day she said that drowning the kittens was not the real answer; she was sorry, she'd miss Tommy, but . . .

However, on this early April day nothing worse than usual had happened at the cottage. Tom was at work and on my way home I went through the field where he was working and had a little talk. He now looked as old as Father had done before he was taken ill. I thought: Yes, that's all that happens to people like us, we get old; and even those who've worked all our days, lose our jobs in the end. I said, "Take care of yourself, Tom."

"You, too, Martha," he said, and smiled. His smile hadn't changed from when he was a little boy.

When I got back to Nethergate it was to find that Mr. Alan had come home, unexpectedly. He'd got leave because his regiment was to go abroad, to the West Indies, the Sugar Islands as they were called.

He'd always been far and away the nicer of Lady Rosaleen's boys. Mr. John, taking after his father in looks, was more like his mother in nature, proud and hard and cold. Mr. Alan was merry and friendly. He had his mother's blue eyes and his hair was an unusual colour; the Franklin ginger, mixed with Lady Rosaleen's black, had come out the colour of a copper beech leaf.

Nethergate was what was called an entailed estate which meant that the land and the house and all that was in it would one day pass to Mr. John. I'd heard enough of those morning conversations to know that Mr. Alan's future had been a matter of concern for both his parents. I could remember hearing her ladyship say that most second sons could count upon something from their mother's side of the family, "But Jack darling, you knew when you married me . . ." And Mr. Franklin said that ever since Alan's birth he'd been trying to save a little here and there, and had enough to set the boy up in business; he thought as a wine merchant; that was a gentleman's trade. As was her way, her ladyship did not contradict; she said of course it all depended upon whether Alan showed any signs of being businesslike; and presently even Mr. Franklin had to admit that he did not. Then how about buying him a commission in the Army: "The plainest man looks his best in uniform. Alan should be quite irresistible and marry an heiress."

Mr. Franklin, whose favourite Alan was, though he did his best to hide the fact, said, "We should see little of him, Rosaleen." And she said, "I know. That is the sacrifice we must make, for his sake."

So Mr. Alan had gone into the Army, and we had not seen much of him.

Now here he was. When he was small he could not say Pratt, only Pwatt, and to that he had held. On this April evening he said, "Pwatt! And not a day older," and gave me a hug that lifted me off my feet. "Do you still make toast, Pwatt? I swear, nobody makes toast like you."

I knew why, after all these years, he remembered my toast. He had not always been as obedient as her ladyship wished her sons to be and had been sent supperless to bed. I knew what it felt like to be hungry and had smuggled him up bits of buttered toast.

His leave had come at a good time; with the roads drying out and the evenings lightening, all in and around Baildon social life was on the stir. Miss Raker had told me about London and Bath and even about Paris, but the Suffolk gentry, on the whole, were content with Baildon and its Assembly Rooms, its new theatre, and the round of entertainment in one another's houses. A self-contained community; everybody remembered that Sir Edward Follesmark had gone to London once and had his pocket picked! About this attitude, even with the rich, there was just an echo of my brother Tom's *We're here and what a good thing*. Yet, though not anxious to go to London, the Suffolk gentry liked to keep up with the times and to follow fashionable movements. Two or three days after Mr. Alan's return there was to be a very splendid concert in the Assembly Rooms in aid of people like Miss Isabella who had been obliged to flee from their homes, but with no relatives in England.

On the day of the concert, just after Mr. Franklin had paid his morning visit to her ladyship, Mr. Alan came in. Miss Isabella had taken away the breakfast tray and I was laying out the day's fresh underwear.

"And how is my lady mother this morning? Morning, Pwatt. Mamma, I want to ask you something. I think Isabella should come with us to the concert this evening."

Her ladyship tried another of her little tricks.

"And what did you wish to *ask*, my dear?"

"Well . . . If she could come. It'd make her feel at home. Scenes from some French play, and a Frog playing the piano."

"Isabella is still in mourning for her father. She would not wish to appear at a public entertainment."

"That be hanged for a tale! Anyway, the six months was up yesterday."

"Really. How quickly time goes. Then it would be permissible: but not, alas, possible. I had the utmost difficulty in procuring an extra ticket for you, Alan."

"She can go instead of me."

"That would give grave offence to Lady Fennel who is organising the concert and actually *made* an extra place for *you*. She would never forgive me."

"And that would break your heart! All right, I'll ride into Baildon and see what can be done by the exercise of charm. Or vile threats."

"You would simply be wasting your time." I knew that she was displeased. So maybe did Mr. Alan, but he'd got out from under her thumb six years before and could bear a little displeasure.

"I have a month's leave," he said. "I can afford to waste a morning."

"You will be disappointed."

"What d'you bet?"

"I never bet. You do far too readily," she said.

He ignored the rebuke and went off and just before dinner came back and into the little room where Miss Isabella and I were at work pressing the last, tiniest crease from the blue silk dress that her ladyship was to wear that evening.

"Now, pretty Coz," he said, "shut your eyes, hold out your hand and see what I have for you."

She looked at the ticket with more dismay than pleasure.

"It is very kind of you, Alan. But I have nothing to wear."

"All women say that on every possible occasion."

"In my case it is true. I have this"—she was wearing the ugly purple, definitely a day dress—"and a black which is even less suitable."

"Oh dear," he said, dashed. "I know what. You shall wear my splendid cloak! Everybody agrees that I have the most gorgeous cloak in the regiment. It'd cover you from neck to toe . . . Wait."

He ran along to his room and came back with the garment; it was cornflower blue, lined with white satin and with a lot of gold lace and cord about it.

Dropping it over her shoulders, he said, "I won it; in a card game. Ferguson of the 8th had it made to his own design and never even wore it. It suits you. You look splendid. Doesn't she, Pwatt?"

Actually she did; the colour matched her eyes and with her short curly hair she looked like a pretty boy.

"I couldn't possibly wear it, Alan," she said, looking helpless. "It would look ridiculous."

"You'd start a new fashion. Everybody would want one. Tailors would be working day and night."

Fashions had started, as well I knew, from some such accident, but Miss Isabella wasn't old enough, or bold enough. So I said:

"If I may say so, Mr. Alan, it is not suitable wear for a young lady. I'm sure that when her ladyship hears that you have obtained a ticket she will know what to do."

All that afternoon I waited for orders to find and work quickly upon some suitable garment. None came. Miss Isabella said, "I suppose I must go as I am; if indeed I go at all." Halfway through her own toilette her ladyship said, "Pratt, could you find that gauze scarf with the squirrel fur ends?" It was a pretty thing in itself, blue, no thicker than a cobweb, a thing meant to be worn over bare shoulders, over silk, over satin. Over the purple day dress it looked much more ridiculous than the military cloak; but Miss Isabella, holding her head high, said, "Thank you, Cousin Rosaleen."

Next week I had something else to think about.

I went home as usual on the Thursday afternoon and there was Tom all crippled up. He'd hurt himself lifting a sack of barley; his head was all on one side and it pained him to move his hand even. I said to Emma, "What have you done to help him?" and she said, "What could I do?" I rounded on her sharply. "Get to the farm," I said, "ask Mr. Rowe to lend you some horse liniment. And be quick."

She could stir if she wanted to; she was soon back with the liniment, which was powerful stuff. I gave Tom a good rub, all round his neck and shoulders and down his arm. He said, "Thank you, Martha. I feel a heap better already." But he still wasn't straight. And Marty's elder girl kept trying to get on Tom's knee, and the baby howled.

Going home that day I thought we'd touched the bottom.

Tom wasn't paid for days he didn't work. There he was, and Emma and Marty, Rosie and Ella, all dependent on what I could provide.

You always think things can't be worse, and then they are.

A fortnight later my free day began badly. Mr. Franklin made his morning visit to her ladyship. I went into the little workroom and whisked up the egg-white mask which did pull her face together, and held it so long as she didn't smile.

Mr. Franklin said, "I don't know whether you've noticed, my dear, but that girl looks poorly."

"What girl, darling?"

"Isabella. Very pale."

"She has a very white skin."

"There's a difference. I don't think she gets out enough. I said so at breakfast. She said she was too busy. Must she be so busy?"

"Jack, darling. Put yourself in her place for a minute. Wouldn't you prefer to think that you were being useful, and not entirely dependent on charity? I know I should. *In fact when Pratt's clumsiness becomes intolerable, I propose to offer her place—and her wage—to Isabella.*"

My death sentence!

Mr. Franklin said that of course she was right. He'd never looked at it in that way.

I was not clumsy. I'd taken enormous care not to be. The complaint was part of a plan to make Miss Isabella into a servant.

Upset by this, I went home. And there was my brother George! He was out of the Army; his left arm had been taken off at the elbow and he had a pension of two shillings a week. Just enough to keep him in bread!

In the twenty-four years since he and William joined the Army we had never had a word from either of them. Of course they couldn't write and had no reason to think that anybody in the family could read; but soldiers can send messages and even presents if they wish. We knew that by Job Fakes. Essie Fakes—she kept The Maybush then—had a bit of a row with her son and he went and joined the Army. One day another soldier, limping home to Lowestoft, had come miles out of his way to give a message and a golden sovereign to Essie. "Tell my mother I'm all right." What that sovereign would have meant to us! Essie, doing well at The Maybush, didn't need it at all. In fact she had a hole bored through it and wore it on a chain round her

29

fat neck; showing it to everybody and saying what a good boy Job was.

From William and George nothing. Now, seeing George, I thought bitterly: They all know where to come when they're out of luck. Not that, apart from his arm, George looked out of luck. He'd put a year on to his age in order to enlist with William, he'd really been fifteen then; so now he was thirty-nine, but he'd worn well. Army food had done him good; he was tall and well set up, very tanned, and as neat as a pin, even in that slovenly cottage where everything he owned was contained in a wooden chest with brass corners. He was quite well-spoken, too. He said he'd learned to read and write and had reached the rank of sergeant; would have been regimental sergeant major but for losing his arm. I suppose I should have admired him, but I could only see him as an addition to my burden, and to Tom's.

Tom, Emma said, was a bit better, but not right yet. Mr. Rowe was keeping him on, doing little jobs about the yard, in the hope that he'd be fit for cutting hay. He was being paid four shillings a week. I groaned in my spirit; six shillings a week coming into the cottage now, and everything that I could bring, in money or food to be divided among six instead of five. It'd be Tom who'd go short, I knew that. I thought: All we need now is for William to turn up with a wooden leg!

However, when I asked about William, George said he'd never got to India, he'd died on the troopship of some sort of fever.

George had already fixed himself up with free beer. Essie Fakes, when she had word that Job was killed and wouldn't be coming home, had retired and sold The Maybush to a couple from Clevely. The man was always drunk and the woman was glad of a bit of help, even from a one-armed man. "And I'm pretty handy," George said. "You never know what you can do till you've tried."

Tom, not working full time, came home before I left that day, and a sorry sight he was; so old, so frail-looking and in the hunched up shape that was to last till the end of his days. Still when I asked how he was, he said, "Mustn't grumble, Martha," and smiled his sweet smile. He said didn't George look well: and wasn't it nice to see him after all this time? Really for the bitterness within me I could hardly drink the tea that I had brought. The cook at Nethergate and I had an arrangement about tea. As her ladyship's maid I was entitled to a good strong cup of tea whenever I wanted it, but I never asked for a pot to myself and when we were all together I made pretend that I liked the weak brew that came after water had been added to the pot. What was saved in this way, the cook put aside for me, a pinch here and there.

In a way that day I realised that for all his worried look, Tom was a happy man. He let Rosie have a sip of his tea and when she said, "More," he gave her more. In fact she drank most of his. When Ella howled he said, "Turn her over, Marty and pat her back. It's wind." In the Bible—Miss Raker had been a great one for the Bible and I actually had learned to read from it—it says, "Blessed are the meek, for they shall inherit the earth." Absolute rubbish; the meek inherit enough earth to be buried in; and that was what Tom would get in the end. Inside myself I was not meek, though I often had to make a pretence of it; there was the difference between Tom and me, and perhaps that was why I loved him.

When it was time for me to go George stood up smartly and said, "I'll walk a bit of the way with you, Martha."

A few steps took us from the cottage to the beginning of the short cut through Layer Wood where the bluebells were in flower and the bracken springing up.

"I wanted a private word with you, Martha," George said. "I wondered if you could lend me a bit of money." It was laugh or cry, so I laughed. "Money, George! Where would I get money from?"

"You've always been in work."

"So I have. Every day of my life as far back as I can remember. And every penny I ever earned, except for buying shoes and having them mended, has gone back to the family. First ours; then Tom's; and now Marty's. How do you think they've lived all these years? How do you think you'll all live now?"

(When Pratt's clumsiness becomes intolerable.)

He said, "Haven't you saved anything?"

"How could I? I tell you, every penny . . ."

"Then it's a pity, Martha." I knew he did not believe me. "I'm on to something that could be a good investment. Essie Fakes told me about it. It's a little inn, down at Ozary. Going for a down payment of a hundred and fifty pounds. Essie regrets selling The Maybush and has been keeping a sharp eye out. She told me about it."

"Let her buy it then."

"So she would, like a shot—if I'd marry her."

31

My burden lightened a bit. A stroke of luck at last!

"It'd be the best thing you could do, George."

"She's old and she's fat. And in her own place she'd be top dog. That wouldn't suit me. A man should be master in his own house."

"If he's got one to be master in," I said.

He gave me a nasty look, but held his tongue, still hoping. "You *sure* you haven't got a bit tucked away?"

I could have hit him.

"If I'd got two shillings in hand d'you think I'd let Tom go about with his head on one side? I'd have got the doctor."

"No use talking about it then," George said in a surly way.

I walked on through the beauty of the springtime wood, worrying in my mind; suppose Tom never got better and able to swing a scythe or guide a plough. Suppose Mr. Franklin's concern for the girl had hardened her ladyship's mind and made her decide to hasten the day when she'd be a paid servant. And George refused, in that pigheaded way, to see on which side his bread was buttered.

As I walked I did what I always did when I had a free moment, worked at my hands, pulling and pressing, massaging the weakening thumbs. If the worst came to the worst I should need my hands, for heavier work than they had done for years. Nobody was going to take on an ageing lady's maid, who'd been sacked after so many years in one place. Oh, dear. I thought: I've worked like a horse, and now, like an old feeble horse, I'm bound for the knacker's.

I rounded a bend in the path as I thought this thought, and there was a horse, tethered to a tree just at the opening of one of the narrow little trails that only gamekeepers used. I knew that horse—it was Mr. Alan's. Rather an unusual colour, buff with a beautiful cream mane and tail. I looked along the trail and there were Miss Isabella and Mr. Alan walking along with their arms around each other. Even as I watched they stopped and kissed, a long, long kiss. Then, still embraced, they sank down into the bracken and were lost to sight.

That morning I'd heard him say that he was going to spend the afternoon and evening at Mortiboys, with Mr. Helmar, and her ladyship had spoken sharply about gambling in such company, and that he could not expect his father to go on paying his debts. To that he had replied in his lighthearted way that he did occasionally win.

I began to put a few other things together. During his first week's leave he'd often come to the workroom, a shirt frill to be ironed, a button sewn on; and he'd lounged about making cheerful talk. He'd insisted upon Miss Isabella attending the concert. Then the visits had stopped. And several times at about this time of the day, or later, after supper, Miss Isabella had not been around. Or not until she was needed by her ladyship.

Now I saw it all and I walked on with another problem. To tell or not to tell?

I had no malice against Miss Isabella; in fact I liked her. It was what she stood for that I minded. And feared. The situation was not of her making; it was her ladyship's doing. If I told, I was certain that her ladyship would have her out of the house before you could whistle. Mr. Alan's leave still had a fortnight to run and there were several engagements fixed. Lady Rosaleen might not be truly fond of her handsome son, but she liked showing him off. She wouldn't send *him* away. It'd be Miss Isabella who would go, and there'd be some cunning excuse for not having her back.

The horrible thing is that once you have decided what is best for *you*, it is all too easy to persuade yourself that it is also best for other people. I'd never had the time or the inclination to have a love affair myself, but I knew enough to see that making love to a young pretty girl in a wood full of bracken and bluebells and loud with cuckoos was something likely to put a young man's mind off the serious business of finding an heiress to marry. Wouldn't it be a pity, I asked myself, if, bound for the Sugar Islands, where, according to her ladyship, heiresses were ten a penny, he kept looking backwards and making comparisons?

And what of Miss Isabella?

Being made love to by Mr. Alan in Layer Wood could do her no good and might well do harm.

However much he might wish to marry her he would not be allowed to. Her ladyship would not wish it, and very few things that her ladyship did not wish ever came about. To be sure she had not wished Miss Isabella to become part of the household, but many things, family pride, public opinion and the warm welcome extended by Mr. Franklin, had made it difficult for her to do other than she had done—appear to accept a situation and then twist it.

There were places where Miss Isabella, young, agreeable, pretty, might be taken in and made much of; the adoption of a French exile was fashionable.

There were places where a lot of French people lived together, supported by the funds raised by such means as the concert at the Assembly Rooms.

There were places where she might find a husband.

Working at my hands I decided that what was best for me was best for everybody.

Her ladyship, when I told her, said, "Thank you, Pratt," exactly as she sometimes did when, her toilette complete, I handed her her gloves or her fan. She turned back to the writing from which I had interrupted her, and anyone who did not know her would have thought that what I had said was of no importance at all.

When, some time later, she came to her bedroom she had several letters in her hand. She separated one from the others and said, "Pratt, will you take this and give it to Long Jim, first thing in the morning? I want it to catch the Colchester mail to London. The rest are merely invitations and a boy can jog round with them later in the day. Now, the weather is warm and I think that Miss Isabella needs summer clothes ..." Miss Isabella was standing there and I saw her mouth tighten and her eyes give that flash. "There is the white muslin with the blue ribbons ..." I knew just where to find it and when I came back with it over my arm, despite herself Miss Isabella looked at it with pleasure. It was a very pretty gown.

"One might call it new," her ladyship said. "I merely tried it on and took a dislike to it. But it will need a good deal of alteration—you have not filled out as I expected, Isabella."

"It is very pretty. Thank you, Cousin Rosaleen."

"And, Pratt, do you remember a rose brocade that was also a mistake? If you could put your hand on it ..." I heard her explaining to Miss Isabella that there was to be a party, here at Nethergate, on Monday evening. "So you will need something rather more formal."

The rose brocade was pretty, too. I could see Miss Isabella planning to get out of her ugly mourning and seem doubly beautiful in the eyes of her lover. But I knew that her ladyship had made her plans and that the girl was being fitted out for going away. Maybe the letter which was so urgent had something to do with it. It was addressed: *Lady Moira Elphinstone, The Old Manor, Egham.*

That was Thursday evening.

On Friday morning, when Mr. Franklin made his after-breakfast visit, her ladyship said, "Jack, darling, I need a little support from you. Would you insist that Alan comes with us to the Whymarks this evening? They know he is home. They will

34

feel hurt. And quite apart from that I feel that he is spending altogether too much time with that gambling set at Mortiboys."

"I agree, my dear. A game of cards is one thing; deep play is another. You insist and you shall have my full support."

"I knew I could rely upon you, darling. Oh, and another thing; I arranged, on the spur of the moment, a little supper party here for Monday. I had no time to consult you. I suddenly realised that Alan has been home a fortnight, and we had not entertained much for him."

"Suits me," Mr. Franklin said. "We're going to be busy. Whymarks this evening, Fennels tomorrow, Rossiters on Sunday. Monday here . . ."

Busy was the word. Miss Isabella busy, stitching away, and no help from me; her ladyship wanted a velvet dress steamed, the lace from a taffeta one washed, ironed, and replaced. Her pillow, she said, felt lumpy, the down must be taken out and teased.

On Monday, about midday, a man, a soldier courier on a sweating horse, rode into the courtyard at the back of the house. He wanted Mr. Alan, Captain Franklin. Leave cancelled.

There was all the muddle of a hurried departure. We stood in a group to wave him away to the wars. Miss Isabella looked stricken, but I doubt if she looked as stricken as I felt. I'd reckoned wrong, after all these years, living close by her ladyship, I'd reckoned wrong. The Bible again: If thine eye offend, pluck it out. Not that Mr. Alan was her eye; but he was her son . . . He had offended her, however, and must be plucked out. And then I said to myself: Martha Pratt, this is nonsense, it simply *happened*. Powerful as she is at Nethergate, her ladyship can't order the British Army about.

On the Wednesday I knew better.

In the country those who live, live long. That same Sam Lockey who had seemed an old man when I was in Baildon and entrusted him to carry my wage and all else that I could scramble together back to Ockley, "That'll be sixpence!" was still on his carrier's round. One day he'd drop dead, or his horse would, or his cart would fall to pieces; so everybody said; but they went on and on, and every Wednesday and Saturday he collected letters and papers from the Hawk in Hand, where the mail coach stopped in Baildon, and delivered them. The papers, when they reached Nethergate, went into the library, to be read by Mr. Franklin and Mr. John. Then Page, the footman, had a glance and brought them to me to be smoothed out with a cool iron before they were passed on to the Rector.

Letters came direct to her ladyship and were sorted by her. Once, long, long ago Mr. Franklin had forgotten to hand her a letter addressed to her and she had said that perhaps in future it would be as well if mail came to her. That had been the rule ever since.

On the Wednesday after Mr. Alan's sudden departure there was a letter which her ladyship read, tore across and across, and dropped into the alabaster urn which stood, open-mouthed, to take anything that was discarded. I retrieved it and pieced it together.

My dear Rosaleen; Before you receive this I hope you will know that we Irish stick together. I acted immediately. A mother of sons myself, I know how very *silly* young men can be. Freddie needed no persuasion. For one of his officers to consort with a French girl. Unthinkable. He believes that all of them who came later are *paid* spies. So he acted at once and I am glad to feel that I have been able to make some slight return for those happy, happy holidays at Barryfergus.

There was more of it; whether the writer should, or should not go to the West Indies with the regiment. If she did dear Rosaleen could rely upon her to keep an eye on Alan.

My scheme had come to nothing; her ladyship's, as usual, had worked perfectly.

One evening Miss Isabella asked, without giving herself away, "Have you heard from Alan, Cousin Rosaleen?"

"I have not. I hardly expect to. Alan is very naughty. He only writes when he wants something."

"I just wondered if he had arrived safely."

"I think we may safely assume that had he not we should have heard."

The hay grew high in the meadows, but Tom, one of the best scythe-swingers in Suffolk, would not this year do more than toss the sweet-smelling stuff, child's work really, and was paid accordingly.

Her ladyship had another letter—at least another letter came—but I had no glance at it. She disposed of it secretly. The warm days lengthened; a beautiful spring. But nothing settled between George and Essie Fakes, though I was glad to hear that she often gave him a meal. Trust George to look after George.

One day Miss Isabella said, "Pratt, do me a favour, will you? *You* ask about my Cousin Alan this evening. I am anxious to know but do not wish to appear insistent."

There was a letter that evening; I saw her ladyship reading it. But that was another of which I never again saw a trace. When at bedtime I ventured my question, her ladyship gave me a sharp look, but said quite good-humouredly, "Of course he was always a favourite of yours, Pratt. But you should know that he is no letter writer."

Presently it was June and on a sultry evening Miss Isabella and I were preparing her ladyship for a reception in Baildon when Page brought up a single letter. Sitting at her dressing table she broke the seal and read the few lines of writing with no change of expression.

"News of Alan, at last," she said.

"Oh. Where is he, Cousin Rosaleen?"

Ever since I had betrayed the secret I had seemed to be more in favour, and on this evening I was doing her ladyship's hair and Miss Isabella was putting away the clothes that had just been discarded. I could see, in the glass, that to ask the question she had paused on her way to the clothes closet.

"At sea," her ladyship said. "He wrote from Plymouth just before sailing. He must now be three days . . ."

There was a thud, soft but quite heavy. I turned and there was Miss Isabella on the floor.

"Ring the bell, Pratt. Madge can administer smelling salts and burnt feathers. We have enough to do if I am to be ready in time."

I rang the bell. But before Madge could answer it, Miss Isabella had come round, clawed herself upright by aid of a nearby chair, tottered around it and sat down. She looked ghastly.

"Give her this," her ladyship said and pointed to the pretty silver-topped smelling bottle, a thing of which she herself had never, in all my time, had the slightest real need. To her it was a weapon to be used on those rare, very rare occasions when she had seemed in some slight danger of not getting her own way. "Jack, darling, you have upset me very much. Hand me my smelling salts."

Miss Isabella sat in the chair, completely limp, her hands hanging over the sides of it. I wrenched the stopper out of the bottle and put it into her hand. Her fingers closed round it, but she did not attempt to use it. Madge came blundering in and her ladyship said:

"It seems that we no longer need you. Pratt, if you could

give me your undivided attention . . . Isabella, you must have been overcome by the heat."

"I am going to have a baby. Alan's baby."

Her ladyship's complexion had already been laid on for the evening; her face did not change colour. Her eyes did. The black centres widened, the blue almost vanished.

She was in every possible way about as far removed as a human being could be from the boy who tumbles a girl in a ditch and two months later hears of the result. Yet she asked the yokel's question:

"Are you sure?"

"Quite sure."

"It will be very difficult to prove that Alan is responsible. Unless, of course, he has admitted it. Did he know? Has he written to you?"

"I did not know myself . . . I have been waiting . . . Waiting to hear . . . He promised." She spoke brokenly. Then she said, almost violently, "A baby must have a father."

"I fully agree. A baby should also have a mother with sense enough to be married before she is pregnant. But it is a little late to think of that. Pratt, this is ill-balanced. You must lower the left or heighten the right." Her eyes were still dark but her manner and her voice were calm. "We must think what to do. Without help from Alan. He is on a long voyage, the exact destination uncertain. By the time a letter reached him and he asked for leave—in the circumstances unlikely to be granted—the baby would be born; fatherless."

"What can we do?" Not *I*, I noticed, but *we*. Asked in that dead voice the use of the word could have two meanings. A challenge: What are you going to do? Or an appeal: What can you do for me?

"We can avoid a scandal. That is better, Pratt. And now I think, my emeralds." She spoke as though her choice of jewels for the evening was fully as important as what they were talking about. "As I see it, two courses are open to you, Isabella." She was having nothing to do with that "we," or with "us." "You could go to London, to one of those French communities and pose as a widow . . ." She paused. Miss Isabella said in a voice not unlike her ladyship's, "That would not be easy. I am Isabella de Savigny. Women who remembered would wish to know who had fathered my father's grandchild. And what had happened to him, that I should be a widow."

"That is a consideration," her ladyship said. "There is an alternative. Immediate marriage to a man of the class where

38

lengthy preliminaries to marriage are dispensed with, and a dowry of a hundred and twenty pounds would be an attraction. Some small farmer, or respectable artisan."

She was wonderfully clever, but ignorant, too. There are no people in the world more respectable than the respectable poor. In the classes she named the rules were very strict; there must never be the slightest hint that the female had been yielding, the man caught. Walking out, invitations to Sunday dinner, inspection by every member of the family, of both families. A courtship never took less than a year, and might take five. Even with us, "We're poor, but we are respectable," had been the motto.

Ignorant again when she said, "Possibly Pratt could help." What small farmer or respectable artisan could I know? Between the smallest farmer, owning or hiring a mere five acres, and a hired labourer like my father or Tom there was a gulf. As wide as the Jordan. Respectable artisans. Little her ladyship knew! Oh, of course, carpenters, builders, bakers, brewers, doffing their caps, saying, "Yes, my lady" . . . "Certainly, my lady." But in their homes, in their families, they were as proud as she was.

In her ignorance, her ladyship said, "A runaway match. That would account for the haste and the secrecy." She stood up, composed, still beautiful if you didn't look too close, and quite formidable. "It must be one or the other, Isabella. And I must warn you. One word that might make Jack suspect and I shall denounce you as a spy, wheedling around Alan in order to gain information of the regiment's movements. Think it over."

I handed her her fan and she said, "Thank you, Pratt," and rustled away.

Apart from my mother, in the old days, and Tom, all the time, I was not given to pitying people, but I did feel sorry for the girl.

I said, "Before I tidy up, I'll bring you a cup of tea."

"Pratt, what shall I do?"

I said, "You must decide that, Miss Isabella."

"My Cousin Franklin is kind, and he loves Alan. I wonder . . ."

I said, "You heard what she said." I think that was the first time that I had ever spoken of her ladyship as *she*. I said, "I know, Miss Isabella. I've been here thirty years and never once have I seen Mr. Franklin stand up to her ladyship over anything that mattered. And I think she meant what she said about spying."

"Yes. Alan said the same. That was why it was all so secret. At the end of his leave he was to go back and ask a friend of his to invite me to stay, and we were to be married. But he never wrote."

Actually I believed that he had, twice. But to mention it would do no good now, even if I had been absolutely sure, which I was not. And it would lead to trouble. I had another thought, too. Anger is a great heartener. She'd stand more chance of being happy in a makeshift marriage, rigged up by her ladyship, if she believed that Mr. Alan had jilted her.

"I'll fetch that tea," I said.

When I came back with it she had lost that limp half-dead look. In fact, for a moment she looked so like her ladyship, not only in shape and colour but in expression, that I wondered to myself: Did something terrible happen to *her* when she was young, to make her so cold and hard and inhuman?

"I have been a fool, Pratt, and must pay for it," Miss Isabella said, and except for the lilt it could have been her ladyship speaking.

I did not feel exactly guilty. I hadn't wished to bring harm to her. I'd simply done the best as I could see it at the moment. Still the fact remained that, unwarned, her ladyship might have handed over any letter addressed to Miss Isabella. If, indeed, any such letter had come. Or again she might have recognised his writing and done, unwarned, exactly what I suspected her of doing. My mind ran this way and that way.

Miss Isabella said, "Can you think of anyone, Pratt? Fairly clean?"

Somebody willing to dispense with preliminaries. Somebody anxious to get hold of a hundred and fifty pounds. Somebody fairly clean.

Who but my brother George?

Narrative by Joanna Drury.

(1793–1796)

I saw the two people alight from the coach when it stopped at Ozary Cross. They'd have been noticeable in a far less lonely place; the man tall and well set up, lacking an arm: old soldier, I guessed; the girl very young, slight, and pretty. I was so busy getting my dropsical patient, Jake Whitton, off the little low cart and into the coach while his wife dealt with the bundles, that I did not notice whether the couple turned towards High Ozary or Outer Ozary. The coach rattled away with Mrs. Whitton crying, "Goodbye, Miss Doctor. Thank you and thank you," and I turned Toby round and led him into the lane, the shortest way to Ozary village which had been my home for thirty-seven years.

The man and the girl were in the lane, well ahead of me. Under his one arm he held a wooden chest and from his other shoulder hung a canvas bag; he stepped out in soldierly fashion. She tottered along, leaning sideways under the weight of quite a small valise; every few steps she twisted an ankle. Her shoes were completely unsuitable, high-heeled and flimsy, and the lane is villainously surfaced as well as steep, running down as it does from the edge of the ordinary land to the marshes.

Toby's hooves and the cart's little iron wheels made quite a clatter, but neither man nor girl looked round, striding and tottering doggedly, like people in a hurry: but as I came nearer they moved aside and I passed and then stopped and said, "Good afternoon," as is the custom in our part of the country, even with strangers. They both looked a bit startled. The girl returned my greeting in a low sweet voice that told me that she came from a long way away; the man said "Afternoon," as though he had no time for civilities. He had a hard, stern face, very deeply tanned; the girl was pale, fragilely pretty.

I said, "You could put your gear on the cart if you liked. I'm going into Ozary."

The girl said, "Oh, thank you," dropped the valise on to the cart, stretched her arm, an arm certainly not meant for carrying things. I waited for the man to shed his load but he said:

"It's no distance. Only to The Unicorn."

"Oh!" I said, "Are you the new owners?"

He said, "Yes. Pratt's my name. This is my wife."

That surprised me; I'd reckoned them to be father and daughter.

"I'm Miss Drury—though you'll never hear me called that. I'm known as Miss Doctor. And you have every right to make use of the cart. It belongs to the inn. I've just taken the Whittons up to the coach and am now taking the cart back."

He ignored this second invitation and walked on, asking:

"You work there?"

I suppose he judged by my clothes. When you're liable to be called out at any hour, when you may have to trudge through farmyard mud, and even, with some low-lying cottages, jump across ditches, you can't go in for fancy clothes. I wear my skirts very short and absolutely plain, double-breasted jackets, with nothing to flop as I bend over a sick bed, or an operation table, and thick soled, ankle-high boots. I can dress myself in less than two minutes. My two winter outfits are made of as good woollen cloth as money can buy, my two summer ones of linen. All my clothes are made by the best tailor in Stoke St. Cross, and Mr. Pratt should have noticed that, and surely realised from what I had said I was called, that I was not an inn servant.

"Oh, no," I said. "My interest in The Unicorn is confined

to the fact that I've been treating Jake Whitton for dropsy."

As a matter of fact I had a far older and more sentimental connection with the inn. In 1743, my father, a fully qualified doctor who had been abroad on some errand that he never mentioned, had been on his way up from the port of Bywater to London and had been taken ill. My grandparents who then owned the inn had taken him in and nursed him; he had fallen in love with the daughter of the house and married her. He learned that in all the vast area south of Stoke St. Cross there was no proper doctor, so he settled down in Ozary, but in the village, not at The Unicorn as my grandparents had wished. Ozary village, he argued, was more central. Actually— I realised this as I grew older—my father disliked the inn, not for any snobbish reason, but because he was a man who set great store on privacy and hated noise. Also he found the marshes, over which the inn had an unbroken view, depressing. So he bought a house, snug in the village, and there, three years after the marriage, I was born. From then until I was five, Mother and I made regular visits. When she died my grandparents offered to take me and for some years after that I was sorry that my father had refused the offer, for in our quiet house the busy man, the strict old housekeeper, had little time for me, and the food was of the plainest. My grandparents always had time, for in those days it seemed they could afford plenty of help about the place; my grandfather knew dozens of fascinating tales and my grandmother was a wonderful cook. The happiest days of my childhood had been spent in the long low building, in the shining busy kitchen, the prim private parlour, and the garden at the rear. I was not allowed into the taproom nor the vast public yard at the side. What went on in the yard, the mustering of cattle that were going down to feed on the drier parts of the marshes for the summer, and remustering when they were brought in for sale in September, the coming and going of the pack-pony strings, I was obliged to watch from the parlour window.

My grandmother was a martinet. Inside the house she did not permit spitting or what she called "foul language." An offender got one warning; if he lapsed again she would say, "If you cannot behave, take your custom elsewhere." There was no inn nearer than five miles away. Once, in one of the booths at the far end of the taproom where she served her wonderful food, a man swore, and she warned him. He then did it again, and she snatched away the beef-steak pudding which she had just set before him and said, "My pudding is too good for your foul tongue, Mr. Beattie. You can eat bread and cheese."

When I was eleven my father decided that he must begin to educate me; he devoted two hours every evening to this task, and then left me so much to learn and to do next day that often I could only get to The Unicorn on Sundays. I did that regularly for the next three years and then my grandparents died within a few days of one another; my father called their sickness influenza, but country people used—and still use—the older name, the sweating sickness. They left the inn and all that was in it, to me. I should have liked to live in it, and one day to run it, authoritative as my grandfather; but my father sold it and invested the money for me. It is, in fact, partly due to my grandparents that I can live as I do, practising medicine without breaking any law, since I never charge a fee. Poor people I treat for nothing; from the others I accept gifts in kind, as and when they are offered.

The steep, stony lane debouched at right angles on to Marsh Road which just skirted the marshes; to the left the road ran to Bywater, to the right into Ozary, Stoke St. Cross, and Colchester. It was not a highway and sometimes in very wet winters it was impassable, but it was a short cut, knocking ten miles off the journey between Bywater and Colchester; it was one reason for the inn's existence.

Pratt set his chest down on the doorstep.

"The woman said she'd leave the key on the sign," he said.

"I saw her do it," I said.

The sign was not one of those painted ones that swing; it was a carved head, fixed just above the doorway. My grandfather had told me that it had once been a ship's figurehead. In his day it had always been painted white, with red nostrils and a golden horn. (One of his stories had concerned a unicorn, lured by some false girl who had tamed it to lie with its trusting head in her lap, so that men could club it to death. The story had haunted me, distressfully, until my father explained that there had never been such an animal as a unicorn; it was just a myth, like the flying horse, Pegasus, and the sheep with the Golden Fleece whom Jason sought.)

Now the unicorn, like the rest of the inn, looked shabby and uncared for. Pratt reached up for the key and opened the door. The stink of stale tobacco, spilled beer, and sheer filth drifted out.

When one attends a patient all one's attention is concentrated and anything irrelevant to his condition is ignored; yet one observes.

44

I said, "I'm afraid you'll find the place a bit of a shambles. Mrs. Whitton was never a good manager and with her husband ill . . ."

"We'll soon clear it up," Pratt said.

We! A man with one arm and this frail-looking girl. It may be a sweeping statement but some people are born fit for hard work and some are not. It has something to do with the neck and the shoulders; an accident of birth yet unrelated to heredity or such circumstance as sufficient or insufficient diet. Girls built like this one born into families where every member must work hard to live, can die of nothing but sheer exhaustion; or they become old and crippled before they are thirty.

On the taproom floor the sawdust, unchanged for a long time, lay clotted with spittle, with mud from boots straight off the marshes, with dogs' droppings. On the bar counter used mugs, blue and white, and pewter tankards stood in puddles.

Pratt stepped in, undeterred. His wife stood in the doorway, staring at the filth not with horror but with complete and absolute helplessness.

I said, "I'll take the cart round to the side. If you'll open that door, I'll bring the mattress and your valise in that way; it is nearer the stairs." As I said that I remembered the state of the bedroom from which I had carried down the mattress to put on the cart in order to make Jake Whitton's journey up the lane as comfortable as possible.

Mrs. Pratt said, "Thank you very much." Pratt turned and asked, "Does the pony belong here, too?"

"No. Toby belongs to me," I said, and was glad to be able to say it. Why, I don't know, unless it is that the process of diagnosis goes on all the time and is not exclusively concerned with the physical. (And Toby was not a *pony!* He was one of that most useful breed, a cross between riding horse and carthorse, thickset, lion-hearted, capable of putting on a spurt of speed in an emergency; unhurried, capable of carrying me—six feet tall, weighing 140 pounds—for hours, for miles and miles on a busy day. I'd had him for six years and he knew his drill. Wherever I went I had no need to tether him. If I said, "Wait," he'd stand until I reappeared, or Gabriel's horn blew. Trivial, perhaps, but if somebody is bleeding to death it is an advantage not to be obliged to look about for a post or a tree to which a horse can be tethered.)

I went round to the yard, unhitched the cart and put it under cover, told Toby to wait, folded the mattress, took up the valise, which in my hand weighed nothing, and went to the side door.

Mrs. Pratt had it opened and was waiting for me. The kitchen had not had a thorough cleaning for years and Mrs. Whitton had not washed so much as a cup for a least a week. Against this background of squalor the poor girl looked helpless and pitiable.

I said, "It's even worse than I thought! Never mind. I'll just take this up and then I'll lend you a hand."

I hauled the mattress upstairs and took the opportunity of emptying the brimming chamber pot out of the window.

When I came down Mrs. Pratt still stood, looking helpless. Pratt came in with four or five mugs hooked by their handles onto his fingers and added them to the clutter on the table.

"Come on, Bella," he said. "First thing, get the fire going."

She said, "I'm sorry. I don't know how. I have never lighted a fire."

It seemed to me an extraordinary thing to say. Never. I have not been called upon to light a fire very often, but I had done it—sometimes on hearths not my own.

"I'll see to the fire," I said.

"And you watch and learn. I'll get the water," he said. "We'll need gallons."

There was something about him that I disliked, yet I found it impossible not to admire him, so brisk and undaunted. He'd pumped three buckets of water and brought them in before I had the fire going. He then took a birch broom and set about the taproom floor, sweeping everything out through the open door. He held the handle between his stump and his body, grasping it lower down with his one hand; very efficient.

When the first kettleful of water was hot, I began to wash up. Mrs. Pratt wiped. She was not exactly clumsy, but she was inept. She'd stand and wipe a thing long after it was dry and then stand and look helplessly about for somewhere to put it. If I had not been so sorry for her I should have been annoyed. As it was I said, "Cups hang on the hooks on the dresser," and "No. Mugs have their own hooks in the taproom."

It struck me that she might be just a bit dim-witted. As we worked I tried to talk. I said, "Have you had a long journey?" She said, "Only from Colchester. That is today . . ." in a vague way. I said, "You are not used to kitchen work," and she said, "No. Before I was . . . before I was married, I was a lady's maid. I mean I was her assistant."

46

That would account for the milk-white hands and the sweet voice. I knew only one of the breed, Lady Thompson's Marion, who was such a deliberate copy of her mistress that when Lady Thompson had to have an ear trumpet, Marion must have one too.

"You'll find this a very different kind of life," I said.

"Yes. I must accustom myself." It did not occur to me then that her answers were deliberately evasive. At intervals she said, "Thank you," and "You are very kind." But she expressed her gratitude with a kind of graciousness which showed me that she had no idea of our relative positions. Here was I, Miss Doctor, every bit as authoritative over a wide area as my grandmother had been in her narrow one, washing dishes, scrubbing the kitchen table.

Pratt, having swept the taproom, took a bucket of hot water and another broom and washed the floor. We'd just got the kitchen fairly shipshape when he came through, went into the yard, emptied the bucket, rinsed it, and the broom—I could hear the pump clunking. When he came in he said, "Mark that. The bucket with the bent handle. Not to be used for drinking water. Now, how's the kettle? I could do with a cup of *char*. Indian for tea." He went to his canvas bag and produced a packet of tea and another of sugar. "The old bitch said she'd include a week's rations in the deal, but I thought better be on the safe side."

(My grandmother would not have approved of that word used in that way!)

Mrs. Pratt was not even adept at making tea. There was the pot, washed clean by me, wiped by her. She hovered over it, helpless and uncertain. She said, "How much?"

Pratt said, "A good pinch for each person and one for the pot."

She made it ineptly, but she poured it with a kind of grace and, handing me my cup, said, "I am sorry. I cannot ask your preference for cream or lemon, having neither."

I was completely baffled. Why had she married him? Why had he married her? I judged him to be forty at least, her sixteen, seventeen at most. He had looks of a sort and she was pretty. Had she been attracted by the attentions of a man so much older; offering an independent life, a place of her own? Or by pity, because he was maimed—women are very susceptible. What in Heaven's name had made him think for one moment that she would be any good at this enterprise?

There is something about tea. It may not rate high on any pharmaceutical list, but I am so convinced of its value that

47

I always carry some with me in my bag. I only produce mine in poor households, where tea is a luxury; in others I simply express a wish. I've seen a cup of tea do more than any words, any prayers could in comforting the bereaved, in combatting shock, soothing tempers.

Over this cup of tea, in the kitchen of The Unicorn, I made an irrevocable mistake.

I began well. I said that his mention of India had confirmed my guess that he had been a soldier. That pleased him, but he lied; he said, yes, seventeen years, ever since he was fifteen which would make him thirty-two; and he was older than that, I knew. He said that he'd reached the rank of sergeant.

Presently I said, "Have you made any arrangements for help about the place, Sergeant Pratt?"

"No. Why should I?"

"I think you will need it. There's a great deal of leeway to make up. And Mrs. Pratt is not very . . . experienced."

Up to then his manner to me had been offhand, now he look at me with hostility.

"She'll learn," he said shortly. "And if you're thinking about *this*"—he touched his stump—"I'm going to have a hook."

"Well," I said, "if you change your mind, let me know. I know everybody in Ozary. I could find you a good strong honest woman."

"I don't want any help," he said, and then added deliberately, "nor any interference."

That angered me. I was only trying to be helpful, and I am not accustomed to incivility. My father began to be infirm when I was eighteen and for four years I acted as go-between, carrying out his instructions. When he died I slipped, almost imperceptibly, into his place, became Miss Doctor, treated everywhere with respect, some gratitude, some awe. The toughest old rogue with a painful boil on his backside learns to be mannerly.

I gave the now tidy kitchen a long, meaningful stare and said, "You will not find me interfering, Sergeant." Then I stood up.

She came with me to the side door and thanked me, said I had been very kind and she did not know how she would have managed without my help. Then she glanced furtively back into the kitchen. He'd returned to the taproom. She said, "Please don't be offended by Pratt. It's just his manner.

48

He's very proud of the way he manages. And I don't think he has money to spare for hired labour."

Seldom have I heard a more unwifely speech. Pratt! She sounded as though she were apologising for some servant's lapse.

I said, "If you ever ail anything, send for me. There's an old man called Ben Stally who looks after Toby; he spends every evening here. He'd bring a message." I had another, interfering thought; my grandfather had kept a horse and cart—not the cart now in the shed, that was specially made and kept for the transport of beer barrels—and had driven to Stoke St. Cross once a fortnight at least, more often if my grandmother so decided. How subsequent owners of the inn had managed I did not know, but I wondered how she would. "If you want any shopping done, let me know," I said. "I go to Stoke St. Cross quite often."

She said, "Thank you *very* much. I think Pratt said that pack ponies would bring our supplies."

"Goodbye, then," I said. "I hope you will be happy here. And prosperous!"

She gave me a look which denied all prospect of such hope being fulfilled. From inside the house Pratt shouted, "Bella," and she gave a little start.

I called to Toby, who came whinneying and nudging. I mounted and rode home.

That was in the first week of July and I did not see Mrs. Pratt again until November; but I heard odds and ends about The Unicorn from Ben Stally, that regular customer. He's a garrulous old man and a gossip, and a bore, since he says everything twice if not three times and in the past I had avoided him as much as possible, giving him orders through Jill, my maid. Now I found myself making excuses to go to the stable when Ben was seeing to Toby.

At first, according to Ben, everybody admired the Sergeant; such a change from old Whitton; cleaned the place up no end. "Wonderful what he do with one hand and a hook." So he'd got his hook! "With one hand and a hook. Wonderful what he do."

Then it was, "A bit strict. Run the place like a barracks. No spitting on *his* sawdust. No, his sawdust ain't for spitting on. And wipe your feet afore you step on his floor. As for dogs they're let in but they do their businesses outside, don't he shout. Yes, he 'on't hev no dog piddle nor droppings on his floor." Probably the old man remembered far enough back to recall that my grandmother had had the same rules. "Language he don't mind. He can swear. Yes, swore at a feller the other night. Feller made the same mistake as we all did. We all made the same mistake, taking the girl for his daughter, not his missus. Natural mistake, her being so young and never answering back as missusses are inclined to. Granted she ain't very handy. No, she ain't handy, but she do do her best. Poor tool, though, yes a poor tool. No life to her like."

Why should this concern me? God knows I have been sorry enough for a lot of women in my time. Pity was nothing new to me. So it must, I thought, be that my curiosity had been aroused. My father had been a great approver of curiosity, he said it was the most single potent element in mankind's development. But he had meant *intellectual* curiosity: Newton seeing an apple fall and asking why? And a hundred other similar questions, asked and answered and of prime importance. My curiosity about The Unicorn was of a baser kind, not so far removed from the twitching aside of a curtain in order to see whether one's neighbour takes one pint of milk or two from the yoked milkmaid.

Despicable, but there it was. I listened, avidly, to Ben Stally's account of the September sales.

At any time the marshes look empty, vast stretches of reeds, bending under the crying wind and the swooping birds. But there is pasture too, and water in plenty. Cattle flourish there. So do the reeds. Much in demand for thatching; cut in late August or early September, baled and sold. What with the reed cutters, those who came to buy the bales, and the butchers, farmers, auctioneers, many coming from such a distance that they must spend a night under the roof of The Unicorn, that poor inept little girl must have had her hands full.

"He managed," Ben Stally said. "She ain't much of a carver. Which is odd, carving being the woman's job. Yes, everywhere I been the woman of the house did the carving, but she ain't handy. She tried. I'm talking now of the busy night. With a bl . . . a great sirloin on the go. She hacked off a couple of slices, very unhandy, then he took over. Lucky he only lost his left hand. Yes, if it came to the point better lose your left, yes, if I was to lose a hand, sooner my left than my right. He took over, hooked the joint with his hook and carved, pink slices no more than paper. Everybody laughed, Miss Doctor. Yes, they laughed, they said he could make a joint of beef go from here to Bywater. Yes, from

50

here to Bywater or as somebody said, in the other direction. Clear away to Colchester. So, as I say, she tried to carve and botched it, so he took over. And, believe it or not then she brought the jug round. Gravy, but she called it sauce. Sauce! It was just gravy, Miss Doctor."

Well, she'd got over the busiest time, and so far as I knew she had ailed nothing. Interest in the newcomers died down so that Ben Stally no longer volunteered information and often I was obliged to listen to his rambling talk for a full ten minutes before I could say, "And how are things at The Unicorn?" and be satisfied with such a reply as "Much of a muchness," or a report of Pratt's activities with whitewash.

Then, well into November, I came home just before dusk. I'd been to Outer Ozary, delivering a child which had an understandable reluctance to enter this world where nothing but hunger awaited it. One risk any doctor who visits hovels runs is the picking up of vermin and the only real precaution I knew was the one my father had always taken when he had spent any time in what he called "a dubious house." In an otherwise empty bedroom I had a wide, shallow tin bath, into which, having removed only my boots, I stepped and stood and undressed, shaking each garment well. The "bag," as people say of a more lively pastime, was on this evening four, and I was in my bedroom, putting on a clean shift, a dressing gown, and slippers when the doorbell rang and Jill pounded up the stairs and said crossly:

"It's that Mrs. Pratt from The Unicorn. No need to hurry, she ain't *ill*. She just want to see you. Shall I hold back your dinner some more?" My usual dinnertime was three o'clock, and though Jill had been with me for full twelve years and I was frequently unpunctual she had never quite resigned herself.

I ran downstairs into the parlour. It would be wrong to say that I should have passed her, unrecognising, had I met her in Stoke St. Cross High Street, but I can say with truth that I have never seen, except in cases of galloping consumption, such a change in four months. In July she had looked so young, so pretty; pale, yes, fragile, yes, but prettily so, like a wood anemone. She had a little cap of black curls, rather like a black lamb's fleece, very glossy. I'd noticed her eyes, too; a beautiful blue with extremely clear whites and that damp look to the lids which is a sign of youth. Now her eyes, like her hair, were dull and there were lines about her mouth. She could have been thirty or more.

I said, "I am very glad to see you, Mrs. Pratt. Do sit down."

"Thank you. I must not stay. I have come to ask you a *very* great favour. You did once say that you would bring anything I needed from Stoke St. Cross."

"Of course. I'm going there tomorrow. What do you want me to bring?"

"Some salt, please. I must explain. Pratt tells me what to order and a man with a pack pony brings the goods. I forgot to order the salt. But Pratt had ordered half a pig, to be put down in brine. He was much annoyed when the pig arrived and the salt did not. I could only think of you, Miss Drury."

Something about her fascinated me. So many contradictions. Referring to her husband as Pratt as to a servant, still, and yet seeming to mind his annoyance: the clarity and lucidity of her speech in such contrast with the cheap shawl that she wore; the dignity and yet the appeal in her manner.

I said, "I am reasonably sure that I can let you have all the salt you need, Mrs. Pratt. I keep a good store." I used it, not only domestically, but medically. I have never understood what makes people wake, writhing and screaming with night cramp, but I do know that a draught of water, heavily salted, is the quickest cure.

She said, "If you would be so kind. I shall not forget again; I will order the salt and repay you. Before bothering you I did try in the village and could only obtain this." She held out the meagre piece, and the shawl slipped. I then saw that she was heavily pregnant; six months at least. Again the contradiction. In early pregnancy—especially an unwelcome one— women tend to lose their looks, but later there is a bloom. I've noticed it dozens of times, even in quite middle-aged women who no more needed another baby than they needed a broken limb. By the third month they become resigned, fill out all over, grow sleek. This girl had not. She was so thin that the bulge was almost obscene.

I said, "I see you are going to have a baby."

"Yes. Sometime in April."

April! Did she take me for a fool? To anybody else who had made such a statement to me I should have said: You're out in your reckoning. February at the latest. But somehow I couldn't say it to her, and why not I could not say. What I did say was:

"You must take care of yourself, Mrs. Pratt, and not get upset over things like salt."

She said, "What happens to me no longer matters. It would be a good thing if we both died, when the time comes."

I had heard that before, but not from a woman so far gone.

"You must not talk like that. You will find that the baby will be a joy to you."

She gave me precisely the same look as she had given me when I hoped she'd be happy and prosperous at The Unicorn. Disbelief, a kind of scorn. Who believes in fairy tales? I felt again that stab of pity, this time mingled with a touch of pique. At the inn door I had merely expressed a conventional wish; now I was speaking from experience of something which I knew. And I was not accustomed to having my opinion questioned, even by a look.

She had evidently hurried out, with her sleeves still rolled to the elbow. To within two inches of her wrist bone the skin was still of a peculiar whiteness; hard work had ruined her hands.

"Do sit down," I said. "I'll fetch the salt."

I told Jill to wrap two blocks—she'd need that much for half a pig. Then I slipped upstairs and hastily dressed in the outer clothes I had not worn that day. I took one block of salt under each arm, looked into the parlour and said, "I'm ready."

"I am imposing on you, Miss Drury. I could carry it. I'm quite accustomed to carrying things—now."

"It's something that women in your condition should avoid as much as possible," I said.

I noticed that she had changed her unsuitable, high-heeled shoes for a pair of what in our district were known as "high-lows," neither shoes nor boots, ankle high, made of leather as hard as wood, the flat heels and thick soles studded with nails. Proper walking wear, but she still seemed to stumble along, as though they were too heavy for her.

"I understand that you've been rather busy," I said.

"Very busy."

I tried one or two other openings, but she was as uncommunicative as she had been on that first day. Then she said:

"I don't suppose you would know anything about the management of a brick oven?"

"I have never used one. But I've watched my grandmother baking in the very one in your kitchen."

"I can fire it," she said. "And I can now make bread dough. Where I fail is in the timing. Sometimes when it is quite brown and looks ready, it is doughy in the middle."

"You test it. Turn a loaf out of the tin and rap it sharply on the underside; then *listen*. If it hisses, however slightly, it is not fully cooked."

"Oh, thank you. Even Pratt didn't know that!"

It was full dark now, and presently we could see the light that hung from the unicorn's horn. She slowed her walk and halted.

"Miss Drury, would you mind if I pretended that I had obtained the salt in the village? Pratt would prefer to think so."

"Why should I mind?" I did though because it sounded as though she were scared of him and I remembered my swift judgement of him as a hard harsh man to whom I wouldn't have cared to hand Toby.

I put a block of salt under each of her arms; then she could not manage the shawl, so I tied its ends in a knot over her breast.

"When your time comes," I said, "send for me, if you can. If not there's an old dame at High Ozary, Mrs. Coppinstall, who is a fairly capable midwife. And Mrs. Pratt . . . Try to think hopefully about the baby. And to look after yourself."

"Thank you very much. You have been so kind."

Encased in her mysterious reserve, she staggered away with her load. I hurried back to my belated dinner.

Anybody who practises medicine must learn detachment or go mad. One may sympathise, and pity; one must not become involved. I had learned this early, while my father was still alive but too tremulous to lift a cup to his lips, too infirm to leave his bed. A man came for help. His dog had bitten him days before; cobwebs had stopped the bleeding, but bread poultices had not healed the suppurating wounds.

"Does it stink, his hand?" my father asked.

"Yes. To high Heaven."

"Sweet and rotten?"

"That exactly describes . . ."

"Then it must be cauterized. And you must do it."

I said, "Father, I can't."

"And who will, if you don't? Must a man lose his hand, his arm, his life, simply because you are squeamish? Give him some brandy while the iron heats. Have some yourself, if you need it; but *afterwards*."

I always remember that operation, because then I was involved. It was *my* flesh that sizzled, *my* hand that changed from the stink of rot to the stink of charring. His pain was mine. But we both survived. The man is alive today with his misshapen and somewhat contracted hand. He is still grateful. He breeds sheep and whenever he kills one for family use he sends me a leg of mutton. And I should be grateful to him, for on that faraway day I learned a valuable lesson. To suffer *with* a patient does nobody any good, least of all the patient. I have cauterized many wounds since then, far more briskly, far more skilfully, because I have learned the art of detachment.

However, on this November evening, hurrying home, eating my dinner, I felt that I was in danger of becoming involved again. I told myself sternly that in the main it was because my curiosity had been quickened. People confide in me; it is not unusual for people to send for me simply in order to confide under cover of some trivial ailment. They waste my time, in a way, but having unburdened themselves they feel better, and *are* better. Mrs. Pratt had confided nothing, at least not directly. Indirectly she had told me a great deal—but nothing that I wanted to know.

"Well, yes," Ben Stally said, "naturally, not being blind we noticed. Couldn't help but notice. But he's a funny man the Sergeant. Way back, must have been September somebody up and congratulated him. Old Coppy—you know, Ma Coppinstall's husband—said something and the Sergeant took it badly. Very badly indeed. Looked as black as thunder and said something about us being a lot of gossiping old women. That's what he said, and us there, drinking beer. You'd have thought a man with his *first*. Knock up nine or ten that's different. And he don't spare her none. No, a hard man is the Sergeant. Hard on hisself, hard on others. Yes, a hard man, he is."

Winter closed in and Christmas came, bringing me, as usual, a plethora of gifts from my better-off patients. Over one present I grinned. Old Sir Charles Thickthorn at Stoke Priory sent me three bottles of port. I'd told him that there was a connection between the drinking of port wine and gout! And I had the answer to that sidelong jibe. Next time he sent for me I should ask him how he would fare if I'd drunk a bottle a night and given myself gout so that I couldn't mount Toby.

Much of what Christmas brought me I passed on to my poor patients whose festive season would otherwise have lacked cheer. I could truly say that Jill and I had more than we could eat. Some, even of the poorest, have their pride and I was pretty skilled at not giving offence.

The New Year, 1794, came in with some of the worst

weather within living memory. But January, however detestable, does hold promise. The days lengthened almost imperceptibly and even when the snow lay and the northeast wind blew, just occasionally in the west the sky would lighten towards evening, with a streak of daffodil yellow, or apple green.

One morning, towards the end of the month, I was dressing and thinking that in a month's time I should not be dressing by candlelight when I had—no, not a premonition, nothing so precise—a kind of feeling about Mrs. Pratt. She'd said April, but I knew better. At least, if I didn't know better I should give up and take to knitting.

Jill said, "Miss Doctor, that Ben Stally wants you." She didn't like Ben and usually referred to him in that way. I ran down. In the bleak, greyish light of dawn, Ben looked grey and shame-faced. He said, "Miss Doctor, I was give a message last night. But I clean forgot it. I was a bit boozed up to tell you the truth." He was not an admirable character; I'd known that for a long time, but he was honest.

"What message?"

"Well, it seems there was a bit of an accident down at the inn, early yesterday. The missus took a tumble on the stairs and started the baby up. And Ma Coppinstall had a job at Outer Ozary so the Sergeant give me a message . . ."

"And you did not deliver it. You *wicked* old man!" I said. "You wait till you want another tooth pulled, God damn you! Go and saddle Toby."

"He ain't had his breakfast."

"You heard me. Saddle him, and be quick."

I darted back into the house, pulled on my boots and reached for my coat, a coachman's coat, three collars, practically impervious, and the beaver tricorne hat which I had adopted long ago, the most practical headwear, shedding rain or melting snow as gullies in a roof shed them. "Best foot forward," I said to Toby.

She was no more built for childbearing than she was for heaving and carrying. So far as I could see she had not hurt herself in the fall. But she had been in labour for a long time, if Ben Stally and Sergeant Pratt were to be believed. Nearly twenty-four hours and nothing to show for it except a failing pulse and the contractions growing weaker and weaker. You can lose both mother and child that way; that old thing about the irresistible pressure meeting the irresistible opposition.

A forcible delivery. Something I'd always hated. It does pose such problems. Mother or child? I had faced that question before. It is sad; one of those choices which must be faced rationally. A good mother with seven young children, in a muddle with her eighth. A comparatively easy decision. Similarly with a young woman, much loved, but with the lung sickness for which there was no cure, due to die in a year, or less. Again easy—she is done for, the baby may have a chance. This was different.

Religion had had no part in my upbringing, but as I set to work that morning I found myself thinking: God help me! No help was forthcoming from any other source. Ordinarily there are relatives, or neighbours. In very outlying places I've known a man to help. But Pratt did not come near. When the baby was born I could do no more than clear its face, wrap it in a blanket from the bed, and lay it aside. Then I turned back to her. As I worked I said, "You've got a lovely little girl." The trite adjective slipped out. Anything less lovely than a newborn baby you would go far to find.

At that point most women, however unwelcome the newcomer may be, show some interest. Mrs. Pratt did not. During the ordeal she had shown great fortitude; now her attitude was one of supreme indifference.

Having settled her I turned back to the baby. A perfectly normal, full-term child, nails on her fingers, hair on her head. I asked myself what had the Pratts been playing at? There was no sign of any preparation; no cradle, no baby clothes. Yet they must have known. He must have known when he repudiated the beer drinkers' congratulations: she must have known when she said, "In April." I thought to myself that the story of a fall on the stairs precipitating the birth might do for public consumption, but I was not deceived. Perhaps that was why I had not been sent for sooner. I remembered her remark about it being a good thing if she and the baby died when the time came. Had her wish to die twisted itself into a determination to do so? And had he concurred? If so, why? I looked back to that summer afternoon when they had alighted from the coach and she'd looked so young and pretty, a wife any man would have been proud of and wished to cherish a bit, at least for a year or two. But his attitude had been far from cherishing even then.

I could think of only one explanation: Not his child?

In that case the prospect of the little mite whom I was now washing was an unhappy one. Men, however rough and hard, usually have some feeling for their own. I'd known a

57

case or two where a child's death had been the cause of a coroner's inquest, but in no case that I could remember had the man concerned been the natural father.

I said to myself: Oh rubbish, Joanna Drury! You are allowing your imagination to run away with you; making a much out of very little. I washed the child and used for a cradle that old makeshift, a drawer; laying the blanket in first and then tucking the flaps over.

Mrs. Pratt appeared to be sleeping, as women generally did even after a normal labour. I went down.

Standing as it does, so little above the marshes, The Unicorn has no proper, underground cellar, too readily flooded. What is called the cellar is no more than three steps down, at the rear of the house. I found Pratt there, grappling with a barrel; not easy for him. As Ben Stally had said, he could dig his hook into a joint and hold it firm, but his hook driven into a barrel might puncture it. I said, "You have a daughter."

"Everything all right?"

"So far as anyone can judge at the moment."

"Good," he said. I then made a grave mistake. Not quite myself. I said, "Can I lend you a hand with this?" It is, after all, a very ordinary expression; lend a hand, but not one, I admit, to be used to a man who has only one.

"I can manage. If you'd get out of the way."

I stood aside and watched as he manhandled the barrel up the three steps, across the kitchen, along the passage and into the taproom. There, using his knees as well as his one hand and his hook, he heaved it onto the stand.

"Well?" he asked, turning to me.

"I did rather wonder," I said, "with the baby coming so suddenly, if you had made any arrangements for a woman to come in and look after things."

"No. I can manage for a day or two."

"It will be rather more than that. A woman should be given a fortnight. As a general rule. And your wife has had a difficult confinement."

"You said she was all right."

"I said as far as one could judge."

"I've known women up and about the next day."

"So have I. But they did themselves damage."

"We don't want hired help." It occurred to me that perhaps he could not afford it. The Whittons were capable of driving a hard bargain; to get possession of The Unicorn, lock, stock, and barrel, ready to move into, he might have been obliged to borrow money.

I said, "Look, in Ozary there is a woman who would come in and do for you, without charge. She'd do it to oblige me."

And indeed why not? Who but me would have taken the risk? She was a widow, with one son. There was the yellow grey film, blocking the windpipe, and the boy dying. I'd done a hasty tracheotomy, on the kitchen table; inserted the broken off stem of a clay pipe. Touch and go. But he'd lived and whatever I asked of Mrs. Dodman she would do.

Pratt said, "I don't want your charity."

In the ordinary way I should have lashed out—I am quite good at invective; but I had her to think of. So I controlled myself.

I said, "As you wish. They are both asleep now. When your wife wakes she should have some nourishment. Have you any broth?"

"There's little call for broth in a place like this. I'll make a cup of tea later on."

He turned away and began to tinker with the bunghole of the newly placed barrel.

I went into the larder. Poor little girl, she had tried. It was all as neat and clean as it had been in my grandmother's time, but it was pitiably ill-stored. The season when there was a demand for meals at The Unicorn was over and it looked to me as though the Pratts had faced the winter on a diet of bread, salt pork, and hard Suffolk cheese. I then remembered that my yesterday's dinner had included a boiled fowl.

Getting into the saddle, I said, "Come on, Toby. Home!" We went even more swiftly than we had come, for he had missed his breakfast. While he ate it, I drank a hasty cup of tea, told Jill to put the liquor in which the fowl had been boiled into a bottle, the remainder of the fowl, some eggs, butter and a jar of honey into a basket, and then I went upstairs to raid a thing seldom found in the homes of middle-aged spinsters—a chest of baby clothes.

There are genuinely premature babies who arrive before preparations are complete; there are even more who come to families so poor that they can only be wrapped in some cast-off bit of clothing. It was my habit in such cases to *lend* layettes, complete even to napkins. They were always faithfully returned, washed, ironed, if needs be mended, and often with some touching little addition. Everybody knew about my baby chest and better-off mothers frequently gave me garments their own children had outgrown. At any given moment I could have clad a dozen children aged from one day to two years. I picked out the best of the smallest size and returned to the inn. Jill, though disliking Ben Stally, was not above gossiping with him and had wanted to know how early the Pratt baby was. I answered obliquely, "It is difficult to say. Mrs. Pratt fell downstairs." Even in the best of working-class people there is a hunger for a bit of scandal. It stems from a lack of drama in their own lives. If for some reason of their own the Pratts wished to pretend that this baby was premature, it was not for me to expose them. But I still could not see *why*. They had arrived out of the blue; they could have been married a year, or eighteen months for all anybody in Ozary knew. Then I saw one possible explanation. Perhaps Pratt had married without being fully in the know and in his early days at the inn might have let slip some incautious word about how long they had been married.

Why then, I asked myself, had his attitude, even on that first day, been so unfond? Because he knew by then that she was not as virginal as she looked, though he did not yet know that she was pregnant? This hypothetical explanation satisfied me.

I said, "Mrs. Pratt, you *must* take this broth. How do you think you're going to feed the baby if you don't take some nourishment yourself?"

"Feed it?" She spoke with genuine astonishment.

"Suckle it. Despite being so thin you are going to have a good breast of milk."

She looked so blank, so helpless that I was obliged to remind myself of what her life had been. A lady's maid and an assistant implied a rich household. Rich women did not breast feed, they put their babies out to nurse. Maids in such households lead sterile lives, or are quickly dismissed. It was just possible that she had never seen a baby being fed.

I explained. "She will wake soon, and she will be hungry. So drink your broth and eat your toast."

While she did so, listlessly, I laid out the baby clothes. Most women respond to anything miniature, but she hardly looked, though she said thank you several times.

"Look at this smocking," I said. "It was done by a woman with hands so coarse from field work that you could hardly believe them capable of such delicate stitching. Her baby was so premature that it was only just not a miscarriage. I lent her an outfit and when she returned it, this was included."

She had not asked to see the child. She was facing the whole complicated business of maternity with that same look of helplessness, tinged with despair, as she had faced the filthy taproom, the cluttered kitchen. But she had managed; had managed surprisingly well. And could again, if she would only rouse herself. If not the infant's prospects were not good.

The baby woke and made little mewing noises. I picked it up, wrapped it in the shawl and laid it in her arms. She looked at the baby with positive distaste.

"Red hair," she said.

"It will rub off, I assure you. Babies seldom keep the hair they are born with. It may grow again in quite a different colour."

Fortunately babies do not know at first whether they are welcome or not. Their instinct is to survive. This was no exception.

Once mouth and nipple were firmly engaged I turned away. I always do.

I am celibate both from force of circumstance and by choice. To begin with, few men wish to marry a woman six feet tall, plain of face, educated on masculine lines and engaged, even when young, on the fringe of a masculine profession. But had I been small and pretty and entirely domesticated, I should still be a spinster because I have never seen a man whom I wished to marry, a man to whose will and preferences, whims, prejudices, habits, I must subject my own for a lifetime. I get along with men very well on the whole and have a liking for some of them. Of a few, like gouty old Sir Charles Thickthorn, I am positively fond, but only on my own terms; they must do what I say. Yet I know very well that a meek, complaisant husband would be one I should despise.

Nevertheless, I should have liked a child; a boy who could perpetuate the name and be a *proper* doctor. I am one of those in full sympathy with Queen Elizabeth Tudor, who when told that Mary Queen of Scots had a son, remarked, "I am but a barren stock." With me, as with her, a line would end. Nobody to whom to pass on the accumulated knowledge of a lifetime, the little tricks, the short cuts. Even my house and my books will pass into the hands of strangers when I die.

About all this I am rational as a rule. Nothing but a virgin birth or a midnight visit from Zeus could solve my problem. I do not brood or grieve; but when I see a woman nursing for the first time, giving the very stuff of life to a scrap of a thing which with luck will one day be a person, a link in the chain . . . Yes, I look away.

When I looked back at the bed a remarkable transformation had taken place. Mrs. Pratt was looking down at her baby with adoration and that complacent, fulfilled look which even poor stray cats wear when they have produced kittens doomed to a terrible life unless they are mercifully drowned.

I said briskly, "Have you thought of a name for her?"

"Yes. You have been so kind. I would like her to be called after you."

I said, "Oh no. My name is Joanna, I always hated it."

"My name is really Isabella. Bella I detest. Could we perhaps compromise? Half yours, half mine. Not Annabella, that might become Bella too; Annabelle. Then however it is shortened it would be pleasant. Annabelle." Her face darkened. "I think Pratt will want her to be called Martha. That is his sister's name, and she did a lot for him."

"More compromise," I said. "Annabelle Martha, Martha Annabelle."

After that I showed her how to fix a napkin and we dressed the baby in the smocked flannel nightshift.

Next morning I went out to the stable to administer the scolding that Ben Stally deserved.

"If ever," I said, "you are given a message for me and are too idle or drunk to deliver it, I shall sack you on the spot." Feeding and grooming Toby, feeding him each morning and mucking out the stable twice a week, leaving a full manger and a filled bucket to await our return was the only regular work the old man had, except in the reed-cutting season. But he seemed more concerned with the threat I had rapped out about the teeth. And indeed from the moment the first one is cut to the moment when the last one is lost teeth are a bugbear; you can tell that by the number of toothache remedies, handed down, orally or in writing; by the number of charms which the superstitious believed to be effective. When a tooth was past remedy, or magic, extraction was the only answer. I could whip out a tooth, swiftly, if not painlessly and I did it often. Blacksmiths, in areas too far from Ozary for a person maddened by pain to travel to me, did a bit of butchery; and once a month a tooth drawer visited Stoke St. Cross, with a little boy who banged a drum, partly to draw attention to his master's patter and partly to drown out the screams of those being operated on.

"You didn't mean that, about the next tooth, did you, Miss Doctor?"

"I most surely did. I shall look in on Mrs. Pratt today, and perhaps tomorrow. After that I cannot give her my full attention. So I must depend upon you. Fail me again and God help you."

"Tell you one thing," Ben said in an attempt to divert me. "Mean. Didn't I say he was mean? The Sergeant. You'd have thought with his first and all right despite the mishap he'd have opened his hand and arst us to wet the baby's head. We waited and nothing happened. Not a word. In the end Old Coppy said, "How about a mug to the baby?" And the Sergeant said the baby was all right and didn't need to be drunk to. Disappointed, I gather, by a girl. Yes, a girl first is a bit of a disappointment; at first, though I've seen a lot of men come round. Come round to liking the little old girls better than their brothers, sometimes."

I did not get down to the inn as early that morning as I should have wished, being called to a deathbed in High Ozary. I walked into the kitchen at about midday and there was Mrs. Pratt at the sink. She was supporting herself by leaning her elbows on its edges while her hands dabbled feebly with some washing. She turned her bleached face to me and smiled.

"What on earth do you think you are doing? Do you want to be an invalid all your life?"

"She must be kept clean."

"I'll see that she is. There are plenty of poor women in Ozary who'd be only too glad to wash those for twopence a dozen. Back to bed with you at once."

At the foot of the stairs I put my arm around her to help her climb and a great wave of protectiveness washed through me. I thought: She shall have a week in bed at least; even if I have to move in and act as watchdog and cook. I'd do my best to make her some dainty little dishes, but that stubborn fellow would wish himself back in the Army!

Her pulse was soft and slow; better so. No sign of fever.

The baby was asleep.

"Is she taking her food?"

"Oh yes, she is very good." Infatuated, like any young mother.

"That's another thing you must bear in mind. If you exert yourself too much and too soon, you may lose your milk. Yesterday I offered your husband a good woman who would come without charge, but he refused. I shall try him again. If he's still so stupid he must manage downstairs as best he can and I'll bring you some food every day. I'll take away the soiled things and bring them back clean. We'll manage somehow."

She said, "Please don't say anything to Pratt. He is already so angry about the clothes."

"The clothes? Oh, the layette. I suppose he regarded that as charity, too. Did you tell him that they were only lent and that I am in the habit of providing in emergencies."

"Of course. But he did not believe it. He accused me . . ." She broke off and looked into the makeshift cradle. "I've been having some strange thoughts. I've never been close to a baby before. We were all like that once, weren't we? Even Pratt. And then life does things to us. He has had a great deal to put up with. Not least from me."

Typical post-parturition sentimentality; but it augured well for the resumption of their life together and of that I was glad. I made up my mind to coax, not scold him into accepting Mrs. Dodman. I went down and cut her a little of the cold fowl and some bread and butter and taking the meal up promised to see her tomorrow. Then I went down and bundled the wet things from the sink into a towel. As I was doing it Pratt came in from the taproom and said, "You! Where's Bella?"

"In bed, Sergeant Pratt. I want her to stay there for at least a week."

"Why? You said she was all right."

I kept hold of my temper. "She is. And we want her to stay so, don't we? I need your co-operation over this. Please, will you not reconsider Mrs. Dodman?"

Cajolery is not my line. I felt silly doing it and did it badly. Or at least unsuccessfully.

He said, "I won't have you making Bella sorry for herself. You did it that very first day. And I warned you. No meddling, I said. And I meant it." He put his hand into his pocket. "Two visits," he said. "What do I owe you?"

"I never charge for my services. And even if I did I would not take money from you, Sergeant. If you cannot afford to feed Mrs. Dodman you certainly cannot afford to pay me."

That stung him; below the burnt-in tan of his face the hot colour rose.

"Get out," he said.

"I am going. When I have fetched something I left upstairs. But now *I* am warning *you*. Unless your wife has at least a week in bed, you may have an ailing woman on your hands."

I ran upstairs. I said, "My dear, I failed. I've been ordered off. Take what care you can. I'll take the washing. I'll get Ben Stally to bring it back clean every night. Put it by the back-door step for him to collect and you'll find clean things there in the morning. Do take care."

For the first time I saw her eyes fill with tears.

"You are so very kind, Joanna. And I can never hope to repay . . ."

Since my father breathed his last nobody had used my given name. Miss Drury, Miss Doctor, Miss, even sometimes, Ma'am. But never Joanna.

I said, "But you can, Isabella, you can. By looking after yourself and taking joy in your baby."

Once again I was dependent upon Ben Stally. It sounds absurd but he seemed to think the carrying back and forth of baby clothes rather beneath his dignity. But I had him in hand, and an extra shilling worked wonders.

"Would you believe, Miss Doctor, there ain't going to be no christening. Coppy and me and a few regulars reckoned he was saving the free drinks. Free drinks for the christening we reckoned, but there ain't going to be no christening. Think of that."

In most parishes the incumbents, however lax in other matters, do try to observe the rites over marriages, christenings and funerals. At Stoke St. Cross the rector had been known to officiate at a funeral with his clerical garb over his hunting gear. But at Ozary the rector, James Thickthorn, cousin to my gouty old patient, had long ago given up. He suffered from a mild form of paralysis agitans and thought he had done his full duty if he went every Sunday morning, supported by a stout manservant, through his garden gate into the church, where he'd haul himself into the pulpit and deliver an incomprehensible sermon, an hourglass by his side and if the sand in it seemed to run too slowly, he'd reverse it. More and more people in Ozary, High Ozary, and Outer Ozary were turning Methodist. And who could blame them? The Reverend James Thickthorn was the last person to chase Sergeant Pratt and suggest that the little girl should be christened.

The christening or the lack of it mattered little to me.

I asked the question which I allowed myself about once a week. "How does Mrs. Pratt look, Ben?"

The answer was almost as much a routine.

"A bit like a washed-out rag. But there never was much to her. She never looked a well woman. No, never a well woman even at her best. But she's doing. Up and about. Funny thing, nobody seen the baby. Coppy did arst. When are we going to have a look at the youngster? he arst. The Sergeant said she was asleep. I s'pose it's all right?" Ben cocked that salacious-gossiping-scandal-hunting eye at me. "Coppy said, what with no drinks and no christening maybe the poor little thing had its legs back to front or something."

I said, "Ben, you may assure Coppinstall and anyone else who is interested that Mrs. Pratt's baby, when I last saw it, was normal and in good shape."

And by mid-March *she* was in good shape enough to send instead of a bundle of washing a little note: *Thank you for everything. I can manage now.*

April, May. The lean, wild-eyed cattle coming down to the peace of the marshes, for most of them the first step towards the shambles. The pony trains on the move. She'd be busy, I thought.

And then Ben said something. "Mean as muck, the Sergeant. On that we all agree. Plain mean. Busy as he is and one handed, I offered, so did Coppy, to drag the cart up to the Cross and meet the dray. We offered, having nothing to do, afternoons. But no. I can manage he says and not even a thank you. I can manage he says, so let him manage we say."

The brewer's dray could come no nearer to The Unicorn than the crossroads, the lane was too narrow, too steep, and too rough. My grandfather had had the little cart made, and would harness his horse to it and go up to the Cross to meet the dray on Tuesday afternoons. That is, if he had an empty barrel to take and a full one to bring back. In the slack season, when the consumption of beer was slow, he would walk up without the cart, just to have a chat with the brewer's man.

I said, teasingly, to Ben, "The Sergeant saw through you two old rogues! He knew you were after free beer by hook and by crook."

Ben grinned. "Why else would we offer? We wouldn't offer for love of him, would we? Not for love, we wouldn't."

"In my grandfather's time the dray came on Tuesdays, if I remember rightly. About two o'clock."

"Still do. But the Sergeant he ain't one for wasting time, not nobody's time. If he want a cask, he go up on the Monday afternoon and tie a red rag to a bush. If he don't put out the rag the dray go straight on."

The arrangement might have been designed for me. On the following Tuesday morning I made it my business to ride by Ozary Cross, and there, in the hedge, the red rag bloomed like a flower.

I reckoned that it would take Pratt twenty minutes to haul the cart up the lane, ten perhaps to unload and load again, fifeen to return, for though then the road would be downhill, the cask must be steadied.

I timed myself so well that as I rode into the yard on one side of the house, I could hear the rattle of the cart in the lane beyond.

She was so pathetically pleased to see me. She was preparing bread for the oven. The baby, still in the makeshift cradle, lay on the hearth. It was specklessly clean and looked well. It had not lost its birth hair, but the colour had darkened slightly. I congratulated her upon her beautiful baby, and for a moment her face lit up, losing its harassed look. I asked how she was herself and she said she was well. She looked far from it, but unless one wishes to frighten a patient into some action it does no good to comment unfavourably.

That morning I had found a south-facing bank studded with cowslips and had picked a handful which I held towards her, saying, "They smell of spring." She couldn't take them with her floury hands, so I looked about on the dresser for a mug to hold them.

"Oh, I mustn't keep them," she said nervously. "He'd know you'd been. Thank you for bringing them, all the same."

"Couldn't you say you found them on the back-door step?"

She looked positively alarmed. "Oh, no. That, if possible, would be worse. He's so jealous. He is affronted if a customer is even civil to me. When the cattle came a young man, who was staying overnight, said, "That was a very nice supper, Mrs. Pratt, thank you." And Pratt called out across the taproom that nobody need be grateful for what he'd paid for." Instantly she seemed to regret having said so much and retreated.

"Excuse me if I get on. The oven is almost ready."

That day I raked out the ashes of the faggot which had heated the oven, turning my face aside from the hot blast of air that met me as I opened the heavy iron door. Everything to do with a brick oven was heavy. The faggot that must be heaved in; the rake for the ashes, the long handled, spade-shaped tool with which the things to be cooked must be placed into the depths of the hot cave. I remembered that my grandmother, with a white apron over her silk dress, had made her own bread and pastries and pies, and had tested the loaves herself, but she had spared herself the heavy work: "Jenny, the oven door, please," she would say.

"Do you always bake bread on Tuesdays?" I asked.

"As a rule. Pratt is a great one for routine."

"Then whenever the red rag is in the hedge I can at least help with the raking out and the putting of the bread in. Or any other little job that you care to save for me, and that can be done in half an hour."

This reminder of time made her throw a hurried glance at the clock which wagged its pendulum against the wall.

I also was aware of the time.

After that I fell into the routine of which Sergeant Pratt was so fond. Every Tuesday morning, a visit to Ozary Cross; if the rag were there, an afternoon visit to the inn. I tried always to take some little treat, something edible, for she still looked ill-nourished to me. I got to know her a bit better, but not really well for quite a long time. She once told me that one of the things she missed most was anything to read. "I always liked reading and at . . . at the place where I worked there was a good library. Now the only printed word I ever see is when something comes wrapped in newspaper. Months old sometimes, but I try to skim through before using the paper to light the fire."

I had many books—not all of them medical. I subscribed to two papers and three magazines, but I could not lend or give her a thing. I told myself that I was in much the same position as a woman whose beloved daughter had made an unfortunate marriage, and who had fallen out with her son-in-law and been forbidden the house.

Once I played a trick on Ben Stalley. While he groomed Toby in warm weather, he hung his disreputable old jacket on a nail just inside the stable door. One morning I slipped a copy of Richardson's *Pamela: or Virtue Rewarded,* into the ragged pocket and then as he straightened up from the grooming, said with feigned surprise, "Why, Ben, I didn't know that you were a reader."

"What you mean, Miss Doctor?"

"Is that not a book I see in your pocket?"

"A *book?*"

"What would you call it? It looks like a book to me. A reward for virtue, it says. Have you been virtuous, Ben?"

"I been cutting reeds."

"Somebody must have done it for a joke," I said.

"Not much of a joke, if you ask me. Not much of a joke. Anybody want to give me something might of give me something a bit useful."

"You are right. Ben, do you know what I should do if I were you? I'd take it back to The Unicorn and put it down on a table. Then whoever put it into your pocket last night would know that you had seen the joke. Virtue rewarded indeed."

"I was a bit foxed last night; just a bit foxed. Reed-cutting is dry work, Miss Doctor. But virtue. Reward for virtue. A bit nasty. Though acsherly last night we was talking about how some people get everything and others get nothing . . ."

It was not a trick that could be tried twice.

In another way I was able to be of service to her. Was there any way, she asked me one Tuesday afternoon, by which she could avoid becoming pregnant again? "I can *just* manage now. With another child I could not, and it would be Annabelle who would suffer neglect. That I could not bear."

I pushed aside the distasteful vision of Pratt, not as a person but as a copulating animal. Above all I wanted her happiness.

I said, "Yes, I can tell you a way. But I think you should give this matter some consideration. Pratt seems not to have taken to this child." Isabella had told me, on a previous visit, how when Annabelle cried in the night with teething pains, Pratt had picked up the drawer and carried it to the farthest room in the house, slammed the door and said she was only making a noise to demand attention. "That may be because of her sex," I now said. "After all, he spent a lot of time in India where females are not valued much. Except as mothers of sons, I understand. If you had another child, and it was a boy . . . It might improve things between you."

"Nothing could, Joanna. Believe me, I have thought. There was even a time, just after Annabelle was born, when I thought that perhaps I owed Pratt a son. I no longer think so. I do three women's work. I cook good food for customers and eat worse than any servant. I owe him nothing, now. My duty is to Annabelle."

"Very well," I said, and told her a method of contraception which I had, on occasion, offered to other women for whom I believed a further pregnancy would be a risk. Not infallible: What is? But I suspect that the failures are largely due to stupidity or sheer carelessness.

Even such an intimate conversation did not make us intimate. She said, "Thank you very much. I am profoundly ignorant about such things," and went on with what she was doing.

Neither stupid nor careless, she had no more children. The

one she had flourished despite the fact that she lived an un-naturally confined life. At a year she could walk quite well, and Pratt decreed that she should spend most of her waking hours tethered, like a dog, to the kitchen table leg. Sometimes during that, her second summer, I'd spend my precious half hour, the highlight of my week, taking her for a brief walk around the garden which, with admirable industry, Pratt had cleared and set down to potatoes, cabbages, onions, and carrots. My grandmother's garden had been full of old-fashioned flowers and herbs. The Whittons, or perhaps their predecessors, had let it run to nettles and thistles.

Then the day came, a Tuesday of course, when I found Isabella with that typical black eye and swollen cheek that is the result of a hard smack across the face. She had the typical excuse too; she had run into a door.

I lost control a bit. I said, "My dear, tell that to your customers! He hit you, didn't he?"

She threw her head up and said, "Yes. I was trying to hide the truth, which to me is very degrading. He struck me."

"Why?"

"I defied him. Annabelle had annoyed him in some way and he would have smacked her. I interposed myself. I dared him to hit her. So he hit me instead." Her blue eyes blazed for a second. "But for her," she said, "I should have hit him back, with the rolling pin or something. Then he would have killed me. And what would have happened to *her?*"

It is unscientific to say that one's heart bled. Hearts do their work, acting as precision pumps, they do not bleed. But mine put in two or three extra thumps and *felt* bruised and bleeding. And my stomach felt sick. I rallied. I said, "No, you should never hit somebody bigger than yourself, even with a rolling pin." How I managed to speak so lightly I simply do not know. The whole picture—with absolutely no justification, a thing of the imagination—unrolled before my inner eye. Pratt had never managed to reduce her; she had cooked and scrubbed, got out of childbed too early and managed, borne everything. But where the child was concerned, she was vulnerable, and he knew it.

I asked, "Is there nobody who would take Annabelle?"

"I have no relatives now. I have no friend in the world except you, Joanna."

At that moment the child, tied to the table leg, said:

"Aunt Joanna. Waisins."

I always brought her a handful of raisins but on that day,

70

seeing her mother's face, I had forgotten to produce them. She was such a sweet little thing; she gave me her entrancing smile and said, "Thank you," before settling down to gobble the goodies.

"And that," Isabella said, as I straightened up, "is another thing I am afraid of. She knows your name. It is a matter of time before she says it. In his hearing."

True.

"You should have let us both die that day," Isabella said. "There is no hope for us. Sometimes I think that the best thing to do would be to drown, both of us, in the river."

I said, "Please, please, put such thoughts away. You've been so brave, so resolute. You must not weaken now. I will think of something, I promise you. Please don't give way to a moment's desperation."

Sir Charles Thickthorn said, "My dear Miss Drury, drink your port and I hope you realise of what pleasure you deprive me when you advise abstention. Back to business. I must say that your unnamed patient has absolutely no redress in the eyes of the law. Unless she, or the child, has been maimed. There is a law about maiming one of His Majesty's subjects. In fact I remember a case, very interesting. It was plainly an attempt at murder, which failed, but in the course of it the victim was maimed. In fact his nose was slit and his assailant was accused, convicted, and hanged, not for attempted murder but for slitting the nose of one of His Majesty's subjects. If the man could be somehow provoked into slitting his wife's nose . . ."

He was taking this very lightly and I was angered. Let him wait, I thought; I'd come along with the colchicum powder, that old cure known to the Romans, and never yet bettered as a specific for gout; but I'd deal very gently with the opium that killed the pain while the colchicum got to work.

"And that is all you can tell me, Sir Charles?"

"Except that a man has a legal right to correct his wife. I believe there is some ancient law about not using a stick thicker than a thumb. And of course thumbs vary in thickness."

I thought: You will get no opium at all! He went on, "She would be well advised, this woman you speak of, not to run away. I seem to remember another case. A woman whose husband consistently beat her, so she ran away and was brought back and sentenced to a public beating. Rather unnecessary, one would have thought . . ."

71

I thought: What a world, in which a beaten woman is beaten for trying to escape from the beater!

"It would have perturbed you more, Sir Charles, if I had reported a poaching offence."

"Illogical, like all women! I thought better of you. Poaching is an offence against property; a very different thing from a domestic squabble. I'll now offer you a word of advice. Take no part in it. To interfere between husband and wife is a thankless task."

I rode home in a mood of depression shot through with questions concerning my own crumb of responsibility. Would things have been better at The Unicorn had I not told Isabella how to avoid another child? Who could answer that? I told myself that perhaps I worried overmuch. This might be an isolated incident; a single blow struck in a fit of temper. My reason might advance this comforting theory but my heart would not accept it. Everything which I had observed for myself, or gained by hearsay, pointed to the existence of a thoroughly bad relationship, now worsening. And she knew it, poor child. "There is no hope for us."

He was unlikely, I thought, to do her any real physical injury—she was too useful. It was her spirit that would be damaged. Imagine the humiliation of having to appear before the customers with that mark upon her face! She had said that the truth degraded her: would have concealed it, even from me, if she could.

Finally I was disappointed by the result of my visit to Sir Charles. He had been a magistrate for as long as I could remember; he knew the law. I had hoped that he would have produced some argument of which I could make use—such as that a woman who had been mistreated had every right to leave the man who abused her. I'd wanted him to say: Tell her to go home to her family. Having no family to go to Isabella could then have come to me and, in the storybook phrase, lived happy ever after.

My next secret visit was my last. Her face was back to normal shape, and the bruise was fading. She said gallantly that she had made too much of it, she had the kind of skin that bruised over-easily. But she had been thinking about Annabelle's growing garrulity and had decided that my visits must cease. "I shall miss you, terribly, Joanna, but I dare not risk giving him any *real* cause for offence."

I was helpless. I, who for so many years had been a source

72

of help to so many people in so many differing ways. There I stood, unable to do anything, able to say no more than, "I hope things will get better. Try not to provoke him."

"We provoke him," she said, "with every breath we draw. I deserve my fate. In fact I invited it." For a second I thought that she was on the brink of confiding in me. "But she is totally innocent. I simply cannot bear to see her unkindly treated."

We both looked at the child. This was November; she would be two in January, an enchanting age. The red hair had darkened to the colour of mahogany and grew prettily on her head, short and curly, and her eyes were beautiful. Apart from those brief walks in the garden with me in the summer she had never been outside the house. Nobody, not even Ben Stally, had seen her. For toys she had a wooden spoon and a few beans tied loosely into a piece of rag.

"It can't go on, can it?" Isabella said, her voice shriller than I had ever heard it. "She can't spend her life tied to a table leg, afraid to make a sound. She is afraid of him now. Sometimes I think of running away . . ."

Oh, to be able to say: Come now. Come home with me. Instead I must say, "My dear, you must not do that. He's unlikely to let you stay away, you are too useful to him. And if you were brought back . . ." I told her what Sir Charles had said.

"Then I shall be driven to kill him."

"No. No. You must not think of that, either. You would be the first suspect; wives always are."

She brushed her dull hair back with her coarsened hand and said, "Of course. You must not mind me, Joanna. It's just that sometimes life seems unbearable."

"I know. I am so desperately sorry." What a note to end upon. I said, "Perhaps when she is a little older and understands what not to do . . ."

That was an endless winter. I tried to be rational. What good did it do to worry and fret until my clothes hung on me like clothes on a scarecrow. I told myself that I must resign myself to impotence, as ageing men do to impotence of another kind. There was nothing I could do. I must forget the poor girl down at The Unicorn, go on living my own life. Doing my own work.

Soon after Christmas, Ben said, "Now he've hurt his leg.

73

Lame as a sheep with the foot-rot he is now. And all his own fault."

"Oh?"

"All due to pride and meanness, meanness and pride. I've told you before how Coppy and me offered to help. But no, he don't need no help. So muddling about with a barrel he hurt his knee. And serve him right."

I had the glimmer of an idea. In pursuit of it, two days later, Tuesday, I looked for the red rag and it was there. In the afternoon, again by careful timing, I arranged to be riding up the lane as Pratt came down. He was indeed extremely lame. He had two casks on the little cart and he was managing it with a dogged dexterity which in any other man I should have found admirable. It was a cold day, but as he came near I could see the sweat shining on his forehead and upper lip.

His last words to me had been an order to get out of his house, but that I pretended to have forgotten. I said quite genially:

"Good afternoon, Sergeant. What has happened to you?"

"No concern of yours," he said, surly as ever. But at least he had halted; glad perhaps of an excuse. He took out the red rag and wiped his face.

"But it is my concern. Is it gout?"

"No. Worse luck. Hurt my knee."

Slipped ligament? Broken patella?

That a man with a broken kneecap should be up and about, tending to his business, was well within the scope of my belief. I knew a man who was loading corn onto a wagon when a wasp stung his horse which started forward, running the wheel over his foot. He kept about and not until the last sheaf was safely in the stackyard did he come to me with his foot wrapped in filthy sacking. Splinters of bone were working out of the grossly swollen foot, and they, he said, were a nuisance. He'd only come to me because his wife didn't fancy the job of pulling them out. In a way I'd admired him, too.

"I might be able to put it right for you," I said. "If nothing's broken."

"It's not broken. Broken bones grate." He looked at me doubtfully, misliking me as much as I misliked him. Finally expedience overcame prejudice. "All right then."

While I dismounted he pulled the cart diagonally across the road, sat down on the front of it, his lame leg stretched stiffly out. He unbuckled his kneeband, rolled his stocking down, his breeches leg up and exposed the injured knee. I explored it gingerly. I was in luck.

"I can do it," I said. "It may hurt a bit."

For the first time I saw a smile on his face. Not a pleasant one. Sardonic amusement.

"I've had an arm off and the stump dipped in hot tar. Anything you could do . . ."

I made the wrench. He did not flinch.

"Now try it," I said. He did so.

"Seems to have done the trick. Thanks."

He was a man to whom even that much gratitude came with difficulty. Standing there in the frosty air, I remembered what Isabella had said about life doing things to people, about even Pratt being a baby once. What had life done to him to hammer him into something so hard? Taken away his arm; plunged him into a marriage which though profoundly unsuitable could, surely, have been happy, or happier, had he brought to it a grain of kindness. But there were vast areas unaccounted for.

With men of his kind—I had known a few, but never such an extreme example—a touch of self-depredation never comes amiss.

"It is really just a trick," I admitted. "And now I am about to fail you. That knee should be bandaged. Most women in emergencies can tear a strip off a petticoat. But I don't wear one."

"No. I didn't reckon you would. Use this." He produced the red rag again. I bound it about his knee, and while I did so he reached into his pocket and brought out a piece of string with which to hold it in place. "There you are," I said, "as good as new."

I rose from my knees. Following that glimmer of an idea, I said, "Now, would you like to do something for me?"

"What?"

"Lend me your little girl." I had cherished the demented idea that if I could get Annabelle out of The Unicorn for a few days he might forget about her; and with the child away he would be disarmed of the one weapon to which Isabella was vulnerable.

"Why'd you want to borrow her?"

"For the simple reason that like all spinsters I dote on little girls. Jill, my maid, feels the same. We should love to have her to stay with us for a little while—if you could spare her . . ."

I'd done my best, but it wasn't good enough.

Pratt said, "Oh. Meddling again. God damn it if it wasn't for the inconvenience I'd put the bloody thing out again. You've heard about young Beattie."

Young Beattie? The name rang a faint bell. Oh yes, the Beattie of my grandmother's time had had his pudding taken away because he defied her and swore a second time.

I said, "I don't know what you are talking about. I've never even seen young Mr. Beattie. And what has he to do with this? I merely thought that I had done you a slight service and that you might feel disposed to do me one, in return. A moment's impulse. Forget it."

"You can't fool me. If it wasn't Beattie it was one of those old sweats, bleating. She's my wife, the brat is mine, and if they need a clip they get it."

"Ben," I said, "what is this I hear about something down at The Unicorn concerning young Mr. Beattie?"

"Well, it was a bit of a rumpus, but we was all agreed, Coppy and me and two're three others, the less said the better. 'Twasn't very nice. Not what you look for when you go for a quiet drink. We all reckoned she wouldn't want it talked about, so we agreed."

"What happeened?"

"Well, since I'm arst . . . Young Mr. Beattie was down taking note of the grazing, what bits had come up and what gone down since last year. Young Mr. Beattie's a gentleman, never mind what his father was, and he bought us all a pint and told us that Lady's Slipper was about twice the size it was last year, whereas Maryland was going under and wouldn't feed a goose this year, leave alone a bullock; not even a goose, he said. Even Old Creekie had changed course, which I could have told him myself. Well, he was staying the night, Mr. Beattie was, and Mrs. Pratt come in with his supper, nice duck on a dish. And the little girl come in behind her. Pretty little thing. We all said so. Sergeant said, 'Who let her off?' Mrs. Pratt said the band broke and she hadn't had time to mend it. Sergeant then said taproom wasn't no place for children and he'd learn her. So he upended her and give her two on the bum, pretty sharp. Yes, sharp for such a little 'un. Mrs. Pratt went for him, dropped the duck and all else. Then he set about her, clipped her both sides of the jaw. Would of done more but for young Mr. Beattie. Mr. Beattie up and took him by the shirt front and shoved him off. Mr. Beattie said was the Sergeant a whole man he'd have knocked him down. But he did more; hit the Sergeant where it hurt most. In his pocket. Went straight out, Mr. Beattie did, got on his horse and rode off. Evening Star, we reckoned." Ben paused and then said ruefully: "All very well for him. He got a horse, a right good horse. Coppy and me and the others we don't hold with hitting women and little children, but five miles is a long way to walk for a beer. We was huffy though; yes, huffy. There laid the duck all in the sawdust and after a bit Sergeant told Coppy he could have it for his dog and Coppy said his dog wouldn't eat duck. So he had to clear it up hisself."

"Does this kind of thing often happen?"

"Well, we have suspicioned it. We've seen a thing or two. But not in the open. Never in the open. That's why we agreed not to talk about it. I mean what's between husband and wife, in private as you might say, is their business. But to clout her like that, as he did, in front of a lot of drinking men, we didn't reckon that was very nice."

Such delicacy of feeling, running directly counter to the tendency to gossip, did not surprise me; it was the measure of their shock.

My house is larger than it appears at first sight. It stands gable end to the village street and runs backwards. I think that my father when he bought it visualized a large family. Weighed down by my thoughts I took a walk through the rooms which were never used and seldom entered. They were partly furnished, largely with what had been my father's stuff before my grandparents died. Their furniture was older and more solid than any he had been able to afford when he married, so the part of the house we used had been refurnished with things from The Unicorn. The disused rooms were in a sad state of disrepair. A leak in the roof in this part of the house was not always discovered immediately. A good deal of work was needed before it would be habitable. As an excuse for putting the work in hand, I told Jill that I had two old cousins who proposed to visit me, hoping to benefit in health from a change of air.

Over my rather elaborate preparations I did not deceive myself. Had I been able at any point to say: Come home with me, I should have said it and we could have lived in cramped conditions for a while. The plastering and the painting, the fresh curtains and covers—all white with a pattern of rosebuds—the search for and the purchase of an elegant, heart-shaped little swing looking-glass for the dressing table, were all concerned with my need of time to think. What I was being forced to do was not easy.

Because of my sex I had never been required to swear to that Hippocratic oath which solemnly affirms: "The regimen I adopt shall be for the benefit of my patients according to my ability and judgement, and not for their hurt . . ."; but its principles had hitherto governed my life. I had never betrayed a confidence; nor entered any house without the determination to do my best. The habits of a lifetime, the ways of thought adhered to for many years, take time to shuffle off. On the other hand it was a case, as with that memorable cauterization; if I didn't do it, who would? Tragedy at The Unicorn was inevitable; I must see to it that it was a controlled tragedy.

By the second Tuesday in April the rooms were ready, and so was I. In the morning I rode to Ozary Cross and there the red rag was in the hedge. The road, as far is I could see in either direction, was empty, so were the fields and meadows on either side. A few minutes later, when I rode away, the red rag looked exactly the same, except that it was more entangled in the thornbush.

It was highly unlikely but not impossible that on this day, of all days, Pratt should have deputed this errand; but one must be prepared for any contingency. Well before time Toby was waiting for me inside a field along the road and I was in the meadow behind the hedge. I could see into the lane if I peeped, cautiously; I was within reach of the rag.

Pratt came himself.

The dray rumbled up and halted.

"You're late," Pratt said. "You may have time to waste, I haven't."

In an equally unpleasant way the drayman retorted:

"We ain't in the Army now, Sergeant." He did not dismount from his seat, high above the two great shining horses, but left Pratt to manage on his own. Admittedly the drayman was not the same one with whom my grandfather had had his cheerful little talks, but he looked good-natured enough, and Pratt was a maimed man. Ill-feeling here, too, I thought. The drayman's attitude was underlined by his talk to his horses; he pretended that they were restive. "Whoa, then, whoa my beauties. Shan't be long now. Nearly done. Whoa there, whoa!"

He said no more to Pratt, nor Pratt to him. Pratt removed the red rag, swearing because it did not come away easily.

He stuffed it into his pocket and went off down the lane.

I went home and waited.

Wednesday. Thursday. Friday morning.

"Sergeant got something else wrong with him now," Ben said. "Started up Tuesday night. Itchy palm he said. Rubbed it on the counter. Rub on wood, sure to come good, he said. Meaning money. But it sort of skinned it. Like when you scratch a gnat bite. So Coppy said he'd bring along some of his missus' green ointment."

I was counting upon that.

Ben's crony, Coppy, could idle away his life because his wife, Ma Coppinstall, in addition to acting as midwife, nurse, layer-out, made herbal remedies and, it was rumoured, love potions and other more dangerous brews. Her grandmother had actually been hanged for witchcraft and around Ozary a good deal of superstition still lingered. My father had been interested in the herbal brews and ointments which, until his coming, had been the only medicines available and he had tried out several of Ma Coppinstall's traditional remedies on himself. Most of them he denounced as quite useless, except that they inspired confidence and the will to recover. Of those moderately effective he deplored the hit-and-miss method by which they were used. She made a heart remedy from foxglove leaves. "Digitalis," he said, "good for a flagging or congested heart, but fatal to one already labouring under pressure." Of her green ointment he had said: "The goose grease which is its base is an effective emollient. The dock-leaves which give it its colour have, for some reason not yet determined, been long recognised as a relief for such inflammations as are caused by nettle stings. But there is something else. I *ate* a little of her green ointment and the result inclines me to suspect arsenic."

Ma Coppinstall and I had never come into head-on competition. There was room for us both. Occasionally a patient of mine would have the idea that what was charged for must be better than what was given free, and would call her in at the last minute.

I could now count upon her unwitting co-operation. Her green ointment with its minute content of arsenic could be depended upon to exacerbate a condition caused by arsenic in the first place. I'd not had the benefit of the classical education which would have been provided, by hook or by crook, for my brother had I ever had one, but I had been allowed to read anything I could read, and I had read about the Renaissance princes of Italy who had sent to an enemy a

79

pair of arsenic-impregnated gloves and then, under pretence of solicitude, an ointment with just enough of the poison in it to worsen the condition. But no Italian Renaissance prince had had quite so much to consider as I had at that moment. However, I was prepared. I said, with an air of complete detachment, "Ma Coppinstall's green ointment may be very effective for a sore hand. It could be dangerous for anyone who handled it, who was not in need of a cure."

"In what way, Miss Doctor?"

"It could be like giving Toby here a drench when he didn't need one. I'm just warning you, Ben. The Sergeant can't very well rub in ointment with his hook. He might ask you to do it, or Coppy."

"So he might. But more likely *her*."

"Whoever does it should be careful. Not to touch mouth or eyes until he or she has rubbed fingers with a greasy rag, and then washed without soap." Soap often contained minimal quantities of arsenic, a bleaching element.

"Soap don't bother me much," Ben said, with great truth.

"Mrs. Pratt might use it."

"So she might. And a bad job it'd be, a very bad job if she did something to herself, wouldn't it? Might have to close down and then where should we be?"

"Where indeed. I think she should be warned, Ben. And Coppy—or anybody else."

Nobody who has not been compelled to work through other people can possibly understand the torment, the hideous uncertainty. It was like trying to drive a team of unbroken horse on reins of cotton.

"I surely will tell her," Ben said. "She should be told. It would be a bad job, a very bad job if they ended up with only one hand between them."

Saturday. Sunday. No news. Perhaps my plan had misfired entirely. Handling an arsenic-impregnated rag might be less damaging than wearing gloves similarly treated. Sergeant Pratt might be tougher than a sixteenth-century Florentine nobleman. Ma Coppinstall might have changed the ingredients for her green ointment.

Monday.

"His hand is a rare old sight now," Ben said, volunteering the information for which I cautiously did not ask. "Like a bit of raw beef. Last night he couldn't draw a pint, couldn't turn the tap. So she had to do it with him growling at her all the time, though she didn't spill much. Kept saying, 'Clumsy bitch,' which wasn't no help. Then he set about

Coppy. Set about Coppy good and hard; said he'd got four-pence for stuff that made it worse. So then I said he should arst you to have a look at it."

"Oh and what did he say to that?"

"Said he reckoned that's what it come to. Swore a bit, but said I could arst you to look in. Suit yourself for time, he said."

"I'll go there first thing, directly after breakfast."

Now that the waiting time was over I was completely calm. Calm enough not to eat my breakfast. Monday was wash-day, therefore dinner invariably consisted of the remains of Sunday's roast, eaten cold. Not very welcoming. I said, "Jill, I've had a skimpy breakfast. I have to go to The Unicorn. Sergeant Pratt has something wrong with him. I'll make it up at dinnertime."

"I'll rig up something a bit extra," Jill said.

Everybody had so far done and said exactly what I had hoped for, planned for: as though they were people in a play, doing the parts assigned them.

Pratt sat at the kitchen table. It was the first time I had ever seen him inactive. He did not look well. Isabella was frying eggs and bacon at the stove. The child was tied to the table leg. I said, "Good morning, Mrs. Pratt. Good morning, Sergeant." I did not speak to Annabelle, but I think she might have spoken to me had Isabella not turned swiftly and given her some crisped-up bacon rinds from the pan. Isa-bella looked even less well than Pratt, very white and harassed. Two breakfast trays at the far end of the table indicated two guests. The wall clock showed the hour to be half-past eight.

Pratt gave me a surly look. He'd obviously hated having to seek my advice.

"I wouldn't have bothered you but I was at my wits' end," he said. Ben Stally's description of his hand was very apt. He laid it out on the table for my inspection and he might have been holding a slice of raw steak in his palm.

"Dear me," I said, "that must be very painful."

Annabelle had dropped one of the frizzled bacon rinds and made a lunge for it; everything on the table rattled. Pratt gave her, perhaps not a real kick, but a hard nudge with his foot; she began to cry. I saw Isabella's shoulders tense.

In my plans I had visualized the taproom, but two people were about to breakfast there. I said, "Could we go into the parlour? The light would be better there."

The parlour had always been my grandmother's special preserve. Only the most favoured and privileged of customers had ever crossed its threshold. This morning both Pratt and I were intruders. To her lingering ambience I said: You would have done the same thing; in the same circumstances! I told Pratt to sit in the chair by the window and I made a pretence of examining his hand.

Masterful, even in this extremity, *he* told *me*. "A job for the knife; I'd have done it myself if I could. Proud flesh this is. A scratch that went nasty."

"We'll try kinder remedies first," I said, in my most soothing voice. "I think it is a condition of the blood; best tackled from within. I have a dose here. I'd suggest that you swigged it down in brandy."

"Well, just this once." I fetched the bottle and one of the little pipkin measures from the bar. I poured the measure, added the dose.

"There, drink that, and your troubles will soon be over."

Soon.

Death from strychnine poisoning is very swift; compared with many other ways it might be said to be merciful.

I have a belief that of all the senses that of hearing is the last to depart. Pratt's body, arching convulsively, overturned the chair. I caught his head and shoulders, knelt, and made a lap for him to die on. I said, over and over, "It is all right. You will be better soon. It is all right." Had I known his given name I would have used it. I went on speaking long after he was dead, long after the rictus, that death's-head grin, had relaxed.

I rinsed the little pipkin with brandy, once, twice, spattering the good liquor about; not that anyone likely to see the corpse in the next few hours was likely to identify strychnine's particular odour, but thoroughness had been bred into me and I was thorough now.

I went into the kitchen and managed to say, rather distantly:

"Isabella, you had better sit down. I have to tell you that Pratt is dead." She did not sit down, she just stood and looked at me. And then, deliberately, slowly, she bent over the child, untied the knot of the string, and said, "Darling, you can run about now."

The child ran about; the clock ticked. Isabella said:

"Was he so ill?"

"It was the worst case of blood poisoning that I have ever seen."

The clock ticked; the child ran about. She said, "I can hardly believe it. So sudden. Just a sore hand." She actually blinked like a prisoner brought out of a dungeon and faced with bright daylight.

I said, "Now you can come home with me." Words I had been longing to say.

Everything so far had gone exactly to plan. Now a little hitch.

"Joanna, that is very kind. Most extremely kind. But . . . It still seems unbelievable . . . but with Pratt dead . . . then the inn must be mine and I must look after it. Until I can sell it."

I said, "But you cannot stay here alone."

"I shall not be alone. Look." She went and unhooked a slate that hung from a nail on the wall, the pencil on a string beside it. Names and dates. "I shall be very busy, with a houseful, for a fortnight."

It was true. Careful men did make visits to see that their cattle were installed upon the site for which they had bid at the grazing auction. Sites varied in value and it was necessary to see that no stray had jumped a ditch or forded a creek in order to enjoy pasture to which it was not entitled. April was also a busy month for the pack-pony trains. Her remark about her ownership of the inn, and the necessity of keeping it going until it was sold, showed sound sense. I was eager to share with her all that I had, but I was not rich. Besides it would be nice for her to have money of her own—to spend on pretty, frivolous things for herself and the child.

Yet, in a way, I was disappointed. I had planned a whisking of her away from work, from the place where she had been so unhappy.

"It would, perhaps, be wise to fulfil these obligations," I said. Baulked of my main purpose, I offered service. "I will see to everything, my dear. I'll see the carpenter and the sexton this morning. This afternoon I must go to Stoke St. Cross to inform the coroner. Is there anything you would like me to bring? You will need a black dress."

"I have a black dress."

It was her working dress, a garment so old, so often washed, so much worn that it was no longer completely black but streaked with grey, with green.

"What I would like is some ribbon, to make a sash for Annabelle. I can now make over my white muslin for her, and she will need a sash. Not blue, please. Any other colour. Oh, and if you could, please, order her a pair of proper shoes." The child had hitherto been shod in little homemade shoes, made from old stockings.

"I'll see to it all," I said. I remembered one other thing I must see to—the red rag. I pulled on my gloves, went into the shed and removed the dangerous one, hanging in its place another, as nearly like it as I could find. I returned to the kitchen and dropped the original into the fire when Isabella's back was turned. "I'll see you this evening," I said.

The coroner knew me well and accepted without question my account of sudden death from blood poisoning. I bought a length of bronze-coloured ribbon, almost matching Anna-belle's hair, and ordered a pair of shoes, in kid of the same colour, leaving with the shoemaker the paper on which I had drawn an outline of her small foot.

Nobody grieved for Pratt. Concern was all centered about what was going to happen to The Unicorn.

"I think we should get in touch with Mr. Beattie," I said to Isabella. "He knows the place and how busy it is at some seasons. But first we must find the deeds."
"Deeds? What are they?"
"Documents that are proof of ownership. Where would Pratt have kept such things?"
"In his army chest."
"Not the deeds. They are a great rolled-up bundle, tied with pink tape." She said she had never seen such a thing, but if it wasn't in the chest it would be in the parlour cupboard. Search there and in every other place, likely or unlikely, failed to reveal them. I knew they existed because during the brief period while the inn belonged to me, my father, with his interest in anything old, had studied them and drawn my attention to one of them, written on a sheepskin, so roughly trimmed that one could see where the neck and legs had been severed. That was a deed of transfer, dated 1666, and drawn up by a Royalist who blithely ignored the interregnum and called that year the seventeenth of our Lord and King, Charles II.

We did not find, either, the hoard of money which Pratt was supposed to have saved. In the army chest there were a few papers and something under £4 in a little linen bag. "But we've worked so hard and lived so sparingly," Isabella said. "What can he have done with the money?"
Finally I said, "I suppose he did buy, not rent this place."
"I don't know. He never spoke to me of such things."
"For rent he would probably have had receipts," I said,

and I turned again to the neatly arranged papers in the chest. Here, with receipts from the brewer and the miller, I found some curious documents. The first was dated June 30, 1793. *Received of George Pratt in accordance with our agreement, the sum of £104. Jacob Whitton.* There were other sums, none so large, but quite considerable, paid at varying intervals. Midway through 1794 the signature changed from Jacob Whitton to Bessie.

I did a rapid sum. In the two years and nine months of his occupancy Pratt had handed over a total of £330. Small wonder that he could not afford hired help, had lived sparingly and refrained from providing free beer!

"What does it mean?" Isabella asked, looking helpless again.

"He was buying The Unicorn by installments. Now, let me think. When my father sold it on my behalf it fetched £450, with nothing much in except things we did not want, the kitchen table and dresser, the worst bedroom furniture. And prices have been rising ever since. The Whittons may have asked as much as £600; in which case you half own it."

"I have earned it," she said simply.

Inconsequently I thought: And so did he! All that whitewashing and mending, the rehanging of the sagging gate, the reclamation of the garden. I also remembered something that had come to me by way of Ben. Ma Coppinstall had laid Pratt out and reported that his hand wasn't the only thing wrong with him; his elbow where it fitted into the cup of the hook, and his shoulder from which the whole thing was suspended were badly galled, she said, worse than any packpony. At the time I had dismissed this, thinking that she exaggerated in order to obscure the effect of her green ointment on his hand. Now I thought of it. The man was financially harassed, subject to a constant rub and chafe of his harness; enough to explain parsimony and ill-temper.

I said, "He was hardly the man to be satisfied with a verbal agreement where so much money was involved. I should think it was drawn up in some lawyer's office. We must find it. We must find Mrs. Whitton, too."

All I knew about the Whittons was that when they found the place too much for them, they had arranged to go and live with their son, who was a farmer, and that they had boarded the northbound coach. Once they were safely on it I had never expected to think, or hear, of them again. And I thought to myself: If I hadn't offered to take them to that northbound coach, nearly three years ago, I should probably never have known anything about the Pratts. How different life would have been.

However, I was trained to concentrate upon the job in hand. Where was this deed drawn up?

"Pratt wasn't a local man. Where did he come from?"

"Does that matter, Joanna? All I know is that he had been a soldier and spent much time in India."

"Yes, my dear. I know that. But later. For instance where did you meet him? Where were you married?"

"In London. Why?"

I tried another tack.

"Can you remember when he first mentioned The Unicorn to you? You were to come and live in it. He must have said something."

"He said he had seen it. And that it was a good place. A place where we could earn a living."

As on that first day, she was being deliberately vague.

"How did he pay over this money? Did he ever go away?"

"Only to the crossroads, on Tuesdays. As you know."

"Well," I said, "we'll start with Mr. Reeve in Stoke St. Cross."

I was reckoning on the fact that Jacob Whitton had been housebound, virtually bedridden. But Mr. Reeve, young, disposed to be helpful, knew nothing of any agreement between Whitton and Pratt. "If such a document, or the record of such document, exists in any lawyer's office, Miss Drury, I can track it down. It will take a little time, of course."

The little time ran well into May. I harassed the poor man, looking in upon him every time I went to Stoke St. Cross, and making any kind of excuse to go there. At last, on a beautiful morning, he said the deed had been located in the office of a Colchester lawyer named Falconer; a copy had been made. He handed it to me and I read it with unbelieving eyes.

For possession of the inn and its contents Pratt had engaged himself to pay £100 down against a total of £800, the remainder to be paid off by installments of not less than £100 a year. If for any reason *whatsoever* he failed to meet his obligation the whole agreement was null and void and the inn reverted to the ownership of Jacob Whitton, his heirs or assignees.

I said, "But this is iniquitous! What it means is that he was paying rent of a hundred pounds a year."

"Oh no, Miss Drury! In effect Whitton made a loan to Pratt of eight hundred pounds—or its worth—for seven years.

What Pratt paid must be regarded not as rent, but as repayment and interest."

"I can't see it so. If Jake Whitton had lent Pratt eight hundred pounds, he would have bought something with it, or invested it and his widow would now have *something*. As it is she has worked—they both worked—saved every penny and now she has absolutely nothing. Is it *legal?*"

"It is an agreement entered into by men of full age, correctly drawn up, signed, witnessed. Yes, it is legal. It is an example of what happens when one party has the benefit of a lawyer's advice and the other has not. Had Pratt consulted a lawyer I have no doubt that some mitigating clause would have been inserted."

No use brooding of what would have been. I did another rapid sum in my head: £470 still to be paid; and then Isabella would own the inn. I could raise that sum. She could then sell The Unicorn for what I thought was its current value, perhaps £550, with luck £600. Something might yet be salvaged. I put this proposition to Mr. Reeve and he said it all depended upon Mrs. Whitton. If she chose to accept such a settlement, well and good. On the other hand she was under no obligation to do so.

I said, "What it amounts to is that Mrs. Whitton has inherited her husband's half of the bargain, but Mrs. Pratt cannot be allowed to assume her husband's obligation."

"She can be allowed to—with Mrs. Whitton's consent; she is not entitled to do so. May I take it that you will explain the situation to her?"

He had always accepted my interference, probably visualising the innkeeper's widow as illiterate.

Mr. Falconer had included the information that Mrs. Whitton was now resident at Cobb's Farm, Fallowfield, in the County of Suffolk. Mr. Reeve obligingly produced a map and I saw that Toby and I could make the journey there and back in daylight if we left at once.

Mrs. Whitton seemed pleased, if surprised, to see me, and I was pleased to find her in more than comfortable circumstances. She was installed in one wing of a roomy old farmhouse, and had a neat maid. In a lilac-coloured silk dress, trimmed with black lace and black bows, she looked about twenty years younger than the harassed woman I had helped on to the coach. We spoke briefly of Jake's death and she used that trite term, "a blessed relief"; he had, she said, been a burden, even to himself towards the end. She said that

87

she had always remembered how very kind I had been to him. I thought that at least I started off with the advantage of having her goodwill.

It vanished when I explained what I had come for. She couldn't possibly accept £470. Nor £500. Nor indeed £600, which was as high as I dare bid. "You must see, Miss Doctor, it'd be better for me to sell it again, in the same way. Only this time I shall ask £900. I can wait. It isn't as though I needed the money." That was obvious. And it was to her advantage. I thought of my poor Isabella with nothing, absolutely nothing to show for all her labour. I said:

"You're unlikely to find another such fool, Mrs. Whitton."

"The world is full of men who want to get on, want to be their own masters, but haven't the money to start off with. Arrangements like Jake made just suit them. We could have sold the place that way a dozen times over and Jake only took Pratt because he could put a hundred pounds down. And didn't look as if he'd last long. I don't mean dying, being able to keep up the payments. With only one arm."

"He couldn't have done it without his wife. Mrs. Whitton, she has worked so hard, never even had a decent meal, and now she has nothing. And a little child to keep."

"Yes," the horrible woman admitted, "it is a rough world. All the more reason to look out for ourselves, Miss Doctor."

Well, she was within her rights. And there was no moving her. This had been a "sleeveless errand" indeed.

Somebody had given Toby a bucket of water. I had not even had so much.

It was after eight when I rode into the inn yard, drew Toby another bucket of water and filched a handful of hay for him. I'd had harder days in my life, but seldom one so exhausting.

I went through the kitchen, through the passage and into the taproom. I said quietly into her ear, "Tell them to help themselves."

"They'd cheat."

"Never mind. They won't be cheating *you*. I have something to tell you. And I badly need a cup of tea." She looked, as always when confronted with a fresh situation, completely helpless. I remembered one of my grandfather's expressions, and used it. "Drink up, boys," I said. "It's on the house."

In the passage she said, "Joanna, what is it? What has happened?"

"I'll tell you," I said.

"Should you have said that? About drinking on the house?"

"My dear, they are drinking *Mrs. Whitton's* beer out of

88

Mrs. Whitton's mugs, under *Mrs. Whitton's* roof." I'd meant to break the horrid news more gently, but I'm only human.

Over the tea, quickly made, I explained. She said, "So! I now do not own even this kitchen table."

I had recovered. I said, "I am afraid that is so. But you must not worry. My home awaits you. Come and live with me and share all I have. I'm not rich, but you shall never want. You shall be comfortable and safe."

I had already decided that although it would be unethical for me to charge for medical services it would be perfectly in order to charge for such services as qualified physicians handed over to barber-surgeons. Cupping, lancing, bone-setting. Even for drawing teeth I should charge, in future, from all but the very poor. Hitherto I had been content to take payment in kind from those who were able to pay and who remembered; a system of which the net result was an overflow of food at certain times of the year, much of it given away. In future for any physical job, there I should be, my hand held out, my voice saying, "That will be sixpence." On a level with blacksmiths and tooth pullers with drums. But never mind. For her sake . . . For her sake I had done worse.

The dusk deepened. In the taproom the effect of unlimited beer was making itself heard. There was loud talk, laughter. In sharp contrast the nightingale poured its liquid silver from the apple tree in the garden.

Isabella said, "At least I have done with that!" She got up suddenly and went along the passage towards the revellers. I thought: She'll never get them out. I heaved myself up, a bit stiffly. I ride every day, I am hardened to the saddle, but Fallowfield was four hours' quite brisk riding, and four back. And, as my father often said, forty years tell their own tale. I heaved myself up and followed her in order to give her the support she did not need.

She stood amongst those merry-making, rather drunken men and said, "I should be much obliged if you would leave now." I recognised, and so did they, the voice of authority. My grandfather would have done it more amiably, "Come along now, I've got a bed to go to. Anybody who hasn't is welcome to the stable." On those rare occasions when he was slightly too drunk to take charge my grandmother had lifted the nearest pewter mug and rapped and said, "All out!" Isabella sounded as though she were dismissing courtiers. They all went, walking, stumbling away. She stooped and shot the bottom bolt, reached up and shot the top one and said, "That is the end of that."

"Yes," I said. "That is the end. Now you can come home with me, and rest, and be happy."

She said, "Joanna, you have been kinder than God to me."

"I'm not sure that that is much of a recommendation," I said. I'm sorry—why sorry?—but when one has seen the terrible and surely undeserved fates that overtake kind, gentle people like my father, and not him alone, others, born blind, or blind at thirty, the decent women with the canker gnawing at breast, at womb, the children born deformed, one is compelled to conclude with, I think it was St. Augustine, that if God is benevolent He is not omnipotent, and if omnipotent, not benevolent. A sorry conclusion, but one which should be faced.

"I meant," she said, "kinder than anybody had ever been."

I said, "I shall always try to be kind to you, my dear. Come now. Bring what you need for the night. Anything else that belongs to you we can fetch tomorrow." After all, I thought that sudden removal, the come-now dramatic gesture, defeated on the day of Pratt's death, had at last been achieved. "Come now," I said.

"It would mean waking Annabelle. And her little frock is washed, but not ironed. She has never been seen. I should like her to make a proper appearance. Tomorrow? Would that be agreeable to you? Tomorrow, Joanna? At about eleven o'clock? Mrs. Whitton has shown herself unwilling to accommodate me, but I should not wish her next victim to find the place as I found it."

I rather liked that phrase, "next victim." It implied an acceptance of circumstance which augured well for the future.

"Very well," I said. "I'll come for you at about eleven o'clock tomorrow morning."

I knew that it was useless to offer to stay with her. I had done it once or twice in the last fortnight when the slate was blank. But she always said that she was not in the least nervous and that it would be very awkward if somebody needed me in the night and I was not there. So I left her; for the last time. Tomorrow, tomorrow, all the tomorrows whenever I returned home I should be going to her.

Jill, with a reproachful look, served my belated dinner. I had told her some days ago that my cousins had decided that the journey would be too much for them, and I could now say, "It was most fortunate that those rooms were prepared. I have invited Mrs. Pratt and her child to live here." Her face brightened. "It'll be nice to have something young about the place. Nice for me, too, when you're called out in the night." All these years and she had never once given a sign that she minded being left alone in the house.

"Mrs. Pratt has had a very hard time lately. She needs a real rest. Later on, if she likes to, she can do little light jobs, like dusting. And if she cares to try I will teach her to roll pills and mix doses." I would indeed invent little jobs for her, so that she should not feel too dependent. My thoughts ran ahead. Annabelle would soon need some simple lessons, and the company of other children; we might well find two or three other small children whom Isabella could teach at the same time—a little dame school with modest charges.

"Well," Ben said next morning, "so we got our free beer, after all. Been a long wait, but we got it. And, Miss Doctor, when you said it was on the house, it could've been your grandfather. Could easily have been your grandfather."

"It was to celebrate the closing of The Unicorn," I said.

"Closing!" He looked as if I had just announced an imminent bereavement. "But it ain't never closed. Never been known to close." He stood there, Toby's brush in hand, and ran through the inn's history since my grandfather's death. "Hired man kept it going till the Somerses took over. Mrs. Somers didn't like it the place, never did, so they sold it to Watts, and he was there a good fortnight before they left, not knowing the trade and needing to learn. Then, let's see, somebody left him a bit of money, a nice bit and off he went and Mr. Beattie, old Mr. Beattie, put a man in to keep it open till it was sold to Jake Whitton. The Whittons went out and the Pratts come in, all in the same day. Except— and I was forgetting that—as a token of respect when your grandparents died, the old Unicorn never closed. And you can't blame us," he said, suddenly angry. "We all behaved with Pratt gone just the same or better, yes better, than when he was there. We was all agreed: never do, we said, never say nothing to make her feel she can't manage on her own. Look at last night. Tight as ticks with the free beer at last, but we left, you seen us, like little lambs. Like little lambs. Didn't you hear us? 'Good night, Missus, and thank you kindly,' and she all the time aiming to shut down on us."

I said, "Mrs. Pratt had no choice. But it will not be shut long." Mrs. Whitton would see to that.

On my way back into the house I noticed that the climbing

tearose had a bud just opening. I plucked it, took it in a vase along to the room that was to be Isabella's and placed it on her dressing table, so that it was reflected in the heart-shaped glass. The glass in which Isabella would see, day by day, her youth and prettiness returning.

It was a beautiful morning, the hawthorns in full blow, oxeye daisies beginning to open in the hayfields, cuckoos calling and answering one another. The cattle on the marshes were out of sight, but one could hear them lowing, a plaintive sound in itself, but in Ozary so associated with summer as to be almost joyful.

I rode as usual into the inn yard and went to the kitchen door. It was locked. She'd had no reason to open it, I supposed. I hammered on it. When there was no answer I thought: Poor girl, she overslept as people do after strain. I stepped back and called, "Isabella!" directing my voice towards the window of the room in which she had borne her child. When there was still no answer, I thought: Fool. Of course she would no longer wish to occupy the room she shared with him. So I walked round to the front. And there on the door, under the unicorn's head, was a piece of paper tacked. It said: *Key in usual place.*

Meant for me? Meant for whom? A little flustered, a little apprehensive I reached up and there the key was. The door which I had seen her bolt on the previous evening was now simply locked and opened with a creak. I stepped into the empty house. I knew it was empty; a house with only one, half-dead old person in it feels different from one totally deserted.

I cannot say exactly what my thoughts were as I hurried through into the kitchen. Muddled. Hovering, afraid to light upon the thought of suicide. The realisation that she now had nothing could well have turned her thoughts back in that direction. I should not have left her. I had overestimated her resilience, and her faith in me.

And there, on the white-scrubbed table, lay a whiter oblong. The suicide note which literate suicides leave, explaining, excusing . . . It was addressed to me and sealed with a blob of candlegrease.

My dear Joanna—After all your kindness to me I feel very sad not to say goodbye properly but I know that if I told you what I propose to do, the gamble I mean to take, you would try to dissuade me. It is for Annabelle's sake and I am not to be dissuaded, so you would be annoyed and our friendship would end upon a note of discord and that would distress us both. For all your kindness to me, all you have done for me, and for your understanding, I thank you from my heart. Isabella.

Not dead. But gone.

Nobody here to offer me the steadying arm, the soothing word that I had offered so often, to so many. Only the clock on the wall, emphasising the silence, echoing the heavy thump of my heart.

All you have done for me. I thought: You wretched woman, I committed murder for you! And at the same time I thought: Oh, my poor little girl, what gamble? Something as witless as marrying Sergeant Pratt?

She had said she had no relatives; no friend but me.

It was eleven o'clock. On summer mornings the first northbound, southbound coaches passed each other at about nine o'clock at Ozary Cross. She was now a full two hours on her way in one direction or the other. Pursuit would be futile—and undignified.

She had vanished into the mystery from which she had emerged. And there was nothing to be done.

I stood there for a moment with my mind like a broken looking glass, reflecting this and that, and nothing whole. The rose in the pretty room, the fowl in the oven; the unicorn, that mythical beast so cruelly betrayed; Pratt with that death's-head grin.

I said to myself: "Pull yourself together, Joanna Drury. You're strong. You still have work to do. This is not the end of the world, merely the end of an episode. What you need is a drink."

That was my head, quite reliable. My heart wailed on, asking where? Asking why? Only on the matter of brandy were they agreed. And of that useful stimulant my father had used that warning word, *afterwards*. Was this not afterwards?

I made my way back to the taproom; once under way oddly shaky, handing myself along the passage, half blind, half paralysed. Very slowly it dawned upon me that the whole thing had done me a damage, worse than I knew.

Narrative by Jack Franklin.

(1796)

I heard the doorbell ring, deep in the house. Nothing to do with me. Nobody came to see me nowadays: visitors were forbidden.

Then I heard, along the gallery, a door open and close; and another. Quite quietly, but on such a still evening sounds carried.

The door of the room to which I have been confined for two years opened. I looked round the wing of my chair and there they stood. I thought: I must have died without noticing it! Rosaleen and Alan!

Just a lapse, of course. I get a bit confused sometimes, but I'm right in my head. It was the girl, the French cousin, Isabella, who'd run away and never sent a word. And a child, a girl I now saw, but so like Alan; so like Alan in the Gainsborough portrait of Rosaleen and the boys.

I motioned to them to come in and to shut the door.

She said, "Oh, Cousin Franklin, I am so sorry to find you like this." She sounded genuinely sorry. She seemed a little unsure of her welcome, too; as well she might be, the way she had behaved. She didn't attempt to touch my hand or kiss me. The mite made a little curtsey and said, "Good evening, Cousin Fwanklin."

There are times when, taking it slowly, I can say a few words quite clearly; but not when I am upset; then I just gibber. I didn't even try. I reached for my pencil and the paper and wrote: *Lost my speech.*

"I am so sorry. Are you ill besides? You are so thin."

I'd learned to be careful. If you laugh when nobody else can see why, they think you're crazy. The thought did occur to me: What would she say if I wrote: *I'm being starved. I* did not write that: I wrote: *Why are you here?*

The child said, "Mamma, I am hungwy."

"You shall have something to eat soon, darling. Go now and look out of the window." As the child moved away Isabella pulled a chair near to me and said in a low, hurried voice:

"I am in such a plight, Cousin Franklin. The man I married is dead. I have no money. I came to ask you to do something, if not for me, for her. For Alan's child."

No, I wrote. *Never say that. Alan is dead. Will not have his name blackened.*

"But it is true. I swear it. You can see for yourself."

Don't believe you. If I did wouldn't admit.

I had to think quickly. Any minute now Chandler would come to take away my supper tray from which I had eaten a small piece of boiled salt fish and a thin slice of household bread. If he saw them, and reported, I should be helpless to help them, as I was to help myself. When you are helpless, you get cunning. I was wondering how her arrival might be turned to my advantage.

Who let you in?

"Nobody. The footman said you could see nobody. But I was desperate. Cousin Franklin, I am desperate. I walked round to the west door."

Out same way, I wrote, *unseen if possible. Go to Dower House. Pratt there. No mention of Alan. Ever. Tomorrow morning, go Baildon. Turnbull, the attorney, bring back here. West door if you can.*

I did not think she could manage it; she looked so helpless. But there was just a chance and a man reduced as I had been could not afford to miss even the slightest, the frailest chance.

At least she moved. She said, "Come along, darling. And thank you, Cousin Franklin. Thank you."

I listened, but there was no outcry, no running about.

She'd managed to go as she had come, unobserved. I sat there, asking myself was it possible that my luck had changed.

Born lucky; yes, that could truly be said of me. Only son, heir to an entailed estate of considerable extent and the house in which I, my father, his, and his had been born. Nethergate. Some fellow who knew about such things once told me that the name meant lower; the house had been the lower, or nether gate of an abbey that had once stood on the site. In addition I was healthy and had, I suppose, a happy disposition. When I was young and then less young, my only trouble had been that I couldn't see a woman I really wanted to marry, to spend the rest of my life with.

And there again I was lucky. Like a good many other country squires with a bit of money to invest, my father had speculated mildly in London property; all the area between Piccadilly and St. James's was being built over. But my father, like me, was a country man and had left all the business of building, leases, rents in the hands of a fellow who was a bit of a rogue. When I was thirty—my father had died when I was twenty-seven—I became tired of receiving less rent, no rent, and long tiresome letters. One day, and it was June, the rogue wrote that one of the houses in Hanover Crescent must have £200 spent on it before it could be relet. I thought maybe I'd better go up and see for myself; as I always did with the farmhouses and cottages, even the cowsheds on the estate. My good friend and neighbour, Sir Evelyn Fennel, hearing that I was going to London, told me to go and introduce myself to a cousin of his, Lady Alyson. I said I would, but I had no intention of doing it. However, when I found that the house, on paper so tumbledown that it needed £200 spent on it, was actually a firm, stout building, I went for the rogue and lost my temper. "You've made your last penny out of me," I said. "I'll sell the lot!" A brazen-faced fellow, if ever there was one. He said that he knew somebody willing to buy. I said . . . well, no matter . . . I told him I'd sell Hanover Crescent without any help from him. And there I was, in London, that horrible, crowded, noisy, stinking place, not knowing quite where to turn, until I thought of this Lady Alyson. I went along to her house meaning to ask her whether she, a Londoner, could recommend me to an honest man. She was entertaining and Rosaleen was there. I just looked at her and was heartily glad that I hadn't married any of the nice girls, neighbours' daughters whom my mother had been trying to force on me.

I don't know what she saw in me. I never did know. I don't

know how Lord Barryfergus in his ruined old castle in Ireland took the news. My mother disliked the match and foretold every kind of disaster. I was marrying out of my class, always a bad thing to do; Rosaleen would forever be wanting to go to London and so on and so on. Then when they'd met she said Rosaleen looked too delicate to be a good breeder and any woman as pretty as that was unlikely to be faithful. All wrong. Wrong as could be. There never was a happier marriage. Rosaleen did not hanker for London: she gave me John within a year, and Alan a year after. We never had a cross word, and though there were thirteen years difference in age, every time she called me "Jack" I felt like a boy again.

She was a wonderful manager, too. Never any fuss, no scolding of servants, yet the house ran like clockwork. Take an example; there was a lady's maid, called Pratt, who came into the house when we married and stayed till the end. Rosaleen even managed to do what few women can. She kept on good terms with our daughter-in-law; under the same roof, too! When I married my mother moved straight out into the Dower House, just across the park. When she died I had it thoroughly done over so that it would be ready for Rosaleen when I died. I was so much older, and women live longer than men anyway. I offered the place to John and Harriet when they married, but they said they'd prefer to live with us; Harriet didn't know much about running a house. In fact none of the Rossiter girls did; their father had spoiled them and they'd grown up a bit harum-scarum, all horses and dogs. The arrangement worked well and we were a happy family while Rosaleen was here.

She died in April 1794 and I mustn't pity myself for the way it happened. We were at one of these things called *soirées* at the Assembly Rooms in Baildon. She looked so young and so beautiful that evening; I remember looking across the room and thinking that there wasn't a woman there to touch her. She left the people she was talking to and came to me and said, "Jack, darling. I need some air." It was a warm evening for the time of year and the room was growing stuffy. I said, "So do I," and gave her my arm. We got out onto the portico and she said, "Much better," and dropped down, before I could catch her. There she lay, just a little heap of blue satin.

Heart failure, Doctor Stamper said.

I think myself she'd secretly grieved over Alan's death. She never was one to make a display of her feelings, and when we heard, in September, that he'd died in Jamaica of yellow fever, she was braver than I was. I hope I'd never shown it, John being my first-born and my heir, but I'd always had a very soft spot for Alan; he had his mother's eyes, and he was gay. John and I got along well, he's a thorough Franklin, interested in the estate ever since he was a boy, but Alan was better company. His death hit me, but Rosaleen's behaviour kept me up: I'd think: If his mother can take such a knock without whining, so can I.

Her death almost finished me. I knew she'd gone the way she would have wished, no damaging illness, no pain, no humiliation; just snuffed out like a candle, but for me it was a shock as well as a grief.

Part of the trouble is that I'm not a religious man. I go to church a few times a year—or did; setting a good example, I pay my tithes cheerfully, ask the parson to dinner two or three times a year, give whenever he's raising a fund for something; but I never had much idea about God, or life after death. It's all beyond me. For me Rosaleen's death was missing her, every day; thinking: I must remember to tell her that; or: Better ask Rosaleen about this, and then realising that she wasn't there. I couldn't sleep, I couldn't eat, and when they lowered her into the ground I simply broke down and howled like a dog.

I might not have got over it but for something I overheard Harriet say.

"*Now,*" she said, "we can have that bedroom. And the drawing room completely done over."

I said, "Eh? What was that?"

She said it again, to me this time, not to John, and I said: "No. Not while I'm alive. They're *her* rooms."

The sale of the London property had enabled me to make some improvements at Nethergate. Nothing fancy; I like the good old timber and brick which people are beginning to despise, and Nethergate wouldn't have seemed the same to me faced up with plaster and a lot of white pillars. What I did do to prepare for Rosaleen was to have the winter parlour, which faced south, and the summer parlour, which faced north, made into one spacious room and furnished afresh with colours and materials of her choice. It was a beautiful, elegant room, hers and nobody else's. So was the bedroom. To suggest alteration only a few days after the funeral sounded heartless.

Harriet took my refusal very badly. She said all the colours in the drawing room, too pale to begin with, had faded and she did not wish to sit amongst wreaths of rosebuds and forget-me-nots. I then pointed out that there were plenty of rooms in the house, she could choose one and furnish it to suit her own taste.

Her having said that about alterations made me begin to think about what would happen when I was gone, and that somehow gave me something to live for. Silly, maybe a little spiteful, living on just to keep Harriet's meddling hands off Rosaleen's things: but anything is better than nothing. I lived on.

Harriet would have meddled in other ways too. John and I, like my father and grandfather, used one end of the library as an estate office. One evening, soon after I had begun to recover a bit, I had something to discuss with him, and Harriet came and sat down at that end and seemed prepared to stay. She was John's wife, and I thought it for him to tell her that we were going to talk business, but he did not, so it was left for me to say:

"My dear, John and I have something to discuss. It won't take long." I got up and moved to open the door for her.

"Harry knows all about this kind of thing," John said. "In fact she has some useful suggestions to make."

I said, "I may be old-fashioned, but I don't like women dabbling in men's affairs. Your mother never did."

I waited, holding the door. Harriet got up, made a little face at John and went out, giving me a sulky look. When she'd gone, I said, "My boy, I'll offer you a word of advice. It doesn't do to put yourself under a woman's thumb. You end up being henpecked."

He said, "Henpecked!" in rather a nasty way. Then he said:

"Actually, Harry's ideas are sound. She thinks all rents should be raised as from Michaelmas. Her father's raised all his."

I said, "When I want Rossiter, or his daughter, to tell me how to run my estate! Look at Fulchurch! Tumbledown buildings, land going back to the waste. Rossiter never did, to my certain knowledge, have a tenant settled for more than two years. Look at ours. There've been Crofts at High Acre and Rayners at Slough Farm almost as long as there've been Franklins at Nethergate. Old Finch moved into Meadow Farm in my grandfather's time and there's a likely young grandson getting ready to take over." That was what mattered to me, the thought of things going on.

John said, "You may not have noticed but Harry did, at the last Meet, Abel Croft had the best horse there. Rayner's just bought a gig. And Finch gave fifty guineas for a cow only the other day."

100

"Shows they're prosperous. That's what I like to hear."

"They're spoiled," John said. And I saw another reason why I must stay alive; to keep things as they were for as long as I could.

Just ordinary day-to-day living was nothing like as comfortable as it had been. Harriet was no sort of manager. The cook we'd had for years came to me crying, "It's the not knowing and everything so sudden, sir. Yesterday that lovely sirloin and only you to eat it, today with a fowl in the oven, I'm told four guests. I can't keep up with it. I'm too old, really I am."

I didn't grumble. I merely suggested hiring a housekeeper. Harriet said that was an insult to her and struck back at me about old Pratt who did, she said, absolutely nothing except potter about in the rooms I was so sentimental over. Also Pratt had upset Phoebe. Phoebe was the young, impertinent maid whom Harriet had brought with her. Pratt had told her that something Harriet used on her face when she dressed up for the evening was positively dangerous.

Maybe I was sentimental about Pratt, too. She'd helped Rosaleen dress on that last evening. She was old and a bit crippled in the hands. But I solved that. I said that Pratt could go and live in the Dower House on board wages, with an allowance of meat and other necessities sent from the house. I said it would save maids going across every week and cleaning and airing the place.

When I said that, Harriet gave John a look and he said:

"Father, we were meaning to speak about the Dower House. Harry thought it would be very suitable for her cousin, Richard, due back from India almost any moment and hard up." I'd heard a bit about this cousin from Rossiter, who in his cups wags a loose tongue, and I didn't fancy him as a tenant. So I stuck to my arrangement for Pratt, who actually cried when I told her and said it was more than she had hoped for and would it be all right for her family to visit?

It was all rather like a nasty game; Harriet scoring a point: I scoring one. She and John had been married in June 1793; no child. One day I said to John, "You know, all this galloping about on horseback, no good for a woman." He took that amiss, and told her, I have no doubt. So when I had my accident, things had gone from bad to worse.

It was an accident. Finch at Meadow Farm, who had given fifty guineas for a cow with a pedigree, presently gave seventy for a bull, bred at Holkham, up in Norfolk. I wanted to see this very special animal—and I had, day by day, discovered that the more I busied and interested myself the better I felt about Rosaleen, about Alan, about everything. I rode my old grey mare that day; she had once been the best steeplechaser for miles around, but now she was, like me, getting old and staid.

It was July, pretty hot. I stopped at High Acre to congratulate Croft on his corn. It promised to be a bumper crop. Croft gave the mare a drink and Mrs. Croft offered me a glass of her blackberry wine.

Jogging round like this I missed Rosaleen less. She had never been a horsewoman, never ridden around with me. When, as on rent days, I'd made little festivities for the tenants, or when John came of age, she had moved about, astonishing everybody by her beauty and being charming, greeting by name people she had not seen for a year, but that was the extent of her interest in the estate.

At Meadow Farm there was less arable land; the present Finch's father had decided to go in for dairy-farming and cattle breeding. I could just remember the time when all but the necessary stock animals had to be slaughtered off when the pasture died down. Turnips had altered that. Finch could bring his beasts into snug byres, stand them knee-deep in straw and stall feed them so that he could send a bullock to market anytime he wished. The straw, well trodden and well dunged, made good manure. What corn he had and his turnips looked extremely well, and his glossy cattle were a sight to see.

Finch came out of the kitchen wiping his mouth on the back of his hand. I apologised for disturbing him at his dinner, but he said he'd just finished. He was a thick-necked, heavily built man, not unlike a bull himself.

I said, "I've come to take a look at this new beast of yours."

"He's a beauty, sir. Bad-tempered brute, though. I got him cheap on account of his temper."

"I never knew a good-tempered bull yet."

"I did. My old fellow, he didn't need no handling. Lead him about on a thread of cotton, I could. But he got past his job and had to go. This one we call Satan. I'll bring him out."

He went into the darkened shed and I heard the clank of a chain.

It occurred to me to think that the lives bulls lead don't make for good nature; too little exercise, good feeding, no company.

The animal came out into the sunshine, and stood, with Finch holding onto the pole which hooked into the nose ring.

I said, "By God, he is a beauty!" And he was.

"He'd have cost a hundred if he wasn't a known killer."

I sat on Meg, to one side of the yard and Finch stood there; we ran over the animal's points. It didn't irk me that a tenant of mine should own such a show beast.

Satan stood placidly enough, perhaps dazzled by the light after the darkness of the shed. Then he suddenly put down his head and lunged towards me where I sat on Meg, the reins loose on her neck. She bucked. I saw the cobbles of the yard come up at me and I thought: God, I'm falling off a horse!

I was not hurt. I was up in a second. Finch was on the ground, the bull, with the pole trailing was just about to toss him. He'd have been a dead man if I hadn't run, grabbed the nearest horn and swung my whole weight on it. I weighed sixteen stone and was strong, but I couldn't do more than turn the great head. I couldn't hold the brute, I could feel my feet slipping. Then Mrs. Finch ran out and threw a dark cloth; Finch got up and grabbed the pole.

"Are you hurt, Bill?"

"No. Bump on the backside," Finch said and led the bull away.

Mrs. Finch began to cry. I patted her on the shoulder and told her how brave she was. "But for you we'd both be dead or maimed," I said.

"And that'd make four," she sobbed. "I begged Bill and begged him . . . I know a mean eye . . ."

She was all of a-tremble. I didn't feel too steady myself; and when Finch joined us his ruddy face was the colour of suet, streaked with red veins.

"You sure you're all right, Bill?"

"Sure. And you, sir? If it hadn't been for you . . ." He reached out a hand as hard as wood and wrung mine. "What we all need is a drink."

We went into the parlour and drank sloe brandy. We drank to Mrs. Finch's courage, to our lucky escape, to Satan's progeny. At least, I proposed that toast and Mrs. Finch said:

"Oh no! Oh no! He's going to the butcher's Wednesday if I have to take him myself!"

"Come, come," Finch said, "you don't mean that, Jenny."

"Oh, don't I? You'll see!" She was a little bit of a thing, but I had a feeling that Satan was on his way to the butcher's.

I took the shorter way home, going through Layer Wood. I thought about life and death. Last April I had, with all honesty, wished myself dead because life without Rosaleen had not seemed worth living. Then Harriet had mentioned alterations and it had seemed worthwhile to live on and defeat her. And this morning, with death so near, as that great neck which we had been admiring, arched and my feet slithered I had fought for life and now was grateful for it.

I was almost at the point where the ride through the woods ended in the thick shrubbery around the Dower House garden, when I began to feel a bit queer. I was surprised, rather as I had been to find myself, Jack Franklin of Nethergate, falling off a horse. Drunk? Not likely. In an evening's mild gaming I could get through a bottle of port wine and feel none the worse and today I had had a glass of homemade blackberry wine at High Acre and three small glasses of Mrs. Finch's sloe brandy. A mere nothing. But I was, if not drunk, about to be sick. So I dismounted to do it tidily . . .

And that was the last I knew until I woke up in a bed not my own. A room not my own. Window in the wrong place. Everything wrong. I tried to say, "Where am I?" and that came out all wrong. I tried to heave myself up and couldn't because half my body, the left half was solid lead.

I had been glad to be alive and was now half dead.

There were faces which I recognised but could not acknowledge, voices which I knew but could not answer. I heard Doctor Stamper who on the portico of the Assembly Rooms had said "Heart failure," now say, "An apoplectic stroke." There was John and there was Harriet and Page, the footman.

They came and went and they said things. It was a bit like those early autumn evenings with patches of mist, suddenly blinding, and a few yards on, clear.

I fumbled my way from dimness to light and back again.

One of the clear things was the pan. I'd always been a bit fussy about such things. In houses I knew, finer and more fashionable than Nethergate, chamber pots were kept in the sideboard so that gentlemen need not interrupt for more than a minute their drinking or their card games. That had never been the custom at Nethergate. There the rule had been— Outside; or since my marriage—Upstairs. For when I tried to make the place fit for Rosaleen to live in I had installed not only a bathroom, with a marble bath so heavy that it took twelve men two days to haul it into place, but a water closet, the first, I think, in Suffolk.

To me the pan was an affront and a humiliation.

I could, then, only gibber and gesture, but Page seemed to understand. He wasn't very big or very strong but he understood. He hauled in a commode one day, and then straining and grunting he heaved me out of bed and onto it, and went away and left me to myself. Better, but still not good.

Another thing that Page did was to talk to me as though I were still a human being. Nobody else did. Not my son, not Harriet; they came and looked at me and talked to each other. But Page talked to me. He said, "I expect you wonder what happened, sir. Long Jim and Sammy were scything the lawn at the Dower House and Miss Pratt saw Meg coming back without you. So she sent them to see what had happened, and they brought you home on a gate. You feel poorly now, sir, but the doctor said a *mild* stroke. If we try, with God's help we'll have you on your feet again."

I had never noticed Page much, or at least only to think that my father had liked his menservants tall. However growth is largely a matter of feeding and when Page was young there had been some hungry years. Rosaleen had engaged him. She said, "He is a Methodist. And Methodists should be methodical, so I propose to try him for a month." At the end of that time she had said she was satisfied and Page became part of the household.

And he was sharp. It occurred to me, after a few days during which I could only mumble and gibber, that my right hand was as good as ever it had been, so I made writing gestures, and Page understood. He understood so well that he did not bring me quill and ink which I might have mismanaged, but the gold encased pencil, a pretty toy from Rosaleen's writing table. With that, and some paper, I could communicate with the world again. I wrote: *Thank you, Page. What date?* I was astounded to hear that I had lived in that blurred world for a fortnight.

John and Harriet never answered questions. They looked in each morning and said things like, "You need not bother," and "The doctor said you must have quiet and rest." One morning I wrote: *Want proper food.* Harriet said, "The doctor advised a light diet." Except in the time of my great misery I'd always been a hearty eater and now with the days so long I thought about food with flavour. I was given a lightly boiled egg, a bowl of thin gruel, a bit of boiled stockfish. Even Page thought I should have more and took to smuggling me stuff from the kitchen.

I couldn't understand why nobody came to visit me. If *my* friends, Edward Follesmark, Tom Rider, George Forrester, had been struck down I'd have been there, trying to cheer them up, taking some kind of sickbed offering.

Why nobody to see me? I wrote and held out the question to John and Harriet.

Harriet said, "Doctor Stamper advised absolute quiet. No visitors."

Cut off like that and knowing that now Harriet was in charge, hostile to me and with John under her thumb, I wondered what changes might be going on, inside the house, outside the house. One morning I wrote and held out to John: *Must see Turnbull.*

"What for? Doctor Stamper said you were not to be bothered about business."

Must make new will, I wrote.

"But you have already made one."

When your mother and Alan were alive. Change needed.

That brought him to attention. Nethergate, the estate, was not mine to will away, but there were other things, bits of money I'd invested not without some scrimping, so that in the Dower House Rosaleen would not lack any comfort, and a little bit for Alan in case he should not, after all, marry for money, but for love, as I had done.

Turnbull was sent for and he came. To me he was still "Young Turnbull," just as the owner of the bull was "Young Finch." As a person I liked Young Turnbull less than I'd liked his old uncle, but he was a good lawyer. He dealt well with Harriet who ushered him in and sat down. Watching. He said, very respectfully, that he wished to be alone with me.

She said, the false hussy, "But what if he needed something?"

"Then I will ring the bell."

When we were alone I wrote: *In my right mind. Ask me anything. Test me.*

He said loss of speech did not imply loss of mind, but to please me he asked a few questions. Then I wrote that I wished to give him power of attorney over certain of my affairs. He was to see to it that Rosaleen's rooms remained as they were; that no rents were to be raised; that no tenant was to be evicted, and that Pratt's circumstances were to stay as they were. He had paper and pen and a portable inkpot with him, took down my instructions without questioning them, and I signed in ink, my signature as firm as ever.

When John and Harriet heard about this they were angry, but I was prepared for that. They said it was the act of a demented old man. Then they set about to prove it.

Page was very good to me. He said I must believe that I should get better, if that was God's will; he said that he prayed for me, and that I should pray, too. Sometimes, dropping to his knees at the foot of the bed, he prayed aloud. I found that a bit embarrassing, but it was interesting too, because Page's manner towards his God was new to me; he addressed Him respectfully, and yet in the manner of a man talking to a neighbour who might, if well-disposed, do him a favour or lend him something he needed.

It didn't do though, Page explained, to leave everything to God. He went all through the miracles in his little black Bible and pointed out that in most cases somebody had taken action. We must take action too. I must try to move my left arm, to stand on my weak leg, to say a word clearly; believing all the time that I could do these things. Belief, prayer, practice; never lose faith, never stop trying. And very, very gradually I did begin to get better; I could move my left arm; supported by Page I could stagger across from my bed to my fireside chair, by taking my time and not getting flustered I could say several words.

It was autumn, the season of game, but I should not have tasted partridge or pheasant or venison had not Page smuggled me up little greasy parcels, tepid, of course, but most welcome after the unvarying round of what Harriet considered invalid diet. It was nothing of the kind, obviously, it was pure spite; I had offended her, so I was to have prison fare and be kept in what was almost solitary confinement.

About that, at least, I could do something. When I could, with some help from Page, get into my clothes and reach my chair, I wrote to Edward Follesmark and asked him to come to see me, and to insist upon being admitted no matter what anyone might say. Page took the letter and waited for the answer which was what I expected, Edward would visit me next day.

Unfortunately Harriet was at home when he arrived, and she brought him up herself. As they entered the room I heard her say that this was one of my better days; she then whisked away the paper I had been reading and put it on a side table at the far end of the room. She then sat down.

Poor old Edward wrung my hand and stared at me with tears in his eyes. He said how sorry he was, how glad to see me on the way to recovery; he mentioned having called several times when I was too ill to see him. I had prepared a few slow careful words but my own excitement and his show of emotion upset me so that I could not speak. But I could write; and I thought I'd write that I wanted Harriet sent away. And then I would write that we would take a glass of brandy together. As I grew better I had begun to crave for a drink and alcohol was one thing Page would not smuggle. His God disapproved of spiritous liquors. The one miracle which was never mentioned was the first one, the turning of water into wine.

I looked for my pencil and paper and they were gone. That sly hussy had whipped them away with the newspaper. I looked at the side table and could see about an inch of the pencil protruding. I pointed, I tried to speak but could make no sensible sound. Harriet jumped up, all willing and helpful and said, "I think perhaps he wishes to draw your attention to something in the paper, Sir Edward. He does look at it sometimes." Look at, mark you, not read! She fetched the paper and at the same time managed to knock my paper and pencil onto the floor. "There you are, Papa Franklin," she said. That had been her name for me until I angered her over the rooms: since then she had not used it. Hearing it now, part of the show put on for Edward's benefit, angered me. I threw the newspaper onto the floor and pointed again, determined to speak and making idiot noises.

"Oh dear," Harriet said, sounding like somebody who has a lot to put up with but bears it patiently. "One never knows . . ." There was now nothing on the far table except a vase containing a single rose which Page had brought in that morning, saying it was the last of the year. "Could it be the rose?" She fetched it and my oldest, my best friend sniffed it and said Nethergate roses were always better than his; they liked the clay. And all the time he had only to turn and look and he'd see what I meant. Great stupid fool. I could have cried from vexation. I did not, I simply kept pointing and shouting, "Yah. Yack. Yah." I sounded and looked like the village idiot.

I'd always known that Edward wasn't exactly clever, but I'd never thought he was so witless. That bitch Harriet said, "I was rather afraid of this. Anything out of the ordinary routine . . ."

Edward heaved himself up. "I'm sorry. I should not have insisted. Poor old Jack." He was speaking to her, not to me. I was so maddened by the way he'd let himself be fooled that when he tried to take my hand again I pulled it away. Harriet said, "Doctor Stamper assures us that he suffers no pain. And he has quite calm spells . . ." At the door she turned back and looked at me, and if ever malice and triumph shone on a human face it did on hers, then.

When I calmed down—which took some time—I thought that in the end I would get even with her; I'd stay alive, I'd stay calm, I'd practise even harder at walking and talking. I'd never make another attempt to see anybody until I was more sure of myself.

All this time Page had been drawing only a footman's wage, so for Christmas I gave him ten pounds. Then *he* had tears in his eyes. Another answer to prayer, he said. The Methodists sent missionaries to work among the black slaves in Virginia and every chapel was supposed to give something to the cause; but the chapel he went to was so small, and all its people were so poor, they'd never been able to spare much. Ten pounds! Hallelujah!

So we came to the end of 1795; and, on the last day of December, Page asked did I think I could manage if he went to what he called a Watch Night Service. He'd been very good about missing his regular Sunday night meetings. God would understand, he said, and hadn't Christ promised that where two or three were gathered together, there He would be in the midst of them? But now, if I could spare him, he would like to go and see the New Year in with his friends, and to hand over his money for the Missionary Fund.

I no longer needed to lean on him, I could manage with my stout stick. And I could speak.

I said, "Go—all—means. Enjoy—yourself."

I thought that even if I had no supper on this New Year's Eve, I shouldn't be missing much. At the rate of progress I was making, by this time next year I'd be downstairs, sitting at the head of my table, entertaining my friends.

Page said, "Effie will bring you your supper, sir. And we shall all pray for you."

Anniversaries do bring memories. It was impossible not to look back, to remember happy times and those who shared them. Rosaleen was dead, so was Alan, and really John, so far as I was concerned, was worse than dead; gone over to the enemy.

I was thinking these sad things when the door opened and in came my supper tray, carried not by Effie but by a man, a stranger to me. I knew that Page's place had been taken by a man named Wilcox, but I had never seen him; now, seeing him, I thought that nobody but Harriet would have engaged him. He was very short, far shorter than Page, but thickset and he had one of those lumpy, bashed about faces that you see on old pugilists at fairs.

I said carefully, "Good—evening—Wil-cox."

"Good evening, sir. Excuse me, my name is Chandler. I

am your new valet, sir." His voice didn't go with his appearance, it was very soft and civil.

"My—new—what?"

"Valet, sir." I'd never had a valet in my life so how could I have a new one. I'd always thought of them as jackanapes dancing attendance on jackanapes. I'd always said that when I couldn't get into my own breeches . . .

"Or nurse, if you prefer the term, sir."

I controlled myself. I said, "Page—looks—after—me."

"I was not aware, sir, that there was a page. Off duty, perhaps . . . Your supper, sir." He put the tray on the table by my chair. A bowl of broth, a finger of coarse bread. I was angry and I was confused. So I did a silly thing. I put my good hand under the table and tipped the tray onto the floor. The dreary thin broth made a puddle, the bread fell into it and immediately swelled. That is why poor people eat such bread. Given a little moisture the rough stuff in it, the bran, swells and they feel full.

Anyone who knew me would have been surprised by my action. Chandler was not. In a businesslike way he mopped up, keeping a wary eye on me. Then he opened my bed, laid out my nightshirt and said he would be back in half an hour to help me to bed.

I started to say that I could put myself to bed, but I was not careful enough; the words came out a bit blurred. He understood though and began to argue in that smooth overcivil voice that it was one of his duties to see me into bed.

I did not, as he reported, hit him, angry as I was. I only lifted my stick and waved it as I tried to say, "Get out!" He was very fast and very strong. In a blink he had the end of the stick in his hand, a twist and he had it entirely. He took it away with him.

When I was alone I sat and regretted my behaviour. Page would be grieved to hear that he couldn't be out of the house one evening without my behaving like a lunatic. But I had reason to lose my temper; hiring a man for one evening was all part of the plot to make me seem more helpless and useless than I was; and the man saying *valet* and *nurse*. And daring to take my stick!

Anyway, I thought, I'd show him that I could put myself to bed. I missed the stick and was obliged to get to the bed by going round by the wall, hanging onto furniture when there was any, or onto the moulding of the wainscotting. It took some time. I was ready for bed, but not in it when Chandler came back. I was actually at the commode, supporting myself, for lack of the stick, by holding the bedpost. He came and stood by me, a thing Page had had the good sense not to do. I tried to say, "Go away," but the whole evening had so upset me that I was back with the gibberish, so I flapped my weak hand at him and upset my balance. He caught and held me. "I wouldn't advise you to be violent, sir. You only hurt yourself." In the end I was put to bed by him, after all.

In the morning I lay and tried over the words, "Happy New Year, Page." I was calm then, and taken slowly the greeting was clear as a bell. I probably shouldn't be able to tell Page the whole story of what had happened last evening, my speech wasn't good enough for that yet, but I could write it. He'd understand.

It wasn't Page who came in when the door opened. It was Chandler with his bruiser's face and his pimp's voice. The truth dawned on me then but I felt that I must hear it said before I could believe it. I said to myself: Steady, Franklin, now. Steady! A bit like taking an unknown fence in the good old days.

"Where—is—Page?"

"I understand now to whom you are referring, sir. Page has left."

I did not then have the second stroke they hoped for, but the blow told. Harriet had some lying tale ready; Page had found looking after me too much for him and had given notice but didn't want me to know because he couldn't bear to see me upset. I knew it was a lie. Page would never, in a thousand years, have done such a thing. They'd sacked him; because he was my friend, was helping me to get better, had brought me tasty little bits of food, carried my letter to Edward.

I did not have a stroke, but I was damaged. Nobody now treated me as a human being. I was an old lunatic, shut away with a keeper. Chandler was Harriet's tool, he did precisely what he had been hired to do; he was very free with his "sirs" but when I did need something he took his time answering the bell. When I tried to speak he made no effort to understand, when I wrote he ignored it.

I lived for months in Limbo, dying by inches; kept alive now by very different things, my wish to spite Harriet and my certainty that wherever he was Page was praying for and believing in the miracle that would restore me. They say that drowning men clutch at straws and it may be true, but unless they find some other support, or are rescued, they drown. I was going under fast by that summer evening when that girl Isabella forced her way in.

It did not occur to me that here was somebody to the rescue. At least, not at first. I was mainly concerned with what she said about the child being Alan's. Nobody could deny the likeness. This child was younger than Alan when that portrait was painted, and she was female, nevertheless the shape of face, the colour of the hair . . . unmistakable.

I know that men do beget bastards. Some of them are lucky. I know one not far from here whose father liked him better than he did his legitimate sons and made him his heir; I know others pushed off and living like peasants. But so far as I knew there'd never been a bastard in our family. We're one-woman men. For instance, when Rosaleen said, after Alan's birth, that she wanted no more children I did not run about fornicating; I was never even tempted to. And now with Alan dead . . . Oh no, I thought.

There was another side to it, too. If I'd said, "Yes, I can see. Come to Grandpa, darling," it would have been worse than useless. Simply further proof of my lunacy.

I speak and I walk with difficulty, but I can still think. And once the surprise and the shock had passed I thought very quickly. Isabella had managed to get in; if she could get out, unseen, and do exactly what I told her, there might be hope for us all.

That night I slept badly, thinking and thinking. In the morning as soon as it was light I scribbled down the main points of the arrangement I had planned.

I would give her power of attorney inside the house; complete control over all domestic matters, so long as she did exactly what I told her. That would put me back in the saddle. I'd pay her a good salary—say £40 a year. The child must stay with old Pratt at the Dower House. Pratt could have ten shillings a week for looking after her and making sure that she did not leave the premises of the Dower House or be seen by anyone likely to notice the resemblance. Later on she could go to school. I'd provide for her future; £1000 on her marriage, or her coming of age, or my death, whichever happened first.

All this must be put into legal words and properly signed because there was something tricky about Isabella. French, of course. I'd liked her when she stayed with us and Rosaleen had been more than kind to her. In return she'd played fast and loose with Alan and then simply run away, causing us distress and anxiety. Rosaleen had not fussed—she never did—but the ingratitude had hurt her, I knew.

112

Looking back over it all I thought how peculiar that the girl hadn't told Rosaleen. Rosaleen was a very moral woman; she'd have made Alan marry the girl, even if she'd had to fetch him back from the ends of the earth to do it. I puzzled over this for a while, as the light brightened, and came to the conclusion that perhaps Isabella had run away before she knew she was pregnant. Perhaps having been made love to by Alan, she couldn't do without it. There are women like that. If she happened to be one of them, then any Tom, Dick, or Harry would do. From the look of her she'd done herself no good.

It then occurred to me that Isabella was still young. No more than twenty, though she looked older. She might want to marry again, or indulge in another *affaire*. I wrote on my paper, *No marrying or playing about*.

By the time Chandler brought me the cup of weak tea and the soft-boiled egg that made my breakfast on my lucky mornings, I thought I had covered everything. All I had to do now was to wait. Waiting, I thought about food; delicious food, in large quantities. How about duck and green peas for dinner?

Narrative by Isabella de Savigny/Pratt/d'Aubigny.

(1796–1804)

We went out by the west door, Annabelle and I, and into the strip of park that divided the main house from the Dower House. The long slow twilight of a June evening was thickening and sweet with the scent of cultivated, civilised ground. So different from Ozary.

Annabelle said, "Mamma, I am hungwy."

I said, "I know, darling. You shall have something to eat very soon. Look, there is a light. That is where we are going."

She said, "I am tired." I stopped and lifted her and carried her towards the light.

I had walked this path before; during my eight months at Nethergate it had sometimes fallen to me to go to the Dower House and supervise the brushing and the dusting and the airing. I knew that the lighted window towards which we moved was the kitchen window. We reached it, and just beside it was the kitchen door, upon which I knocked.

Pratt opened it. We could neither of us see the other very well, to me she was a shape, solid against the firelight, the candlelight inside the kitchen; to her I was a shape, looming up out of the dusk. I said quickly, "Pratt, it's me. Mr. Franklin sent me."

When I said "Pratt," the child in my arms jerked and stiffened. She had been frightened of him—as in fact I had been until I realised that I was useful to him and that he would no more disable me than a man would his donkey or his pack pony. Superficial hurt, yes, danger, no.

"Miss Isabella," Pratt said, knowing my voice. "Come in."

I saw in a glance how comfortably Pratt was placed. It was parlour as well as kitchen. On the hearth a fire, low enough to heat a kettle, without overwarming the evening air, and before it a rug, two easy chairs, a low table bearing a three-branched silver candlestick, a tea tray, and a piece of knitting.

I staggered across and put Annabelle into a chair. Pratt, having closed the door, came across and took a long look at the child and nodded her head. Then she looked at me, and I looked at her. She'd grown slightly plumper and her anxious expression had smoothed out; she looked younger and happier than I remembered.

She said, "Are you by yourselves?"

"Yes. I'll tell you everything, presently. Annabelle is hungry and I should welcome a cup of tea."

In slightly over twenty-four hours I had sustained the shock of learning that I owned nothing; had made a difficult decision; made a journey from Ozary to Baildon on the coach; walked from Baildon to Nethergate, carrying Annabelle when she tired; and then I had found, not the hearty, powerful man to whom I had meant to appeal, but a frail, helpless, *furtive* old man.

Still, he had referred to Turnbull, his lawyer; he had made some sort of plan for tomorrow.

Pratt made tea and produced bread, butter, cheese, and a piece of plum cake. She was all agog with curiosity.

"Fancy Mr. John sending you here," she said.

"It was my Cousin Franklin who sent me."

Pratt looked alarmed. "But he's out of his mind, poor man." She told me what she had heard; he'd gone crazy, had worn Page out, now had a keeper who made no secret of the fact that he had once worked in a lunatic asylum and who had been threatened with a razor, struck by a stick.

I said, "That is gossip, Pratt. Mr. Franklin has lost his power of speech and is physically infirm, but he is quite sane."

As I said it I wondered. The instant repudiation of my story, the haste, the secrecy . . .

"Well, I hear otherwise," Pratt said. "I was lucky. He arranged for me to live here, with ten shillings a week and stuff sent over from the house every week, meat and such, *before* he went off his head. And all legal, too. All looked after by Mr. Turnbull."

"Mr. Turnbull?"

"That's right. Mr. John would have had me out in the blink of an eye. He and Miss Harriet wanted this place . . . That's why I said *fancy,* thinking it was Mr. John sent you. It didn't seem to make sense. But if the master said . . . But then you say he can't speak . . . ?"

"He can write," I said.

Annabelle had begun to eat avidly, but the sharpest edge from her hunger gone, more and more slowly; now she was falling asleep with a piece of cake clutched in her hand.

I asked was there a bed aired and Pratt said that she had kept the Dower House as it always had been kept. "I like to think I earn my keep," she said. She picked up the candlestick and led the way. I carried Annabelle.

For once the child lay in fine linen, on a down-stuffed bed, a down-stuffed pillow. She was too sleepy to know. But I knew. From the moment, not of her birth, but from my recognition of her as *my* child, not as something foisted upon me by Alan, the seducer, I had wanted the best for her, and seen no hope of attaining it. No hope at all, until Pratt died.

Back in the kitchen, Martha Pratt took up her knitting, handling it awkwardly with her knotted fingers.

"Now," she said. "What happened to George?"

"He died." The news would not grieve her. She had never given any sign of fondness for Pratt as she had for her brother Tom, and fixing up the match which was to his advantage she had said frankly that she'd done it to get George off Tom's back.

"Well," she said calmly, "he wasn't as young as he made out. What ailed him?" I told her. I then added something over which I had been brooding. "That was in the spring. Since then I have been married again. To one of my own countrymen, Monsieur d'Aubigny."

I could say that now with confidence. It was a bitter thought but the squalid, farcical marriage in London had shown me that there had been no need to marry Pratt at all. Clergymen imprisoned in the Fleet gaol for debt would marry any couple who presented themselves, and no questions asked. Such marriages were legal though they broke almost every accepted rule; witnesses could be bought—fellow prisoners, glad to oblige for a measure of gin. Even partners could be hired. In my ignorance I had shrunk from the idea of joining the French colony in London with nothing but a fictitious marriage behind me: too late I had learned that for a guinea I could have hired a man to stand up with me and bestow upon me married status, and any name I chose to select.

"And where is he?" Pratt asked.

To say that he was dead, too, seemed somewhat extreme.

"He has returned to France. He is a kind of link between the exiles and the French government. He was in London only long enough to marry me and formally adopt Annabelle." I enlarged a little. "I have known Monsieur d'Aubigny for a long time, he was a friend of our family. He entertains some slight hope of recovering some portion of his property."

"Then you'd be all right," Pratt said. I may have imagined it but it seemed to me that as she said that Pratt regarded me with a touch more respect.

"Eventually, I hope. But it will take time."

Well, I had rid myself and my child of the hated name.

Pratt switched to another subject.

"If Mr. Franklin is, as you say, in his right mind, I can understand his sending you to sleep here. There wouldn't be a bed or a room in the house fit to use at a minute's notice. Everything is at sixes and sevens, so I hear. Ever since her ladyship . . . Of course, you knew about that?"

"Yes. I read about it in the newspaper."

Kneeling by the stove, hastily running my eye over a page of the Baildon *Free Press,* months old, before I lit the fire and heated the kettle for Pratt's shaving water, for which he must not be kept waiting one minute. The obituary notice was extremely eulogistic; and it made reference to the sad bereavement suffered by Lady Rosaleen in the previous year. So Alan was dead, too! I set light to the paper and watched it burn. I thought: Between them they ruined my life! I am here in this hateful place, in this hopeless situation, because of them. I was glad then that they were dead; and still more glad when my plan began to shape in my mind . . .

Presently I told Pratt that I would go to bed because I had to get up early in the morning, as my Cousin Franklin had entrusted me with an errand to do in Baildon. I did not tell her what.

I'd slept very little the previous night and had had a hard day; I expected to sleep as soon as I crept into bed beside Annabelle, but I did not. Instead I began to suffer not exactly a fit of conscience but that need for self-justification which is its near kin.

I knew that I had behaved with marked ingratitude towards Joanna Drury who had been so unfailingly kind to me. But I had my reasons.

First and foremost I had Annabelle's future to consider. What would it be if I accepted Joanna's invitation to stay with her in Ozary? Happy enough, while childhood lasted. She'd get a little education, perhaps from Joanna who was very learned, perhaps from a short spell at the kind of school that Joanna could afford. She might then become a governess. She might even drift—as Joanna had drifted—into amateur medical practice, a hard life, though Joanna made nothing of it; a desperately lonely life, halfway between gentry and peasant, halfway between male and female. Or, since there would be no dowry, and no social life, she might marry a farmer, at best an auctioneer. That was definitely not what I wanted for my daughter: nor would it be suitable for a girl of her breeding. My family were aristocrats, of long lineage—a de Savigny had gone with King Louis on the Third Crusade; the Franklins though less distinguished belonged, and had for many generations belonged, to the peculiarly English class—the squirearchy. Blood alone entitled Annabelle to something more than Joanna could offer.

There was another reason, too. Facts must be faced, hateful as they may be. There had never been, between Joanna and me, that kind of relationship said, rightly or wrongly, to have existed between Marie Antoinette and some of her women friends. But I felt that it lurked there, biding its time. Base of me to suspect, perhaps, but one has one's instincts. Nothing obvious, nothing explicit, but *there*. "You can come and live with me," she had said as soon as Pratt was dead. Oddly enough, Pratt who hadn't a sensitive nerve in his body, but who knocked about the world a lot, had also been alert from the first day. He *said* he hated meddlers, but he also said, "I know that sort and I hate them."

When the time of decision began with his death and she was so kind, taking charge of everything for me, I knew that any future Joanna and I might share would be disastrous. Not because of my scruples. I had none. Not because of distaste. Anybody who could go to bed with Pratt had lost all fastidiousness; and I swear that if it could have benefitted Annabelle in any way, I'd have bedded with a gorilla. But what Joanna wanted of me was love, and I had none to give. In a few brief days Alan had taken all I had of one kind, Annabelle, from the moment I first fed her, had taken all the rest. Joanna would have suffered a grievous disappointment and become either terribly wretched, or dangerously resentful.

Dangerous?

Sleepless, in the first comfortable bed I had known for three years, balancing between self-justification and a kind of remorse, I considered again the possibliity, the likelihood, that she had killed Pratt. (If she had done so I was grateful to her. I certainly had no moral judgement to make. Hundreds of men far better than Pratt—my father amongst them—had gone to the guillotine: thousands more, young, conscripted, were dying in the war.) I suspected Joanna of killing Pratt partly because she had been *prepared* for his death. Over their beer men talk and I had heard them. Miss Doctor was having rooms made ready for cousins from London; yet she had once told me that she hadn't a living relative in the world. She'd sent me a warning message about the green ointment. And on that morning, Pratt, though not in his usual health and in worse than his usual temper because of his sore hand, had not been so ill that he could not eat his breakfast. Then, alone with Joanna in the parlour, in ten, fifteen minutes he was dead and she was saying that I could go home with her.

I needed time to think. Twice before in my life, making my escape from France, marrying Pratt, I'd had no time to think at all. Now I took my time. And yet, in the end the decision had been hurried. Tomorrow morning, I said, at eleven o'clock, I said . . . And I thought: I must take this risk; I must let my Cousin Franklin see Annabelle, see how like Alan she is. That was not a sudden thought, I had been thinking about it for a month.

Once I had decided upon it the ruthless way seemed best. I had loved Alan, but the manner in which he had deserted me had killed my love dead. Chop! Like the fall of the guillotine. I thought: I will desert Joanna in the same way. Chop! And she can think of me as an ingrate, just as I thought of Alan as a seducer. Pratt had once said about amputations, "Better the quick than the careful." So I wrote my letter and I hoped, I *genuinely* hoped, because she had been so kind to me that Joanna would read it, think me ingrate, cut me off. Hate me, as I had hated Alan . . .

Mr. Turnbull kept saying, "Yes, sir," and "I have that, sir." They sat, both scribbling away, passing papers back and forth. I sat by the window, sweating a little. I'd managed what Cousin Franklin had told me to do; gone into Baildon in Sam

Lockey's cart, brought Mr. Turnbull back with me, riding in his gig, smuggled him in through the west door. Now I waited, quite sure that though my Cousin Franklin had not been prepared to recognise Annabelle as his grandchild, he was now making some provision for her in the way men do for children who cannot be acknowledged but must be cared for.

At one point a servant had looked in. Not one I knew. He had a face that reminded me of some I had seen, in or around the Fleet prison. On my wedding day! He halted when he saw Mr. Turnbull. My Cousin Franklin wrote something and Mr. Turnbull said, "Your master will ring when he wants you, Chandler." The man went away and I resumed my staring out of the window, from which the chimneys of the Dower House were just visible. I'd left Annabelle asleep; for the first time in her life she would wake and not find me. A strange house. A strange face. I became agitated. I looked at the two men with impatience. What could they be doing that took so much time?

At last Mr. Turnbull scattered sand on the wet ink and said, "Now, Madame d'Aubigny, if you will read this and make sure that you understand each condition and agree to it, and then sign . . ."

When did anything ever go right for me?

This was a most disappointing document. In a way it made provision for Annabelle but it was not what I had hoped for. It was twisted and inhumane. Perhaps those who said that my Cousin Franklin's mind was affected were right. Annabelle and I would be separated; she virtually a prisoner at the Dower House, I virtually a slave here, committed to obeying "every wish and command." Still, I had no choice; this gave us a roof—but separate roofs—over our heads and food to put in our mouths; £40 a year, with my keep, was far more than I could earn in any other capacity, and at the end of it there would be £1000, a useful if not generous dowry.

The clause about my not remarrying or having anything to do with men I found insulting, but amusing, too, in a sour way.

Fresh from my experience of an agreement that was deliberately one-sided, I had a sharp eye for loopholes, and saw two.

"What happens if Pratt should die?" I asked.

Cousin Franklin scribbled, *You appoint suitable person.*

"And if I die?"

Cousin Franklin held out the four words to Mr. Turnbull who pursed his lips and then said, "Very well."

I said, "I should like those two eventualities included in the contract. And one other. That no matter what circumstances arise in this house, I visit my child every day."

Mr. Turnbull wrote some more and then I signed.

The moment the lawyer had gone Cousin Franklin wrote: *Dinner. Duck. Sage and onion stuffing. Green peas; new potatoes. Gravy.*

It was the first sign of an obsession that was to continue for a long time. I could sympathise with it; I had often been hungry at The Unicorn, cooking and serving good substantial meals to customers and then eating bread and hard cheese. Had Cousin Franklin dealt with me differently, had he only allowed me to have Annabelle with me, here in Nethergate, I should have thought: Poor old man, and taken some pleasure in seeing to it that he had nice things to eat, gluttony being now about the only pleasure left to him.

And send Clamp to me, he wrote.

During my former stay at Nethergate I had not been into the kitchen often, but I remembered it as specklessly clean. It had to be. Cousin Rosaleen did not visit it regularly, she made sudden appearances and unless everything was in perfect order she was displeased.

It was different now.

The cook was not the one I remembered, but I could tell which of the three women in the kitchen was cook, the oldest, the fattest, the one doing nothing.

I said, "Good morning. My name is Madame d'Aubigny. I have come to keep house for Mr. Franklin."

She gave me a pitying look. "Chandler did say something about a woman . . . Housekeeper! Just another of his daft tricks."

I said, "I should be obliged if you would stand up when you speak to me."

Somewhat to my surprise she got to her feet, but rather with an air of humouring me than of acknowledging my authority, which indeed at that moment had little foundation. When I told her what Mr. Franklin wished to eat she said, "You mean the old man? He ain't allowed no such things."

I said, "What is your name?"

"Blencoe. Mrs." I had a notion that she was about as much entitled to *Mrs.* as I was to *Madame.*

"Mrs. Blencoe, Mr. Franklin wishes for duck. In future he

will order whatever he wishes and if you wish to retain your post you will prepare it."

"We'll see what Mrs. Franklin has to say about that."

"Mrs. Franklin will have no say in the matter whatever. This is Mr. Franklin's house and he has engaged me to run it."

She still did not believe me, at least not fully, but she compromised to the extent of sending one of her handmaidens to tell Long Jim to catch and kill a duck.

I knew where I should find Clamp; in the room that served both as butler's pantry and upper-servants' sitting room. Chandler was with him; they were taking their ease, smoking little clay pipes and drinking not the ale which was allowed them, but either sherry or Madeira.

". . . a woman, I tell you," Chandler was saying. "Think I don't know a woman when I see one?"

"Depend whether she'd got her clothes on or not," Clamp said, laughing at his own witticism.

I said, "Clamp!" and he turned, jumped to his feet. Gaped.

"There you are! What'd I tell you?" Chandler asked.

"Miss Isabella! Come back?"

"Yes." At least he had recognised me, and when I said that Mr. Franklin wanted him, he did not argue. "You'd better take the wine book with you," I said.

It was typical of the slovenliness that had fallen upon Nethergate that the wine book, which in the old days had been so meticulously kept that a glance through it showed exactly what was in the cellar, and where, now took almost ten minutes to find. But it was found, and I thought that with the duck being prepared and Cousin Franklin busy—doubtless happily busy—choosing his wine to go with it, I could just run across to the Dower House.

Annabelle was pleased to see me, but she seemed quite happy with Pratt. And Pratt was more than happy when I gave her a brief outline of the arrangements Cousin Franklin had made.

"Ten shillings a week, just for looking after her," she said. "Oh, that will be such a help to Tom. And she's no trouble, very obedient. Not like some."

Annabelle had learned, very early, that obedience was wise, and though she had lately enjoyed more freedom she was still very amenable. Pratt, of course, knew all, and when I mentioned that Annabelle must stay on the Dower House premises she nodded and said, "I'll be careful about that."

I went back to the house, hurrying over the grass in which,

presently, my feet were to wear a definite track. I had, I knew, another ordeal to face. Telling John and Harriet.

John had never taken any notice of me. A poor relative, exiled from France. Nobody! Harriet, at our first meeting, had given me the up-and-down look which any woman not yet firmly betrothed gives any female who might constitute a threat. Danger here? Not me, in that ill-fitting dress. Shy and unsure. Nobody!

Now I was somebody—the housekeeper with extraordinary powers.

Harriet flared. "Didn't I say from the first that he should have been put away? Are you seriously meaning to tell us"—she swung round to me—"that *you* can decide whether we eat beef or mutton?"

"I *could*," I said. "The document which Mr. Turnbull drew up this morning gives me absolute control. But I assure you that any wish you may have, provided it does not run counter to my Cousin Franklin's desires, will be observed by me."

John said, "I simply don't believe it. It's a trick of some sort. I'll go down and tackle Turnbull at once."

Harriet said, "Just wait till my Papa hears of this insult!"

I said, "Wait, before you say or do anything. Many people in houses smaller than this employ housekeepers. Unless you choose to make it seem otherwise this is a perfectly ordinary arrangement. It relieves you, Harriet, of the burden of house-keeping; it provides employment for a poor relative. Nobody will see anything unusual about it. I shall not intrude. I shall take your orders—so long, as I said, that they do not conflict with those of the master of the house."

That seemed to me to be the basis of a reasonable settlement. But John said he must see Turnbull. And did, and was told that the situation was exactly as I had described it. Harriet decided not to speak to her father.

Rancour remained. For quite a long time I had to endure something too petty to be called persecution, too petty really to be noticed except that it shows how petty people can be. From what was known as the small drawing room, an ugly room, all stripes of dried blood colour and buff, the bell would ring. Wilcox would answer it and then plod along to tell me that Mr. Franklin, or Mrs. Franklin, wished to speak with me. And it would be some trivial thing, heavily sarcastic. The log basket was empty, had they my permission to have it replenished. Had they my permission to invite guests for a meal, for a night. There were constant complaints, too; the steak was tough, the roast either over- or undercooked. Would I do them a favour and speak to Cook?

These, however, were mere pinpricks and there were adequate compensations. I had great authority which I enjoyed exercising and for the first time since my escape from France I had money to spend, household money, and my own. After the penny-pinching routine at The Unicorn it was delightful to me to go into Baildon and place lavish orders and receive the almost servile respect accorded to those whose custom is valued. Even more delightful was the spending of my own money, some on myself, more on Annabelle. There was no proper toy shop in Baildon, but I found a stall on the market which sold toys as well as trinkets. The first thing I bought there was a doll, a very pretty thing with a wax face—a development of Madame Tussaud's famous death masks at her museum in Paris—flaxen hair which the stall-holder assured me was real, and eyes of blue glass. Annabelle had never had a doll, never a proper toy at all, and she was enchanted. I said that a doll must have a name; what should we call her? It was a stupid question, for Annabelle had led such a restricted life that she knew no names, except those in the stories and rhymes with which I had tried to enliven the tedium of being tied to a table leg. She thought for a second or two and then said, "Aunt Joanna." I imagined then that every time I heard the name I should suffer a little pang and be obliged to go through the process of self-justification all over again: but the truth is that human nature is definitely adaptable; soon I was using the name, hearing the name used, without a thought of its original owner.

At Nethergate I installed myself comfortably; upstairs a proper guest room, near to the one to which Cousin Franklin had been carried; downstairs a room that had hitherto been used only for lumber. It opened off the back hall and was almost opposite the kitchen. It had glass panels in the upper half of the door, so that without moving from my chair, I could keep an eye on comings and goings. I had it cleared of all the lumber except one thing, a narrow, very solid old table, once perhaps the dining table, long enough for me to take my meals at one end, and use the other for housekeeping business. I then spent a happy hour or two going through the house and selecting other furniture and trimmings, a winged chair, a high-backed sofa, almost a settle but upholstered in worn velvet. With a rich-coloured rug in front of the hearth, two pictures—both of flowers—and a gilt-framed looking glass, my room was not only snug, but as far as its proportions allowed, elegant.

When I say that I prepared it happily I discount my one discontent. All the time I was thinking: If only Annabelle could come and share with me. She was my child, I loved her, and in addition the circumstances of our life at Ozary had created a special bond between us. Rich people see little of their children; they put them out to nurse, hand them over to governesses or tutors: the poor tend to have large families, so that affection is diffused and to women who are obliged to work a young child is often a nuisance. I had worked as hard as any woman alive, but Annabelle had been with me; we had been all in all to each other, lately I had protected her against Pratt. Now I missed her at every turn. The highlight of my day came when I could run across to the Dower House, see her, play with her and put her to bed. On every day except Sunday my hour was between about half-past five and half-past six. On Sundays I went later, so as not to intrude upon Pratt's family; her brother Tom, his wife, his daughter and her two children who came from Ockley to share her mid-day meal. I had no wish to see them—my relatives by marriage.

Proper food had made a remarkable difference in Cousin Franklin, and the change of atmosphere helped, too. I had had a straight talk with Chandler; I told him that Mr. Franklin's bell must be answered promptly, that anything Mr. Franklin wrote must be regarded as of the utmost importance. I had, in fact, restored Cousin Franklin to his rightful place as master in his own house.

As he grew less pitiable it was easier for me to cherish my grudge against him and resist his invitations to sit down and have a little chat, by which he meant that he would say a few halting words and write others and that I should talk. I refused to drink his wine, or play cards with him. Often when he made a friendly gesture I would think: If only you had allowed me to keep the child we could all be together and happy; *you* created this situation and you must put up with it.

Once he gave me a present. It was on the day when I first wore my housekeeper's dress, a stiff, rustling black silk.

"Nice," he said, "but—needs yah yah." He wrote, *Gold chain and watch.* He then wrote where I should find a certain box. It contained all Rosaleen's jewel cases and a chamois leather bag from which he took a long, thick gold chain and a pretty little watch. These he presented to me with a smile and just a touch of gallantry. I thanked him, but I hardened my heart by thinking that no amount of trinkets could make up to me what he had deprived me of, and when he showed an inclination to linger over the jewels, opening a case which held some sapphires and saying, "But—her—eyes—were—bluer," I refused to share this nostalgic pastime and asked briskly whether he wished to keep the box by him or should I hide it again?

"Hide," he said. And then, "Page . . ." While I disposed of the box he wrote: *Find Page. Get him back. Better than Chandler.* I promised to do my best. Unfortunately nobody knew anything about Page except that he was not a local man and had never spoken of his family or his home. Cousin Franklin remembered that Page had been a Methodist and went to chapel. I followed that trail and eventually learned that Page had become a missionary.

"Pity. Pity," Cousin Franklin said when I told him this. Then he wrote: *Still I have you now. Very thankful.*

He had indeed my time, my services; I had thoroughly re-organised his household and put an end to the pilfering that had certainly been going on. I was keeping my side of the bargain, but I should have served him more wholeheartedly but for that stupid clause about Annabelle.

Very soon I had something more than our separation to worry about.

Pratt, speaking of her family and their weekly visit, had said, "Marty's girls are some bit older, but they'll be company for her in a way." And on the evening of the first Sunday she reported that the children had got on well together. Annabelle talked a good deal about Ella and Wosie, the first children with whom she had ever had contact. Wosie said this and Wosie said that. Amongst other things that Wosie said was that they never went to bed till it was dark.

Pratt said, a little defensively, "Well they can't. Only two bedrooms and one no more than a passage." Pratt was always slightly on the defensive on Sunday evenings when her usually neat kitchen was in disorder. "They have a longish walk," she said, "and are glad to sit down. Besides, if they did help to clear up they'd put everything in the wrong place."

On the occasion when Annabelle, for the first time, de-murred about going early to bed I said, "Darling, Rosie and Ella are both older than you. Besides I cannot stay long. Say good night to Pratt and come along, or we shall have no time for a story."

Annabelle said, "Good night, Aunt Marfa."

Defensive again, Pratt said, "They call me that, naturally. And children do copy."

I thought: Yes, and if a Fleet wedding is legal and a child born in wedlock is regarded as the legitimate offspring of the husband, Annabelle is perfectly correct!

It hurt; but as I had once said to Joanna, I had invited any hurt that came to me.

Children do copy. With unbelievable rapidity Annabelle's pronunciation deteriorated; and what can one say to a loving child who says, "Oy wuz looking owett for yew, Mamma." I let it go; a temporary thing, merely a sign of how well Annabelle got on with these, her half cousins. Pratt's speech was extremely precise; I flattered myself that I spoke perfect English; six days must eventually triumph over one.

Then came the day when, from the toy stall, I bought Annabelle a coloured ball and because it was a wet evening we played with it in the kitchen. She missed a catch and said, "Bugger it!"

Pratt looked up from her knitting and said, very sternly, "What did I say I would do to you if you ever said that again?"

Annabelle said jauntily, "Yew said yew'd slap me. But Mamma wouldn't let yew."

"I would, darling. What is more if Pr . . . if Aunt Martha ever has to slap you, I shall slap you again, and harder."

Annabelle looked at me with hostility. Pratt said, "They play about on the Green, you see. I don't know; Tom and me never had time for playing. And our father was strict. He used to say we may be poor but we don't have to be rough. Now things are different and Emma and Marty don't care and I don't like to spoil Tom's day with carping."

This whole business of swearing, of deciding what are forbidden words is a bit confusing to any rational person and doubly so to one who is completely bilingual. It is an arbitrary thing. All I could say to Annabelle, when I had her to myself, was that there were some words which nice little girls mustn't say. "And if Pr . . . Aunt Martha ever tells you not to use a word, darling, you will know that it is not one that nice little girls should use. Do you understand me?"

I went home—if Nethergate could be called my home, thinking how ridiculous the whole thing was. *Nomme du nomme. Merde.* Words no gently reared person would use. And the English *damn;* I will build a dam in this stream, absolutely permissible; this stream is a damn nuisance; this cow's dam was so-and-so. Where, really, was the difference?

But these were my frivolous thoughts, thrown up to protect me from what was real and urgent: What to do about Annabelle on Sunday?

I was very meek. I said, "Cousin Franklin, I have a great favour to ask. Would you relax the rule about Annabelle so far as to allow her to spend part of Sunday here? From about twelve o'clock till half-past five? I promise she should stay in my room, nobody should see her."

He managed to say, "No. It—was—agreed."

"I know. I know. But when I agreed I did not realise . . ." I told him exactly what was happening, why I asked this favour. I said, "She is your granddaughter, whether you wish to acknowledge her or not. Surely you would not wish your granddaughter, Alan's child . . ."

He lifted his stick—the stick that I had returned to him—and beat on the floor. "I—said—not—to—mention. Yah, blah, bloof, yack."

I said, "Very well. In future I shall be absent from this house on Sunday, from twelve o'clock until five. It was written into the agreement that I should see Annabelle every day. No specific hours were mentioned."

He received this information with a frown but made no protest.

I tried to be tactful with Pratt. I told her that I now had things at the house so well under control that I could absent myself on Sundays. I said that, after all, I saw Annabelle very little during the week, and would take her for a picnic on Sunday.

Pratt understood, but all she said was, "She'll miss a good hot dinner."

The garden at the Dower House was quite spacious and in it was a pretty little pavilion, just the place for a make-believe house. The garden on one side ended in a thick shrubbery which, I discovered that afternoon, became, on its far side, Layer Wood. There was nothing to mark the boundary. So where did the Dower House premises end? Indulging in this piece of sophistry I went into the wood where we played Hide-and-Seek amongst the trees and ate a few early black-berries. It was a very happy outing, a taste of what life could have been had Cousin Franklin been less intransigent. When it was over and we went back to the kitchen, again untidy, Pratt said, "Rosie and Ella missed her. After dinner they went into the garden to look for her."

"We must have been in the shrubbery," I said.

The problem was no problem while the fine weather lasted,

as it did that year, well into October. I took good care that if the Pratt children came into the garden Annabelle and I were elsewhere. Her vowel sounds had recovered by the time the weather broke.

I took a rug and we ate our picnic huddled together in its shelter, inside the little pavilion which was draughty now; we warmed ourselves playing ball and other games on the fringe of the wood. But we were doomed; the days grew shorter as well as colder.

One Sunday morning, with a chilly fog lingering, Pratt said: "If you take her out in this, she'll surely catch a cold."

"It is not a very nice day," I agreed. "Do you think your family will venture?"

"They wouldn't miss for anything. Tom knows what his visits mean to me. The others come for the food. But they're hardy."

Annabelle did catch cold that day and was snuffling on Monday, in bed on Tuesday and Wednesday. Pratt, without saying anything, managed to make rebuke and reproach felt. On Saturday Annabelle was better, but still slightly hoarse, so I made one last attempt to have her to myself. Would it not be wise, I asked Pratt, to keep her in her room on Sunday, in case the other children should catch the cold.

"Bless you," Pratt said, "they have colds all the time from Michaelmas to Easter."

Comforting hearing!

Very gradually I was becoming aware of the fact that there were two Pratts. Even over her grandnieces she was of divided mind. She would admit that they were rough, so potentially destructive that during their visits she always kept the door between the kitchen and the main part of the house locked. At the same time they were Tom's grandchildren and therefore to be cherished and not to be criticised however tacitly by an outsider. Her attitude to me was ambivalent. I was Miss Isabella, I was Madame d'Aubigny, but I was also her brother George's wife, a woman saved from the shame of bearing an illegitimate child by Pratt's timely intervention. Now and again she put gentle pressure upon me.

I had bought some fine soft blue cloth and made Annabelle two little frocks and a cloak. The sight of them roused the Pratt in Pratt; I saw it happen.

"I wonder now, whether next time you're in Baildon, you'd buy me some stuff. Then I could make cloaks for Rosie and Ella. We don't want jealousy, do we?" I said, "But of course," and she said, "I'd pay." But she said it in such a way that it was plain she had no intention of doing so.

I said, "Oh, no, Pratt. I'll buy the material. A kind of early Christmas present." I did not buy such good cloth, nor did I buy blue. I bought crimson.

On another occasion Pratt said, "You having charge of everything up at the house now, could we have beef for Sunday? We've had pork so far and that isn't such a treat for Tom. When they *do* get meat at home they get pork."

Prior to my arrival Pratt had received certain supplies from the house; tea, sugar, flour, meat, delivered on Saturday. The meat had always been pork and I had not changed that arrangement. During the week I had myself taken across the extras demanded by Annabelle's presence. Beef, a chicken, lamb chops as well as things like honey and butter and eggs. Here again the favouritism that must be avoided. I agreed that in future Pratt should have beef to cook on Sunday.

Once or twice Pratt also referred to Monsieur d'Aubigny. One could not exactly say that when she did so she looked sly, but there was something not quite like her usual look or manner when she asked had I heard from my husband. This again was a situation for which I had only myself to blame. I said, No, it was still rather early to expect news; and then, No, perhaps something had gone wrong, France was a dangerous place, and finally, No, I was becoming anxious. One day I should be able to tell her that I feared the worst . . .

At Nethergate, Cousin Franklin flourished; he was regaining his speech a little more every day and moving less clumsily on his stick. He began to entertain and I organised his little card and supper parties for him to the very best of my ability. Downstairs Harriet and John entertained, too. I was very busy as the year ran downhill.

I had now reverted to my usual time for Sunday visits and one Sunday in December I arrived to find Annabelle in tears. She ran to me and held out Aunt Joanna, in two pieces, her head and her body.

Pratt said, with a touch of irritation, "I *told* you I'd mend it as soon as I'd tidied up a bit."

"They did it. Wosie and Ella," Annabelle said.

"It was an accident," Pratt said. Perhaps she had had a trying day. "A lot of fuss about nothing. Crying over a doll!"

"They hurt Aunt Joanna," Annabelle said. "Ella pulled and Wosie pulled. Wosie is wough."

The doll's waxen head, neck, and about an inch of torso

had been attached by stitches to her leathern body. It was the stitches that had given way, not the tiny holes in the wax through which the stitches had been inserted. I could see that it would be the work of moment to mend the doll. Then I saw in the accident the wax on the nose had been injured, so that whatever the head was made of, some dark, leaden substance, showed through. Like a bruise. The thought took me straight back to Ozary . . . Annabelle and I had been through hard times together; she, at least, deserved better than this.

I put in the necessary stitches, and then, warming the waxen face to just the right consistency, I worked on the nose, stealing a little from the surrounding areas and covering the bruise. Pratt watched with a touch of scorn and I thought she should have understood me better; she was no stranger to love; she loved her brother Tom much as I loved Annabelle. Yet my gestures of love seemed to her contemptible.

When I came down from putting Annabelle to bed, happy with Aunt Joanna, almost as good as new, beside her, Pratt said:

"I have been thinking. It might save trouble if they had a doll each. I'd pay, if you'd look out for them for me."

I said I certainly would look out for dolls, and pay for them. But two dolls would not solve the problem. I tried once again. I asked Pratt wouldn't it be a pleasant change for her to visit her family instead of their plodding, in bad weather, to visit her, and going home in the dark. "You could have the gig, Pratt, and take whatever you wished to take. I'd look after Annabelle. Wouldn't that be easier for everybody?"

"So it might *seem*," Pratt said. "But for one thing they've got no oven at Ockley. For another it's a treat for them to come here. It'd be no treat for me to go there, half the size of this"—she looked round the kitchen—"and all of a clutter."

Defeated again!

Shortly after that Pratt wondered whether she could have a turkey for Christmas. "Tom never tasted it. It'd be such a treat for him."

Tom Pratt was far from being alone in never having tasted turkey; it was a luxury dish which those who could afford it were adopting not as a substitute for the Christmas roast beef, but as a supplementary dish. I said, "Very well." I felt that Pratt was encroaching, but there was nothing I could do about it.

On the day when I bought the dolls—nothing like Aunt Joanna, stout wooden creatures that would stand up to ill-usage—I found on the stall the ideal Christmas gift for Anna-belle, a tiny tea set, the cups hardly bigger than a thimble, each item decorated with a miniature rose. For Pratt at another stall I bought a roll of grey flannel. Then, my Christmas shopping done, I gave my attention to the celebrations at Nethergate.

John and Harriet, pursuing their policy of making everything as difficult as possible, wanted four, no, two, no, six, no four after all, house guests, and four, no, six, possibly even eight neighbours to come for Christmas dinner. Cousin Franklin wished to entertain, too; three old friends who for various reasons lacked the family background so desirable at the festive season; after the meal he proposed to play cards. The fact that there would be two separate parties did not bother me much; Chandler was quite capable of serving the meal upstairs and the whole thing was eased by the fact that on Christmas Day everybody would dine at the same time.

Perhaps it was the influence of my fellow exiles that had brought about a change in the eating habits of the English, dinner being pushed later and later, its daytime place being taken by the lighter meal called luncheon. Harriet and John, being young and wishing to be fashionable, had adopted the new régime, Cousin Franklin stuck stubbornly to the old. He dined at one o'clock and took supper in the evening. Not that it made much difference, he was now so greedy that his two meals were indistinguishable. However, on Christmas Day everybody would dine at one o'clock; the servants would make merry in the evening; the house guests would manage with a cold buffet supper and if Cousin Franklin, having eaten roast beef and turkey, plum pudding and mince pies, demanded a hot meal in the evening, as he was quite capable of doing, I would prepare it myself, *after* I had visited Annabelle.

The Pratt family not only ignored the weather, they seemed able to see in the dark; they never left for home until half-past five; even on the shortest day.

On Christmas Eve when I left the Dower House, I gave the box containing the little tea set to Pratt, asking her to put it by Annabelle's bed when she went to bed herself. I wanted Christmas to begin happily for Annabelle. I had another present for her, a pair of little boots, made to her measure, and blue, like her cloak. They had white fur around their tops and would please her—but not so much as the tea set.

I said, "Happy Christmas, Cousin Franklin."
"The—same—to—you—my—dear." I had my inevitable,

my inescapable thought: How happy it could have been . . .

"Box," he said, "Bring—the—box."

This time he delved about in it and brought out a case of velvet, slightly worn.

My Cousin Rosaleen's jewels had never impressed me very much because, good as they were, they were very modest compared with those which my mother had owned. One of my remote ancestors had gone on Crusade with Louis II of France and amongst the many other things he had brought back from the East was the largest known ruby in the world; or so it was said. It was also said that two Kings, Louis XIV and Louis XV, had coveted the jewel, wishing it as a gift, not for their wives but for the mistress of the moment. It was as large as a pullet's egg and of perfect colour; not set, it would have been difficult to set, simply pierced at its narrower end and worn on a slim gold chain. There was a tradition in the family that whenever it was worn it should be worn alone, nothing, not even a ring to detract attention from it. In addition to this famous de Savigny ruby, there were the emeralds, reputed to be the first to come from Brazil. All to be mine, one day. But I was only thirteen when the world turned upside down and the jewels became not merely unfashionable but rather dangerous—a diamond necklace had played a large part in Queen Marie Antoinette's mounting unpopularity. So, when my father and I went to Paris, he to take his seat with the Moderate Party, all I took with me was a single string of pearls—permissible wear to any ordinary *citoyenne* because some clever man had perfected the art of making artificial pearls, within the reach of all but the very poor. Mine happened to be genuine and they—with some aid from a faithful servant—had undoubtedly saved my life. The great ruby and all the rest were locked up in our château in the village where, my father said, no one to whom he had always been a kind and generous landlord would dream of touching anything that was his. What happened to those jewels I did not know, should never know.

However, the string of pearls in the blue velvet case was almost a replica of the one which had provided me with the means to escape and live on—in a life which had more than once, especially in Ozary, seemed hardly worth living.

"Present," Cousin Franklin said. "For—little—girl."

It was touching and it was infuriating. To give Annabelle something of value, not only in itself of value but something that had belonged to Rosaleen, was an acknowledgement of what he would not acknowledge. Just across that strip of park

Annabelle was keeping Christmas with the Pratt family; and she could have been here!

I said, rather stiffly, "That is very kind of you, Cousin Franklin. She is too young to wear them at present. I will put them away for a while." (We don't want jealousy, do we?) "Shall I put the box back?"

"No—leave—it."

I then looked about his room. When he had begun to entertain I had moved in two tables, one a gateleg which, opened out, seated four comfortably but could at other times stand folded against the wall and take the place of a side table, the other a foldover card table.

I said, "I will tell Chandler to make ready."

"He—has—his—orders. I—am—ready."

"Oh yes, so I see," I said, observing for the first time that he was wearing the blue jacket, the embroidered waistcoat which in the old days had constituted his best wear. He had worn these clothes to that concert in Baildon.

"You look very grand," I said. He gave a kind of smirk of self-satisfaction.

I locked away the pearls and went downstairs. There, when I saw Chandler, I reminded him about preparing Cousin Franklin's room and he gave me a sly look and said everything was ready which I knew to be untrue but took to mean that the trays were laden and needed only to be carried up. I spent a little time in the kitchen where Mrs. Blencoe and the assistant I had hired for her as soon as I realised that Cousin Franklin required two full meals a day were very busy. Everything was under way there; I had earlier overlooked the setting of the table, my duty was done for the moment and I was free to retire to my sitting room, eat my lonely Christmas dinner from a tray and wish, as I always wished, that Annabelle could have been with me.

Chandler found me there. "If you please, madame, the master would like a word with you."

Something wrong upstairs? Or did my Cousin Franklin wish to ask me, yet again, to drink a glass of wine with him? Chandler followed me upstairs and into the room where Cousin Franklin stood, his good hand on his stick, his weaker one on the back of his chair. Nothing in the room showed that guests were expected here.

"Coming—down," he said. "Give—everybody—surprise. Sit—head—of my—own—table."

He was already a little flushed. He had in the last week or two managed to get along the gallery to the water closet, but he had never ventured farther and never even mentioned trying the stairs. I thought his plan a piece of folly, something which if he failed to achieve it would spoil his day, but I had been hired to obey his orders, not to dictate to him.

"And—you—" he said, "place—of honour—my right—hand."

I said, "Oh, no, Cousin Franklin. I beg to be excused. It would embarrass me."

The thing that made him so difficult to deal with was that the slightest opposition to his wishes deprived him of speech. It did so now; he yah-yahed a bit, let go his hold on the chair back and sat down, took the stick between his knees and snatched up his pencil.

But for you, dead by now, he scribbled. *Christmas Day. Show everybody. You promised. Do what I say.*

It was true; I had promised. And I certainly had no wish to provoke the stroke which might kill him. I hoped he would live many years; out of my £40 a year, I could save something; Annabelle and I had our keep. In the bond there had been some mention of school; if he lived long enough he would pay for her education.

And did I really mind a few country squires and their wives thinking that I did not know my place? I had, after all, sat at that table before.

I said, "Very well."

Chandler went down the stairs first, walking backwards, strong and alert. Cousin Franklin, his stick in his weaker hand and his right clutching the bannister rail, went down as a child does; one foot on the step, the other foot following, feet together on the stair, and then the process all over again.

His aim to give everybody a surprise was fully achieved. There were outcries of pleasure, some genuine, some spurious, and, of course, a chorus of greetings. Harriet gave me a dark look. She held me responsible for this melodrama. The truth, I think, is that my Cousin Franklin, under his mild, kindly manner, had always needed to assert himself. While Rosaleen was alive he had never been able to do so, and before he could really reorganise himself and his life after her death he had been smitten down and rendered completely helpless. Now he was almost himself again and he had certainly caused a stir.

Actually, if I were to be at this table at all, there was no reason why I should not take the place of honour; kinswoman by marriage, de Savigny by birth. Who had a better right?

I had forgotten my Cousin Franklin's amiable custom of presenting every lady at his Christmas dinner table with a gift.

I had only spent one Christmas at Nethergate and then I had hardly found my feet in a strange environment; since then a lot had happened. Alan, George Pratt, Ozary, Joanna, Annabelle ... life and death. But here on the long table where men for once outnumbered women, were the gifts for the women, wrapped in that fine white paper used by milliners and dressmakers and called "tissue" and bedecked with ribbon.

The Christmas that I remembered every lady had received a scent bottle; Amber Water was contained in amber-coloured glass, Hungary Water in blue, Eau de Cologne in green; pretty toys with silver stoppers. Today every tissue-wrapped parcel was oblong, except mine which was square. It occurred to me that the idea of demanding my presence at this table had been an afterthought and that my table gift might be some makeshift thing. I could not have been more wrong. Harriet, her sister Sylvia, now Mrs. Martin, her cousin's wife—the wife of the only man who had come out of India with nothing—and the two other young women who, with their husbands, were here for the meal, they all opened their presents and displayed fans, very pretty, with ivory sticks, hand painted with flowers, birds, butterflies.

I opened my present, saw what it was and shut it smartly. Rosaleen's sapphire earrings.

How could he do this to me? What harm had I ever done him?

"Open—it. Wear—them," he said, softly but with insistence.

Hot-faced, but trying to maintain composure, I obeyed, under a battery of eyes. I was wearing my housekeeper's dress, my uniform, my armour; with my high-collared black dress and small plain cap, these ornaments looked ridiculously incongruous. On each there was a sapphire at the lobe of the ear, and three little strings of diamonds supporting other sapphires. Showy things, and, of course, recognisable.

"Cousin Franklin, I don't know what I have done to deserve such a gift."

"I—know," he said.

Two of the women at the table were Harriet's relatives and had doubtless been told that Harriet had been denied Rosaleen's jewels as well as her rooms. The dinner guests, all four of them young and not long established in the district, may not have understood the situation, but Harriet managed to say, "Well!" in a very eloquent voice. Old Sir Edward Follesmark, Cousin Franklin's friend, said in a kindly way, "Very becoming, my dear. And well deserved." Other eyes at the table asked: How earned? It was particularly unfortunate that one of the men who should have been eating upstairs was Mr. Helmar who had a very bad reputation where women, particularly housekeepers, were concerned. My Cousin Franklin was not very fond of him, but he, like Sir Edward and Mr. Rider, were men on their own and so free to, and glad to, accept an invitation for Christmas Day. The look he gave me was especially offensive.

However, the bad moment—and it may have been even less than that—passed. It was, after all, a gathering of people with some pretensions to good breeding. The ladies began to flutter their fans and thank Cousin Franklin, uttering little cries of appreciation. Ordinary talk began again. I justified my presence at the table, and perhaps my position there by cutting Cousin Franklin's meat for him. He could cut well enough, but his left hand was not reliable on the fork.

Presently somebody said, "The snow has begun." Everybody turned to the windows and said things like, "Seasonal," or "Proper Christmas weather." Harriet's cousin, who sat on my right, exerted himself to be civil to me, asking from what part of France I came and hoping that I did not suffer so much from the English climate as he did after years in India. His sufferings, he said, were increased by the fact that he and his wife had failed in their search for a suitable house and been obliged to take one which was draughty and damp. Perhaps the earrings had given him a false idea of my power and he thought that if I cared to try I could oust Pratt and instal them in the Dower House, after all.

After the meal I saw the dining room cleared and the cold supper laid out. I supervised the serving of tea. Everybody, including Cousin Franklin, was engrossed in gambling games.

Just before half-past five, carrying Annabelle's boots and Pratt's flannel, lighting my way with a lantern, I made my way through the darkness and the snow, to the place where my heart had really been all day.

So much was going on in the Dower House kitchen that I was able to take a long look before anybody noticed me.

The kitchen table had not been properly cleared after dinner, everything, including the almost stripped turkey carcass, had been pushed towards the centre of it. At each end a tea party was in progress; Pratt, her brother Tom, his wife and daughter were drinking real tea at the end nearest the fire; Rosie, Ella, and Annabelle were holding a dolls' tea party at the other. Tom Pratt bore not the least resemblance to his brother; he was grey and small and looked hunchbacked; the two women were fat and blowsy and might have been sisters rather than mother and daughter. They were all talking and laughing, Pratt as loudly as any, her prim manner completely abandoned.

As I stood there, Rosie Pratt reached for the turkey dish and snatched up a fragment of the meat. She crammed it into her mouth and said, through the mouthful, "Thass moy turn tew pour owett."

Annabelle said, "Naow, it ain't. Thass moyn."

Rosie grabbed the little teapot which slipped through her greasy fingers and shattered on the pammented floor. Ella, using her doll as a weapon, aimed a blow at her sister and said, "Clumsy sod! Look what you done!"

Annabelle simply wailed.

Tom Pratt, without turning his head, said, "Can't you lot play quieter?"

Then they were all aware of me. Annabelle's wail grew louder, she hurled herself at me.

I dropped my two parcels and picked her up, saying into her ear, "You shall have another. Be quiet now, darling, please. Quiet."

Pratt stood up, looking flustered. "This is Miss Isabella. Madame d'Aubigny, I should say."

The two women stared, cowlike; but Tom Pratt had the instinctive good manners which I had noticed among the working men at Ozary. He stood up, "Hev a chair, ma'am. Less take your cloak." He took it, shook off what snow clung to it and hung it on a peg. I sat down with Annabelle on my lap.

Pratt said, prim again and apologetic, "It turned out such a bad night and Tom is free tomorrow . . . so I said they could stay."

"Very sensible," I said.

In the eyes of God—and of Pratt—my relatives by marriage.

"Well," I said with a geniality I did not feel, "I hope you have had a happy Christmas." The women just stared. Pratt said:

"We all enjoyed the turkey."

Tom Pratt said, "We hope you did, ma'am." And he smiled. I saw then why Pratt was so much attached to him; he was gentle and mannerly, and had a singularly sweet smile. Anything less like his brother . . . I said that I had had a very nice day, though busy. I'd had a horrible day, and now this. Their staying the night meant that Annabelle would have another day in company which was not only detrimental but not even happy. Rosie and Ella were thumping each other with the dolls which Pratt had believed would bring peace.

Tom Pratt said, "Anything left in the pot, Martha?" Thus prompted she offered me a cup of tea. It had been very black to start with and was now stewed as well.

"Aunt Joanna never got no tea," Annabelle said with a whine.

"Bring her here; she shall have some of mine," I said.

For a moment we sat there, she and I, pretending. Pretending that all was well, pretending that a doll could drink tea. Then Rosie and Ella thought they'd join in, too; they brought their dolls, already somewhat the worse for wear.

"Moyn tew. She's dry."

"So's moyn."

I did my best; I included them in the game. I tried to make conversation, but Pratt was plainly uncomfortable. Only Tom made any effort.

"The snow," he said, "come just in time. They say a green Christmas make a full churchyard and there's truth in a lot of old sayings. This being white should mean a healthy year."

"I sincerely hope it will prove so, for us all."

One of the women then broke silence, "You can't go by that. White as wool it was when we buried your mother."

Oh dear. Oh dear. I had so looked forward to having an hour of Christmas with Annabelle, to giving her the little blue boots, even to seeing Pratt pleased with her roll of flannel. The mention of the coming year depressed me—there would be a lot of Sundays before the weather was suitable for the picnics to be resumed. And up at the house, where manners were superficially more agreeable, a good deal of evil-thinking was going on. A horrid world, but the child was here, warm, growing heavy, trustful, loving; my one consolation . . .

As soon as was seemly I ended the session by taking Annabelle up to bed. A whispered bribe, "Darling, I have another present for you. A secret one."

She was delighted, as I had thought she would be, with the blue boots and it hurt me to say: "Don't wear them tomorrow. Rosie and Ella would want the same and I cannot afford to give them, every time, what I give you." That, of course, was beyond the understanding of a child one month short of being three years old; but Joanna had once said that Annabelle was precocious. She now said, "Moyn. Not Wosie's; not Ella's. Moyn." I thought: This is not what I wanted for her; not what I visualised; something must be done, and quickly otherwise she will be as aggressive, as "wough" as Rosie and Ella.

Tom Pratt offered to walk home with me. He looked so frail. I thanked him, I said I should be quite all right, it was only a little way and I had my lantern.

At the door I drew Pratt's attention to the roll of flannel and she forgot everything in joy. "I can make Tom some good warm shirts," she said.

My Christmas Day ended with getting Cousin Franklin back to his room and that was difficult since it was now his weak hand that was on the side of the bannister rail and Chandler, called from the kitchen celebrations, was more than slightly drunk.

It was not until I was at last in bed that the thought struck me that, unsatisfactory as this Christmas Day had been, it had, in effect, been profitable. I had not had a happy moment, but I had, locked away in the top drawer of my chest, a string of pearls, a pair of sapphire earrings.

On the following day, with Cousin Franklin very pleased with himself and his adventure and how well he had managed, but in fact exhausted and quite glad to stay in his bed, and with Harriet and John more venomous than ever, nicely gauging their demands for my presence to remarks meant to be overheard: ". . . exploiting a senile old man . . ." ". . . one wonders what next . . ." I went in the evening to the Dower House and found Pratt almost in tears.

"I do blame myself. I didn't realise that once upstairs they were free of the house, there being no door to lock there between back and front."

Rosie and Ella had found their way down the front stairs and managed, in the course of a game, or a fight, to break one of a pair of lamps in the hall. She took me to survey the damage.

Pratt had exerted pressure on me and on the previous evening when Annabelle had cried, with considerable justification, she had turned a deaf ear, so I said, coldly:

"This is no concern of mine. Mr. Turnbull looks after things outside the main house."

"I know," she said dolefully. "I suppose I'll have to tell him."

"You know best about that."

"Or could we match it?"

"I should think it highly unlikely."

The Dower House was beautifully furnished, the more elegant part of Nethergate on a small scale. The lamps were of cut glass with free-hanging pieces, like those on some chandeliers; they stood on pedestals of onyx, not easily tilted.

"I towd yew, Mamma, Wosie is wough. She's wough to Ella and me and Aunt Joanna."

It struck me that about the only word she now pronounced in the ordinary way was "Mamma," which, of course, the Pratt children did not use.

"They get excited," Pratt said. "There isn't much space where *they* live."

"Yew said yourself Wosie was wough and orta hev a smack on the bum."

"And I told you not to use that word," Pratt said. Annabelle made a face and stuck out her tongue.

It was a hopeless situation and could only get worse. Some action must be taken immediately.

Mrs. Twysdale, the head of the Female Academy for Girls, looked at me as though I were a criminal and insane into the bargain.

"Three, Madame d'Aubigny? Three! This is a school, not a nursery! We have sometimes taken a child just under ten, but only in the most exceptional circumstances."

"My circumstances are exceptionally exceptional," I said. I tried to explain: I was housekeeping for an elderly relative who did not want a child about the place. Mrs. Twysdale glanced through the window and there was the gig, the glossy horse, Long Jim waiting. She took me for an idle rich woman who did not want to be bothered with the care of a child. I had dressed myself carefully; I hoped to look, and sound, respectable. I said, "I know that three is very young, but Annabelle is very forward for her age, very self-dependent, very amenable . . ."

"And like any child of that age she needs either her mother or a reliable substitute. Could you not provide that? A school in which ten is the lowest age for admittance is certainly not the answer."

I humbled myself. I said, "Mrs. Twysdale, mine is a very real problem. I am a stranger . . . Could you recommend me to any place, any person? I cannot leave my child where she is."

She said, "I am sorry, I cannot help you, Madame d'Aubigny."

All the way home the cob's hoofs beat a rhythm: A child needs its mother; a child needs its mother.

On Saturday, having made my decision, I said to Pratt, "I have arranged for Annabelle to spend Sundays with me, in future. I shall call for her tomorrow morning at eleven."

"But you said Mr. Franklin said . . ."

"Mr. Franklin, like everybody else, is capable of changing his mind," I said.

Pratt understood, as she had understood the picnic scheme. She accepted and at the same time resented. She said, "I admit they're rough. But you can't blame Tom." That sounded rather pathetic. I relented over the lamp and told her that in a spare room at Nethergate there was one that was almost a match.

On Sunday morning I fetched Annabelle. She carried Aunt Joanna and I bore what remained of the tea set—there had been further breakages on the day after Christmas. I told her that we were now playing a new game: we had to get into this house without being seen. We managed that.

I had changed my room a little, shifting the high-backed sofa so that it formed almost a partition. If Annabelle stayed on the far side of it, near the fire, she was invisible from the door. I explained that the game now was to have an indoor picnic, a secret one, nobody must know that she was here. I removed her cloak and kissed her and hugged her and resolutely pushed away the thought: If only . . . Today was ours, we must make the most of it.

"Can Oy maike towast? Wosie allus maide the towast and Oy allus got the burnt bits."

I said, "Darling, you can make as much toast as you like. Toast, not towast."

"Wosie and Ella said I talked funny," she explained.

We had such a happy, happy day and our secret remained secret. When Wilcox tapped on my door—bringing word that Mrs. Franklin wished to speak to me—I did not call "Come in," but went to the door and took the message there. I locked my room when obliged to leave it unguarded. I had planned the day carefully, bringing down a chamber pot for Annabelle's use. I met my luncheon tray at the door and Annabelle ate all that it held before I returned it to the kitchen myself. Later we had a tea party with real tea and toast.

We slipped out of the house unobserved and, as we went towards the Dower House, Annabelle said, "That *was* a nice game, Mamma. Can we play it again?" I said I hoped so.

"Tomorrow?"

"No, not tomorrow. Next Sunday."

Through January and February and March. Into April. For once luck seemed to be with us. I never relaxed my precautions and the end, when it came, was in no way due to carelessness. On the second Sunday in April we were prepared to leave as usual; I always went and opened the outer door, made sure that no one was in the back hall, and then said, "Quick!" and Annabelle shot out. On this evening she was dressed and I was putting on my outdoor shoes when she said, "Oh, look, Mamma. Snowing and shining all at once."

It had been a day of sunshine, but with a sharp wind. I had thought that morning, seeing the daffodils and the first flecks of green on the hawthorns, that Spring was here—but for the wind. Maybe by next Sunday we should be able to picnic in the pavilion. These indoor Sundays had been delightful, but I was always conscious of a sense of strain, *and* of guilt. Moreover, Cousin Franklin, who since Christmas had seemed content to remain in his room, was now talking about trying the stairs again. He was now so much better, both in speech and movement, that this was a feasible plan. I was afraid that, once on the ground floor, he might take a fancy to see my room, and it might be on a Sunday.

Now, with the sun still bright in the west, snow was falling and the effect was must unusual. The light struck all the prismatic colours from each snowflake so that it looked as though a shower of diamonds was falling. I had never seen such a sight before, nor have I seen it since. It was enough to take one's mind off being careful. I went and stood, with Annabelle, in the square bay of the window and watched the spectacle which lasted only a minute or two. The angle of light changed and the snow was just snow. However, during that brief time Chandler passed the window and saw us.

I told myself that it did not matter. Everybody at Nethergate knew that I had a child boarded out at the Dower House: only Cousin Franklin, Mr. Turnbull, Pratt, and I knew that she was supposed to stay there and not set foot off the premises. To Chandler there could seem nothing extraordinary or worthy of mention, in my having my child in my room. So I comforted myself. But . . . There remained the fact that Annabelle's visits had been completely secret; if Chandler should mention the child, however casually, to Mrs. Blencoe for example, two and two might be put together; something funny going on?

That may have happened, in which case perhaps Chandler was prompted by malice, a getting-back at me for keeping him up to his duties. On the other hand it may have been simply a desire to ingratiate himself. I only know that on Monday morning when I went to take Cousin Franklin's orders for the day, Chandler was in the room, clearing up the wash-hand-stand. I said, "Good morning, Cousin Franklin. I hope you slept well. Good morning, Chandler." He slightly turned and said, "Good morning, madame. If I may say so, what a pretty little girl!"

I had one frail hope—that Cousin Franklin, engrossed as he always was at this time of day with what he should eat and drink—might not have noticed the remark, or made the connection. He did, of course. In fact, though many who thought they knew him, including his own son, regarded him as a typical simple, slow-witted country squire, inside his bulk, when he was bulky, inside his bones when he was starving, there was something ferret-sharp. It sprang to attention now.

"Eh, Chandler, what's that? What pretty little girl?"

"Madame's," Chandler said. "Very pretty indeed, sir. I said to myself, seeing them in the window, Just like a picture, I said."

If his intention had been to flatter and please, Chandler had failed.

Cousin Franklin said, "Get out." Chandler went, quickly.

"You've had her here," Cousin Franklin said angrily. "You cheated. You're a false, French hussy!"

"I was desperate. I tried to explain to you once. Things grew worse. I tried to find some solution." I related what shifts I had tried and how they had all failed. "So there was nothing to do but bring her here. Nobody has seen her, Cousin Franklin, except Chandler."

"And he knew. Everybody will know. You heard what he said, Just like the picture."

"He said a picture."

"Don't argue with me! You went dead against my orders. You broke your given word. Well, two can play at that game. The bargain's off!"

I thought of the wretched state in which I had found him, only last summer, of all the organising I had done on his behalf, and all the worry I had endured because of the one stupid rule.

"Very well. Had I known what the bargain involved I should never have made it. I can find a post where I am allowed to have my child with me. And Heaven help you if you fall ill again."

Straightway he did, under my eyes. The flesh of his face, mulberry-coloured with anger, seemed to slip sideways, twisting his mouth. His eyes bulged. The anger died out of his stare leaving just vacancy. When he sagged in his chair I thought he was dead.

I thought—as I rang the bell—of the £1000. Enough to set me up in business; enough to start a school . . .

He was not dead; he had simply suffered a second and far more incapacitating stroke. I helped Chandler to get him into bed while Long Jim rode helter-skelter for the doctor.

Well, our bargain was broken and I was free. Free to make the most of the time between now and the moment when he recovered—if he did recover—and could decide whether he wished to dispense with my services, or make a new bargain, on *my* terms.

That evening I took Annabelle back to Nethergate with me. I offered Pratt the plausible excuse that Mr. Franklin was now so ill as to need constant attention, so that, as I should not be able to visit regularly, I must have Annabelle in the house.

Pratt said, "What about what he said?"

I said, and it was true, "Oh, Mr. Franklin and I were talking about that just before he was taken ill."

"I see. I shall miss the ten shillings. It's been such a help to Tom." That gentle pressure was there again. But after all, Pratt *knew*.

"So long as I am at Nethergate, Pratt, you shall have your ten shillings."

I expected to be at Nethergate only a short time. Doctor Stamper had warned me; in his experience, he said, people who survived two strokes, invariably had a third and fatal one within a matter of months. Cousin Franklin might die, he might live and remember that he was angry with me, he might live and recognise my value and come to terms. In the meantime I had Annabelle, and Annabelle had me and much of Nethergate. Poor child, it seemed to me that there must always be some restriction on her freedom. I had no wish to provoke John and Harriet, so I forbade her to go to the front of the house, except when with me. I could choose times. A child of three, the only child in a houseful of servants, is bound to be made much of; everybody spoiled her. "Little Missy" had the first ripe strawberry that year; for "Little Missy" Mrs. Blencoe made gingerbread men.

The happiness of those stolen Sundays extended to weeks, to months, to years.

The first thing my Cousin Franklin did when he recovered consciousness was to grope for his pencil and write in a shaky scrawl, *Don't leave me*. I assured him that I should never leave him so long as he needed me. I dared not add—and as long as I can have Annabelle here. The very name might provoke another stroke. So there began a conspiracy of silence about her. She was never mentioned and he never saw her. He was not, indeed, a sight fit for a sensitive child, for his face remained twisted, the mouth pulled up on one side, the eye pulled down. His speech was completely unintelligible and his left leg so useless that it was only with the utmost difficulty that he could be heaved into a bedside chair.

Harriet, who had tried to kill him by slow starvation, accused me of bringing him to this sorry state. "All that rich heavy food," she said. "All that wine and brandy." One can learn, even from one's enemies. I saw to it that he had less to eat, but what he had was tasty; he had his wine and brandy, too, but well watered. He had visitors, though these grew rarer as the years passed.

I now had no grudge against him; happy myself, I cared for him tenderly and indulged him wholeheartedly. I spent hours reading to him, his left hand being so weak that to hold the paper was difficult for him. We played cards a great deal, his "hand" laid out on a tray held on his knees below table level and so out of my sight.

I kept him alive for almost seven years, and when in March of the year 1804 he died, Doctor Stamper said that he could not recall a case when a third stroke had been so long deferred. He congratulated me.

That was small comfort. In fact in the upheaval and confusion which followed, the only comforting reflection was that Annabelle and I had had these happy years, and that I had saved a little. We were rather better equipped than we had been in 1796 to face what was, without doubt, a very hostile world. And a world in which there was no justice. I had broken the contract between Cousin Franklin and me in only one respect—in bringing Annabelle into the house. And that, surely, was justifiable, an act of desperation. Apart from that I had kept my bargain, and done many things not demanded by our agreement; but at sometime or another he had seen fit to alter his will entirely and leave us nothing. There was a peculiar bitterness in the thought that *I* had kept the old cheat alive long enough to enable him to make a new will; and that *I* was the one who always admitted Mr. Turnbull, welcoming him with a smile, saying how glad Cousin Franklin would be to have a little business talk. One such smiling welcome, one such little business talk had ended in Annabelle being disinherited. She would have nothing now—except what I could get for her . . .

Narrative by Annabelle d'Aubigny

(1804-1815)

I said, "Mamma, are we really going to live *here*? It's a horrible house."

"It's a very horrible house. Not worth half what I was obliged to pay for it. But we are lucky to have a house at all."

It stood in a lane, Hawk Lane, that led from the Saltgate in Baildon to the river; there was a smithy on one side of it, a timber yard on the other and between the two it was so pinched and narrow that its door and one window took up most of its front.

Mamma unlocked the door and we went in. One tiny square whitewashed room and behind it a kitchen so small that even I could not stand in it with both arms outstretched. The back door opened into a yard of hard-trodden earth with a lean-to shelter for fuel and a little necessary house not recently cleaned. Upstairs there were two small rooms. Even from the upper windows there was not a tree nor a blade of grass to be seen. At the back the timber yard, and the rear of houses similar to ours, and at the front the lane and some cottages with sagging thatched roofs.

Misery gripped me; and a feeling of being stifled. I said:

"Mamma, we can't. We can't live here. Even if we are now so poor . . . Couldn't we have a little house in the country? This is so *ugly*."

"There would be no work suitable for me in the country," Mamma said. She looked about bravely. "This will look better when it has furniture in it. And that we must see about. We own nothing. *Nothing*."

The world had broken down under us. All because an old man had died. One minute we'd been at Nethergate, happy and comfortable and rich; and the next we were here. I did not understand what had happened and Mamma, who had never failed, as far as I can remember, to answer any question I asked, had said, "Darling, I cannot speak of it, *yet*. It is all too disgusting."

She now said, "We must have beds and some crockery. Sam Lockey told me of a place."

That was another thing. So far back as I could remember, whenever we came into Baildon we had come in a gig, driven by Long Jim, drawn by a shining fat horse. We went to shops and Long Jim tapped the window with a whip and the shop-keepers came out and called Mamma Madame and were very polite. This time we came, with our clothes and a few things I treasured, in the carrier's cart.

This time we did not go for our furniture to a shop, but to a kind of yard surrounded by sheds. An old bent man, who seemed humble until Mamma questioned his prices and then turned nasty and said, "Take it or leave it," sold us two beds, some sheets and blankets, a table, some chairs and a few other necessities and said he would deliver them as soon as the donkey was back.

Mamma was very quick that day. From the crockery stall on the market, cups, a teapot, plates, from another a kettle, a saucepan and a frying pan; knives and forks. Another yard, two cauldrons of coal, two bushels of wood and a faggot; from a shop, tea, sugar, candles, bread, cheese . . .

No time to think; no time to feel anything much until evening when, the wretched furniture in place and a meal of a sort eaten, Mamma said, "Well, thank God, I saved what I could. We have a roof over our heads."

I was so silly—so out of this world that I did not even know what she meant by saying that she had saved. All I knew was that this was a roof I did not wish to have over my head; and when I was in the rather hard but well-aired bed—

Mamma had been very careful about the airing—I tried to think back and arrange things in my mind.

Before Nethergate I did not remember much. Sometimes Mamma would send me across with a little present for Pratt, and if I went in I did vaguely remember being there, with a girl called Rosie who had broken my doll. And sometimes, saying *Pratt*, I had a half memory of another Pratt of whom I was frightened, and of being tied to a table leg. Not the table in the Dower House. Another. Perhaps something I had dreamed about. Anyway, such memories were of no help at all when I looked back and asked myself: What happened?

There was Nethergate. Upstairs the old sick man to whom Mamma gave so much attention; downstairs there were two people who, because they had no children of their own, didn't like to see me about. But there was still a lot of space to run about in; and there was one most beautiful room into which Mamma took me one day in order to teach me to play the piano. Poor Mamma; that was perhaps her first failure with me. It was such a beautiful room—all cream coloured, and rose coloured, and blue, rosebuds and forget-me-nots on the curtains and the chairs and the sofas—that I simply could not give my attention to the piano. I could only think how I would like to sit in this room and have, not a doll's tea party but a real one, with friends who would admire it as much as I did.

I did not attend, all Mamma's efforts were in vain and one day she threw up her hands and said, "Darling, you are tone deaf. Like your father. He once told me that he only knew when the National Anthem was being played because everybody stood up!"

So there were no more lessons, but the people who didn't like the children never went into that room, therefore I could use it as my own.

In fact, until whatever happened did happen, I had had a happy life, taking it for granted; only now, looking back, seeing, realising how much I had had, and how much I had lost.

I did not know the word "homesick," but that was my affliction. Even Pratt, when she came along on the Wednesday afternoon when we had been in the horrid house for a week, looked like a link with the old life, bringing a bunch of wilting primroses, a reminder of last year, when I had picked them. This year I had helped Mamma to whitewash the tiny parlour and the kitchen.

Mamma seemed surprised, and not overmuch pleased to

see Pratt, and this surprised me, since they had always been on good terms.

Pratt looked round and said, "What a nice, snug little place you have, Miss Isabella."

Mamma has a nose which can express things. The nose said: It is detestable! But Mamma said, "It will be habitable when I have finished. Have you time for a cup of tea?" It rather sounded as though she hoped that Pratt would decline.

"I've all the time in the world," Pratt said. "In fact I've come to ask you to let me stay with you."

"Stay *here?*"

"I'd work. I know I'm old, but I'm active. I'd cook and wash for you. I wouldn't mind what I did, so long as I could get away from Ockley. I'm fond of Tom, but the place is all mess and muddle. And there's no room for me."

"Nor here, I'm afraid. There are two bedrooms, but I shall be obliged to take a lodger in order to make ends meet." This was the first time she had mentioned this plan.

"I could sleep downstairs," Pratt said humbly. "In fact I am doing it now."

"But I am taking a parlour lodger."

"I'd sleep in the kitchen."

"Look at it," Mamma said, in a bitter voice. She rose and threw open the door. There was no need for Pratt to move in order to see the whole of that dismal place. In addition to being so small it contained three doors, one to the parlour, one to the yard, one to the steep, narrow stairs. It would have been impossible to have all three open at the same time. In the fourth wall there was a small grate—no oven—and a shelf at which one could wash up. Alongside the door to the yard were some more shelves which served as china pantry and as larder.

"No," Pratt said in a doleful way. "I see."

"I'll make the tea," Mamma said with a shade more kindliness in her voice. Pratt did indeed look pitiable, shrunken, and old suddenly.

"Oh, what a come-down for you, Miss Isabella. And a blow to me. I thought I was settled for life."

"For my Cousin Franklin's life!"

Mamma's Cousin Franklin was an old sick man who never left his room. Mamma had looked after him and spent much of her time with him. He owned Nethergate and it was his death that had changed everything.

"The way you'd looked after him, too," Pratt said. "Shameful I call it."

"I prefer not to talk about it," Mamma said. In a way it seemed as though Pratt were somehow to blame for what had happened.

We all drank tea. Even that was different here, cheap, coarse stuff with a rough flavour. After drinking a cup in silence Pratt said, "Well, I must think what to do. I can't stay there. It looks as if I shall have to hire myself out again, though who'll have me at my age . . ."

"I have found myself a post, of a kind," Mamma said. And that was the first time she had mentioned this either. "I am going to give French lessons at the Female Academy."

"Lucky," Pratt said. She had often told me, when I visited her, that I was lucky, comparing my lot with that of her grandnieces, Rosie and Ella: "Not all that much older than you, and both out at work." I could remember Rose Pratt as being a good deal older and bigger than I was, and rather nasty.

After her second cup of tea, Pratt said:

"I think I'll try the Grammar School. I could patch and mend and help about. Just for my room and my keep. I had my first living-in place there. It'd be funny if I ended where I began, wouldn't it?"

"I only wish there was some prospect of doing so myself," Mamma said.

"Yes, you've had your disappointments. But at least you've got a place you can't be turned out of. I think I'll go along to the school now. I can't afford to keep running in and out."

Before she went I thanked her for the primroses, which I had placed in a cup of water.

When she had gone I said, "Mamma, has Pratt offended you in any way?"

"Why should you ask that?"

"You didn't seem very . . . pleased to see her."

"I was not. The sight of her reminded me that if she had not been so besotted . . . I can't explain now, Annabelle. I will tell you all about it one day. When you are older."

"Are we really going to have a lodger?"

"That depends. It may come to that. In the meantime it was an excellent excuse."

She then went to fetch a bucket of water from the pump which stood in the lane, just below the smithy. It served the cottages as well and was a kind of meeting place for the men who were waiting for their horses to be shod and the people who were our neighbours. Mamma had forbidden me to go near it. I was to take no notice at all of the children who lived

153

in the lane; if an adult spoke to me, I was to say "Good morning," or whatever the time of day might be, and walk straight on.

She had made her attitude towards the people of the lane clear from the start. On our first day a slatternly woman had come across and said, "Just moving in? If you ain't got your fire going yet you can bring your kettle across to mine."

"Thank you very much," Mamma said. "That will not be necessary."

Then, when the donkey cart arrived and the driver simply heaved the things off onto the cobbles, a man slouched across and said:

"Lend you a hand, missus?"

"A little help with the beds would be welcome," Mamma said. He helped and when the beds were, with some difficulty, got up the steep narrow stairway, she took out and offered him sixpence.

"I weren't looking for nothing," the man said.

"I wish you to have it."

In some manner not easy to describe, she had changed; she had always been very dignified, and people had respected and obeyed her, but she had not been sharp or harsh. Now she was, to everybody except me. It was as though she and I were alone against the world.

Pratt obtained a post as sewing woman and general help at the Grammar School and took to making unexpected visits in the evening. And almost always there was, sooner or later, a jarring note.

Pratt was glad to have found a living-in post, but she earned very little and grieved because she could now do less to help her brother than she had done before.

"You take altogether too serious a view of your responsibilities towards him," Mamma said. "After all, he's a grown man, not a child." The sharp tone was there.

"If he lived to be a hundred he'd seem like a child to me," Pratt said.

Then, soon after Mamma had started work at the Female Academy—every afternoon except Saturday and Sunday—Pratt came and said:

"You know, I've been thinking, Miss Isabella, how our lives seem to have run alongside. Now we're both at schools." She spoke quite cheerfully. Mamma said, in a crushing way:

"I think you have had the best of it, Pratt. Patching breeches and mending sheets is far easier than trying to teach arrogant, boneheaded girls something they have no wish to learn." She had disliked her work almost from the first day.

Then, of course, there was Pratt's curiosity about the lodger.

"Have you found a suitable person yet?"

"Yes, indeed. His name is Mr. Wade."

"Has he come yet?"

"No. I expect him next week."

"What does he do?"

"I did not inquire. It seemed not to be my business."

Undeterred Pratt asked how old he was. Mamma said of middle-age. Would he be sharing the parlour with us. Mamma said naturally, where else could we sit? "Then I expect I shall be seeing him," Pratt said.

Mr. Wade became our secret joke; we invented characteristics for him. Pratt herself, looking around the parlour and seeing no sign of him, remarked that he must be a very tidy man.

"I insist upon it; down here. His bedroom is a pigstye."

We told Pratt that he was working late; that he had just gone out to supper; that he was having a holiday.

Perhaps we were punished for these jokes; for by midsummer we were obliged to take the first of a long succession of lodgers.

Mamma came home one afternoon in high spirits.

"Darling, I have made an arrangement that I hardly dared hope for. In September, when the new term begins, you are to enter the Academy as a pupil. Mrs. Twysdale has agreed to accept my work in place of your fees."

I was horrified. I had never had anything to do with any other children except the Pratts, and nothing that Mamma had said about her pupils had made them sound other than horrid. The idea of living with them, all day and all night—the Academy had no day pupils—really frightened me.

I said, "Oh, Mamma, please. I don't want to."

This is what I mean about the change in Mamma; at Nethergate she would have said, "Darling, if you don't want to, you need not." At Nethergate, apart from a few rules, learned when I was so young that I no more thought of questioning them than I did the colour of my hair, I had done almost exactly what I liked. All those with whom I came in contact had spoiled me, Mamma first and foremost. But now she said:

"It is a chance of a lifetime. *Whatever* the future may hold a good education must be an advantage."

I wept. She said, "Don't be so stupid, darling. Crying never did anybody any good. What we must do now is look about for Mr. Wade since I shall not be taking my wages in money; and even I must eat! Actually the arrangement is very much to our advantage. It costs more to board and educate a girl than it does to pay a Mamzelle."

I sobbed, "I am educated. I can read and write. You taught me, Mamma."

"There is history," she said, "and geography, and arithmetic which I never had the heart to force upon you. And other things—how to get along with other people . . . making friends."

Actually I had friends, all as imaginary as Mr. Wade. They were people I had imagined, or read about. It had begun, I suppose, with my doll, Aunt Joanna, who had been a very real person to me, so real that when she was hurt, I was hurt. Then there had been that beautiful room in Nethergate, where beautiful people visited me in their beautiful clothes, with their beautiful voices.

The real people in the front of the house, who did not like to see me because they had no children, never used that room, so even after Mamma had given up hope of teaching me to play the piano, I could go there provided I did no damage. Which I never did, because from the first moment, to me it had been a magic place; holy. I was homesick for it now. Homesick for all Nethergate, even the part into which I had never been allowed. But, ten-and-a-half, I realised that there were other troubles, real ones, in a real world; a place I disliked very much.

Mamma set about finding a real Mr. Wade, who turned out to be a Miss Graham, and to providing me with what was needed for school. She said, "You must be properly equipped, that is important," and properly equipped I was, down to the two black sateen aprons to be worn over dresses to protect them from inkspots.

"I saved," Mamma said, "and it is well that I did." She had had to buy all my school equipment, and also to provide an oven. Mr. Wade, that fanciful person, might be content with boiled or fried food, Miss Graham, the real lodger, wanted baked meats once a week at least. The oven and the flue that connected it with the chimney cost Mamma £9, and having paid the bill she gave me a wild look and pushed back her hair and said, "I could have robbed them. It will take them six months to find where the things are. And there was no list. But I could not stoop so low; not even for you, my darling."

I was her darling, but she put me into the Baildon Female

Academy for Young Ladies, where I was thoroughly miserable.

Somebody said, "What is your name?"

"Annabelle d'Aubigny."

"Daubeny. Are you a frog?"

"I beg your pardon?"

"A frog. A Froggie? A Frenchie?"

I said, "Yes, I am French. I do not understand the allusion to frogs. I rather dislike them, harmless as they are."

"Who's your father?"

"He is dead. While he was alive he was Monsieur d'Aubigny."

"Daubeny. Like Mamzelle?"

"Madame d'Aubigny is my Mamma."

"She's a frog, your father was a frog, and you're a tadpole!"

In the Female Academy at Baildon that kind of remark was considered to be witty. I understood what Mamma had said to Pratt: arrogant girls and bone-headed. And, all but two of them related to one another, either by blood, a kinship carried to the utmost extreme, or by social relationships almost as binding.

It was a curiously closed community; the girls seemed all to come from the same background; even their reasons for being sent to school were similar; they were only daughters of their family, or far divided by age and to keep a governess for a girl was only a little less expensive than sending her to school where she would have the company of her own kind. During the holidays they stayed with or visited one another, attended the same functions, had the same amusements—or so it seemed to me, listening as they compared notes.

I was the outsider, set apart by my nationality, my different background and the fact that I was Mamzelle's daughter. In addition to the fact that there was, apparently, a long tradition of despising the French teacher, the girls disliked Mamma as much as she disliked them. That new sharpness of hers was nowhere more in evidence than in the classroom.

There were two other outsiders, a girl called Jassy Woodroffe and Mr. Helmar's daughter, Dilys, but they were too old to be of use to me and their exclusion was not total, as mine was; Jassy was both admired and feared. Dilys's difference lay in her home, to which nobody was ever invited, and her father's reputation, which was bad. Also—and though this may sound contradictory—most girls were rather sorry for Jassy and Dilys because they were not always well-equipped; it was easier to adopt the attitude: Poor thing, she has no mother to see to her clothes! than to be tolerant of Mamzelle's daughter who had everything, and of the best. Mamma had spared nothing; my pencil box was of red and gold lacquer, my hairbrush silver-backed.

Even as regards lessons I was a misfit. What Mamma had taught me she taught well. I read and wrote as well as anybody, and better than most. There were plenty of books—never used—in the library at Nethergate and provided I chose my times for taking a book away and returning it, all was well. In my lonely life, with Mamma spending so much time looking after and amusing the sick old man, I had read a good deal.

I was a dunce at arithmetic. I could add a column of figures three times and get three differing answers. For some things I had a good memory; I could memorise a piece of poetry, or even of prose, with no difficulty at all; but when it came to "Kings and Queens of England" or "Capes and Bays of England" my memory seemed to refuse to have anything to do with them. If Kings and Queens wished to be remembered they should vary their names more; in England six Edwards and eight Henrys. (In France even worse, seventeen named Louis!)

At the Academy there were three subjects for which parents paid extra: Art, Dancing, and Music. It was really an excuse for adding to the fees; everybody except Jassy and Dilys, for instance, took dancing lessons, and at least one of the other extras. Mamma, having decided that I had no ear for music, decided that I should have lessons in art and in dancing; for which she would pay. "I will manage somehow," she said. "A young lady must have *some* accomplishments."

All the three extra subjects were taught by the same visiting master. I think he was French. His English was as good as Mamma's, but with the same faint lilt. His name was Eagle; perhaps he had prudently modified it slightly.

I wished to paint. I had tried on my own with a splendid box of paints, a present from Mamma on my eighth birthday. I wanted to paint flowers because it seemed to me to be so sad that a flower should be so beautiful one day and dead the next. I wished, by painting its portrait, to preserve it. But I failed; and even under Mr. Eagle's tuition I failed again and more dishearteningly. At dancing I did better, for a very curious reason. At the Academy there were only females, and as we entered for the dancing class we dipped into a bag of marbles, red and blue; and nobody knew, holding her marble whether Mr. Eagle would say, "And now, young ladies, for this evening those holding red marbles will act as gentlemen," or whether he would say blue. Whichever he decided, gentlemen chose their partners and nobody ever chose me unless forced to it by the fact that the class was composed of an even number. The enrolled number was, for most of my time, uneven and since everybody enjoyed the dancing lessons it took more than a heavy cold to make a girl absent herself. So often I danced with Mr. Eagle, who was conscientious; a girl whose mother had paid could not be left out. At the same time he had his duty to the others, so he danced with me in a very abstracted manner, calling directions over my shoulder, halting suddenly, rushing to correct. So far as dancing was concerned I had a qualification that was rare; I knew what it was to be abandoned in the middle of the floor; and another, perhaps less rare, to know what it was to accommodate myself to a partner whose real attention was distracted. I became a good dancer.

But not a good needlewoman. Mrs. Twysdale, the head of the Academy, taught needlework, plain and fancy, and I could never please her. I could sew; Mamma had taught me that too, but Mrs. Twysdale's standard of excellence was to make stitches that were completely invisible. Once she said to me, "Will you compare your work with Cecily's?" A futile request; I could not even *see* Cecily Drew's stitches. And what did it matter? The object of sewing seemed to me to join two pieces of material together, or to convert a rough edge into a firm hem; for such purposes surely visible stitches served as well as invisible ones.

In the main, misery. And while I struggled with mine, taking refuge in my dreams, Mamma struggled with hers, about which I knew nothing until I went home for holidays since Mamma had decreed from the first that within the walls of the Academy we must confine ourselves to the relationship between mistress and pupil. This was undoubtedly wise, but it seemed harsh to me at first. I wanted to run to her, throw my arms around her, call her "Mamma"; and all I could do was to stand with the rest, make the perfunctory little curtsey and join in the chant, *"Bon jour, Mamzelle."*

Mamma disliked her lodgers as she disliked her pupils and her neighbours. They all ate too much; the young because they were hearty, the old because they had nothing else to think about; quiet old ladies who stayed in the house all day needed fires, young men kept irregular hours and sometimes returned intoxicated. There were constant changes during the

159

first two years and then, when I was twelve and a half, Mamma found a lodger to her liking. His name was Mr. Bricey and she put it succinctly: "He is out a great deal and seldom comes home emptyhanded."

Mr. Bricey worked at the brewery and knew a great deal about barley. He could tell, he claimed, from the look of a standing crop whether it was fit for malting, or for milling. "Always making allowances for the weather, of course." His work brought him into close contact with farmers and he received many presents: fowls, hams, rabbits, hares, butter, cheese, and honey.

"I rather think," Mamma said, "that a certain amount of bribery is involved, but that is not my concern." Nor, I thought, mine. During the first week of that summer vacation I ate better than I had since leaving Nethergate. School food was good; Mrs. Twysdale, who kept house as well as being Head and needlework instructress, saw to that; but it was rather dull. Mr. Bricey had evidently eaten well all his life. He had a broad red face, fingers like sausages, and a rounded paunch.

He was not a person whom I would have entertained, in my dreams, in that beautiful room at Nethergate, but he was amiable and almost the first lodger whom Mamma had felt herself able to tolerate for more than six weeks. He was extremely polite; he always called Mamma "Madam" and me "Miss."

I had been home rather more than a week when Pratt made one of her visits. Supper had been deferred because Mr. Bricey was late and we were still at table. Eating plums.

Mamma's slightly astringent attitude towards Pratt had not changed; she said, "Good evening, Pratt. I expect you would like a cup of tea."

"Well, I would," Pratt said. "I had a bit of worrying news today. I went to Sam Lockey, sending out what I could to Tom. And he told me there's the smallpox out there . . . Hessington, Nettleton, Ockley, Clevely. Spreading like wildfire. I'm anxious about Tom. He never had it. I did when I was very young and my mother had the sense to hang a red petticoat at the window. So I lived and wasn't marked. But I doubt whether Bessie or Marty . . ."

Mamma said, "Pratt, I've said it before. You worry too much about your brother. Elderly people seldom contract smallpox."

"He's not all that elderly," Pratt said.

Mr. Bricey was more sympathetic. He said, "Excuse me,

madam. I have a better cure for fretting than tea, so don't bother to make it."

Pratt, who had obviously met Mr. Bricey before, said:

"Anything that'd stop me fretting about Tom would be the death of me." But when Mr. Bricey had gone into the kitchen and mounted the steep stairs and come down again with a kind of flask in his hand and from it poured a measure, Pratt drank it. Mamma refused, "Thank you, Mr. Bricey, as you should know, I do not drink distilled spirits."

She began in her new, impatient way to clear the table. I helped; also with the washing up and the putting away. As we worked we could hear Pratt's voice, thin and mournful, and now and again Mr. Bricey's, heavier, consoling.

We went back into the little front room which Mamma insisted upon calling a parlour and Pratt was saying in an almost tearful voice:

"I've always looked out for Tom as well as I could. And I never neglected my duty to others. I looked after Annabelle when she lived with me. Aunt Martha she used to call me. I even did my best for my brother George . . ."

Mamma said, "Pratt, you are becoming intoxicated!"

"Oh, come ma'am. Granted it's good whisky—I wish you'd try a sip—but even so two little tots wouldn't make anyone drunk."

"It might, if that person were totally inexperienced with drinking."

"I'm not," Pratt said almost truculently. "There was always ale. At Nethergate. Wine too. Christmas and birthdays. Her ladyship's, the master's, Mr. John's, and Mr. Alan's . . ."

"I think it is time you went home," Mamma said. "I have no wish to appear inhospitable, but it is late and will soon be dark."

"I'll just finish this, then I'll go." Trying to drink quickly, she slopped some of the whisky which ran down her chin. She fumbled for her handkerchief, failed to find it and wiped the drops off with the back of her hand. Mamma watched with icy disapproval.

Then Pratt stood up, and tottered, caught at the back of her chair, almost pulled it over, reached for the table and managed to lower herself back into the chair.

"Well, well," Mr. Bricey said, interested and surprised. "Seems you were right, ma'am."

"She's in no state to go home alone. That bridge is very narrow. She might fall into the water."

She waited for Mr. Bricey to offer. Then she said, "After

all, Mr. Bricey, you are responsible for her being in this condition."

"Sorry, ma'am, I got work to do before I sleep."

"I'll take Pratt home, Mamma," I said.

"You will do no such thing. You will go to bed. Come along, Pratt. Pull yourself together." Mamma took her by the arm, not gently, and hustled her towards the door. It was much lighter in the lane than in the low, small-windowed room.

I said, "Good night, Mr. Bricey," and went upstairs and undressed. I was in my nightgown when I heard him in the kitchen below. Then the stairs door opened and he called:

"Miss, I want a candle and I can't find one."

I ran straight down as I was.

There followed something that I do not care to remember, that I *will* not remember while I am awake, though in dreams I sometimes relive the moment and wake yelling.

I was so utterly ignorant that for a second or two, when he laid hold of me I thought that he, like Pratt, was drunk and needed support . . . He stank of whisky, tobacco, sweat. He was very strong. In that tiny space, even if I could have freed myself, there was nowhere to run, nothing to dodge behind. All I could do was to scream and push. I could not even kick, having run down barefoot.

He had his back towards the door of the parlour, which stood open. And suddenly there was Mamma.

Nobody would have credited her with such strength. She took him by the back of his collar and heaved him into the parlour, across it, and out by the front door which she had left open. She flung him with such force that he fell on the cobbles. She slammed and bolted the door. Then, with what might have been her dying breath, she said, "Are you hurt?"

"No, Mamma. Only frightened."

She ran upstairs and threw out of the front bedroom window everything that Mr. Bricey owned. I sat, shaking, in the parlour and watched things fall past the window. Solid things like boots, his razor, his valises, his barley record books fell straight down and thudded. Handkerchiefs, shirts, and loose papers took their time, floating down, like wounded birds.

From the cottages opposite came the sound of doors and of voices.

"That will give them something to talk about for a year," Mamma said, coming back into the parlour and dropping into a chair. She was shaking too. But not from fright; from exertion and fury.

162

I recovered first. I lit the candle—which stood there in plain view; I made the tea—which made an hour earlier would have prevented all this. Mamma talked. She blamed me a little for coming down barefoot in my nightdress; she blamed herself more for leaving me alone with "that pig." She said she hadn't realised . . . Most bitterly she blamed Pratt. "At every turn of the road she has been my evil angel. I hope her precious Tom dies!"

Tom Pratt did not die; but the two people at Nethergate, those who had no children and disliked the sight of them, did.

Pratt brought us that news on her last visit; for on that occasion Mamma said, quite amiably:

"Pratt, I am afraid this will have to be your last visit. I shall not be here in the evenings in future. I have decided that there is no profit to be made out of lodgers. I propose to attend private pupils in their homes."

"Every evening?"

"Every evening. Most mornings . . . or so I hope."

Pratt said simply, "Well, I shall miss coming." And that was that.

Was I the only one who noticed that when Mamma said that she intended to take no more lodgers, but to be out, working most of the day, Pratt did not ask to come, to live in, to wash and cook, as she had done two years earlier?

There was the new term. It opened badly for me, with what Mrs. Twysdale called a "little talk." She was, she said, somewhat concerned about my future. So far as she could see I had a choice. I could, by applying myself to the art of making invisible stitches, become an apprentice to a dressmaker, possibly Miss Borrowdale who did a great deal of work for the Academy and with whom, Mrs. Twysdale said, she had "a certain amount of influence," or I could apply myself more industriously to my lessons and qualify myself to be a governess. "After all, Annabelle," she said in a kindly voice that forgave me all those visible stitches, "this is something which must be considered. You will soon be thirteen and you cannot remain at school forever."

Nobody could remain at school forever. Of course I knew that. Who, indeed, would wish to do so? But there I was, forced to admit that I had never given my future any serious thought. To more practical-minded people, like Mrs. Twysdale, my thoughts about the future would, I knew, sound absurd. No plan. Just a dream, based upon nothing. Absurd, but the truth was that whenever I visualised the future I was back in the past; seeing myself at Nethergate, in that beautiful room, entertaining the beautiful people, with beautiful clothes, beautiful voices. I knew it was ridiculous; I should never be there, I could never be there and yet, whenever I looked ahead that was what I saw. I saw it now, under Mrs. Twysdale's eye, as she offered me the choice, dressmaker or governess. I tried. I tried very hard to see myself stitching away, miles of tiny invisible stitches; or—the only alternative— teaching some small child how to read, how to count, the Kings and Queens of England; the Capes and Bays.

I simply could not see the future in such terms. And yet I knew that what my mind refused and shrank from was the reality and must be faced . . .

I said, "I think, ma'am, that I should prefer to be a governess."

She said, "Very well. You still have a good deal of leeway to make up, on the academic side. You will no longer be required to attend needlework classes."

The term was not very old when everything in the Academy changed. One day Jassy Woodroffe and Dilys Helmar left quite suddenly; the word "expelled" was used, but nobody was certain. Then Mrs. Twysdale left too and there was a good deal of confusion. Miss Hamilton, who had hitherto simply taught, became Head and all was changed, not always for the better. The food was definitely worse.

Miss Hamilton was very learned, a scholar. One day, having given us a lesson about John Milton and his great poem, *Paradise Lost,* she set us, as an exercise, to write a poem of our own, on the same subject. The loss of joy. "And that," she said, "will stretch whatever imagination you have! I wish no reference to Adam, Eve, or the serpent. Understand that. I am easily bored."

I sat and thought. All around me girls were grumbling; how could anybody write a poem about paradise lost without mentioning Adam, Eve, the serpent?

I knew, because I was the only one there who had lost a paradise, the only one who had been exiled.

I could see it. Adam and Eve thrust out of Eden as Mamma and I had been dismissed from Nethergate.

I wanted to catch the thought. I took my pencil and wrote: *Outside the gates of Eden, the world is hard and cold . . .* Absolutely true, but as I developed the theme it became more than a lament for bygone comfort and turned into the cry of an exiled heart.

It made Miss Hamilton notice me. One day, after that exercise had been handed in, she asked me to remain behind.

"Have you written verse before, Annabelle?"

I told her, no.

"For a first attempt, quite remarkable. Is it for France that you suffer such homesickness?"

"No, Miss Hamilton. I have never been there."

"Some other place then?"

She looked at me kindly, seriously, and as though she were prepared to understand; but something in me retreated. I could not speak of Nethergate, or the beautiful room: so I evaded the question:

"I tried to imagine how they would feel, Miss Hamilton. Adam and Eve . . ."

Her look changed to what I thought was pity. She said:

"Imagination can be a very hard master, my dear."

I had never thought of it in that way; for me it had always been a way of escape; even when I was in the beautiful room itself I had been alone, obliged to escape from loneliness by filling it with people conjured up out of my imagination; and now that I had lost it forever, and was lonely in another way, lonely with people all around me, I had retreated more and more. In my mind running away from school where I had no friend, and from the home where I spent such dismal holidays. Dismal through no fault of Mamma's . . .

Having thrown out Mr. Bricey and made up her mind to take no more lodgers she had advertised her willingness to take private pupils for French and for the pianoforte, at sixpence an hour. The response had been good. She said herself, "If only I were a witch and could fly on a broomstick . . . The getting from place to place is the problem." Baildon was growing, partly because people who plied trades that prospered were no longer content to live over their business premises in the heart of the town. The old town had had six gates, four named after the points of the compass, Saltgate, Watergate. The gates and the walls had long since fallen into ruin and the town had crept outwards along the roads, where in new houses, or old ones much altered, there lived people who wished their daughters to acquire some accomplishments. Mamma had as many pupils as she could handle, allowing for the walking from place to place; her mornings and early evenings were fully occupied.

In the holidays at the Academy one would have assumed that she would have been free, but she seldom was. When the Academy was closed Mr. Eagle gave dancing lessons—again sixpence an hour per pupil, and Mamma went to play the piano for him. I asked could I not accompany her and she said, "Most definitely not!" She did other things, too. Seaside holidays were all the rage just then and some of the families to whose daughters she taught French and the piano asked her to keep an eye on their houses and their servants, while they were at Yarmouth or Southwold. Sometimes they chose to have rooms papered and painted during their absence, and then Mamma overlooked the workmen, too.

All I could do was to clean the horrid little house, shop, cook, read, and exercise my imagination.

The remarkable thing was that I never exercised it where Mamma was concerned. I could feel for a stray dog, nosing round for the market stalls; for horses and donkeys, dragging heavy loads and being whipped but my own mother . . . No, to me she did not seem an object of pity; she was too masterful, too scornful, brisk and sharp.

She was sharp even to me when I tried once—never again—to discuss the future with her. I was aware that nobody could stay at school forever, and that my time was running out. So I said something which made Mamma bristle. She said:

"Darling, you may leave all that to me. I have always done what I thought best for you. I shall continue to do so."

So time went on. In January 1809 I had my fifteenth birthday. We had celebrated it beforehand, during the Christmas vacation, on a Sunday, which was Mamma's free day. She had astonished me very much by presenting me with a string of pearls. Or, as I thought at the time, a string of pearl beads from the stall on the market; the stall from which, when we lived at Nethergate I was always free to choose anything that took my fancy, and then, suddenly, with the move to Baildon, was advised not even to look at. "We cannot afford toys or trinkets," Mamma had said, "so it is wiser not to tempt oneself." However, even a string of false pearls cost five shillings, a large sum in our narrow budget, so, having thanked her, I said, "Are you sure you can afford them, Mamma?" She gave a peculiar smile and said, "I did not buy them, darling. They are genuine. They belonged to your grandmother; your grandfather gave them to me and I promised to give them to you when you were old enough to take care of them."

This piece of information was as startling as the gift itself. I knew hardly anything about my ancestry; just that Mamma's father had been a great aristocrat, guillotined before I was born; and that my father had been in England, had returned to France and died there. I could remember Mamma telling Pratt this.

This gift from the past, from a grandfather now mentioned for the first time, spurred my curiosity.

"Did he ever see me?" I asked.

"Once only. Let me show you how the clasp works." It was obvious that questions on the subject were not welcome.

I was wearing a new dress upon which Mamma and I had both worked during that holiday. It was the new "best" dress required by the Academy rules. Deciding that the time had come for my old one to be discarded, Mamma had looked at me with a certain dissatisfaction.

"I do hope that you are not going to be *too* tall. I wish you would stop growing upwards and fill out a bit." To compensate for my lack of figure, she had made the short bodice of the dress rather full and gathered. It was very becoming, and the pearls gave the right, finishing touch. Like most girls of my age I was at once pleased with and displeased by my looks. Nice eyes, blue, with dark lashes; complexion good as regards texture—I was never spotted or freckled as so many girls were—but too white; nose, I thought, too high-bridged and narrow. Mamma's nose was high-bridged, a sign of breeding, she once said, but her nostrils were less pinched looking; mouth undoubtedly too large. Secretly I rather admired my hair, unusual as the colour was. Before I became resigned to being called Froggie or Tadpole, I had protested against the nicknames and somebody had said, "Red hair for temper!" It was not really red, it was more the colour of the mahogany table which had stood in Mrs. Twysdale's sitting room and which she had taken with her when she left. I wore it short, as was the fashion, and was lucky in that it curled naturally and grew very slowly; I did not have to bother with curling irons, and a close crop every holiday, made by Mamma, sufficed. She said on one occasion that except for its colour it was just like hers, and that it had taken her a long time to grow hers long enough to be dressed in a style, "more suitable to my age and position." Hers was black as night, and though she wore it straitly brushed back and pinned at the back of her head, a curly strand would escape now and then, to be brushed back impatiently. Perhaps if I had seen her less regularly I should have observed that the black was now silvering.

On this, my premature birthday, turning away from the sizable but rather spotted looking glass, I did notice something, and that was that of the two of us, she was the one who was in more need of a new dress. She had never, even at Nethergate, spent much on herself and she had two gowns, one black, one mulberry colour. When the sick old man whom she called her cousin died, she had bought some black crepe and converted the black into a mourning gown. When we came to Baildon she had removed the crepe, ripping it away so impatiently that in places the silk had frayed. To this had been added the wear and tear of almost five years. She wore the mulberry coloured dress only on occasions, or when the black one was being sponged and pressed or mended. The black was now very shabby.

I said, "Thank you, Mamma for the dress and for the necklace. The next new dress must be yours, look!" I put my finger on the place where the gathered silk had cut itself through, as good silk will, even when laid away and not worn.

She gave an impatient jerk and said, "What I wear now does not matter in the least."

So, with my new dress and my string of real pearls, I went back to school. January was a horrible month and February was worse, bitter winds bringing storms of sleet. The room which had once been Mrs. Twysdale's and which had seemed so cosy, even in winter, was now a classroom because the school had grown in numbers, and several times that month, what with the sleet against the windows and the rattling of the nearby front door, one could hardly hear what was being said. There was a fire, but it seemed to give out no heat and every now and then a gust of smoke billowed out into the room. Girls shifted and coughed and whispered; Miss Smithers twirled the globe.

I took refuge in my dream where it was always summer. I was so far away that I did not notice the arrival of a maid. When Miss Smithers said, "Annabelle d'Aubigny," I looked up, ready to say that I was sorry, but I had not quite heard her question.

"Miss Hamilton wishes to see you in her room."

Miss Hamilton's room, like Mrs. Twysdale's, had once seemed cosy in winter, cool in summer, neat and shining at all seasons; it was different now. Miss Hamilton had, within three months of Mrs. Twysdale's departure, engaged a woman, Mrs. Doughty, to act as housekeeper and matron, and the food which had been very bad had during the interval improved. It was now better than it had ever been, but the house as a whole, Miss Hamilton's room in particular, had lost its cared-for look.

"Oh, Annabelle, my dear, come in, sit down. I wished to speak to you before the end of your class, before you heard any alarming talk. I can assure you that there is no need for alarm . . ."

"Mamma!" I interrupted. What else, in my life, could be a source of alarm?

"Yes. She arrived this afternoon in a state of collapse. This horrible weather. And I think she had been hurrying. But she is all right now. Mrs. Doughty resuscitated her with brandy and beef tea and I advised her to go home and get to bed, and not to venture out tomorrow. As I said, there is no cause for *alarm*. There *is* reason for concern . . ." She broke off and made one of her habitual gestures, pressing her eyes with the thumb and forefinger of her left hand. "I have for some time suspected that she was overworking. I know now that she is underfed. Something must be done about it, my dear."

I said, "What? What can I do? I would do anything . . ."

"I know. So would I. But I am in such a predicament. I am such a deuced bad manager. Or too stupid to see that if fifty girls meant no profit, sixty made loss inevitable. I am now quite deeply in debt. Never mind that. I mention it only that you may understand. I would most gladly pay your mother a salary, but I cannot do it unless I have your bed, your place at table, your place in class to offer to a fee-paying pupil. Do you understand?"

"I must leave?"

"I am afraid that that is what it amounts to. I have been thinking about it all afternoon, ever since . . . And I have thought of a solution. Annabelle, this sounds brutal . . . You are neither old enough nor versatile enough to take a post as governess. What you can do, you do very well, but your arithmetic is elementary, and faulty at that, you cannot play the piano, or draw. If you obtained a post in a private household you would hold it for no longer than a month." She rubbed her eyes again and said, "The same could be said of me. But I have been thinking . . . In a school, in an establishment somewhat similar to this but catering for younger pupils —to whom you would seem quite grown up—you could teach what you *do* know, earn your keep and possibly five pounds a year. I think . . ." She raked through the litter of papers on her bureau, once so neatly arranged, found what she was looking for and said, "I am almost certain that Miss Pollinger at North Walsham would consider anyone warmly recommended by me. We are friends, by correspondence. Will you think about it, Annabelle?"

"Of course," I said. "Miss Hamilton, would it be possible for me to go home? Now?"

Nobody ever went home except for holidays. That was a law, laid down long ago, I suspect by Mrs. Twysdale, and as irrevocable as the laws of the Medes and Persians in the Bible. Girls who lived near Baildon might if allowed to, go home and come back crammed with unsuitable food and be sick, or bring back some contagious ailment. Envy, from those who lived within less easy distance, was inevitable. So nobody went home—except in cases of severe illness, or death, during term time. And nobody ever went out alone. Even in daylight.

I knew, as soon as I asked it, that I was asking the impossible.

However, Miss Hamilton said, "Of course. Naturally you are anxious. And certainly the suggestion I have made would come better from you . . . You may find your mother in a less intransigent mood . . . But be tactful. And, Annabelle, take your supper." She looked at her watch. "Otherwise you will miss it. You have until eight . . ."

I had never, in the whole of my life, been out alone after nightfall. Once, twice a term, during the last three years, as a senior, I had gone with the rest of the seniors to a concert or a puppet show in the Assembly Rooms, or to the newly opened theatre. Back at Nethergate on almost equally rare occasions, when "they" were away, Mamma and I would walk in the gathering dusk amongst the roses in that part of the pleasure garden from which I was ordinarily banned. This new experience might have made me nervous but for the fact that my mind was absorbed by thoughts of Mamma, and my body concerned with battling against the wind which seemed to blow from all directions.

There was a rule that householders should hang a lantern outside their premises at night, and in respectable areas this rule was observed. I was not really in darkness until I turned into Hawk Lane where, as Mamma had said, when considering the rule, anything left out of doors would be stolen within five minutes.

I had expected to see a light in the upper window, for Mamma had moved into the bigger, front bedroom after Mr. Bricey's leaving. But the whole house front was in darkness.

If she were in bed and asleep would it be kind to disturb her? I rapped on the door gently, just enough to attract the attention of a wakeful person, not so loud as to disturb a sleeper. Almost instantly, the window creaked open a little and Mamma called in a challenging voice, "Who is it? What do you want?"

I announced myself and in no time at all, Mamma tore open the door, saying, "Darling! What has happened? What is wrong?"

Like me on a former occasion she had run down in her nightgown. The little parlour was frigid and in the light of the candle she carried, dreary in the extreme. I had never before seen it on a winter evening without a fire in its narrow grate.

"Nothing is wrong. Miss Hamilton gave me leave to come and see you. To see how you were."

"What a coil about nothing!" she said, displeased. "Am I to believe that she allowed you out, alone, after dark?"

I lied, I said, "No, Mamma. One of the maids had an errand in Saltgate. Come back to bed."

"It is the warmest place," she admitted.

She led the way upstairs and set the candle on the chest of drawers. "You're dreadfully wet, darling. Oh, if you catch cold through this I shall never forgive that ridiculous woman. Hang your cloak on the door. Get into bed with me." She huddled over to the wall side of the bed and reached, from the rail at the foot, an old shawl and flung it round her shoulders. I remembered with a pang that until recently she had owned a dressing gown, a relic of our well-to-do days, very warm and fleecy; but she had insisted upon my taking it back to school with me, because like so many of my things mine was outgrown.

I kicked off my shoes and got into bed with her. She put her arm around me and said, "We shall soon be warm. Darling, I hope she didn't frighten you. It was nothing. I had hurried, in the teeth of the wind. That stupid Mrs. Shafto delayed me, coming in at the last minute and demanding that Angela recite for her. Had I been given a moment to recover my breath . . ."

I realised how thin she was; even through my clothing I could feel the sharpness of her arm bones.

"So I suppose you missed your lunch," I said.

"I never lunch on Thursdays. Even if I get away from the Shaftos' promptly, I can only just manage to reach the Academy on time." I had never seen the Shaftos' fine new house; I only knew that it stood a good way out on the road towards Norwich.

Overworked and underfed!

Mamma's arm tightened convulsively and then relaxed.

"Darling, I have nothing to offer you. The weather was so horrible, I came straight home and did no shopping. Pure idleness! I do apologise."

I told her that I had brought supper for two. That was almost true, for when I went to collect my supper Mrs. Doughty was in the kitchen and she had cut the homemade brawn and the bread with a lavish hand.

Mamma said suspiciously, "Why for two?"

I lied again. "Because half of it was supposed to be the maid's; but she said her family would expect her and that they always had liver and bacon for Thursday supper. I left the packet on the parlour table. Shall I fetch it?"

Mamma said gaily, "We can have a picnic!" The fact that she did not demur at the prospect of eating a servant girl's supper informed me that, as well as missing her lunch, she had not eaten, or not eaten much, upon her return. But even this conclusion did not prepare me for what I found, when I went down, taking the candle.

I thought I would make tea.

The kitchen hearth was clean, the fire half-laid; paper, twigs, a few slightly larger pieces of wood; just about enough to boil the kettle, in time. But I was in a hurry; I wanted a good fire, a kettle quickly boiled, so I opened the back door and looked under the lean-to. There was no coal at all; just enough twigs and wood pieces to boil another kettle. I left them there— Mamma would need them in the morning.

In the tobacco jar which served us as a tea caddy there was about enough tea for two brewings; there was a little milk in a jug; in the bread crock a single crust of bread, very hard and stale. Nothing else at all. Miss Hamilton, impractical as she often seemed, had summed up the situation correctly.

Waiting for the tardy kettle I occupied my hands with the making of two thick slices of bread and a wedge of brawn into as impossible a plateful as possible, and my mind with calculating the best possible approach to the suggestion which would end this impossible situation. The suggestion would come better from you!

I carried up the tray.

Mamma said, "Oh tea! I wondered why you were so long. Delightful! Darling, I am afraid you found supplies very low. As I said, I shirked the shopping this afternoon. This is a lovely picnic. I don't suppose you remember those happy Sunday picnics we had in the little pavilion at the Dower House, or in the wood?"

"Did we pick blackberries?"

"We did indeed."

She ate bread and brawn avidly.

Presently I said, "Mamma, I *did* come to see how you were. But there was something else I wanted to talk to you about. I wish to leave the Academy."

"Oh! Why?"

"Mamma, I have never been happy there. And now I am *bored*. I cannot say that I have learned all there is to learn, but I have learned as much as I am capable of learning. If I stayed on another year, or even two, I should never understand arithmetic or latitude and longitude and such things."

"Poor darling," Mamma said. She sounded amused and not annoyed, as I had feared. "And what, having left the Academy, do you propose to do with yourself?"

"Well," I said cautiously. "I ventured to speak to Miss Hamilton about my wish to leave and she said . . ." I told her what Miss Hamilton had said. Mamma laughed.

"So!" she said, "I have worked myself to the bone in order to provide the world with another Miss Smithers—or another Miss Hamilton! Galley slaves. Oh no! I had hoped to do better. I *will* do better. I had intended to speak of this at Christmas, but you seemed so young, so immature. I deferred it, thinking Easter early enough and hoping that your figure would develop. But now . . ." She gave me a key which opened the bottom drawer of the chest where, under a layer of sheets, old when they came into our possession and now much mended, lay another key which opened a wall cupboard in which a third key was hidden.

Mamma said, "One thing I learned from my Cousin Franklin. A treasure hunt must be a hunt. Now, open the left-hand top drawer of the chest."

In it there was a letter and a square case.

"Bring them here and I will show you," Mamma said.

She opened the case first and showed me a pair of earrings, very splendid; even in the light of one candle they shone; blue, rainbow coloured. I faintly remembered something; standing by a window, looking out at snowflakes, drifting down through sunshine.

"Sapphires," Mamma said, "and diamonds. Valuable enough to pay for a season in London. Where we have a friend. Read the letter, darling."

After that everything went mad.

The letter said that indeed, most certainly, Madame d'Aubigny was right. A good marriage to an Englishman of substance was the best that could be hoped for, in these troublous times. The writer had contrived more than one and was prepared to act again for the granddaughter of the man who had gone to the guillotine because he had spoken up so boldly in defence of the King. She would do her very utmost . . .

Mamma said, "If only I had been bolder, upon my arrival in England . . . I had looks then . . . But had I done so, I should not have *you*, my darling."

I was completely confused. Even the signature at the bottom of the letter, though bold and imposing, was quite indecipherable.

"Who wrote this?" I asked.

"Madame la Marquise de Lacratelle," Mamma said. "She was singularly fortunate. She left France in 1789, at the beginning, one of the so-called joyous immigrants. She found a protector, Lord Dunwich, a man so very old that not the slightest scandal could be inferred. With what she brought with her and what he provided—he has been dead for many years—she is quite rich. And very charitable. Not that we need charity. All that we need is a measure of social recognition and some introductions. These, as you see, she is willing to provide."

"How do you know so much about her, Mamma?"

"From the papers. When she entertains, formally, it is always remarked. So I took the risk of writing to her. After all, darling, nobody is going to knock on a door in Hawk Lane, Baildon, to inquire whether a pretty girl, well-reared despite everything, and of high lineage lives here." She huddled herself into the shawl. "I entertained a faint hope that you would make a friend, be invited, meet some susceptible elder brother . . . I underestimated the prejudice, the snobbery of this clodhopping society. In London we shall do better."

Stupid I might be about arithmetic, latitude, and longitude, but I was not obtuse.

I said, "Mamma, a very long time ago, once when Mrs. Twysdale was cross with me—do you remember her? She asked me what I thought would happen to me unless I sewed better. And I said, it was all I could think of, that I might get married. Then she said, quite angrily, that girls with no dowries who went husband hunting, got themselves bad names and were avoided. I never forgot that."

"Mrs. Twysdale was bourgeoise to the tips of her fingers!

174

What could she know? There were the two Gunning girls who came out of Ireland, with little but their looks. They both married Dukes. There was my Cousin Rosaleen, who came with nothing and made a marriage not spectacular, but secure, happy. All I ask is that you should do the same. And in order to do it, we must go to London. As we shall, in May."

In that small, low, whitewashed room, lit by a single candle, the whole thing sounded fantastic. It even sounded absurd to say, "But, Mamma, I have no wish to be married." It sounded like saying I had no wish to fly.

Mamma said, "That is ridiculous. How can you express an opinion on a subject about which you know absolutely nothing? In this world marriage is the only alternative to slavery if a woman has no money." She paused and seemed to consider that remark and amended it. "A *good* marriage. And you may depend upon me to choose a man of substance, with a good reputation, and kind . . ." She went on to describe the delights of the London season, the balls, the concerts, operas, receptions. She had never before mentioned London, but I did not inquire how she knew; her past was a mystery to me; she might have lived there. Or perhaps she was remembering Paris. "All this," she said, waving a skeleton hand, "will seem like a bad dream. We shall make no pretence at being other than we are, French exiles of good family, in penurious circumstances, but we shall hire comfortable apartments at some respectable address, entertain modestly."

"How shall we afford it?"

"By selling these earrings. And this house, of course. I gave a hundred pounds for it and I have had the roof repaired. All that whitewashing, too. I might obtain a hundred and twenty."

She chatted on. Nobody listening would have, could have, possibly believed that this afternoon she had collapsed from inanition, come home to a house without food in it and gone to bed in order to keep warm. I realised with a shock that she too, had sustained herself with her dreams.

I sat and listened and knew that the thing she planned, putting her dream into action, did not attract me. Why? At fifteen one has little self-knowledge and I had not until that moment thought of myself as being shy. Now I knew that I was. The idea of meeting with and mingling with a lot of strangers did something to my stomach. But if Mamma had not conceived this wild scheme I should be facing strangers in North Walsham, and without Mamma's support and company. And then I had another thought which, as well as making my stomach lurch, stopped my breath.

I said, "Mamma . . . suppose, having sold your jewels and the house . . . nothing came of it?"

"That," she said, "I refuse to contemplate. It is too frightening a thought. And one must not be frightened, that is one thing I have learned. Twice in my life I have erred through being timid." That was not easy to believe!

"The thought does frighten me," I said. "Would it not be better if we kept what we have. Suppose I left school and found some work—not in a school as Miss Hamilton suggested, I confess the idea of standing up in front of a class appalls me . . . Perhaps I could find some pupils for French, or take some of yours so that you need not rush about so much. You would be paid for your work at the Academy. We should have the earrings to fall back upon."

"Counsel of despair," Mamma said. "It would condemn us both to a life of toil, ill-paid. And that is not what I wish for you, darling. Ever since you were two and I was free to plan, this is what I have planned for you, what I have worked for, schemed for. You will never know what lengths I went to just to ensure that when you were old enough to be presented to the world you would be *presentable*."

"You mean sending me to school?"

"That and much more."

"All the more horrible if we fail."

"We must not fail."

She then began to worry about my getting back to school in time. She looked at her watch. It was not the gold one on the gold chain which had done something to set off the sombreness of the black dress. At some point that had vanished and been replaced by a watch of some dull metal slung on a black cord. I had asked about it and Mamma had said that the gold watch had ceased to keep good time. Blind, blind, sunk in self-pity, seeking comfort from my dreams, I had missed the implication.

It was a quarter to eight.

"Yes," I said, "I must go."

"What about the girl? Will she call for you?"

"I arranged to meet her on the corner. Thursday is her short evening."

"I'll come down," Mamma said. "I shall stand by the door until you reach the corner and call to me. Call if she is there. If not come back and I will walk with you."

"She will be there. She only went home to take a pair of shoes to be mended and to eat liver and bacon."

"Then you must not keep her waiting."

As I put on my shoes and my cloak she gave me civil messages for Miss Hamilton; she would take her classes as usual tomorrow afternoon, and then if Miss Hamilton could spare ten minutes, discuss the future.

At the corner I looked back; from the open door, behind which Mamma shuddered in her nightgown and shawl, the faint light of one candle showed, not yellow, not even primrose colour, just a strip of something not quite dark against the blackness of the lane. Like hope, I thought, nothing very positive, just a faint lightening of the hopelessness.

I called, "Bertha is here!"

I needed to cry. Somewhere back in the past Mamma had told me that crying did no good; that tears altered nothing. But I had proved by experience that this statement, though superficially true was, at a lower level, false. Tears served no practical purpose, they altered nothing, but they eased the pressure inside one's head, inside one's throat.

I felt so sorry for her—trying to bring a dream to reality; like me going to Nethergate sitting down in the beautiful room and saying: I belong here; this belongs to me. I was shocked by the revelation of how she lived when alone. I was frightened by her plan.

I had to cry or choke. I could not go back in tears to the Academy. So I began to cry as I walked along the Saltgate; and once having started I could not stop. Cold sleet and hot tears ran down my face as I blundered along, up Tun's Hill into the wide open market place. On one side of it the inn, The Hawk in Hand, stood lighted. The Assembly Rooms were dark. So was the church from whose tower a single booming sound announced the quarter hour. I was already late. On the fourth side of the square was the gateway to the Abbey, behind it the ruins, and on either side bits of ruined wall, some waist high, some knee high. I felt along, found a piece to sit upon and prepared to cry until I could cry no more.

I still tried to be sensible. Annabelle d'Aubigny, what is this all about? Would you have cried if you had trotted home with your bread and your brawn and your Mamma had said: What an opportunity; how kind of Miss Hamilton; and I hope you will be happy at North Walsham? Yes, I should have cried. From simple self-pity. Now I cried because it was all such a muddle; because she was so brave and so determined, and so frail; because I had not noticed; because the watchful, warding light had been so faint in the dark night. Less than a star . . .

Incredible as it may sound, a bit of my mind slipped off:

177

Less than a star, but held by a steadier hand against the dark. Less than a lantern, but held higher into the night. I was positively ashamed that something inside my head should run off, making out of this evening's experience a package of words. That thought put the final touch to my awareness of being heartless and callous. Not noting how Mamma was wasting away, taking without question everything she had given me all these years.

I was crying so hard, so lost in my misery that I did not know that I was not alone in this deserted space until a wavering circle of lantern light passed near my feet and a man's tread, firm and brisk, went past me. Some paces on he stopped, turned and came back. I had time to think, in panic, that Mamma and Mrs. Twysdale were right, Miss Hamilton mistaken.

"What's wrong?"

"Nothing." The word came out like a hiccup.

"Something must be or you wouldn't sit here, in such weather, crying your eyes out." He sounded concerned and kind, but then Mr. Bricey had always been kind to me: until that last evening. The man directed the beam of the lantern upon me. "Has somebody attacked you?"

"No."

"It's no business of mine, I know, but you can't just sit there. You'll catch your death. You're already soaked. Come along. You must go home. Where do you live?"

"St. Matt . . . Matthew's Square."

"I'm bound in that direction myself. Here, take my arm."

The sleet made a dancing halo around the lantern beam and I was dizzy from crying. I was glad of the support. Even with it I lurched a bit. And the sobs kept coming.

"You are in a poor way," he said. "You seem very young to have such woes. Is it anything anybody could do anything about?"

"Life," I said, stumbling. "The world. Everything. . . ."

"Once you start crying about that you could go on forever," he said.

I gulped out, "I think—perhaps—I shall."

"Oh, come," he said, "it can't be as bad as that! Things are never as bad as they seem."

"You don't know."

"How could I? You've told me nothing, except that life and the world have gone wrong with you . . ." We had now reached the corner of the Square and the full blast of the blizzard struck us, my hood blew off, the loose side of my cloak sprang up like a wing. But for the fact that I was clutching his arm I might have been airborne, like a bird, like a leaf. As it was we staggered together round the corner and into the comparative shelter of the Square, with the first householder's lantern swinging but still alight over our heads.

The man said, "You're very young." My hair was all over the place, I grabbed at my hood and pulled it as far forward as I could. "Couldn't you tell me what is wrong? It helps to tell, you know. I can't alter life, or the world for you, but I'd do anything I could, within reason."

I had a strange feeling that he would; that if I'd been, say, an apprentice running from ill-treatment or a servant girl summarily dismissed, in fact if my problem had been anything on an ordinary level, he would have dealt with it, sensibly and kindly.

I had another feeling, too, rather vague in all the muddle but there sure enough, a wish to lean, a wish to confide. (I didn't think this then, but I did afterwards, explaining myself to myself. There had been no men of any substance in my life; no father, no brother, no uncle or cousin; only servants, Pratt's brother Tom, Mamma's Cousin Franklin, upstairs in bed, never seen and his son who must never see me. None with authority. There *was* actually, but only in bad dreams, a man who did have authority, but was not friendly, a nightmare figure with a hook where a hand should be. So perhaps, I thought, afterwards, I was unduly vulnerable to the support and the comfort that a friendly male could offer. But, as I said, that thought came later.)

Moving away from the corner lantern, I said, "It is very kind of you, but to tell you what I was crying about would take at least a fortnight. And there is nothing that anybody could do about it."

And I thought, even could I bring myself to tell, who would believe Mamma's story. Who would believe that a woman with a pair of sapphire earrings in a drawer would be starving to death, planning a London season for her daughter?

He said, "Very well. Now which house is it?"

"That one. With the lighted fanlight and the window."

Why the window? I asked myself. The light in the hall, yes. Left on for me. But the window on the left was the window of the room which had once been Mrs. Twysdale's sitting room and was now a classroom. Why should that be lighted? Was Miss Hamilton sitting there, waiting for me? Before I had time to sort over what Mamma had said and prepare something that sounded moderately reasonable.

I suppose my step slowed. He said, "What is it? Are you afraid to go in?"

I said, "No. No." Panic. I knew that if I said I was afraid he'd say he'd come with me and then where should I be? Not only late and failing in self-control, but picking up men in the street. As bad as what was said about Dilys Helmar and Jassy Woodroffe.

"No. Thank you very much. You have been so very kind," I said. And up rushed the tears again.

He said, "You really do need a shoulder to cry on. Is there one in there?"

"Oh yes. I shall be all right now."

"I sincerely hope so. Then I'll wish you good night. And I hope that your troubles will sort themselves out."

He directed the beam of his lantern on to the steps, the doorway, the knob. Making it easy for me. With my hand on the knob I turned back and said "Thank you" again, and he lifted his hat; the sleet fell on his sand-coloured hair. Absurdity upon absurdity; at that moment I loved him with all my heart.

Miss Hamilton came out of the classroom. She said, "Almost an hour late . . . My dear, what is it? Is she . . . worse?"

I knew then that there is a stage beyond which crying cannot go; it turns into laughter that is not laughter at all, a painful paroxysm that takes you by the throat, by the shoulders and shakes you to pieces. It is known as hysteria and the traditional remedy is a smart slap across the face. Miss Hamilton did not apply it. She put her arm around me, took me up to her own room, where, although the fire was dying, it was warm, and gave me something to drink. She said, "There, there. You're chilled to the bone." She lifted my sodden cloak and hung it over the back of a chair and then threw another log on the fire. Whatever she had given me to drink had a calming effect; it also loosened my tongue and when she at last asked, "Now, Annabelle, what is the matter?" I told her everything.

Her attitude surprised me. She had always seemed rather impractical and unworldly; in the interim between Mrs. Twysdale's going and the installation of the cook-housekeeper, though the food had been more varied it had not been served well and the kitchen was ill-supervised: this very evening she had confessed that the school was not prosperous; I should not have expected her to take a favourable view of Mamma's crack-brained scheme, concerned as it was with life in high society and the mercenary intention of marrying me off to somebody rich. Yet, when I had finished my blurted-out tale, she said calmly: "If your Mamma has the resources you speak of, and influential friends, I think she is doing the best thing for you, my dear. Security through marriage is much the best fate that could befall you. That is one thing life has taught me." Was she perhaps regretting her own unmarried state? Her own lack of security? She went on speaking sensibly and soothingly. She exculpated me from blame for not noticing Mamma's physical deterioration. "One does not notice such things in people one sees often." She approved of London, the best place, she said, for finding a husband rich enough to overlook the fact that I had no dowry. "Which fact in itself will spare you the attentions of a fortunehunter and should ensure that whoever marries you is attracted by *you*." She urged upon me the need to co-operate with Mamma, "bearing in mind that you will attain security for her as well as for yourself. She has plainly made repeated sacrifices for you." Everything she said was almost exactly the opposite of what I should have expected, but it was very heartening. Finally she said, "If the prospect of marriage upsets you, Annabelle, you must consider that marriage, like everything else, is a matter of living one day at a time. Of small adjustments. If someone had told me when I was your age that I should spend my life, end my life, as a not very successful schoolmistress, I should have dropped dead, I think, of shock and repugnance."

Her calm invaded me; as the stranger had said, it did help to tell somebody. I went off to bed in a state of mind capable of reflecting that all along Mamma had done what was best for me, and was about to do so again.

The childish habit of making my last waking thought centre about Nethergate, of imagining myself back there, occupying the beautiful room, remained with me. But tonight, amongst all the delightful imaginary people who kept me company there, there was a real one, the stranger who had befriended me. I was well aware that I should never see him again, never see Nethergate again; but somewhere in the future which had so abruptly been unrolled before my eyes that evening, I could at least hope to occupy another pretty room, with a man who was kind and strong and who cared what happened to me.

In the morning I woke not only resigned to, but enthusiastic about Mamma's plan. I was able to look around upon the girls who had never endeared themselves to me with a feeling of superiority. How many of them were going to have a season in London this summer, sponsored by a French

Marquise? Now and again my complacency was shot through by that particular anguish known only to the congenitally shy, but I pushed that aside, remembering that to stand up before a class of children, however young, in Miss Pollinger's school at North Walsham would have been equally trying.

Our venture began badly by our encountering some difficulty in selling the house. Only one really serious buyer appeared, the man from the timber yard, most appropriately named Sawyer, and he offered fifty pounds.

"But Mr. Sawyer," Mamma said, "I gave a hundred pounds for it."

"So you did. And as I told Bob Tanner, he was blamed lucky. You wanted a roof over your head, ma'am, you had the money in hand. There ain't many like you. I'm offering you fifty, like I offered him at the time. Take it or leave it."

"I shouldn't dream of taking it. In the five years I have lived here everything, down to a candle, has increased in price. I entirely fail to see why a house should have halved in value."

"I been telling you," he said, and went away.

Mamma advertised the house in the Baildon *Free Press*, pricing it at a hundred and fifty; she engaged the services of an auctioneer who also sold houses privately. A few people came to look, some I suspect from idle curiosity, some genuinely wanting a home and thinking that the price, a hundred and fifty pounds for a house in Hawk Lane must be a clerical error. It seemed to me that whenever anybody came to inspect the horrid little house the sawmill was unusually noisy and the smithy more malodorous than usual.

Mr. Sawyer bided his time and then renewed his offer. Poor Mamma, it was now April, well on into April; she wanted, she needed, to be in London by early May. She was desperate, but she did not show it except that her always pale face turned a little paler. She said, "No."

"But look at it," the man said crossly. "You ain't sold it. Who'd give more for a place in Hawk Lane, set betwixt a sawmill and a smithy and sharing a pump. Sharing a pump. Not even a well of its own? Fifty-five then?"

"Mr. Sawyer I cannot accept fifty-five pounds for a house that cost me a hundred—and has had money spent on it."

"A lick of whitewash."

"And the thatch mended."

"All right, I'll grant you the thatch. Sixty?"

Even paler, Mamma said, "No." She looked as though she were about to faint, but she spoke firmly and I remembered that Miss Hamilton had said something about her high spirit.

Mr. Sawyer said, "Have it your own way then," and went to the door, tugged it open so roughly that the whole house shuddered. Then he turned and said, between his teeth, "Seventy. And that's my last word."

Mamma said, "I might consider seventy, Mr. Sawyer, but we cannot conduct business in the street."

Afterwards she pointed out to me that in effect we had lived in Hawk Lane for five years at the cost of £30; £6 a year, a reasonable rent.

I said, "You were marvellous! You made him pay an extra twenty pounds."

"If one is forced to act like a huckstering old market woman, one might as well do it properly," she said.

The man who had sold us the furniture bought it back for a hundredth of the price we had paid and took it away and we boarded the coach for London.

I had never been in any place larger than Baildon, a quiet country town; I was quite stupefied by the noise, the bustle and the smell of a great city; but Mamma had lived in Paris and seemed to know exactly what to do. From the yard in the inn which was the end of the coach stage, and fully as busy as Baildon on a market day, she sent a ragged little boy to find and bring back a hired conveyance. She gave the address in a confident voice and we rattled away to a quieter part of the town, through streets and squares lined with pleasant houses; there were gardens, there were trees. But our final destination was disappointing, a narrow, dim—even on this sunny day— side street. We drew up outside a kind of cook-shop. Mamma said there must be some mistake, but there was not; this was the address which she had given the man, and inside the shop which smelt strongly of hot fat and onions a rather dirty, rat-faced woman announced herself as Madame Laurier and led us up to the apartments that had been reserved for us. It was a tall house and had perhaps once been pleasant, but the two rooms assigned us had been made from one, so that they were far too high for their size; it was like being at the bottom of a well. What furniture there was was very inferior and there was a lack of cleanliness of which the nose as well as the eye was aware. Mamma looked round in disgust. "Madame la Marquise must have misunderstood me," she said. "I told her that my means were very limited; I did not say that I was a pauper. Unpack only what is necessary to make ourselves tidy. I do not propose to stay here."

Madame la Marquise received us very graciously, but I found her formidable. She wore her dead white hair in the old-fashioned style, piled high; her eyes were so black that there seemed to be no difference between iris and pupil, they were as black as coal, and as bright. She was dressed in black—perpetual mourning for the King and Queen of France, I later discovered. I should not have cared to find fault with any arrangement she had made quite so early in the first meeting, or in such a forthright way, but Mamma was quite intrepid. Madame seemed hurt.

"My dear Madame d'Aubigny, I considered myself fortunate to find an apartment vacant in this district. The demand is enormous. And prices are extortionate. I understood that you had but slender resources. I hesitated to engage anything costing more than four guineas a week . . ."

Mamma gave a little gasp. "Four guineas? For those rooms?"

"I was given to understand that there is a water closet. A rare amenity. There is also the cook-shop, or café, which will be convenient for your meals, will it not? But what I thought the singular advantage is that you will be so near me. Since you have no carriage . . ."

Mamma said, "I am sorry, madame. Four guineas is certainly as much as I can afford. More than I should perhaps. I apologise for my complaint."

Madame inclined her head. "You are a stranger to London," she said, as though that excused all. "Now let us consider more important matters." She turned that bright, penetrating look upon me. Not unfriendly, dispassionate, critical, as though I were something she might possibly consider buying but was not quite sure about.

"She looks very *young*."

"Annabelle is sixteen," Mamma said swiftly, adding half a year to my age.

"And very shy." How did she know that? She said to me, "Child, you will shortly come under scrutiny far more severe than mine. You must be prepared for it. You must hold up your head. You must say—inaudibly, of course—I am the granddaughter of the Marquis de Savigny; who are you? Remember that." To Mamma, she said, "What accomplishments?"

Mamma explained that I was unmusical, could not sing, played no instrument.

"Perhaps as well. Unless there is real talent such things are better not attempted. Can she dance?"

"She has had lessons, regularly. Little practice, of course."

Madame's coal-bright eyes raked over me again and I tried on her the trick she had advised: I am the granddaughter of the Marquis de Savigny; who are you? She closed her eyes for a second; she had extraordinarily deep upper eyelids.

"I think the motif must be simplicity. Young, straight from school, shy. White muslin. I will give you the name of a fellow exile who makes the most delectable dresses, embroidered, absurdly cheap. No ornaments except a posy, or wreath of flowers, either real or artificial. There is another unfortunate who makes artificial flowers of such perfection that sometimes even the English, who love their gardens beyond all, are occasionally deceived. Ornaments. That reminds me. You wrote that you had jewels to dispose of. What exactly?"

"I have them here," Mamma said, and she took the square case from her reticule. Madame la Marquise turned upon the sapphire and diamond earrings precisely the critical look that she had turned upon me.

"Quite good," she said, "but in no way exceptional. What else?"

"That is all I have," Mamma said. Madame la Marquise gave her a very funny look, amazement, pity, and admiration, yes, admiration, all in one, or following one another so closely that they seemed one.

She said, "You are indeed a stranger to London. The market for this kind of thing is glutted. So many of the first émigrés—of whom I was one—brought out spectacular pieces, jewels of pedigree. There was great demand then, both for their intrinsic value and for their associations. But it is different now. Every English lady of quality is the proud possessor of some jewel which, if it did not actually belong to Queen Marie Antoinette was worn at Versailles . . . For these"—she dismissed the earrings with a glance—"some stout English burgher or country squire, wishing to favour his wife and outdo his neighbour, might give forty pounds."

Mamma did not flinch. She simply turned pale. "Then we must sell Annabelle's pearls."

"Oh," Madame said. "Yes, that would be wise. If they are genuine. Nowadays the imitations are so clever. But for real pearls there is still a market. Little English girls have twelfth birthdays, or recover from chicken pox. Such occasions must be marked and how better than by a gift of a simple string of pearls? May I suggest that I should undertake to dispose of these trinkets for you, Madame d'Aubigny? I do not conduct

185

the transactions myself, but I have a servant, very shrewd, very experienced."

Mamma laid the box containing the despised earrings on a table nearby. I unfastened the pearls and laid them alongside.

"If you would be so kind," Mamma said.

Madame then showed a flash of sympathetic understanding for me: "You will not feel the lack of them, my dear. Very few French girls have any trinkets left and despite your English upbringing, you are French. And that reminds me of another thing." She turned back to Mamma. "Your own antecedents are, of course, impeccable. Your father stayed in France and tried to compromise with the rogues, but his end redeemed that error. In fact it is generally held that until de Savigny's head was in the basket the King's was safe. Who exactly was Monsieur d'Aubigny?"

The question was rapped out suddenly; almost as though it were intended to confuse and trap. And indeed Madame la Marquise, so central a figure of émigré society, so charitable and energetic in the exiles' cause, may have been imposed upon.

Mamma said calmly, "You would not have heard of him, madame. A younger son of a younger son, but of a good family. A Breton. He was killed at Quiberon."

Had she intended to divert attention from my father's obscure status she succeeded admirably.

"Ah, Quiberon!" Madame la Marquise exclaimed. "Had we but succeeded there!"

At Quiberon there had been a rising in the Royalist cause; one of the dead King's younger brothers had taken part in it. It had been a failure, but to have died at Quiberon made a man a hero. In fact throughout my season in London, every introduction made by Madame la Marquise took an explanatory form: This is Mademoiselle Annabelle d'Aubigny. Her grandfather was the Marquis de Savigny. Her father was killed at Quiberon.

Mamma, for so long cut off from polite society, seemed to know exactly what to do and what to say. In fact she was back in her own world, and quite at home, in a way that I, I felt, should never be.

"Well," said Madame la Marquise, "you may be sure of a warm welcome from the French community; and that is most important, for the English aristocrats frequent our salons, thinking—quite correctly—that there they come in touch with a culture superior to their own. And one introduction leads to another. I trust that Annabelle understands that an *English* marriage must be our aim. She will meet many Frenchmen, well-bred, charming, the rightful heirs to great estates. But frankly I do not believe that even should the monarchy be restored, the property will ever be returned. It would mean taking it away from the peasants who now hold it; and when did a peasant ever yield up anything he had his hands on? The only real prospect for a young Frenchman is to marry an English heiress, as indeed one of my protégés did very recently. A rather plain girl, no longer very young, but with a dowry of thirty thousand pounds. I am happy to think that I made the introduction."

Over the tea which arrived at that moment, the talk turned to clothes. For me Madame had decreed white muslin and white muslin had been best and Sunday wear during summer at the Academy. I was actually wearing one of the stipulated three. I had, however, grown since last summer, and though simplicity and youth were to be the motives, Madame said, rightly, that the dress I was wearing was not designed to be attractive. I should need six new ones, she thought, three for day wear, three for evening; I should need scarves of lace or gauze for wear on chilly evenings. She knew a woman who made beautiful ones; the fashion was to have the ends trimmed —and weighted—by bands of fur, too expensive, of course, so this ingenious woman had found a way of using wool, instead, so teased about and then clipped that it gave exactly the same effect.

As for Mamma, Madame's coal-black glance flickered over the worn black silk and repudiated it.

"We are all poor," she said, "and we admit to being poor, but of Frenchwomen a certain style is expected. It is a challenge, and as you will see, it is gallantly met. What you are wearing now, my dear Madame d'Aubigny, was certainly made of excellent material—otherwise it would not have stood up to such hard wear—but it was made by a country dressmaker, was it not? Madame Chateaurellant, to whom I propose to take you this very afternoon, will make you, from much inferior material, a much more stylish gown. You, too, will need something for evening wear."

I do not think that she intentionally exploited us. When I came to know her better I realised that she was, absolutely heart and soul, devoted to the cause of helping her fellow exiles in every possible way and by whatever means. If Peter must be robbed a little in order that Paul should benefit, then Peter must be robbed, always in the lively hope that Paul, having benefitted, could in his turn be robbed for Peter's sake. In fact Madame la Marquise de Lactratelle was not unlike a juggler whom I saw at Vauxhall Gardens, keeping about a dozen plates in the air; he used his hands, his feet, his shoulders, his knees, anything so long as no plate should fall. Here we were, not destitute, not old, not ailing; there was the not impossible hope that I should find a husband. If, in order to bring this about some outlay was required, then Madame Chateaurellant must be given the chance to make a little profit.

One thing which this visit to Madame Chateaurellant did for us was to make us heartily thankful for the accommodation which Madame la Marquise had found for us. Compared with the damp, stinking, semi-basement room in Somers Town where these beautiful, stylish clothes were made and three people lived, slept, cooked, even the horrid little house in Hawk Lane seemed palatial in retrospect.

Driving back—the first garments of the order promised for the evening after next, and the shock of what we had seen still lively in our minds—Madame la Marquise said, "You may perhaps wonder why, with people living in such abominable conditions, I keep my house to myself. The point is that I cannot accommodate all and I cannot make invidious distinctions. I have guest rooms, I accept guests who can afford to pay. Of the rents I give every penny to the Abbé Carron's Chambre de la Providence which helps the old and the ailing. I saw, quite early, that it was more necessary to help the many than to pamper the few."

Mamma and I went back to our apartments and next day set about cleaning them. Every cushion, every upholstered surface given a smart slap exuded a cloud of foul-smelling dust. We beat, we scoured and polished. Mamma, tucking in her mouth, an expression of disgust and determination, even tackled the amenity, the communal water closet which because it had been used by everybody and was owned by nobody had fallen into a sorry state.

Madame Laurier looked upon these activities with disfavour, a criticism of her management, and took her revenge. During these two days we ate at the café tables, cautiously requesting the cheapest food. It was never available. We were always just too early or just too late for anything but the *coq au vin*, the most expensive thing on the menu. Mamma, indomitable, found a place a little farther along the dismal, dung-scented street where take-away food was available; very cheap. She bought bread and cheese and ham. Madame Laurier climbed the stairs to inform us that Mr. Stokes had a rule against tenants having food in their rooms; it encouraged mice.

"And who is Mr. Stokes?" Mamma asked haughtily.

Mr. Stokes was the landlord. We never saw him; we had no real proof of his existence, but we heard a lot about him and his prejudices ruled our lives, to our cost. He did not approve, for instance, of any washing being done on his property, it lowered the tone of the apartments, and since, in London, I needed a clean white muslin dress every day, and sometimes two, we were obliged to spend a good deal upon laundry.

However, once the first of our new dresses were delivered and we were invited to spend an evening at Madame la Marquise's house, life changed. As she herself had said, one invitation led to another and we were soon in the thick of a society where all the English seemed to be very rich and all the French very poor.

What amazed me about the French was their gaiety. They had, with very few exceptions, lost all they possessed and were exiles in a strange land, many of them earning a meagre living in ways more menial and less certain than Mamma's teaching, but once they were together, given a thin biscuit and a glass of cheap wine or a cup of tea, animation and wit and gallantry abounded. There was an unwritten rule that misfortune must not be talked about, except as a joke; and another that any chance good fortune should be shared as far as possible, the sharing usually taking the form of a party where food of a fairly substantial kind was served. For such events Madame la Marquise's drawing room was always available, since almost everybody else lived in an attic or a cellar or an overcrowded room. A good many of the men gambled when they could afford it; I remember one, a delightful young man who worked in a barber's shop and one day backed the winner in a horse race; he took about a dozen of us to Vauxhall Gardens and gave us a wonderful supper with very good wine. Another, older man, had some luck at the card table and took a party of us to a very gay café owned by the Comtesse de Guery who had discovered within herself a talent for making ice cream and from very modest beginnings had built up a thriving business. Her contribution to French solidarity was to charge her fellow countrymen half what she charged her English customers. The Prince of Wales frequented the Café Guery a great deal and she overcharged him and his friends quite shamelessly.

Madame la Marquise's hospitality was generous without ever being ostentatious; one could, however, be certain of not coming away from one of her receptions feeling hungry as one often did when she lent her room and some other lady played hostess. In the English houses to which we were invited the food was always superb. One's stomach learned to adjust itself; now a bowl of soup and a slice of bread in the café below our apartments, Madame Laurier having found that Mamma was not to be bullied, and now a buffet supper at Devonshire House with every delicacy under the sun.

It was a curious life but there were things in it that I should have enjoyed but for the fact that Mamma became, for the first time in my life, extremely critical of me. As day followed day and then week followed week, it seemed to me that most of our outings ended in bedtime recriminations.

I had danced three times and taken supper with a young Frenchman. "The very thing Madame la Marquise warned you against on that first day."

Louis de Vaudreul meant nothing to me except that with him for some reason I did not feel at all shy.

"He had heard about Papa being at Quiberon," I said defensively. "He was there, too, and survived. He seemed to wish to talk about it."

"I am not saying that any gentleman should be *discouraged*," Mamma said, unmollified. "To appear to be in demand is essential to popularity. But three dances and then supper. Most unwise."

On another occasion I erred because I had spent too long in the company of a very beautiful girl, Marie Latour, who was even more at sea in this fashionable world than I was. She came from Martinique where there had been a slave revolt. Her escape had been dramatic, and her account of it interested me—she had not been in London long enough to know the rule about making a joke of misfortune. Also she was terribly homesick, and I, having suffered such agonies over Nethergate, could lend a sympathetic, perhaps too sympathetic ear.

"You must see," Mamma said, "that she eclipses you absolutely. You are pretty, she is beautiful. To stand there and invite comparison . . ."

I also made the mistake—this on my second visit to Devonshire House—of talking to a woman of dubious reputation.

"People," Mamma said, "are known by the company they keep. Mrs. Grant-Thomas is notorious."

In my inmost mind I knew that this carping was simply the outward expression of Mamma's disappointment at the fact that so far no rich English gentleman had flung himself at my feet and also that she was worried about money. But that she, always so doting and indulgent, should attack me for talking to a woman whose name, leave alone whose reputation, I did not know, was too much. I too have a temper.

"How could I know? Mrs. Whatever-her-name-is came up and asked was my posy made of real or artificial flowers and I told her artificial and she said she should have known, they looked too real to be real. That doesn't sound amusing now, but it did at the time. So I laughed and then she asked me where I obtained them and I told her and she said flowers real or artificial were not her style, that she looked and felt her best in riding kit. And she asked did I ride. And I said no and she said it was a pity, I had the figure for it. So then I said . . ."

"Very well," Mamma said quellingly. "I think that in future it would be advisable if you looked at me every now and then. If you are acting indiscreetly, I shall touch my hair. So. You will then excuse yourself and come straight to me."

After that an uninformed observer might have imagined that Madame d'Aubigny was unduly anxious about her coiffure. And once a very civil man said to me, "I observe that you are interested in the lady by the door. If you wish it I could effect an introduction."

I said, "She is my Mamma." I wondered what he would have said had I explained.

The awareness of a constant, vigilant and not altogether approving eye on me did little to inculcate the poise, confidence, and grace that were so desirable. In the company of French women I was always conscious of a lack of animation; gestures, smiles, overemphasis on certain words came so naturally to them that they made me feel stiff and dull. In the company of English people another disadvantage obtruded itself—ignorance, of a kind; straight from school, straight from the country how could I talk about the last play, the latest book, the latest scandal? Even my vocabulary seemed defective. Who was Prinny? What did my partner at a ball mean by saying, "I see the butcher has arrived."? I learned, of course, in time; Prinny was the Prince of Wales, the Butcher his brother the Duke of Cumberland, but during the learning I lost confidence and gained for myself a reputation for being a good dancer but dull to talk to. Nobody so described me—at least in my hearing—but I could judge by the fact that I never lacked partners at a ball, but at the end of each dance was returned promptly to Mamma, who sat with other non-dancers on rows of uncomfortable little gilt chairs, being very animated indeed; she had become much more Frenchified since coming to London, and certainly nobody seeing her in public could have guessed how anxiety and disappointment and presently a kind of despair were gnawing at her.

Curiously enough, my one comfort during these trying days was that intimidating woman, Madame la Marquise. Where Mamma criticised, she praised; she told me that I was pretty and had dignity, "a rare quality and perhaps slightly out of fashion these days, but we shall find somebody who will appreciate you, my dear. It is early days yet." When Marie Latour, homesickness forgotten, became engaged, after a whirlwind courtship, to Sir Hugo Jepson, and Mamma moaned with envy, Madame said privately to me that Marie was greatly to be pitied. "He is a most dissolute young man, and nobody but that old aunt of hers who is anxious to be rid of her at all costs, would have contemplated such a match."

I thought, in my heart, that Mamma probably would have done. Not perhaps that she was eager to be rid of me but because time, and money, were running out. By mid-July everybody who was anybody would be leaving London. Where should we go?

It was in the third week of June that Madame issued an invitation to us to accompany her to Hampstead to see an exhibition of pictures painted by a Madame de Goncourt.

"She is a very good artist. Her best work is fully equal to that of Vigée le Brun, but of course she is obliged to paint these small hasty pictures in order to support herself and her old mother."

"My dear Madeleine"—they were now on Christian name terms—"you must know that I cannot afford to buy a picture however small. I have no wall upon which to hang a picture."

"Nobody expects you to buy a picture," Madame said, "but I think you should be there. It is a fashionable event, for Madame de Goncourt is generous with the one thing she has, which is space. There will be many other things on sale. A new straw hat for this child, for example. Ten shillings and vastly becoming. The carriage will call for you at two o'clock. I must be early as I am helping."

Hampstead was a village, standing high outside London; I should see the real country, for which I hungered. And a sale of pictures and other things could hardly be an exercise in social aptitude or a popularity competition; so I rather looked forward to the outing though Mamma was sour about it.

"That was practically an *order* to spend ten shillings. I can only hope that when we are reduced to making straw hats, Madeleine will be equally assiduous on our behalf." That was the kind of thing she said, more and more often, nowadays. There were times when I felt completely bereft; I'd lost Nethergate; the only man for whom I had ever felt anything at all had walked away, nameless in the sleety night, and now Mamma had changed so much that she seemed not to be the same person. I seemed to have lost everything.

As the carriage mounted the slope the air grew fresher and the light clearer; I could understand why an artist should choose to live there. There were a number of pretty cottages, their gardens bright with flowers, but Madame de Goncourt lived in a stark, ugly house, its plaster and paint peeling, its windows without curtains. The front door stood open and we alighted and went in. Madame's coachman drove into the shade of a row of elm trees on the opposite side of the road.

Immediately inside the door was a studio with whitewashed walls hung with small, very pretty pictures, bright flowers, birds, landscapes. There was no furniture except a plain wooden table and a chair, a harp and a stool. This room was connected by folding doors, now thrown back, to another at the rear. That room was full of chairs, sofas, stools, set closely together, and on its farther side was a long table covered with a white cloth and dozens of tea cups. Another door, to the side of the studio, opened upon a verandah, from which came the sound of voices and movement.

We were no sooner inside than an incredibly old man, dressed in seedy black, came creaking in. He made a deep bow and Madame said:

"Good afternoon, François. Where is your mistress?" She spoke very loudly.

"Madame is making ready, madame."

In her ordinary voice Madame la Marquise said, "Absolutely no sense of time at all! That is François, once her steward. He chose to be exiled with her and what she would have done without him I just do not know. He cooks and shops and frames the pictures. He is very deaf."

As she spoke, she ran her piercing black eyes over the pictures, assessing, assigning. Mamma gave them an apathetic glance. I was more attentive; there was one, a bowl of pale pink roses, which would have been exactly right in Nethergate's pretty room.

Outside a carriage drew up.

"Really," Madame exclaimed. "To be so diligent and yet so

dilatory! Fortunately I am here. Oh, good afternoon, Lady Dossiter. I am so relieved to see you early! Had you not been I should have faced a most embarrassing situation. Everybody will want those pink roses! But I know that there is only one place for them; between the long windows in your drawing room. An exact match for your curtains, are they not? I was contemplating being obliged to tell a lie and to say that they were bespoke. I felt I must reserve them for you."

What could Lady Dossiter say?

Mamma and I had now circled the room and come to the door that gave upon the verandah. Here other goods were on display on various tables, each with its attendant.

All the things offered for sale had this in common—the maximum possible work and ingenuity had combined with the minimum possible outlay on material. Many émigré ladies had been convent reared and did needlework and embroidery of the kind that would have won Mrs. Twysdale's most hearty approval, but with a few exceptions the stuff was unworthy of the work; beautiful designs in drawn-thread work executed not upon linen but on cheap cotton cloth, lovely lace made of cheap thread. There was also a lot of carved work, worthy of ivory, but done on bone or wood, artificial flowers that should have been of silk or velvet made of calico or felt.

Infinitely, infinitely depressing. I thought: And Mamma has nothing to sell, except me and I also am of inferior stuff!

And then I had another, more lively thought. I thought: However well managed, there must be an end to this. There must be a limit to people's willingness to buy what they really do not need, simply through charity. Half this skill and industry, applied to proper purposes, would have been a hundred times more effective. All these people, Mamma and I and Madame la Marquise, have simply been wasting time! I thought that this evening I would ask Madame la Marquise to cease looking for a husband for me, and to begin to ask about whether anybody needed a young governess, fluent in French. I remembered that little room in Hawk Lane when Mamma had called my sensible ideas a counsel of despair. I had been too easily persuaded, for as events had proved, I was right, she was wrong. Now, our small substance wasted, our groundless hopes withered, we were faced with this makeshift, make-believe life, in which I wished to have no more lot or part. In fact, if Madame la Marquise could not help me I would choke down my pride and apply to Miss Hamilton.

There were more tables in the garden. The long one bearing the hats was at the very end and Mamma moved towards it reluctantly. "I suppose we must buy one," she said, "though I see nothing wrong with the one you are wearing."

"Nor do I. I don't need a new hat." Actually I found our progress amongst the laden tables rather embarrassing; the people who were selling always looked up so hopefully, with a civil greeting, and then were disappointed when we spent nothing. Being early we were conspicuous. However, people were beginning to arrive, one could tell by the noise.

"I think Madeleine may take it amiss if we do not buy a hat," Mamma said glumly. So we came to the stall. The hats were undeniably pretty, very wide in the brim and shallow in the crown and trimmed, some with artificial flowers and ribbon, some with ribbon only. The stately old lady behind the table greeted us with a narrow smile and said, "Are they not delectable? Is not Madame Lucien clever?" It was customary on such occasions for people to sell other people's work, so that praise, not being self-praise, could be used freely.

I decided to take my time about choosing the hat, so that when we walked through the garden again we should pass unnoticed in the crowd. Had I had nothing to think of except buying a hat I knew which one I should have chosen; it had a wreath of forget-me-nots made of what looked like velvet, and ribbons of the same colour to tie under the chin to keep it anchored on the head. But the stately lady murmured that the hats with flowers were fifteen shillings. However, in this curious world it was not quite correct to admit openly that five shillings made the difference between what one could, or could not afford, so I tried it on.

"Please not to tie the ribbons," the stately lady said sensibly. "Until, that is, you have made your choice." She had a square looking glass which she obligingly held up so that I might see myself.

Mamma was too low-spirited to pretend even to take much interest in the procedure; my mime of indecision went disregarded by her. I hovered, an unflowered hat with cornflower blue ribbons, one with rose pink ones?

"Which shall I have, Mamma?"

"Whichever you prefer, darling." Despite the term of endearment the voice said: It makes no difference. Seven weeks and not so much as a nibble!

The pretence could not be indefinitely prolonged; even the seller of hats was beginning to think me capricious and held the glass rather wearily.

I said, "I will have this one." It was much like the one I should have chosen, lacking only the flowers.

It was then that I became aware—the way one does—that I was under observation. I half-turned and saw a man looking at me very intently. As our eyes met he bowed and smiled and said in a pleasantly, definitely English voice:

"Permit me to say—quite charming!"

"It is becoming is it not?" Mamma asked, springing to attention like a good soldier.

The stately lady said, "It would be a favour to Madame Lucien if you would wear it, mademoiselle. Everyone, seeing you, would wish such a hat."

The man said, "Since there is no one else to do it, may I introduce myself? Lord Bowdegrave."

"I am Madame d'Aubigny. My daughter, Annabelle."

Any girl, however ignorant, knows when a man is interested—and when he is not. No man except the ineligible young Frenchman with whom I had danced three times and taken supper had been interested in me, since that night in Baildon in the sleet. Lord Bowdegrave was. I knew instantly.

He was not young, forty perhaps, extremely elegant, fleshy without being fat, quite nice-looking though with contradictory features, a kind, good-humoured mouth, an arrogant nose, rather sad eyes now studying me with a rather wistful admiration, now turning to Mamma with interested curiosity.

The stately lady rearranged the hats a little and looked at Lord Bowdegrave invitingly. He said:

"I regret, madame. My only female relative is ninety years of age."

I tied the ribbons of the new hat and picked up the one I had discarded. It had no ribbons by which I could sling it on my arm, being a deep-crowned, narrow-brimmed one which needed no ties. As I took it up, a trifle awkwardly, Lord Bowdegrave reached for it and held it between his left arm and his body. Mamma, with more goodwill than she would have shown a few minutes earlier, put half a sovereign in the flower vase which stood waiting. She then laid her hand lightly on his proffered arm, and thus escorted we made our return journey through the garden, which was now crowded.

Although to us he was a stranger, he appeared to be well-known; a good many people greeted him, some with ill-concealed surprise. This was explained when a handsome man, younger, but no longer very young, halted and said, "My dear Charles. What has dragged you from Abhurst?"

"A matter of business—which as you see has turned into pleasure. May I present Lord Alyson? Madame d'Aubigny, Mademoiselle d'Aubigny. I should add that Lord Alyson is my neighbour in Kent and a villainously bad one, too! I swear that every time an Abhurst pheasant sees a gun it takes flight to the Fernhurst wilderness where it dies of old age."

"When a man is married," Lord Alyson said with a shrug. "Poor Maude would die without her quacks and witch doctors." Lord Bowdegrave then inquired about Lady Alyson's health and was told that she was trying some new treatment, connected with magnetism. "I'm afraid I can't keep up with her medical foibles," Lord Alyson said rather callously.

"Please commend me to her, warmly," said Lord Bowdegrave, and we moved on.

He spent freely, buying only the best on offer, the finest of the lace-edged handkerchiefs, the most elaborately carved bone snuffbox, the biggest bottle of perfume, two exquisitely painted fans. As he received each package he placed it in my discarded hat, after asking me if I minded it being used as a basket. But when we came again to the most shaded part of the verandah, where the homemade confectionery was displayed, and he bought the largest box of fondants, there was no room in the hat, so apologising for making me carry anything, but saying it was not really heavy, he placed the beribboned box in my hands. Just at that moment I saw Madame la Marquise appear at the door to the studio. She halted, stared at us not only with surprise but with a look of horror, turned and went back.

By this time I had learned some of the facts of life and they included a knowledge of mistresses, kept women. It occurred to me that a man of Lord Bowdegrave's age, apparently well-to-do, whose nearest female relative was aged ninety, might well be one who went in for mistresses. I remembered that his approach to Mamma and me had been unconventional. A man with serious intentions would have been more likely to have sought out amongst the many people here with whom he was acquainted, someone who knew us, or knew someone who knew whom we were, and obtained an introduction in a more orthodox fashion.

I began to think seriously; which was to be preferred, a job as a governess, all hard work and respectability, or a life of ease and shame? And what about Emma Hamilton? Then I saw the absurdity of asking that question on the grounds of a single afternoon's acquaintanceship. Inwardly I laughed at myself.

Of Mamma's social expertise there could be no question. By the hat stall there was nobody to add the explanatory words to the bare introduction, but by the time we were in the back room where tea was being served, she had managed, in the most natural way in the world, to present Lord Bowdegrave with all the facts. And in case de Savigny and Quiberon were not enough, she brought in our English connections. "I feel so very sorry for all these people," she said. "When I was obliged to flee from France I was singularly fortunate. I was able to go to my cousin, Lady Rosaleen Franklin, in Suffolk." That placed us. Lady Franklin might have been the wife of a knight or baronet; Lady *Rosaleen* Franklin meant more. "Unfortunately she died some years ago and since then I have learned what it means to be an exile, living in poverty. However, Madame la Marquise de Lactratelle has been a very staunch friend."

Early as it was for hope, poor Mamma, on whom failure had had such a souring effect, was already in a softer, more benign mood. When we came face to face to Marie Latour and she said, "Honey child, what a beautiful hat. Did you buy it here?" and I said, "Yes, at the very end of the garden. Under the beech tree. And there was one with cherry-coloured ribbons that might have been made for you," Mamma said amiably, "That is so." And then, "Annabelle, that was sweet of you!"

We found seats, and with Lord Bowdegrave sitting between us we drank tea and ate biscuits so small and so thin that it was difficult to take two bites at one. Then we listened to the harp, played by a very young man, lately a pupil at the school established by the French Jesuits at Stonyhurst.

As Mamma had so early discovered, I was not musical, but I found the harp, gently played, more agreeable than any music I had ever known; though sad; though recalling somehow all that was lost, an innocent childhood at Nethergate, dreams of that beautiful room, even the faint and yet compulsive memory of the moment when I looked with love upon a rugged face and head of sandy hair, all haloed in the sleet.

Lord Bowdegrave said, "You enjoy music, mademoiselle?" I came out of my trance and said, "I enjoyed this."

"Then I wonder," he said, switching his rather wistful look from me to Mamma, "whether you would do me the favour of accompanying me to the opera tomorrow evening? I have a box, seldom used because I am not fond of London, but I like to think that it is there should I ever need it."

Mamma said, "That is immensely kind of you. Gluck, is it not? Marie Antoinette's favourite composer."

"Splendid," he said. "Then I will make a further suggestion. An early dinner at my house. If that is agreeable to you I will send my carriage . . ." Mamma told him where we lodged. "Meanwhile . . ." He stood up and went away, forcing a path through the milling crowd, nothing wistful or sad about him now, the arrogant nose in charge, towards the studio. In the opening the young harpist still stood, smiling and bowing, acknowledging some belated applause, hoping for a sponsor. Everybody was on the move, duty done, pleasure beckoning. Mamma and I were left there for a moment or two; she now holding the box of bon-bons, I clutching the hatful of purchases. Then the very old man, François, hobbled in and said, "Madame d'Aubigny? If you would please to come this way." We went into the studio, its walls almost denuded. There stood Lord Bowdegrave, Madame la Marquise, and a gaunt, untidy woman with wild eyes.

Madame said, "Madame de Goncourt, Madame d'Aubigny, Mademoiselle Annabelle d'Aubigny. We have had a most successful afternoon! Of thirty pictures, twenty-four sold. But, alas, no commission for a portrait until Lord Bowdegrave suggested that Annabelle should be painted." I had never before seen her otherwise than absolutely sure of herself, completely in control of the situation. Now she was not sure, she was not in control. She was indeed torn between the desire to see Madame de Goncourt given a commission that would earn her twenty-five guineas and whatever it was that she held against Lord Bowdegrave.

However, in this now almost bare whitewashed room we none of us really mattered. Madame de Goncourt took charge.

"Take off that hat," she said to me. And if Madame la Marquise had once looked at me as though I were something for sale, Madame de Goncourt looked at me as though I were something she had bought and was now absolutely disgusted with.

"I do not," she said, having looked at me from all angles, "paint pretty little misses in white muslin."

Forgetting perhaps that Mamma was French by birth, that I had a knowledge of the language, that even Lord Bowdegrave might not be completely ignorant of it, Madame la Marquise burst into an angry tirade in that language. *Sottise* —stupidity—was the mildest term. How long, she demanded, did Gabrielle dream that she could live here, secluded in Hampstead, painting silly little pictures which nobody really wanted to buy, which, in fact, had only been sold with immense effort? What about the winter, most surely coming; think how much coal, how much food twenty-five guineas would buy!

It would have been embarrassing except that Madame de Goncourt seemed not to mind. "I did not say I would not paint the girl. I said I would not paint a pretty miss in muslin. Wait."

She went out and whisked in again carrying a blue cloak; somewhat faded, the darker, original colour showed where epaulettes and froggings and the lace on the collar had been removed. She shook it out and flung it over my shoulders. She then ruffled my hair.

"There. So I shall paint her—if I paint her at all."

Lord Bowdegrave said, "Not so fast! I made a suggestion only. Mademoiselle's wishes must be consulted." I looked at Mamma who said, "I have always wished to have a portrait of Annabelle, but have never been able to afford it. I am not sure that I approve of the cloak."

He looked at it, and at me, and said, "I—think—I—do," speaking slowly; speaking also as though that were the last word to be said on the subject."

"I can paint it as it was," Madame de Goncourt said, almost eagerly. "I can remember every detail. It was so beautiful!" She stood back a little and studied me again. "Youth," she said, "gallantry, idealism. All doomed."

It was then briskly arranged that Lord Bowdegrave's carriage should convey me to Hampstead next morning and that I should sit from half-past ten until twelve.

After her tirade Madame la Marquise had fallen silent and she remained silent and thoughtful as we went out to the carriages. I tried to give Lord Bowdegrave the things he had bought, but he said, "Oh no, please keep them. They're all rubbish really but you could give them away perhaps."

Perhaps the word rubbish offended Madame la Marquise; she took leave of him very coolly, and as the carriage bowled downhill to noisy smoky London she seemed indisposed to discuss what Mamma was plainly longing to.

"I understand that Lord Bowdegrave has a house in Kent."

"That is so. And one in Norfolk. And one in Hanover Square."

"He was kind enough to invite us to attend the opera with him."

"Indeed."

After a few more exchanges like that I tried.

"To sell so many pictures, madame, you must have worked very hard."

"I did," she said. Yet she was not offended with us, for as

we neared Argylle Square, she invited us in to share what she called a simple meal.

Indoors she flung herself on to one of the sofas and invited Mamma to take the other. She kicked off her shoes. Her feet and ankles were swollen. "Annabelle, my dear, befriend me. Take these and dispose of them for me. Louise is out today. You will find the proper place for each article if you look through my chests. And then be so kind as to bring me a pair of very old slippers with little velvet bows."

She had bought lavishly, a pair of gloves, yards of lace, handkerchiefs, a fan, cosmetics, and perfumes. What she had said about finding a proper place for everything was true, she even had a drawer devoted entirely to fans. Each drawer when opened emitted a sweet scent. I had been in her bedroom before, but always with other people, prinking before the looking glasses, no time to stop and stare. Now I did. It was not such a pretty room as the blue-and-white bedroom over the very beautiful drawing room at Nethergate, the furniture was heavier, the colours more sombre, but it was impressive.

The slippers took me a long time to find; they were tucked away at the back of the cupboard. With them in my hand I returned to the drawing room where Madame was speaking so earnestly and Mamma listening so intently that I had opened the door and entered the room before they were aware of me. ". . . warning you, most *seriously*," Madame said. "I happen to be very fond of Annabelle and I should *hate* . . . Oh, there you are, my dear. Thank you. And now, if you would ring the bell."

I did so and her old servitor came, unfolded a table between the two sofas and served a delicious cold meal. Now the balance had changed, it was Mamma who was quiet and distrait while Madame talked animatedly about the afternoon's event and how she had absolutely forced people to buy pictures. Lord Bowdegrave's name was not mentioned.

Walking home, a mere few steps, for the streets in which we lodged, opened out of Argylle Square, I said, "Mamma, what does Madame hold against Lord Bowdegrave?"

"Nothing—except that he did not call upon her to make the introductions. Or so I suspect. People who are accustomed to pulling strings do resent it when something happens which they have not manipulated."

Evasive.

My mind still running upon this matter of mistresses—and that idea did link with the few words I had overheard, while Mamma's explanation did not—I said, "Then what was she

201

warning you about, saying she was fond of me and would hate . . . ?"

We were now within the aura of the cook-shop, its hot fat stink and the other which I now knew to be garlic, far more penetrating and lingering than onion, engulfed us.

Mamma said, "Warning—yes, she said that time was short. And had she finished the sentence I am quite sure it would have been to say that she would hate to see you left, in three weeks' time, no better off than when we arrived."

That at least did fit.

Well truly, there seemed no danger of that. Marie Latour had certainly had a whirlwind courtship from Sir Hugo Jepson, but it was nothing to mine. It was enough to turn any girl's head.

The next morning the carriage called for me. Mamma came too, but Madame de Goncourt said she could not possibly work with anyone else in the room, so she sat out on the shady part of the verandah and read a magazine. It was a very hot morning and I found the cloak heavy. The sessions were called "sittings" but I was required to stand bolt upright with my chin held high and my eyes fixed on what Madame de Goncourt called "the far distance." I had always had a disability—shared with Mamma—which prevented me standing quite still on one spot for any length of time. I could walk long distances and dance all night, obliged to stand I soon began to wilt. "Hold the pose," Madame de Goncourt said mercilessly. "Keep your head up." "Don't droop." Presently I reeled and only just saved myself from falling by sitting down, heavily and quickly, on the one chair. With obvious impatience Madame de Goncourt called to François to bring me a glass of cold well water, and allowed me to sit for five much grudged minutes. I then resumed the pose and was about to collapse again when Lord Bowdegrave arrived, dismounting by the door—propped open to admit air—and walked straight in.

Madame de Goncourt was not pleased to see him, and when he said that he had come to see how the work was progressing, growled that she never showed a piece of work unfinished. "And how long it will take I cannot foresee. I had no idea the child was so delicate."

Mamma, who had hurried in at the sound of his voice, said, "Delicate? Annabelle? I fail to understand you. Annabelle has always enjoyed perfect health." She divided her look of disfavour between me and Madame de Goncourt, blaming

202

her for the disparaging remark and me for having been the occasion of it.

"She may be healthy; she cannot stand for an hour without swooning."

"Nonsense. Annabelle has never swooned in her life."

It seemed to me that only Lord Bowdegrave had any thought for me. "You look pale, mademoiselle," he said. He put his hand under my elbow and led me to the chair, lifting away the cloak.

"This is too heavy," he pronounced. "I would suggest that some sturdy girl should be hired to wear it." He glanced around as though expecting a sturdy girl to appear by magic. "Then mademoiselle's head could be painted in a few short, untiring sittings."

Madame de Goncourt looked at him with disgust. "It is *intended* to be heavy, my lord. A burden to be borne, and *resisted*. Such a subterfuge as you suggest would destroy the integrity, the symbolism."

"I know nothing of such matters. What I do know is that Mademoiselle d'Aubigny has had enough for today and I propose to take her away."

Madame de Goncourt was on the very verge of saying: Take her away forever; I could see that in the flash of her wild eye; but she probably remembered that winter would come with its need for fuel and solid food.

"Very well," she said. "But she must wear the cloak. She can sit down every half hour."

He tried to woo her back to good humour. "If, when the picture is complete, madame, it does justice to the subject, I shall have it hung in the Long Gallery at Abhurst. I shall give a party for the picture. A valuable advertisement for you and one that should result in many commissions."

Uncajoled the artist said, "When I paint from my heart it is not of money that I think."

"Naturally not. Now, we will go to the Café Guery and refresh ourselves with ice cream."

When, after this outing, we returned to our dismal rooms it was to find them all aflower with roses, and Madame Laurier's manner had undergone a remarkable change. If we wished to take lunch and did not favour the *coq au vin*, she was prepared to make omelettes. Her attitude was the first little straw that announced a change of wind.

That evening there was dinner in the house in Hanover Square—unbelievably magnificent, a footman in livery behind each chair. Then the opera, where our box seemed to attract a good many curious glances. One person would look, nudge his or her neighbour, whisper, and another head would turn. (I am the granddaughter of the Marquis de Savigny. Who are you?) Mamma's composure came naturally; mine had to be fortified.

From that evening on, through the last week of June and the first two weeks of July—the season virtually ended with Madame la Marquise's annual Ball, given on the 14th— Mamma and I were the objects of Lord Bowdegrave's indefatigable attention. There was a subtle shift of circle; we met, in his house, or in houses to which he took us, or on outings which he arranged, people slightly different from those to whom Madame la Marquise had introduced us, people decidedly less stylish, less Frenchified, less gay, but very solid and very rich and, in the main, like the girls at the Academy, all related to one another in some way or other. With such people, Mamma, with astounding gift of adaptability, laid less emphasis on de Savigny and Quiberon, and more on Lady Rosaleen Franklin. Once we met a couple—a General, lately retired, and his wife, Lady Moira. Rather odd, rather mothy; but at the mention of Lady Rosaleen's name Lady Moira became alert and lively. "She was my best friend. I often think that my happiest days were the holidays I spent with her at dear Barryfergus. And what a tragedy about Alan! A blow from which she never recovered. And how strange . . . Actually I said to Freddie, didn't I? Oh dear, poor darling he is so very deaf! When I saw your daughter I said, 'Freddie, I have never seen exactly that colour of hair except on Alan Franklin.' Poor Alan, so charming!"

Sometimes, in the midst of the whirl, I would stop and think. Charles—we were now all using our given names— certainly had no intention of making me his mistress. Mistresses, actual or potential, are kept well into the background of a man's life. I was all the time on display, almost ostentatiously on display. And it certainly was not one of those passing flirtations that leave a girl with a sullied name. Mamma was always there.

I was not, after the first couple of days, shy with him. He loved Abhurst as I had loved Nethergate and we could always talk about the country. We were both interested in *old* things. As a young man he had made the Grand Tour, which in his case had included visits to Pompeii and Herculaneum. He remembered what he had seen and could talk interestingly about his experiences. He was also a great reader and, thanks to Miss Hamilton, I had read a little more widely than the average schoolgirl. We never lacked things to talk about.

What appealed to me most, however, was his limitless, unfailing kindness to me. It was always what would I like to do, where did I wish to go, whom would I like to invite for dinner, for supper, a picnic. My comfort, my well-being were now of the first importance, as indeed they had been with Mamma until very recently, with this difference, that he had power, money, influence. I never, for instance, had to stand again for Madame de Goncourt. Next time the carriage came to take me to Hampstead, he was in it, with a girl, almost exactly my height and size. "Daisy," he said, "is accustomed to standing. I found her on her father's whelk stall and hired her for an indefinite period. Madame de Goncourt must surely see that I chose the model well and excuse you from further exertions."

I was not in love with him; fond of, yes. Grateful to, yes. Prepared to marry, yes. Prepared? Anxious, rather. Of love, outside books, I knew nothing, except that one pang . . . And even that seemed long ago, put away, no longer real, like Nethergate. This was a flinty world in which, all unwittingly, I had lived buffered by Mamma's devotion all these years; but with my apparent failure even she had changed. I was only too happy to accept the new buffer of Charles's devotion.

My portrait was completed. I suppose we all have delusions about our appearance—even in a looking glass we see our right side to the left and vice versa; but although nobody had ever called me beautiful I was generally regarded as pretty and of prettiness in this picture there was no trace. I did not voice my disappointment, waiting for Mamma and Charles to give their opinion. Mamma said, "I still hold that the cloak was a mistake." Charles said he was delighted with it and congratulated Madame de Goncourt on a most impressive piece of work. He was paying for it, if he were pleased with his twenty-five guineas' worth it was hardly for me to say that had I come upon the picture suddenly I should not have recognised myself. I should merely have thought: Oh, somebody with hair the same colour as mine. So I also congratulated her. Charles then invited her—and her old mother—to join the house-party at Abhurst on the 15th of July. The party in honour of the picture's hanging was to be on the 16th.

Madame la Marquise's Ball had a touch of the macabre about it. It was held as celebration of what was generally held to be the real outbreak of the French Revolution—the storming of the Bastille in 1789. "People have very short memories," Madame said. "It is right that they should be reminded once a year, and the dead remembered."

The dead were remembered by the name of the Ball, *bal à la victime,* and had I heard about such a thing before coming into close contact with the French community I should have imagined that it would be a dismal affair. All those who had lost a relative to the guillotine were to wear black or white, unrelieved by any decoration except a narrow red ribbon tied around the neck at the point where the blade would fall. Perversely enough, this was a most coveted distinction and everybody, even English people, were anxious to claim a relationship, however remote, to someone who had gone to death in La Place de la Guillotine. Madame, with her vast knowledge of pedigrees, submitted all such claims to severe scrutiny and anyone proffering a false one was never invited again.

Madame's hospitality, though generous, was never lavish: in many ways she seemed to be careful not to stress the difference in her circumstances and those of most of her compatriots; but on the occasion of her *bal à la victime* no expense was spared; she hired a ballroom and transformed it into fairyland, differing the theme each year. Last year, she explained, she had employed several artists, all French, Madame de Goncourt one of them, to cover acres of canvas with the device known as *"trompe l'oeil";* this year the theme was The Arbour and the people who benefitted by it were the makers of artificial flowers. The rows of gilt chairs were banished, and all around the vast room there were cubicles made of trellis-work up which living ivy and other climbing plants, planted in pots, had been trained; attached to the living greenery were the most skilful examples of the artificial flowermaker's art; roses, clematis, honeysuckle, convolvulus. The size of the arbours varied, some seated two, some four, a few six. The ballroom itself was brilliantly lighted, hundreds of candles in glittering chandeliers, but since each arbour was roofed, the light within was muted, very romantic. Three weeks earlier Mamma would have been perturbed by the setting, and by the fact that dowagers and chaperones were gathering in another room: but now all was different; Charles was in charge of me and could be trusted to see that I did not dance three times or take supper with the wrong person.

Charles's dancing was exactly what one might expect of a man of his age and solidity and not much in practice; a trifle staid, a trifle old-fashioned. But correct. I danced with him, and then sat out in an arbour for two where a waiter immediately appeared with real champagne. The setting, the whole atmosphere was right. I thought to myself: Now! Now! But nothing was said. In fact, he had never said a word to me that could not have been said in the presence of others, although Mamma had more than once in the last week manoeuvred so that we should be alone.

I then danced with the young man who had got me such a scolding. He said, "I understand that you are to be married. Would you welcome congratulations?"

"I would—had anybody bothered to inform me." He laughed, so did I. And as I did so I saw Charles, standing in the doorway and watching, much as Mamma had watched in the early days, but with a different expression; not critical, sad, rather. In love with me? Aware of his age? As the progress of the dance brought us near him I smiled, moved my hand in a gesture of assurance.

Louis de Vaudreille said in a matter-of-fact way, "In this regard I think the advantage lies with the lady. Husbands should be older and what does a year or two matter? You will not be obliged to pretend you are thirty-five."

"Will you?"

"I rather fear so. The lady who seems disposed to share her fortune with me is a widow with three children, the eldest about my age."

Despite all that commonsense might say, there was something a little chilling about this talk. It was inconsistent of me to think "mercenary," but I did think it and was then ashamed, for who was I to use the term, even in thought, about anybody else? I said, "I hope you will be happy."

"Oh, I shall indeed. To have again a horse. Of all that I have missed in England, I have missed horses most. Was it not a King of England who exclaimed, 'My kingdom for a horse!' In my case, my name, my title for a horse."

After that I went back to Charles and we looked for an arbour. They were all occupied, but when we reached one furnished for four and now occupied by three people, there was Lord Alyson, another man, and a young woman, none of them wearing the distinctive ribbon.

"Come in, come in," Lord Alyson exclaimed, jumping up. "My dears, sit closer. Make way so that Mademoiselle d'Aubigny, wearing her ribbon, may shed her effulgence upon us. May I introduce my cousins from the country: Sir Stephen and Lady Fennel; Mademoiselle d'Aubigny; my neighbour, Lord Bowdegrave."

I was skilled now in that all-embracing glance—Lord Alyson very slightly drunk; Sir Stephen Fennel solemn and polite, almost a younger edition of Charles; Lady Fennel absolutely beautiful. Pink and white complexion and hair the colour of honey and the substance of spun silk.

She said, "D'Aubigny? Annabelle?" Then I knew why in this beautiful place that honey-coloured halo of hair had taken me back and make me think of the Academy, of Mrs. Twysdale, of Jassy Woodroffe and of Dilys Helmar.

I said, "Dilys?" a bit tentatively, and Lady Fennel began immediately to act in that exaggerated manner which qualifies for the term "animation." So far as I could remember she had never addressed a word to me at school; now one would have thought that we had been inseparable, had been torn apart by cruel circumstance, and were miraculously restored to each other. "To think," she cried, "that we were at school together! Annabelle must sit by me. Darling, how wonderful to see you again! And looking so lovely. Would you not all agree that Annabelle is lovely?" Two pairs of eyes—those of her husband, those of Lord Alyson—regarded me briefly, not without approval but of a mild kind, and then slid back to her. It was, as Mamma had said of Marie Latour, that she was beautiful, I was simply pretty; she eclipsed me. In other circumstances I should have done well to avoid her. Tonight, however, I had my admirer whose gaze, if it lacked the rather fevered look which both the other men turned upon her, was at least steadfast.

I could now recall that at the Academy she had been pretty, rather delicate-looking, and afflicted with a slight stammer, a favourite of Mrs. Twysdale's, and a great friend of Jassy Woodroffe. She was greatly changed. A cousin up from the country she might be but she knew every fashionable trick and was now capable of entertaining—with just the right touch of flirtatiousness—three men simultaneously. "Do you remember how I was *expelled?* Stephen, darling, don't look so shocked! Had I not been I should probably have been lingering to this day in that house of correction. Then you would never have met me and would now be married to some absolutely worthy girl who hated London as much as you do. Happy ever after."

"Stephen," Lord Alyson said, "is a model landlord. Like you, Charles. He can just bring himself to London when the hay is safely in and the harvest three weeks away. Dear Dilys, were I a model landlord, I might be able to afford to hire you a London house for the full season."

"What a very cousinly gesture that would be," Dilys said, with animation.

Sir Stephen said in a flat prosaic voice, "You'd be robbing yourself, Chris."

"So I should. Your contribution to our household expenses is the one bit of ready money that I do not have to sit up and beg for. Unfortunately I anticipated it and backed three wooden horses in a row. Maude was *not* pleased."

In the pretty little cubicle, over the wine, there was a faint sense of chat having taken the wrong turning. Dilys was aware of it and leaning forward said, "Lord Bowdegrave, did you ever encounter a real live witch?"

"No, Lady Fennel. I believe that a neighbour of mine, a Mr. Foxley, was once obliged to look into a case of suspected witchcraft, which he dismissed summarily."

"Annabelle and I were at school with one," Dilys said.

Sir Stephen said, "Darling, must we go into all that again?"

"But it is true! The one story I have that nobody can cap. Annabelle and I were at school with a girl called Jassy Woodroffe. When I was expelled, so was she, and I took her home with me. Can you imagine what she did? She bewitched my father. He married her and then she poisoned him and cheated me out of Mortiboys. Had that come to me, as it should have done, I could have afforded a London house for a full season. I would have backed some wooden horses, too."

There was one of those uncomfortable little silences. I said, "What happened to Jassy?"

"She was hanged. Did you not know? Oh, of course not. Anything of real interest was carefully cut out of the papers before pupils were allowed to peruse them. And no gossip allowed." She flashed her bright eyes, her embracing smile, "I'd be willing to guarantee that you don't even know what happened to Mrs. Twysdale. No? Well, she retired to a little cottage where, as you can imagine, everything was kept in perfect order, meals served punctually, everything done to timetable. Just the thing to appeal to the military mind. It did! She married a retired Brigadier. Now, tell me all your news, darling."

Tell me, in fact, how it has happened that you, the daughter of an impoverished French teacher, should be here at the most fashionable Ball of the year. And in such company.

"There is nothing much to tell," I said.

"I hear that you have had your portrait painted. I should most dearly love to see it." She knew who owned the portrait, too, for the last words were not addressed to me. As she spoke them she threw Charles a most cajoling glance.

"The picture has been despatched to Abhurst," Charles said. "I propose to make a little ceremony of its hanging. If you and Sir Stephen would care to be present, I should be delighted."

"Oh, how very kind! Stephen, darling, is it not a most kind, most delectable invitation?"

"Am I included?" Lord Alyson asked.

Charles said, "Of course. Will you stay at Fernhurst?"

Lord Alyson said, "No, only the caretaker's room will be habitable. You give me a bed."

Sir Stephen made no remark at all.

In the supper room I encountered Marie Latour, who drew me a little aside and told me that my good fortune must be attributed to a spell which she had worked on my behalf. "You were the only female who ever spoke kindly to me when I was so miserable," she said. "So I worked one of my old mammy's very best on your behalf. It is infallible. The ring is already as good as on your finger." She was wearing hers, an enormous emerald, as green as her eyes.

After supper, in the retiring room, I encountered Dilys again. She was making some tiny repair to her complexion and, unobserved as she thought, she wore a different look. An expression of almost tragic discontent, a yearning sadness, strangely at odds with all that animation. I could not help thinking that amongst the things which had changed her from a pretty, stammering schoolgirl into a lively, sophisticated woman, there had been something sad.

The look vanished as soon as she became aware of me.

"I think your Charles is quite delightful," she said. "Tell me, as an old friend, *has* he spoken?"

I could only say, "No." I said it unwillingly.

"An understanding perhaps."

"Perhaps."

"The odds are on you, anyway, darling. And what a feather in your cap! One of the richest men in England. And known to be fickle."

My heart gave a jerk. Fickle, changeable, uncertain of purpose.

"Fickle? In what way?"

"Well, I have this from Maude, Chris's wife. She is a great gossip and when Chris came home from somewhere and mentioned seeing Charles with you—though he did not catch your name, he said—Maude said that on two occasions to her certain knowledge he'd been attentive enough to raise hopes and then backed away. Not that that is likely to happen to you, darling. Absolutely devoted, I should say. No eyes for me at all."

No eyes, in fact, for anyone else. And no word for me.

Going into our bedroom at the hour of three o'clock in the morning I attacked, where I had so often been attacked.

"Mamma, did you know that Charles has, on at least two occasions, behaved to girls much as he has been behaving to me, and that nothing came of it?"

She did not immediately answer. Then she said, "Yes. Madame la Marquise warned me on that afternoon. She wished, she said, to guard me against overoptimism. But this very evening she admitted that she was wrong; that neither of the former *affaires* had gone so far. Neither of the young women concerned had, for example, ever been asked to stay at Abhurst nor been made the focus of such attention as this hanging of your portrait involves."

I looked about the room; our valises yawned on the floor, awaiting only the clothes we were wearing now and the things needed for the last night. Our rent had been paid up to the next morning and our notice given; for one thing at least was certain: if, after the Abhurst visit, we needed hired accommodation we must find it in some cheaper place.

I said, "I am worried. I hate the idea of being made a laughingstock. Had we never met Charles we could simply have disappeared, quite unnoticed. As it is we might be made to look very silly. Are you aware that wagers are being made? Think how detestable!"

"We must take the risk," Mamma said. "Three, no, four times in my life I have taken enormous risks. We must take this, because there is no alternative."

"There is, there is. We are both able-bodied." That was true now. Despite all our devious shifts to feed ourselves when we were not being entertained during our first weeks in London, latterly we had been entertained so much that Mamma had become quite plump. "We could earn a living," I said.

"Darling, I have earned my living—and yours, in varied ways. None agreeable. Believe me, only those ignorant of it—as you are—would speak of it so lightly. I am reasonably certain that Charles intends to combine the hanging of your portrait with the announcement of your engagement. He is fanatically devoted to Abhurst. The Attbury family have been there for seven hundred years. Charles is a traditionalist and sentimental. I think he will speak, he *must* speak at Abhurst."

"And if he should not?" I asked brutally.

"Then God alone knows what will happen to us," Mamma said.

Narrative by Sir Stephen Fennel, Bart.

(1816)

The last thing in the world that I wished to do was to go to Abhurst as the guest of a man I hardly knew, in order to look at the portrait of a dumb, simpering little girl who had happened to be at school with Dilys.

I said so, reminding Dilys that we had already prolonged our stay in London by two days so that she could attend that ghastly Ball. However she argued and coaxed and finally said that if getting home to Suffolk was so important to me, I could go and she would make the visit alone. Alone meant with Chris. Highly likely!

If she hasn't already cuckolded me, she surely will one day, but not with my cousin Chris and not with my connivance.

One should never expose one's weak flank, so when she said she was willing to go to Abhurst alone I did not immediately react by saying that I would go too. I waited until she said, with a pathetic look, "After all this has been a most disappointing visit."

That was true. In order to be entertained one must entertain—or be entertaining, and this year our stay with Chris and with Maude his wife had been singularly devoid of what I call proper invitations. Maude had advanced her imaginary ill-health from a hobby to a full-time occupation and as a result had been dropped by all but the faithful few. I had done my best to make up to Dilys by patronising everything into which one could buy one's way; we'd been to the opera, to several plays, two or three concerts and several affairs arranged for charitable purposes, but it was not the same. It would be wrong to say that for me the visit was disappointing, I always came to London unwillingly and went home gladly; for me life did not centre about Carleton Terrace, Devonshire House, or Hanover Square. I belonged to Ockley and Ockley belonged to me. But women are different; pretty women, like Dilys, like to be seen, in new dresses, with new hair-styles. So ever since our marriage I had made an annual concession to Dilys's desire to be gay and fashionable.

Our stay in London did Chris a bit of good too.

Chris Fennel, Lord Alyson, is the head of our family. He inherited the title, and what remained of the estate, but very little money. In fact that branch of the family never fully recovered from the effect of the Civil War when they had been on the Royalist side, fighting for the King, melting down their silver, pledging their jewels. When Cromwell and his Ironsides won, every inch of the Alyson estates had been sequestrated, and when Charles II took the throne not all had been restored. So that branch of the family, though grander, had always been poorer than mine. My seventeenth-century ancestor had hedged his bets carefully; he'd been a Parliament man until the wind showed signs of shifting. When it did, he quickly arranged a marriage between some obscure cousin of his and an equally obscure cousin of General Monk who played such an important part in the Restoration.

Turncoat?

Woud I not do the same? To save Ockley?

This is all irrelevant; an attempt to explain why poor old Chris was so glad to give Dilys and me house room every July.

Chris was ten years older than I and even as a boy he had been wild. At Eton the name Fennel was remembered and stood for feats I could never attain. Did not even wish to emulate.

Chris married well—or so everybody thought. Maude's grandfather had been in trade—the Bristol trade to be precise, a slave dealer; but he had made a respectable marriage and his daughter had done even better, marrying into an old Shropshire family. She died in childbed and Maude became not only the old Bristol merchant's heir but the apple of his eye. Maude was very rich indeed and the old grandfather had taken steps to see that she remained so; Chris couldn't touch a penny. Maude paid all expenses, made him a derisory small allowance and occasionally settled his debts. This was not the basis of a happy marriage. Chris was glad enough to get his hands on the twenty guineas a week I paid him during our annual stay in his house.

There had never been anything between Chris and Dilys until this year. Then it happened. I always know; there is the underlying note in the bantering talk, the communication between eyes. It may sound whimsical but I swear that when she is on the hunt Dilys even *smells* differently. What gets into people I cannot understand, and certainly am in no position to judge, for I fell in love with Dilys the first time I saw her when I was an adult, and I married her in circumstances that would have made any other man have second thoughts. Marriage to her has been, and probably will always be, a very uneasy business but I love her still, I always shall. At her very worst she is rather like a naughty child, and although she does not realise it, poor darling, she has never bamboozled me for a minute. That suggestion that I should go home to Suffolk while she went to Abhurst was typical of her idea of subterfuge.

Dilys, Chris, and I drove down together, using my carriage. Dilys and I took all our baggage since we intended to leave early on the morning after the party and make straight for Suffolk without going back into the west side of London. It was a beautiful day and I was glad to be in the country again—the only town I really like is Cambridge. I was interested to see hop fields, and oast houses.

My own home, Ockley Manor, is a sizeable house, and I am familiar with others, much larger, in the neighbourhood; Merravy and Mortiboys, Cleveley and Nethergate; but Abhurst is as big as any three of them put together—a great Tudor house flanked by additions in every known style. The effect might have been displeasing, but homogeneity was achieved by the atmosphere of loving care expended and no expense spared. The gardens were equally varied, and equally well-kept; even the part known as the Wild Garden had had its wildness well tamed.

Our fellow guests included Madame de Goncourt who had

215

painted the portrait, a gruff, unfeminine-looking woman, a living contradiction to the belief that a Frenchwoman can look stylish in anything. With her was her ancient mother who spoke no English—but she understood it; nobody listens as avidly as she did to conversations that mean nothing. There was a dashing-looking woman of about thirty, called Mrs. Grant-Thomas, accompanied by a Colonel Rowlands—I scented intrigue there: the Duke and Duchess of Romney, two other married couples, several unattached men, none very young.

Bowdegrave, on his own ground, showed to better advantage than he had done at the Ball, a kindly and generous host against a background of great magnificence. I noticed his footmen particularly; they were as well-matched as carriage horses, all exactly of a height, all blue-eyed and pink-cheeked. There were so many of them that if time had rolled backwards to the Middle Ages and some warrior king like Edward I or Henry V had called Lord Bowdegrave to report in battle array, bringing all his followers, just the indoor staff would have made a sizeable contingent. At Ockley we employ a butler and a footman, and that is about average.

At dinner I found myself seated between Madame de Goncourt's mother and Madame d'Aubigny, the mother of the little girl whose portrait was the *raison d'être* of this visit. Like many another little English boy I had once had a French governess who had ruled my life until I was old enough to ride out and take lessons with an old clergyman who prepared boys for public school. He had never heard of French, Latin was his language; as it was the language of Eton and Cambridge. Conditions on the continent, by the time I was of an age to travel, were such as to make staying at home advisable, and so now, seated by an old lady who had no English, I was obliged to fall back on a few trite phrases, ill remembered and worse spoken. She soon tired of me and, with the ungraciousness that her daughter had inherited, turned her back, leaving me with Madame d'Aubigny.

She at least was amiable, though, I thought, slightly odd. We did not lack subject for talk. She knew Suffolk well; she had, she said, kept house for her cousin by marriage, old Jack Franklin of Nethergate, and she remembered my father, one of his visitors, and a number of other people, like old Sir Edward Follesmark. She knew Baildon, she had taught Dilys, we could have had a rather better than average dinner table talk if she could have given it her full attention. But that she simply could not do. Every now and then her eyes would take on a blank, inward centred look and she'd say, "Really?" "Indeed." "Oh, yes." Very much like a parrot one of my grandmothers had once owned. These lapses of hers spoiled what could have been an enjoyable dinner for me, Dilys and Chris well within view.

After the meal there was music for those who liked it, cards for those who wished to play and Bowdegrave himself came up to me and said, "Sir Stephen, your cousin tells me that you are fond of books. Would you care to look at my library? I have a few quite interesting things . . ."

I thought: Yes, immure me in the library! I thanked him and said that perhaps some other time, and went and took Dilys by the elbow. "Darling, what would you like to do now?" Knowing the answer. Frustrated, she chose to play cards. And in that she was wise, for about the only thing her father, Nick Helmar, had bequeathed her was a card sense, a thing as indefinable as a nose for weather. Nick Helmar had, it was said, won Mortiboys in a card game . . . Let's not think about all that resulted from that.

"Very well then," I said, "we will play."

So that was the evening safely negotiated.

The next morning brought its own little problem.

Bowdegrave, that careful host, had planned an outing and a picnic lunch to a nearby place called Beauclaire. It had once been a castle, much damaged during the Wars of the Roses in the fifteenth century, later turned into a Benedictine monastery and then dissolved by Henry VIII. All the land appertaining to it had been given away or sold but the building had stood and rotted until a reviving interest in antiquities had encouraged a few sharp businessmen to invest a little money in it and to make it a show place, open to the public. Amongst its attractions was a maze, far older and more intricate than the one at Hampton Court.

Dilys said, "It all sounds most interesting, darling. But Chris seems to feel that being so near he should just go and look at Fernhurst. I've never seen it. How would it be . . ."

My dear, my darling, my dim-witted girl. How would it be if I went to see this interesting ruin at Beauclaire and you went to Fernhurst with Chris? Transparent as a pane of glass!

"Come to think of it," I said, "I have never seen Fernhurst. My grandfather was born there. It would interest me more than Beauclaire."

God knows this kind of countermove gives me little pleasure.

So instead of visiting a reclaimed ruin, I saw one in the

making. Fernhurst was a sorry sight. Houses shelter people and in return people, merely by living in houses, keep them alive. If anything more depressing were the farms and cottages of the estate, all in poor repair and in the hands of shiftless, hopeless tenants. Good husbandry begins at the top and permeates downwards. I am myself a conscientious landlord and I have always thought that affairs in France would not have gone the way they did had there been more like me and fewer like Chris.

On the whole a rather dismal day, but I had won another round.

The picture about which such a fuss was being made had presumably been hung in the Long Gallery which was part of the original house at Abhurst. The door to it had been locked and nobody had had so much as a glimpse of the picture. Bowdegrave's neighbours had been invited to present themselves at half-past six, so that the picture could be seen while the light was still good. We all assembled in the hall, which was like the nave of a church except that it was full of flowers. The dining room used on the previous evening was far too small to accommodate such a crowd, but to one side of the hall I could see an enormous room set out with tables of varying size and lined along the walls with sideboards laden with examples of culinary art.

Dilys and I were fortunate in being with Chris who knew all the locals, most of whom were men of my own stamp. I feel at home with a man who says that if only this good weather continues it should be a bumper harvest.

We all went up the stairs and into the Long Gallery, a very magnificent place, with a coffered ceiling and some fine plastering. The whole of the wall on the left, the west, was windowed; like Hardwicke Hall, of which it was said, "more glass than wall." Bowdegrave had chosen his moment well; at this time on a mid-July evening, the whole place was light but not in direct sunlight, which would have cast shadows.

The walls without windows were hung with pictures rather oddly mixed. I do not pretend to be an expert, but I know a Rembrandt, a Titian, a Rubens when I see one. Here, interspersed with the work of the masters, were family portraits, some good, some bad, and a few so dark with age that the subject was indiscernible.

The picture we had come to see was hung on the wall facing the door. It was covered with one of those Oriental shawls and it had obviously been hung in the place of another, larger picture; one could see the marks on the wall. I thought: So this is to be an unveiling, how pompous! I also had another thought. If I really liked the picture and considered it to be a faithful portrayal of that rather dim little girl, I'd offer Madame de Goncourt a commission to paint Dilys, an infinitely more promising subject. But she would have to come to Ockley to do it. I wasn't going to have Dilys running to and fro.

The footmen, all so much alike, wove about skilfully, proffering champagne. I looked about and saw Dilys with an elderly little grey man who was giving her some instruction about the pictures. He talked and pointed, she nodded and smiled, exuding charm as effortlessly as honeysuckle in a hedge exudes scent. Chris, looking extremely miserable, was being lectured by a powerful woman in plum-coloured silk. So far, so good. Just behind me Madame de Goncourt said gruffly, "And the peaches alone must have cost ten times as much as the portrait." True enough.

We stood about, glasses in hand, nobody quite certain what to do. Madame de Goncourt, Madame d'Aubigny, and her daughter moved towards the front of the crowd and stood waiting. Presently somewhere a clock boomed. Seven o'clock. The two identical brothers in livery who had been standing under the picture faltered for a second and then, obedient to orders, pulled the cords. The shawl which had looked whole but was actually in two halves fell away. There was a ripple of noise. *Oohs* and *Ahs*. The moment, so carefully planned—as someone within my hearing said, "Nobody can set a scene like Charles"—lacked the directing presence. Quite obviously the liveried brothers had been told to unveil the picture at seven o'clock and they had obeyed. But Bowdegrave, who should have been there, was not. So there was a hiatus.

I had time to think: Madame de Goncourt will get no commission from me! Annabelle d'Aubigny was quite a pretty little creature, apart from the cropped hair, a fashion which Dilys would have liked to try but I forbade it. I said that if she dared to have her hair cut in that outlandish fashion, I'd shave half her head while she was asleep. Of Annabelle's prettiness Madame de Goncourt had caught no glimmer. There it was, a portrait of a boy, young, defiant, suffering, sagging under and yet bearing up against the weight of a military coat laden down with enough gold buttons and braid to keep the Mint busy for a week. It was quite preposterous, especially when you looked from the portrait to the girl it pretended to portray—young and meek in white muslin with a little bunch of moss roses on her breast.

My immediate neighbour said, "It does not flatter her, does it?" I was saved from making any comment by, of all people, Mrs. Grant-Thomas, who took charge. In her loud, ringing voice she said, "Madame de Goncourt, we all congratulate you on a wonderful portrait. And you, Mademoiselle d'Aubigny, on having been immortalised by it. Shall we drink to them?"

Everybody drank, happy to be given some direction. People said, "I must have a closer look," and pushed forward, or they said, "Some pictures are better viewed from a distance," and moved backward.

Somebody said in my ear, "Sir Stephen! Please, sir, would you come?" I turned and saw one of the liveried brothers, who had lost the family likeness in that his look of well-being had vanished. His pink cheeks were the colour of suet, his blue eyes almost black.

"What is it?" I asked. Some hitch, some contretemps. I think I must have a *reliable* look. Even in London where I am a virtual stranger, people have stopped me and asked me the way.

"If you would please come. Please, sir." I followed him out. I said again, "What is it?" He said, "An accident." "Your master?" He said, "Yes," and hurried along, leading me through what seemed miles of corridor, down some stairs, more corridor and finally into a room which I judged to be as far as possible from the Long Gallery. And there, on the floor, near a glass-fronted gun case, lay Charles Attbury, Marquess of Bowdegrave, with his brains blown out.

Perhaps the man had done rightly in choosing me; I was shocked, but not shattered, for I was looking upon one I knew but slightly. However, it was a nasty sight; and it was obviously suicide. From the position of the gun and the nature of his injuries I deduced that he had placed the barrel in his mouth.

The man who had fetched me began to cry with a hard, choking sound. I stood for a moment thinking hard, recalling little bits and pieces of gossip I had heard, things which had not interested me much at the time. On two former occasions, apparently, he had got himself almost to the point of proposing and then withdrawn. This time I guessed that he felt he had gone too far; only one way out was left to him. And suddenly I thought of that poor little girl standing there under her picture. People would say: He *shot* himself rather than marry her! She would know and remember all her life.

Not, I thought, if I could help it.

"Who else knows about this?" I asked.

The man gulped. "Nobody, sir. His lordship welcomed his guests, and then said he would come in here and have a quiet moment—and a drink—before the ceremony. Brandy, sir . . ." The decanter and a glass stood on the table. "He asked me to tell him when everybody was assembled. So I came and I . . ."

Poor wretch, I thought. Perhaps up to the very last moment he had intended all to go as planned. A little time in this quiet place to compose himself, a stiff brandy to lend him Dutch courage.

I said, "Now, you are a sensible fellow. You saw at once that it was an accident. Try to pull yourself together. Is there, upstairs among the guests, a local gentleman who is a Justice of the Peace?"

"There's Mr. Foxley, sir."

I could not send him, in his present state, on a discreet errand. So I asked, "Where is the Steward?"

"Overlooking . . . In the dining room, sir."

"Go to him, as quietly as possible, and tell him to fetch Mr. Foxley here. With the least possible fuss. You understand."

"He was the best master . . . The kindest man in the world."

I thought: Up to a point, no doubt; but a bad man, a cruel man could hardly have had inflicted more hurt upon that poor little girl—and her mother.

Left to myself I got busy. Gun rooms, small like mine, large like this, are much of a muchness. Five minutes sufficed. When Mr. Foxley arrived there was the wadding, the pull-through, the oil, concrete evidence that Bowdegrave had been cleaning his gun.

Mr. Foxley was the man who had made the remark about the weather and the harvest. He was an old friend and near neighbour of the dead man and he was deeply shocked, but sensible, too. When he could speak coherently, he said, "Rabbits. He was getting ready for rabbits. The oats are almost fit to cut. And he never liked to see them chased and clubbed. He always shot . . . shot as many as he could."

The Steward, an incredibly impressive figure, was crying like a baby and repeating what the other servant had said about the kindest, best master in the world. Mr. Foxley, having mastered his own emotion, had little sympathy.

"Be quiet, man, and let me think. This is going to cause great commotion. Upwards of a hundred people. And some have come from a considerable distance. He . . . he would not have wished them to go away unfed. I think the news should be broken gradually. Martingale, use your handkerchief and pull yourself together. Go upstairs and say that supper is served. Tell Sir Godfrey Talbot that your master has had a slight accident. You"—he turned to the servant who had fetched me—"can you ride? Good. Get a horse and go for Doctor Doughty."

When we were alone he said:

"Sir, I never catch names at first go . . ."

"Fennel. Sir Stephen Fennel."

"Permit me to say, Sir Stephen, that you have handled things most discreetly." He gave the cleaning apparatus an eloquent look. "Poor Charles, what an end!" He cleared his throat fiercely. "And what a shock, what a dreadful disappointment for that poor child. Everyone was confident that the engagement would be announced this evening . . . I think she and her mother should be told. Told the truth. What do you think?"

"They'll have to know."

"Exactly. Everybody will have to know. But I think tomorrow. In their own homes. Women do so tend to scream and faint and encourage one another to drama. Are you married?"

"Yes."

"Is your wife here? Would she be capable of breaking the news?"

"She is rather young." And God knew she'd had enough horror in her life. "I think I know somebody who would do it competently."

"I'll leave that to you, then."

Supper was getting under way in a great buzz of talk; a slight accident; what kind of accident? The Steward, having obeyed Mr. Foxley, had withdrawn, not trusting his self-control. The band of liveried brothers, bustling about with wine and quite outlandish food could only say in answer to questions, "I do not know, sir." "I have no information, madam."

I looked first for Dilys and found her, just as I expected, with Chris, at a corner table, under a potted palm, drinking and exchanging long, lecherous looks.

Mrs. Grant-Thomas was not flirting with her cavalier; they were far past that stage. She was at a bigger table, with Madame de Goncourt and her mother, of course, Annabelle d'Aubigny and Madame d'Aubigny and two people I did not know.

Madame de Goncourt was saying, "So it would happen. He

was to make a speech. Advertisement for me. Then this happens. A slight accident. What accident? Tomorrow the picture will be forgotten, the accident remembered. This would happen to me. If, when I die, I can afford a tombstone, on it I would ask to be carved, "This would happen to me!"

"A universal complaint," Mrs. Grant-Thomas said.

I leaned over the back of her chair, noting, as one does in critical moments some absolutely irrelevant thing. In this case it was the lobster. A lobster reconstructed, the perfectly modelled shell made of pastry, paper thin and coloured red, the eyes a single bead of caviare. I was not, at that moment, partial to anything red, nor to white, creamed chicken in aspic. Averting my eyes, I said, "Mrs. Grant-Thomas, may I have a word with you?" She stood up at once. I backed away a little and in a muted voice told her the truth. "Will you break it to them, please," I said, looking towards the girl, never to be Lady Bowdegrave, and her mother whose hopes and ambitions were to be shattered, temporarily, at least.

"My God!" Mrs. Grant-Thomas said. "Why me? Haven't I done enough for one evening?"

She was not the kind of woman I cared for at all, but I had thought of her. Competent, levelheaded.

"Somebody must do it," I said.

"Very well. I'll get them into the library. Send one of those blue-eyed boys with some brandy. I shall need it if they don't. How could it have happened? Charlie wouldn't have an accident *with a gun.*"

"He did."

"I see." She gave me a look, infinitely old, infinitely knowing, and then she turned back to the table, whispered to the girl and her mother and took them away .

One of the blue-eyed boys approached me—I had already despatched one with brandy to the library. "Sir Stephen, please, sir, Mr. Foxley would like you to go to the gun room."

My mind echoed Mrs. Grant-Thomas's words precisely: Haven't I done enough for one evening?

It seemed not. First on the scene, I must go through it all again, first for the benefit of two other men, plainly people of substance and influence, and then for Doctor Doughty, so much in awe of us all that had we said that the injuries were due to a simple fall I doubt if he would have made any protest.

There was the question of relatives to be informed. Only the old aunt, somewhere in Cumberland, ninety years old and so senile that she did not know her own name.

"The last of a long line, a very long line," Mr. Foxley said, sadly. "The first Bowdegrave came over with William the Conqueror."

"Pity Ralph died so young," one of the other men said. "Poor old Charlie once told me that he never wanted the title, or the place. He would have liked to live in Italy."

"Humph; humph," Mr. Foxley said. "Still, he was an excellent landlord—and a good neighbour."

It then occurred to me that Dilys and Chris had been a long time alone, unsupervised. I hurried back to the older part of the house.

The last of the evening visitors were about to leave, the supper room deserted. By this time, in some mysterious way, news of what was to be regarded as the truth had spread; there was an air of gloom, shot through with a kind of half-shamefaced excitement that follows any untoward event. Of Dilys and Chris there was no sign. In this vast house, as large as a small village, and with everyone's attention focussed elsewhere . . . So many beds . . .

This would happen to me!

Actually Dilys was in our room—the last place to which my futile search led me. She was slumped in a chair. Ordinarily the pale rose and cream of her complexion blend imperceptibly, now her face was very pale except for patches of deep rose high on her cheekbones. Her hair was tumbling, her eyes looked wide and dark. Confirmation of my worst fears.

Before I could say anything, she said, "Where *have* you been? I've been looking for you everywhere."

Attack the best defence?

"It's an ideal house for playing hide-and-seek. I've been looking for you. Where have you been?"

"Having a horrible time. First Annabelle and her mother; then with Chris."

"Oh, what happened?"

"Diana—Mrs. Grant-Thomas—sent for me to help her. To comfort Annabelle. Madame d'Aubigny just fell down in a swoon. We thought she was dead too, and Annabelle was quite distraught. Diana needed somebody. We couldn't bring Madame d'Aubigny round. It must have been an hour. Brandy, smelling salts, burnt feathers. Nothing worked. And when she did recover she was very odd. She didn't seem to know where she was, or what had happened."

"Just as well. My poor sweet, how horrible for you."

As always when I have suspected her I was overcome by remorse and self-hatred. By this time I was on the arm of the chair with my arms around her and she was leaning against me. "I sent somebody to find you and you couldn't be found."

"I'm sorry," I said. "I'm terribly sorry." I told her where I had been, ending: "And then I had to make a statement, in writing. But that will at least excuse me from the inquest. So we can go home tomorrow."

"I've never been so glad to go home in all my life. This has been a hateful visit. And Chris has behaved abominably."

"Oh?"

"They've absolutely nowhere to go—Annabelle and her mother. And no money at all. In fact, Annabelle, upset as she was when we thought her mother was dead, said maybe it was just as well. They seem to have only one real friend in the world—that Marquise woman who gave the Ball, and she's gone to Bath. So then"—Dilys straightened up a bit—"I said I'd see what I could do—arrange something. And I thought of Chris with Fernhurst empty. It's horrid, I know, but it would be somewhere to live until . . . And we could give them a little money, couldn't we? So I found Chris and asked him. Do you know what he said? Impossible. Maude would not approve. Maude!"

She began to laugh, on that high note and in the jerky way that presages hysteria.

I pulled her close again and said, "Darling, don't! You've had a hateful evening and borne up well. Don't give way now. Look, slip off your frock and I'll brush your hair for you." She liked having her hair brushed, and I liked to do it. It was like living silk, crisping and crackling under one's hand and shining in the light.

"Pretending," she said, "to be so devoted to me and then the first, tiny, tiny thing I ask as a favour, taking refuge behind Maude. She'd never even have known they were there."

We're all mixtures. It is only in stories or plays that one person is assigned a part, with a few basic characteristics, the brave consistently brave and so on. Real people are rather like the Comtesse de Guéry's ice cream, layer upon layer. Under the fluff, the flirtatiousness and all the rest of it, Dilys has a genuinely kind streak. Quite a lot of the mess she had made of her life just before she married me was due to the fact that she had taken that vile creature, Jassy Woodroffe, home with her because she had nowhere else to go. Annabelle d'Aubigny seemed, on the face of it, unlikely to turn out to be another Jassy, but then, like everybody else she was a mixture, otherwise she would not have been human.

Dilys was kind; she was also at this moment—and I knew it—suffering from wounded vanity. Chris had failed her. She had imagined that she had him wound around her little finger. And I had no doubt that he felt that she had failed him; there had been an almost perfect opportunity for a bit of illicit love-making and all that had come of it was the asking of a favour, summarily refused in a moment of irritation.

I am as much a mixture as anyone else; capable of thinking: My darling, you will eventually learn from experience; capable of thinking that her concern for an old school friend did her credit, and capable of refraining from making the offer to take Annabelle and her mother back to Ockley with us. If I did that and for any reason the thing turned out badly, Dilys would turn to me—her kind streak in abeyance—and say that it had been my idea.

Presently we were ready for bed. Then Dilys said, "Darling, I really do feel sorry for Annabelle. Would you consider having them to stay with us for just a short time? Until they can come to some arrangement?"

"Most willingly, if that would please you, darling."

Like a piece of accurate construing, that took me straight to the top of the form.

Dilys had said that when Madame d'Aubigny regained consciousness she had seemed very odd. What none of us had visualised was that she would remain so. Not mad; the down-right mad are, I think, easier to deal with; you can lock them away, hire a keeper, put them in a straitjacket. What happened to her was that the vague, not-quite-attentive attitude which had been intermittent during that first dinner at Abhurst was now more or less her permanent state. She was lost, but she never raved, never said anything which, in the right context, would have sounded absurd; she always behaved impeccably, even with dignity. She'd just lost all sense of time and place.

We had our first experience of this on the way home. From Kent to Suffolk is too long a journey to be made in one day without pressing the horses unduly; even on our shorter journeys Dilys and I had always taken two days to get to London and had found a comfortable hostelry in which to lodge. To reach it we took a right-hand turn, off the main road, and as we did so Madame d'Aubigny, who had been so far very quiet, suddenly became alert. "Not Ozary!" she said sharply. "I can assure you, from personal experience, it is a detestable place. And Joanna would absolutely gloat!"

Oddly enough this byroad into which we had turned would, if followed far enough, have taken us to a place called Ozary, which I knew by name, marshland to which some people sent cattle for the summer.

At that stage I did not think that there was anything much wrong with Madame d'Aubigny; she had had an immense shock, a terrible disappointment and was still a little stunned; so I leaned forward and told her that we had no intention of going to Ozary which would be miles out of our way; we were bound for Stoke St. Cross. She said, "Yes. I have heard of it. I have never been there." And that was that. She settled back into passivity and later seemed to enjoy her supper.

It was Dilys—so like a flower, so like a butterfly—who one day, soon after we were home, asked about the possibility of Lord Bowdegrave having left Annabelle any money.

"Most unlikely," I said. "He gave every indication of being about to marry her, in which case she would have been provided for."

"Chris thought otherwise. Did you know that? He was so certain that there would be no marriage that he bet against it. All I was thinking, darling, was that if by any chance he had left Annabelle a fortune, nobody at Abhurst would know where she was. We left so early."

I thought it just worthwhile to write to Mr. Foxley. My own opinion was that Bowdegrave had committed suicide on the spur of the moment; unable to face the engagement which everyone expected. On the other hand, why, out of all the rooms in that great house, choose the distant gun room in which to have five minutes' privacy and a bracing drink? And if he had planned to do what he did, it was possible that he had spared a thought as to what would happen to Annabelle. He could have scribbled a will. But it seemed that he had not. His will, Mr. Foxley informed me, had been made ten years earlier; he had been magnificently generous to tenants and servants; he had made provision for any horse or dog that he owned at the time of his death: the bulk of his money went to the ninety-year-old aunt who did not even know her own name. So much for kindness!

So far as I was concerned Annabelle was welcome to stay with us for as long as she liked. We had room enough, and when two-thirds of what you eat is produced on your own estate or in your own garden, two extra mouths do not matter. Dilys's kind good will towards Annabelle showed no sign of running out and I was, privately, trying to make up in hospitality for my misjudgement of the girl whom I had considered dumb and missish. In fact she was the very reverse. What had happened at Abhurst had been a shock to her, but she bore it well and quickly recovered. It is a test of personality to be dependent, to show gratitude without becoming subservient. She had that quality, with sound good sense and the kind of wit as indescribable as a flash of lightning. Dilys, like most women, is deficient in a sense of humour. Sometimes I'd look at Annabelle and think what a fool—or how deeply perverse—Bowdegrave must have been.

Maybe Dilys and I had made a mistake in treating Annabelle and Madame d'Aubigny as guests. It seemed natural at the time and when Madame was in her abstracted state of mind nobody cared. But she had other moods and usually when we had company. Once she stood up while several of us were taking coffee in the drawing room and said, apropos of nothing, "Now I will play the piano for you and perhaps Mrs. Shafto will decide whether she wishes her sausage-fingered daughter to take lessons or not." That kind of remark leaves people at a loss, even more at a loss because she then sat down and played beautifully.

The common, ordinary people have a limited vocabulary, but perhaps for that very reason every word must carry its weight and they speak of those who are not quite normal as "cracked." The amount of crackedness varied; a bit cracked, right cracked, wholly cracked. (In Suffolk wholly rhymes with woolly.) It began to be evident that Madame d'Aubigny qualified for the third category, and the term was apt.

We asked Doctor Stamper to see her. She recognised him, but was under the delusion that he had called to see old Jack Franklin of Nethergate, of whose condition she gave quite a lucid description. Informed that on this occasion she was herself the patient she looked confused and was silent for a moment. Then she said, "I am quite well. Overworked, of course by being obliged to hurry so much from place to place, but if overwork could have damaged me I should have died long ago. However, that is not to be spoken about."

Doctor Stamper reported that she was in good physical condition and that with time and kind patient treatment her mental state would improve.

We were all kind and patient and Annabelle was superb. There were small, trying scenes, however.

We had four people to dinner and Madame d'Aubigny remarked, "People who have never been hungry cannot really appreciate food. There are times when, as I serve delicious meals, my mouth literally waters. I flatter myself, however, on my self-control. Whatever is left over that is edible, Annabelle must have. After all, she is growing."

Annabelle said, with composure, "Mamma's mind wanders a little at times. Mamma, eat your dinner."

Two of our guests that evening had not been in the district long and had not visited Ockley before. Did they go away with dark suspicions that Madame d'Aubigny was not well fed except when we had company; that ordinarily she served meals? It was not unknown for people to exploit a poor relative.

On another occasion, having been blessedly silent, except for an abstracted reply or two, she suddenly leaned forward and regarded a brooch that Dilys was wearing.

"Quite pretty," she said, "but virtually worthless. Unless, which is not unlikely, Madame la Marquise's lackey was a cheat."

After a few more of such embarrassments Annabelle suggested that when we had guests she and Mamma should eat from a tray in their room; which, as Dilys said, was very dull for Annabelle. Annabelle, though she never showed a sign of impatience or self-pity, was indeed having a trying time, always on watch. Dilys, who was fond of riding, wished Annabelle to learn, and they went out once together, Annabelle mounted on a steady old mare, safe as a rocking horse. They left Mamma in the garden with a book—she was an avid reader; but while they were away she went into the kitchen and made a disturbance about a duck and that upset our Mrs. Horner, the kingpin of our household.

Dilys was no housekeeper; she had never even lived in a well-ordered household; her father had invariably chosen his female staff for other reasons than their domestic virtues, with favouritism, quarrels, sudden sackings as a result. The only servant who stayed at Mortiboys was a man named Moult, of the familiar insolent-servile type, and Dilys once told me that she was scared to give him an order. She was, in fact, a little scared of all servants. We were extremely fortunate in having Mrs. Horner, and Mrs. Horner knew it; she had only to manifest the slightest displeasure or express a wish for something, and Dilys and I both jumped to attention.

On this particular day she was displeased indeed. "I can't do with Madame Dauby in the kitchen. If she wanted a duck I should've been told. Nobody said nothing to me about duck. It was cutlets. So she comes into the kitchen and says duck for luncheon and Long Jim can dress it; and I say to her, there ain't no Long Jim round here so far as I know. So then she says she can dress a duck, if she has to, and she'll cook it in the brick oven. Which, as you know, ain't been used for twenty years, judging by the cobwebs. The long and short of it is, I can't do with Madame Dauby in my kitchen."

That would have stopped the rides immediately; with Annabelle saying she was extremely sorry, and that in future she would stay at home and see that Mamma did not invade the kitchen again. But I had my own, secret, shameful reason for wishing Annabelle to ride. It was now just on harvest time . . . So I made a suggestion: Dilys and Annabelle should ride, and Mamma should be taken for a drive in the carriage.

It would have been a great deal easier if she'd looked crazy or behaved crazily. In fact her manner was calm and rather grand. When the outing was proposed she said, "How agreeable! Actually I prefer the gig."

"Then the gig it shall be," I said, and gave the requisite orders: a nice long, roundabout drive.

"But, sir, she wanted to go to Baildon. And she set everybody by the ears. I couldn't stop her, could I? Sir, I didn't realise, till she started ordering a lot of stuff for Nethergate . . ."

I thought: Oh dear!

I knew this latest John Franklin of Nethergate, but not well. Nobody knew him well. Somebody once said that for the English foreigners began at Dover; in Suffolk foreigners begin at the end of the lane, the verge of the village green, at the farm gateway, the cottage door. Old Jack Franklin, my father's friend, had died, leaving, in perfect order, all he owned to his son John, who was married to one of those helter-skelter Rossiter girls. They'd had no children and they'd died together in a small-pox epidemic. (Enviable in a way; I hoped that Dilys and I might die together like that, but not before we had a child.) John and Harriet had no child, so Nethergate—an entailed estate—passed to another John Franklin who already had an estate in Wiltshire. He was quite a good fellow, curiously like the Suffolk Franklins in appearance, but he was a foreigner and the fact that he was so often in Wiltshire, so seldom in Suffolk had prevented his full adoption into our circle. Mothers of marriageable daughters had done their best and then fallen back on rather romantic tales, quite baseless so far as I could see. One was that he had been in love with a girl who had died, very young. The other was that he was in love with a married woman, in Wiltshire, and was simply waiting for her husband —much older—to die. I thought myself, having met him a few times, that the truth was that he was a typical Franklin; a late marrier. Old Jack Franklin, I'd heard my father say, was a full thirty when he went to London and fell in love. John was hard on thirty when he married Harriet Rossiter, and Alan must have been in his late twenties when he died, unmarried, in the West Indies.

Now, hearing that Madame d'Aubigny had ordered a lot of stuff for Nethergate, I felt it my duty to ride over and explain, pay for the stuff, whatever it was, and bring it away.

He wasn't there. He was in Wiltshire. A pleasant woman, not unlike our Mrs. Horner when she was in a good temper, said she couldn't think what had happened when a ham, so much beef, so many sausages, a whole Stilton cheese and various other things had arrived. "We'd got all that we needed, sir. For a minute I had the notion that the master might be coming back unexpected. But then I thought: He'd have let us know. Very considerate, he is."

I explained as best I could.

But that evening Dilys said to me, "This can't go on, can it? She defeats us at every turn and it is awful for Annabelle."

"Awful for everybody," I said.

"Poor Stephen . . . I know you only did it to oblige me. And it was a mistake . . . I don't suppose you have noticed but Annabelle is beginning to look like that horrible portrait. She has come to realise that Mamma is never going to be any better."

"I'm afraid that that is so."

"Then we must think of something," Dilys said. "But not now. Have you forgotten? Colonel Frisby is coming to dinner, and to play whist."

I had, in fact, forgotten. To cover my lapse I said:

"That takes four."

"As though I didn't know," Dilys said. "It is all arranged. Annabelle is going to put Mamma to bed early and then sneak out to join us."

We were in the middle of the game, relatively new and therefore engrossing, when Mrs. Horner came storming in.

"That Madame Dauby," she said, rather like Savonarola denouncing the pleasure-loving Florentines, "is there in my kitchen again! In her nightgown. Wanting to make a beef-steak pudding. And pudding beef I ain't got, it being a dish for cold weather."

Annabelle laid down her cards neatly and rose. "I am sorry Dilys, Stephen, Colonel Frisby . . ." I could see what Dilys meant about her beginning to look like her portrait, a bearing up under strain. I could hear her beginning to apologise to Mrs. Horner as they went through the door.

At bedtime that night Dilys said, "I have been thinking. When people hardly know where they are it can hardly matter *where* they are. Couldn't we board her out? With some reliable widow or single woman who wouldn't mind when she went into the kitchen. Near enough so that Annabelle could visit her every day. Try to think of somebody, darling."

I did try, for the situation was beginning to get on my nerves. I was very sorry for the poor woman, but the truth is that pity is an expendable thing and not proof against constant irritation. However, in order to house and look after a slightly demented woman for hire the reliable widow or spinster must be poor and very few such had houses of their own. Most poor widows and unmarried women went to live with sons or brothers, or they took living-in jobs. I raked through my mind; within easy reach of our house there were two widows, one spinster, all quite comfortably off.

Harvest was now in full swing and I began my annual round to the fields. It is indisputable fact that even the most independent-minded tenant, like Rowe at Top Farm, welcomes a visit and a show of interest. And the men and women, for once altogether in one place, welcome it even more. I usually timed my visits for eleven o'clock in the morning or four in the afternoon. Work halted then for refreshments. Any capable farmer's wife provided home-brewed beer and a comestible—midway between bread and cake, a kind of bun, spiced, studded with currants more or less according to her generosity. Even when they were eaten at eleven o'clock in the morning they were known as "fourses cakes." (I was, as Dilys had said, wanting me to take myself off to Beauclaire, interested in anything old and that did not apply only to buildings or books. Old customs, old words or sayings had a fascination for me. The real fourses cake was much bigger than a hot cross bun, but marked in the same way. And there was a ritual about breaking it. "North, South, East, West; May our harvest be the best." There was a variant, less often used, "Matthew, Mark, Luke and John, and one for the Pope.")

Standing there in Rowe's field, drinking the home-brew and eating the fourses cake—both very good—I looked about and again thought of France and how unlikely it was that if the revolutionary ideas ever reached England, as some pessimists prophesied, anybody in this field would want to chop off my head. They knew me, I knew them. Then I realised that a familiar figure was missing and I said to Rowe, "Hullo! What happened to that little bent-over fellow?"

"Pratt? He died," Rowe said. "Week before last. I miss him a bit. It's some time since he could handle a scythe, but he was good at binding and stooking."

"What ailed him?"

"Nothing you could name, sir. He had a sister. Some bit older they say. She dropped dead, doing a bit of sewing according to Sam Lockey. He brought word and Tom just went to bed and died."

"Leaving a widow?"

"Yes, and a daughter. Both dead lazy. They could be out here now, binding and stooking, or gleaning at the least. But Tom spoilt them rotten. I said so to him, more than once. And I think the old sister helped, so far as she could. Otherwise I can't see how he managed. Children and grandchildren all over the place. Well, they'll soon learn which way the wind blows. I've given them notice and I've hired a young lively chap who'll want the cottage."

"When?" I asked.

"End of the week, sir."

It was then that I thought of what we always called the House in the Woods—that is when we spoke or thought of it, which was seldom. My grandfather had built it for his head gamekeeper, a great favourite of his. It was built of dressed flint, two rooms and a kitchen on the ground floor, three bedrooms upstairs. It had its own well, a garden, and an orchard. A very desirable house, in which for some obscure reason, nobody seemed very anxious to live. Too lonely, had always been the complaint. Having been built for a gamekeeper, it was naturally in the wood, remote from the village, with our house the only one within easy reach, and time after time men I had installed there, either free or at a peppercorn rent, had moved out again; women didn't like it, too far from the village, and no neighbours. The last time it had been occupied was at least two years earlier; the man, another gamekeeper, had liked it well enough, but when he married

233

his wife refused to consider it and he had gone to live with her parents in a crowded, far inferior dwelling. I now thought: Just the place for the Pratt women and Mamma; three together could not complain of being lonely, and Annabelle could easily make a visit every day. The house might need a bit done to it, so I said, "Look, Rowe, do me a favour, will you. Let the Pratts stay on for a week or ten days. I might be able to arrange something for them."

If *my* father had said that to *his* father, the answer would have been instant, eager compliance, but Rowe hesitated. Within his rights of course, since the labourers' cottages in one of which the Pratts lived went with the farm and were his to do what he liked with, so long as he kept them in reasonable repair.

"I don't want to seem disobliging, sir," he said, "but the new man's coming on Saturday and I did promise him."

"Is he married?"

"Aiming to, as soon as he's got the cottage."

"Then board him at The Maybush and knock the charge off your rent in September."

I thought to myself: And whether you wanted to be disobliging or not, my good man, you have been. Your own rent will go up in September! I have always been rational about rent; not like old Jack Franklin who would never make an increase, nor like John who during his brief rule raised rents all around, a flat 5 percent which came hard on his smaller, less prosperous tenants. I try to use judgement.

I couldn't say anything to the Pratt women until I had spoken to Annabelle, but I could take a look at them. I could go along and say that I was sorry about Pratt. Their cottage, with the others that went with Top Farm, stood in a little bit of a lane which I did not ordinarily use; the sight of the hovels was a shock to me and strengthened my sense of grievance against Rowe. They were not in reasonable repair, in fact they were damned near derelict. Mr. Uppity Rowe would hear about them next time we met.

Pratt's widow and his daughter were almost indistinguishable from each other, slovenly, bovine creatures, living in a sluttish muddle. But they looked amiable enough. Madame d'Aubigny, who had rather a masterful way with underlings, would soon smarten them up; and she certainly would not get on their nerves, for they had none. Even their recent bereavement seemed to affect them only in so far as they wondered what was going to happen to them now: "With Martha and

Tom both going together, sir," the widow said. "Martha didn't earn like she used to, but she always helped."

I made no promises; I simply said, "We must see what can be done," put five shillings on the cluttered table and left, turning my horse's head in the direction that would bring me to the House in the Woods. Unoccupied as it was, and had been, it was a palace compared with Rowe's cottages. The garden was a wilderness, blackberry brambles had encroached, and there were several self-seeded little beeches and hazels. A few marigolds had survived and the climbing rose over the little porch bore some late flowers. In the orchard apples were reddening, and there was a plum tree laden with fruit, bigger than any our trees had produced that year.

Outside the house was in good repair; I wondered about the interior. The front door was barred or locked, but the back one opened easily. The place had been left empty and very clean. It struck cold, but that was natural enough, a house with flint walls and a good thick thatch is cool on the hottest day. I went all over the house, finding nothing which a lick of whitewash or paint could not put right. Downstairs again I paused in the larger of the two rooms, calculating with my eye whether it would take a piano. I decided that it would. Freshly painted, properly furnished, this would, I decided, make Madame d'Aubigny a very comfortable home.

And then something happened. I am not a fanciful man but as I stood there I suddenly knew what a succession of women had, in their inarticulate way, called "loneliness," and had fled from. Depression, melancholia would have been apter words. Abruptly, everything that was right with me and with my life vanished. All that was wrong rushed in. Why it should happen just then and just there I could not possibly explain; nor could I account for this reduction of myself, from a singularly fortunate young man, of rather more than adequate means, married to the sweetest, most lovable girl in the world—and on the verge of shuffling out of the embarrassing situation in which he had placed himself, in order to please her—to a kind of buffoon, married for four years but with no child, obliged to exercise constant vigilance, bound to be defeated in the end . . . Every vile thought, avoided, evaded, now revived; together with the cold, severe enough to make my teeth chatter. Peripheral thoughts, too, about being not physically impressive, medium height, medium size, sallow, brown eyed, while every man who had caused me uneasiness, from Barney Hatton to my cousin Chris, had been a great lout, blond . . .

Outside I recovered myself; the sultry late August evening warmth comforted my bones and I thought that if only Annabelle would agree, I had virtually solved the problem in a way that would please Dilys. I knew, from the way in which, when we were alone, she used the word "Mamma," in that mocking, derisory way, that she would be glad to have Madame d'Aubigny out of the house. I was a little late, so I washed and changed hastily.

The four of us were alone for dinner and when Dilys asked where I had been and what I had been doing, I told her the Pratt story. Nothing about my plans for them; Annabelle must first be consulted; but when I said, "He left a widow and a daughter, middle-aged," I did shoot a look at Dilys—she'd told me to find a widow and I had done so.

Madame d'Aubigny said in that conversational voice which characterised even her least relevant remarks, "Pratt has been dead for years. Ask Joanna if you disbelieve me."

"Another Pratt perhaps," I said, sticking to the rule we all observed—to return sensible answers when possible. "The ones I heard about today were called"—I grappled in my memory—"Tom and Martha."

"Pratt's name was . . ." She broke off. "They were a detestable family. The damage they did was incalculable." For the first time she showed signs of aggressiveness towards me. (Mrs. Horner had said that Madame Dauby could be nasty at times.) "Really, I rather wonder at you, Sir Stephen, raising such a subject at the dinner table. Well-bred people, if they can find nothing pleasant to say, remain silent."

She remained in an ill-humour for the rest of the evening, grumbling because we had not complied with her request to have the piano tuned. "I have mentioned it repeatedly," she said. "Unless it is done this week, I shall refuse to come again." It was not only the piano that she criticised, she was very peevish towards Annabelle. "If you held yourself properly your figure would show to greater advantage. Look at Dilys, quite the most stupid girl it has ever been my misfortune to deal with, but at least she does not slouch!"

Poor Annabelle coaxed her away as soon as possible, and when we were alone Dilys said to me, "She gets worse, doesn't she?"

"Yes. But I see an end to it. Did you catch what I meant when I mentioned the Pratt women?"

"Well, no. I wondered what was so important about them."

I told her about their being without support, the likelihood of their being homeless in a matter of days, and of my visit to the House in the Woods. "If only Annabelle will agree," I ended.

"She must," Dilys said. "She must see that we cannot go on like this. I know I suggested it, darling, but how could I foresee?"

"Nobody could have done. I'm wondering how best to set about it. Talk to Annabelle first, or get the place trimmed up a bit, show it to her and then tell her what we propose?"

"Talk to Annabelle first. It would be a waste to get the house in order before we know. Actually I think Annabelle will insist on going too. Ever since we mentioned this plan, I've been watching. Annabelle is very much attached, in a funny kind of way. Rather as though she were the mother and Mamma a half-witted child for whom she felt responsible. And the word Pratt is no help. You saw how it upset Mamma this evening. I've never really understood. Joanna I do know about; I once asked Annabelle and she said she once had a doll called Aunt Joanna."

I said, "I hope Annabelle will not be awkward. She's such company for you."

She was company. She was also a little fence against what a man in my situation must be perpetually on his guard against. A kind of duenna. That was why I had been anxious for her to ride. I was so often obliged to give a bit of attention to other matters. The Home Farm—I had a splendid foreman, but nothing can be left safely in hirelings' hands. I was a Justice of the Peace—that was why, in an emergency, I had sent for Mr. Foxley at Abhurst. JP's still have power. They also have duties. In addition I had been elected to be one of six men—known as Guildhall Feoffees in Baildon. Four hundred years ago an old wool merchant, dying rich and childless, had left all his money to what was known as the Feoffment Trust. It supported a school for boys and paid for their apprenticeship; it kept up twelve almshouses and provided at Christmas and on Maunday Thursday gifts for the aged poor not accommodated in the almshouses.

These things made demands on my time. I hate to admit it, but each of the four times—prior to Chris—when my suspicion had been aroused, the root cause had been Dilys's riding, or making a visit alone while I was busy with my private or public duties.

I am not a fool. I knew from that atrocious, fantastic story which Dilys had blurted out to me on the morning when I asked her to marry me, that she had once used Jassy Woodroffe as a kind of stalking horse. I knew that women do connive. One of Dilys's near-affairs had been actively fostered by Sylvia Martin, one of the Rossiter girls, sister to the Harriet whom John Franklin had married and completely well. But Annabelle d'Aubigny was different; she had good sense. I felt that she could be trusted. I did not want her immured in the House in the Woods; I wanted her at Ockley.

Dilys said, "She is company. Good company. But frankly I am prepared to dispense with her company if it means getting Mamma out of the house. I have almost run out of patience. Stephen, honestly, I sometimes feel a desire to *slap* her. I've come to the point where I do wonder whether a smart slap across the face and somebody saying, 'Oh, talk sense or shut up,' might not be the best cure."

I said, "Darling, if that were so, Bedlam and every other lunatic asylum would be empty. The lunatics are regularly beaten. People go to watch. But the lunatics remain lunatics."

"Madame d'Aubigny is not a lunatic," Dilys said with conviction. "She had a great shock. I was sorry for her—and for Annabelle. But the fact is she's never made the slightest effort. We could all behave like that if we said the first thing that came into our heads, and did whatever we thought of. And I think Annabelle encourages her."

It was unlike Dilys to speak with such acerbity.

"In that case it would be as well if they were separated for a bit. Who shall make the suggestion to Annabelle; you or I?"

"It would come better from you." Dilys was always willing to leave anything even slightly unpleasant to somebody else.

I made the scheme sound as attractive as I could. I slightly exaggerated the charm of the House in the Woods, spoke of the Pratt women as servants, not keepers, and by saying that Annabelle could walk or ride to make a visit every day, showed as clearly as I could that she was expected to stay in our house. I ended, "Now, how do you feel about it?"

"As I always have," she said, looking extraordinarily like that portrait. "Mamma and I cannot live on charity forever. When we first came I thought: A week. Then a fortnight. I now feel that she will never be better."

She then surprised me by telling me that she had made attempts—during her hopeful period—to obtain posts for herself and her mother. "I wrote to Miss Hamilton, at the Academy, and she was very helpful. The trouble is, Stephen, the question of accommodation; teachers of French and Music are not supposed to live in. Cooks are and even now I feel—I still feel—that Mamma is capable of cooking, if I were there

238

to watch . . . I have asked myself whether her visits to the kitchen which naturally upset Mrs. Horner so much aren't something in Mamma trying to get out. She always led a very busy life, you know. Even in London, there was the social round, and trying to make a penny do the work of two; walking about to find some cheap place where we could eat, or have our clothes washed. This is the first time that I can remember when she has been unoccupied."

"In the House in the Woods she could busy herself, Annabelle. It would be *her* kitchen, *her* house; *her* garden. She might take to gardening."

"You would still be supporting us, Stephen. You and Dilys have been infinitely kind. Mamma and I can never be sufficiently grateful. But apart from all else, I must stay with Mamma. I certainly could not hand her over to people called Pratt; the very name upsets her as you saw last evening. I cannot explain, it would take too long and anyway, it should be forgotten. Martha Pratt, in herself a harmless old woman, once forced Mamma to take an action that damaged her—or so she believes . . ." Suddenly her face altered. "Pratt had a job. She obtained it when she was old and far from able-bodied. Mending and helping about generally at the Grammar School. Stephen, surely Mamma and I, between us, could fill her place."

I said, "Annabelle, don't be ridiculous. Just because I made a simple suggestion, something that I thought would benefit your mother, you go shooting off and talking about being a scullery maid."

I didn't like the idea that somebody under my roof, under my protection as it were, had been writing about for jobs.

She said, "You don't realise. Just for once I would like something *real* in my life. There was Nethergate and school and London, and Abhurst. None of them real! Nor is this. All part of a dream! Mamma and I both need to come back to earth. If she did mending, and cooking sometimes, and I did whatever else there was to do, we should at least be earning our bread."

I have in me a weak streak of which I am well aware. I feel sorry for people. In the moments when I really face myself I know that all my strong emotions, whatever form they grow into later, have been rooted in pity; and I am actually not certain that where people are concerned pity is not often adulterated by a kind of . . . well, condescension. You pity those who are poorer, less happy, less able than yourself; you help, you protect and advise very often out of a feeling of superiority. Once this superiority is challenged, your help, protection, advice refused, irritation is apt to result. My pity for Madame d'Aubigny had worn thin under the friction of nervous strain and now my pity for Annabelle lessened in the face of her refusal to accept what I considered my good arrangement.

I said, "Very well. You must act as you think best. The gig is at your disposal."

And, of course, the Grammar School had no wish to employ two people, one of them a bit off her head, in place of one. Nor did anyone else. As the disappointments mounted my pity revived. To have an independent nature and be forced to accept charity—however well disguised—must be very hard; to wish for work and be repeatedly refused must undermine one's self-esteem. Thinking in this way I deliberately refrained from mentioning the House in the Woods for a while. I did act about it though.

The short time of grace which Rowe had granted ran out. I moved the Pratt women, who really seemed as trusting and supine as animals, into the house where the garden had been scythed and some painting and whitewashing done. I explained that the kitchen, one room downstairs and one bedroom were to be theirs, but that I might have need for the rest of the space, and that whoever came to occupy the best rooms must be regarded as the mistress of the house. I was not more specific than that. They said, "Yes, sir," "Thank you, sir," and "That'll suit us, sir." I lent a light cart to transport their belongings, such as they were. Anybody visiting their hovel would have doubted that they had anything that could be called furniture and I was prepared, as soon as they had made their move, to provide what they needed as well as what, eventually, Annabelle and Madame d'Aubigny would need. However, people are amazing; the Pratts took with them a full load of what one could only call rubbish, and by the end of the first day when I looked in to make arrangements for their sustenance, the freshly whitewashed kitchen was every bit as cluttered and dirty-looking as their hovel had been. I looked round and thought: If Mamma needs occupation to settle her mind, she will surely find it here.

They stayed exactly four days. They moved in on Tuesday and when one of my men went along on Saturday to take the supplies I had promised, meat, groceries, and so forth, they had gone, taking presumably what they could carry, leaving behind a lot of their rubbish.

I was very much incensed and my temper was not improved when Dilys told me Madame d'Aubigny had somehow escaped supervision and gone into the linen room and found things not to her liking there. As a result Mrs. Horner had half-given notice. "Either her or me."

"That settles it then," I said to Dilys. "They'll just have to go to the House in the Woods and manage as best they can."

"I had another idea. Annabelle should be married."

"I entirely agree. She'd make any man an excellent wife. If Bowdegrave hadn't been"—I checked myself just in time—"fooling about with that gun, she would be married and we should have been spared all this. But who's likely to marry her now, with Mamma in tow?"

"Somebody with a big house, so that she wasn't always underfoot. Somebody who *needs* his kitchen looked after and his sheets rearranged. As well as a nice little wife."

"Humph!" I said. "And how many men like that do we know? I mean suitable for a girl like Annabelle?" I was feeling protective again. I know the silly little creature had been prepared to take a menial job, but marriage was a bit different. Some farmhouses are large and it might not have been too difficult to find a farmer whose kitchen and sheets could do with some attention, but how could one visualise Annabelle spending the rest of her life with somebody who sat down to table in his shirt sleeves and had never read a book in his life? I *like* farmers, get on well with them, but . . .

"I know one," Dilys said.

"Then you have the advantage of me, darling. Who is it?"

"Barney," she said. "Barney Hatton."

It was like an explosion in the quiet room. An explosion inside my head. And after the noise the silence. And after the silence my voice, not my ordinary voice, but mine, saying:

"Didn't we agree never to mention his name? Never to think of him again. How can you sit there and suggest . . ."

We had agreed not to mention him. My boyhood friend; in every respect except one—he was poor—the person I should have wished to be, big, handsome, clever—when he chose to be—and endowed with that indefinable thing known as personality. He was poor, because his father was a frantic gambler and unlucky, a ruinous combination. Years before Barney and I ever met, his father had lost Mortiboys, a really beautiful house, to Dilys's father, Nick Helmar, in a card game. Barney had always dreamed of getting it back; and in the end he did. But in a terrible way. The whole thing, even after more than four years, a little more than four years, sounded unbelievable. It surpassed anything Mrs. Radcliffe ever wrote in her Gothic romantic novels. Barney was living, when Dilys and Jassy Woodroffe were expelled from school, in a very humble farmhouse, the one piece of his mother's property that his father had not been able to gamble away. Both the girls—and in my mind I have never evaded this truth—were in love with him, but when they appeared at Mortiboys it looked as though Dilys would inherit the place while Jassy Woodroffe was a pauper. So he chose Dilys, seduced her and then did his best to persuade her to marry him and would have succeeded had she been able to face life as a farm-wife. She drove herself almost crazy with indecision. That was the situation when I asked her to marry me; she was too far gone then, poor girl, to have any reserve about the affair, and I actually married her not knowing whether she was pregnant or not.

Then Nick Helmar died—poisoned, as it was proved—and we learned that he and Jassy Woodroffe had been secretly married. By law a person is not supposed to benefit from committing a crime and in the ordinary way Mortiboys would have passed to Dilys, not to the witch. But she'd been very cunning. Mortiboys had been made over to her when she married; so it was hers to do what she liked with; and she willed it to Barney Hatton!

Out of all this sordid muddle one good thing had emerged—I am married to Dilys, and in all but one small area, happily married. That small area is concerned with her recurring interest in other men. This and the fact that we have as yet no child might be taken to indicate my inadequacy as a lover. Entirely untrue. If I'd had her first we should have been a completely happy couple. The truth is that she was so young, so innocent, that Barney left his mark. She did not love him or she'd have married him and shared a life of poverty and hard work; his attraction for her was purely sexual but strong enough to result in echoes whenever she meets a great blond lout who shows an interest in her. My cousin Chris is a great blond lout, but he had never, until this year, shown himself to be interested in that particular way.

I accept this situation, perhaps because I understand it so completely; I can even see what, for Dilys, would be an ideal life, me, with my devotion, my title, my possessions almost all the time, and a bed session with Barney Hatton, or failing him somebody of the same stamp, about once a week . . . Except when she is obviously straining at the leash this does not perturb me very much. I chose her, she belongs to me,

242

I have her to look at; she is amiable, easily pleased: and easily outwitted as a rule. I have bad moments, of course . . .

I had one now. It was impossible not to ask myself: Has this been a long-planned thing? Had she seen in Annabelle another stalking horse, or at the very least an excuse for resuming contact with the man whom we had both agreed should be wiped out, forgotten, even his name never mentioned. It had been mentioned now; the first small breach in the rampart.

She said, "Darling I couldn't not use his name, could I? And I made the suggestion because I have been thinking and thinking. And I think that if it could be arranged, it would be perfect. Bar . . . all right, I'll just say *he*. He has that huge house and nobody to look after it but that old, old, deaf Meggie. Surely he'd welcome Mamma's ministrations. And he must need a wife. He's so crazy about Mortiboys, did you realise that every minute he can spare from Green Farm he gives to restoring the place, working like a bricklayer, like a carpenter, like a glazier?"

"So I have heard." It was common knowledge. The lovely old house had been in an advanced state of dilapidation when Barney inherited it. A white elephant if ever there was one.

"By now," Dilys said, "he must be wondering about the future. He was always such a one for the past—Hattons at Mortiboys for Heaven knows how many years. So he must think of the future, too. And who could he find to marry? Suitable, I mean?"

One part of my mind detached itself for a minute and examined that question. Out of the past, out of boyhood memories, usually a bit obscured by the interests of the present and the future (laying in wait for old men to whom the present was unacceptable and the future a blank?), I could remember how often Barney, on his rough-coated cob, I even remembered the name—Joby—had ridden off, when class was dismissed, to take the long way round to his home and look at Mortiboys. He had been obsessed with it, and still was, and doubtless its future did concern him—as the future of Ockley concerned me, and as, had he been a normal man, the future of Abhurst would have concerned Bowdegrave. Any man with property longs for an heir, and when the property is entwined with a family tradition the longing is sharpened.

I said, "Very logical, my dear. But that is no concern of ours. I do not propose to have any contact, however indirect, made between Mortiboys and Ockley. And I hope that you have not forgotten that you gave me your word, your most solemn word, never to see or speak . . ."

"I've kept it," she said quickly.

"That I don't doubt. But you made this preposterous suggestion; you mentioned his name."

"Oh well," she said. "It was all such a long time ago. And it seemed such a good arrangement. I can't think of anybody else. Can you?"

I could not.

I said, "That's enough matchmaking for one evening. Come to bed."

I was in my what-the-hell-has-Barney-Hatton-got-that-I-haven't-got mood.

As usual it seemed quite satisfactory, but I did not, as I usually did, drop off to sleep. I lay and worried, not about me and Dilys, but about Annabelle. I had said lightly enough that she and her mother must go to the House in the Woods, but my own curious little experience there had given me a feeling of something wrong. Even those bovine Pratt women, offered the place rent-free and all found, hadn't stayed. Was it a place in which to put two women of a more sensitive kind, one of whom was not quite right in the head? The answer was: No! There was no other place vacant in Ockley. Tomorrow I must start riding round and spying out the land. Tomorrow Mrs. Horner must be placated, told that something was being done, asked to be patient.

Placating was not very easy. Mrs. Horner knew her worth. "I'm not saying, Sir Stephen, that I ain't sorry for the afflicted. What I am saying is I can't do with her about. There's things I haven't bothered her ladyship with, little things, but bothersome when you're busy. And after all, if she know her own name she should remember that she's a lady and keep out of the kitchen. Well, all right then, sir. Just to oblige, just a week or two."

I had absolutely no luck at all. Not a house or a cottage to let in the neighbourhood, Cleveley, the Minshams, Nettleton, Muchanger. I'm on good terms with my neighbours, they would have helped me if they could. The point was that agriculture was booming, partly as a result of the war with France which meant that marginal land, once given over to sheep, was coming under the plough: and where one man can tend three hundred acres or more, devoted to sheep, the same acreage made arable demands twenty: and partly because the new method of overwintering stock, a method in which I was in full agreement and practised myself, meant that cattle could be stall fed; another demand on labour.

As abortive attempt followed abortive attempt, I began to ask myself: What is so wrong with the House in the Woods? Perhaps just some silly old story, handed on, whispered about. Nobody who has not tried to keep in touch—as I had done—with ordinary people can possibly know how deeply, how darkly the roots go. Perhaps, well before my time, something had happened in that solid little house and every woman who lived in it afterwards had been affected by the story, imagining things. And where did that leave me? Knowing no story; simply feeling cold and miserable and stripped down, reduced.

Finally I decided that the only thing to do was to make a test on Annabelle. Ridiculing the whole business I still felt that I should not be easy in my mind until she had seen the house, been alone in it for a few minutes and remained cheerful. If she found the place depressing, I should know—I was now almost as attuned to her moods as to Dilys's; if she said so little as, "It is rather lonely," I should abandon the scheme and set about something that perhaps I should have considered before—turning a bit of my own house into a self-contained unit with its own entrance, its own kitchen. This, because Ockley Manor is a compact, not rambling house, not many rooms but those there are large and well-proportioned, would not be an easy task, and it would cost money; but I could not doom Annabelle to live in a house which had the capacity to lower one's spirits and destroy one's self-esteem; poor little girl, she'd been through so much lately.

As always, at this point my thoughts came full circle and I thought: How ludicrous; it's a perfectly good house!

It was now September and one of those beautiful days which, though acknowledging that high summer is past and autumn bound to come, have a special charm, a mellowness. I invited her to see the house, and decided that we would walk so that she might judge for herself exactly how remote the place was. On the way we picked and ate blackberries and she talked cheerfully; resigned to the move, sure that Mamma would enjoy having a kitchen to herself.

The second-flowering of roses on the little porch was over now, but the garden had been cleared of briars and seedlings and a few hardy wild flowers had taken advantage of the clearance to spring up and add their colour to that of the indestructible marigolds.

"What a delightful little house," Annabelle said. The rubbish the Pratt women had left behind had been disposed of, the fresh whitewash and paint that had been applied shone. It was a delightful little house.

"Properly furnished," I said, a trifle apologetically, "I'm sure that in here"—I opened the door of the room which had so much depressed me—"there is room for a piano."

"Mamma will appreciate that," Annabelle said. Did I imagine it, or had her voice taken on a flatness? I did not imagine that she gave a slight shiver and glanced around as though searching for some source of draught. I myself had felt the cold as soon as I entered the house.

"With a carpet," I said, and my voice had gone flat, too: "I thought a really gay Oriental one. And velvet curtains . . ."

She said, "Stephen, we have been nothing but a nuisance to you. And an expense. I have tried—God knows I tried—but Mamma and I were born to be unfortunate. Think what her life has been. She lost her father and her property, even her country. Then she married. Perhaps that was happy; she never refers to her married life, or to my father, but he died very soon; when I was about two. So she went back to Nethergate and worked, keeping that old cousin alive and he treated her cruelly, going back on his promise. She slaved, she almost killed herself in Baildon keeping me alive and at school . . ."

I—for whom life had been easy, and on the whole pleasant —said, "Life is hard, my dear."

She turned and looked out of the window beyond which the green wood loomed.

"Look at Abhurst," she said. "I had no *feeling* for Charles apart from gratitude for kindness, but Mamma had done so much and she so longed for security. I intended to be a good wife to him. So here we are, after all that striving, a burden to you. It makes one wonder what it is all about . . ."

Was this the effect of that uncheerful house? I was feeling it myself. In fact on me this morning the stripping down process went to the limit. I looked at Annabelle d'Aubigny and thought: Yes, you would have been a good wife, not just a beautiful, pampered doll. Not somebody always to be anxiously watched. I thought: If I hadn't met Dilys and become as infatuated with her as she is with . . .

I abandoned my intention of leaving Annabelle alone in the place: I said, "Come on, Annabelle, let's get into the sunshine."

She gave another little shiver and said, "It *is* rather chilly."

Outside we were ourselves again. She said, "Stephen, I'm sorry. I spoke too freely. I should not complain. I should be—

and I am—grateful for your kindness and generosity. I've made you look quite sad."

Not since my mother died, three years earlier, had anyone noticed any change of expression on my face. I was the watchful one.

"I'm not sad. Just thoughtful. That little house is more isolated than I realised. I had no idea that it was so far from us. I'd always ridden, you see. Walking you notice more." I was edging into a position where I could abandon this scheme and offer a substitute.

"Mamma will not mind," Annabelle said. "People don't mean much to her, living in the past as she does."

"What about you?"

"So long as Mamma is happy. *And* Mrs. Horner!"

I looked sideways at her and thought again of the portrait which I had thought so unlike her. Madame de Goncourt had an artist's insight which might make her a great portrait painter, but hardly a popular one! She had seen the fortitude, the bearing-up-bravely quality. I thought: No, you shall *not* be condemned to a lonely life in that uncheerful house. Ockley must be refashioned so that Mamma can have her own establishment; damn the inconvenience and the cost!

Still preparing the ground for my change of plan, I said:

"I was visualising Dilys paying you frequent visits. She has so few friends of her own age. But now I realise, I think it would be too far."

Annabelle gave me a quick look, seemed about to say something and then decided not to. We walked on. It was almost lunchtime when we reached the house.

The door of the morning room was half-open and as soon as we were in the hall Dilys said, "Oh, here they are," from within the room.

Annabelle said, "I expect Mamma has tired her," and went in, prepared to take over. I followed.

Madame d'Aubigny was not in the room. John Franklin was.

Then what happened? It was rather like being a witness to an accident. You see everything but find it difficult afterwards to believe or to remember what you have seen.

Franklin stood up. Dilys said, "Annabelle, dear, this is . . ." And then stopped, aware of something wrong, or at least peculiar.

It was a bit like that nursery game called "Attitudes" where everybody assumes grotesque postures and somebody claps hands or blows a whistle and there you stand, petrified.

They just stared at each other, rigid in attitudes of amazement and disbelief. If I remember rightly they both blenched. They stood there, static, staring. And the thing was catching; for a second or two Dilys and I stood staring and dumb too. She recovered first.

"You have already met?" she asked, hitting upon the likeliest explanation.

Franklin said, "Yes. In a blizzard."

"It was February," Annabelle said.

He broke his pose, moved towards her. "I looked for you," he said. "I left for Wiltshire the next day. I was delayed there. When I got back it was Easter. The school was closed. Then I went again and you'd gone. Nobody seemed to know . . ."

Annabelle said, "I . . . Mamma and I went to London."

"Ah," he said.

Dilys and I might not have been there. She is not accustomed to being ignored.

"Mr. Franklin very kindly came over to tell you that he has a cottage," she said.

I had not included Nethergate in my search, mainly because it is not a village; simply a big house and estate with, I had imagined, all the cottages let with the farms on an arrangement similar to the one existing between me and Rowe.

"That was very civil of you," I said. With an effort he dragged his attention from Annabelle and muttered that somebody had told him that I was looking for a place. Then back to Annabelle again. "I kept wondering about you—and the world and everything. And whether you ever found that shoulder."

"I did. In an unexpected place. And you were quite right."

They spoke as though they had known one another for years; actually they didn't even know each other's names. Annabelle, making some attempt to include me and Dilys, said, "Mr. . . . Mr. . . ." and stopped, laughing a little. Dilys completed the introduction, adding that she had invited him to stay for luncheon.

That made me think of Mamma.

Love at first sight is not as rare as people think and this was obviously a case of it. Mutual, too. But could he stomach Mamma?

I said softly to Dilys, "Where is Madame d'Aubigny?"

"Gracious! She must have slipped out. Not, I hope, to the kitchen."

"Is there any way of preventing her coming to table?"

Dilys looked at the pair, now saying in amazement that for the last fortnight—ever since his return from Wiltshire—they'd been living within a few miles of each other and not known!

Dilys said sagely, "He might as well know the worst."

We did not know it then, but Madame d'Aubigny had been interfering again, this time with old Pike, our butler; a more easygoing character than Mrs. Horner. (I said to her, sir, I said, all right then; have it your own way. You have to humour the mad.) Fresh from her triumph she was in a fairly benevolent mood and took the word *Franklin* pretty well.

"Not a real cousin," she explained. "Lady Rosaleen was my relative. She died very suddenly. I was lighting the fire. You may not have observed this, but any familiar name, either of a place or a person, seems to leap from a page of even the closest print. I could never explain to Joanna."

Franklin looked a bit confused: Who wouldn't? But not aghast. She was in a talkative mood and rambled on, making what sounded like sensible statements followed by irrelevancies. He quickly adopted the technique which it had taken us—even Annabelle—some time to perfect, enough attention to seem civil, a reply when one was needed, a tactful ignoring of the incoherence.

We managed some ordinary conversation, during which he informed us that he had sold his Wiltshire estate. "It was my home and I was attached to it, but I found it impossible to run both places properly. I seemed to be forever on the road . . ."

"Precisely," Madame d'Aubigny interrupted. "Such a waste of time. I once remarked that only a witch on a broomstick could keep such a schedule."

I noticed something for the first time; enlightened by what Annabelle had said that morning. Madame d'Aubigny's mind wandered, she lived in the past, but her memory seemed to be selective and mainly concerned with rather trivial things. The name *Franklin*, for example, had elicited a remark or two about Lady Rosaleen, nothing about her work at Nethergate or a broken promise. So far as I knew she never spoke of her father, her husband, or even of Abhurst, or the penny-pinching in London. It was as though her mind, having cracked, retained only what was tolerable. Nothing very happy; perhaps, poor woman, she had nothing happy to recall; but on the other hand nothing really distressing.

Nevertheless, when John Franklin was gone, after offering a pressing invitation for us all to go and dine at Nethergate next day, I shared Annabelle's anxiety as to the effect the visit might have on Mamma. "So far," Annabelle said, looking worried, "apart from that visit to Baildon, she has been nowhere that had any meaning for her. Finding herself back at Nethergate might upset her."

Dilys said, a trifle callously, I thought, "You need not worry, Annabelle dear. If she suddenly went rabid and *bit* him it would make no difference. In all my days I've never seen anybody take such a toss."

I thought: Oh no? What about me? Another case of remembering only what was tolerable? I also thought: Jealous?

I said, "You never know, Annabelle. Finding herself in familiar surroundings might be beneficial."

She gave me a little, grateful smile. "They will be familiar," she said. "I asked had anything been changed and he said not. Harriet and John had great plans, becoming more and more ambitious, so that in the end . . ."

"Well," I said, "we shall see . . ."

We saw.

The outing began badly. Dilys said, "Believe it or not, Mamma absolutely refuses to leave the house without her pearls. No woman is safe in this wicked world without a string of pearls. I was obliged to lend her mine. My mother's; you may not remember."

I did. My memory did not exercise the censorship that exists with Dilys, who is quite sane, and with Madame d'Aubigny, who is not. On the day when Dilys and I went back to Mortiboys to collect the few things that were rightly hers, the dumb girl who had been Jassy Woodroffe's bewitched slave, and who had hanged with her, had hit me with a sweeping brush. Not a thing a man is likely to forget.

"I can only hope," Dilys said, "that they marry as soon as possible. I cannot bear very much more."

I said, "I think they will."

"If it can be done quickly enough. Before he realises what he is taking on. *He* certainly does not need a mother-in-law who can cook and mend sheets. I said what I did to Annabelle—about rabies—to give her confidence. This is no time to be missish."

Nethergate is rather like Abhurst's oldest part, smaller of course. Franklin had made no attempt to conceal his eagerness and was waiting for us, outside the house with the main door open. Madame d'Aubigny greeted him, politely but without the slightest sign of recognition. We all went into the hall, where a footman took the women's wraps—in September even a golden day can become a chilly evening. We then went on into the drawing room, which at Nethergate is on the ground floor.

Annabelle said, in a voice of ecstasy, "It is exactly the same. I am so glad! The most beautiful room in the world!"

I had never seen much to admire in it and her appreciation of it had nothing to do with her sex; Dilys had called it cold and shabby. It was pallid, what it had ever had of colour was faded and the marble-topped tables contributed to the cold effect.

Madame d'Aubigny, in a rather distant voice, refused a glass of Madeira, and when Annabelle and Dilys seated themselves she remained standing, looking more and more troubled and patting at herself as though she expected to find something concealed in her bodice or in the folds of her skirt. Finally she said, "Where are my keys?"

Dilys made a little face at me. Annabelle said, "Don't worry about them, Mamma. Come and sit down." She patted the sofa beside her.

Franklin seemed to understand.

"I think I know where they are, ma'am. Wait here, I shan't be a minute."

He went out quickly. Mamma moved to one of the windows and ran her finger along a glazing bar, then studied the finger with disgust.

"Here you are," Franklin said, hurrying in and handing her a jingling bunch of keys, some labelled.

Her face lit up. "Thank you." She scrutinised the labels. "Yes, all in order." She moved purposefully to the door. Annabelle said "Mamma" in a sharper voice than she usually used towards her mother, and jumped up to pursue her, but John Franklin put out his hand and took her, firmly but gently by the arm.

"Let her go," he said. "She'll come to no harm."

"She'll do some." Annabelle said. "You don't understand. People can't bear her meddling. At Ockley the cook gave notice . . ."

"Well, what of it? If they all give notice, we can get new ones. Come and sit down and don't worry." I noticed the use of the word *we*, and the tacit assumption that Madame d'Aubigny was going to be at Nethergate long enough to set everybody by the ears. When he began to explain that the property he had come to offer me yesterday was in fact the Dower House, until lately occupied by one of Harriet's impoverished relatives, I thanked him warmly for the offer and said that I had been doing a little preliminary scouting and might not actually need the accommodation at all. It became increasingly plain that I should not.

Presently the butler sidled in, looking slightly flustered.

"Would it be convenient for me to have a word with you, sir?"

"Go ahead." The man placed himself at the far side of the sofa which Franklin shared with Annabelle and spoke so quietly that I caught only the words, "Madame d'Aubigny"— he had at least got the name right, which none of my lot ever had, and something about "the table," and "wine."

"That's all right. You just do exactly as Madame d'Aubigny tells you and that will suit me. You may tell everybody that."

Had I adopted this masterful attitude and not tried to please Mrs. Horner, had I not felt that the House in the Woods was not quite suitable, then I should not have gone house-hunting, and Franklin and Annabelle might not have met again. He was not a very close friend, and even had he come to dine with us Annabelle would have been out of sight, controlling Mamma and eating off a tray. If he'd heard that some people named d'Aubigny were staying at Ockley it would have conveyed nothing to him, since he did not know the name. I suppose a belief in Fate is the last remnant of superstition and deplorable in a man of reason; but I felt it strongly then. It had ramifications, too; if Dilys and Chris hadn't been hell-bent on an *affaire*, we should never have gone to Abhurst. Then what would have become of those two helpless women? Sobering thought. To escape from it I looked about, noting that in this room, too, little had been changed. I had not been a frequent guest at this table; too young to share old Jack Franklin's legendary hospitality, not on close terms with his heir; but I could remember the Gainsborough portrait—a very good one—of Lady Rosaleen and her two sons, which had always hung over the fireplace. This evening it was not there. In its place hung a rather mediocre landscape with some cows in the foreground and a church steeple showing above a line of trees. Possibly a memento of Franklin's Wiltshire home. I could understand that the portrait would have little sentimental value for the present owner, still it had been a beautiful picture and the change was no improvement.

When the ladies had left us I said, "I see you've moved the Gainsborough."

"The what?"

I nodded.

"Bless me!" he said. "I hadn't noticed. It was here this morning . . . It's a funny thing, until I'd met Annabelle—I mean the first time, in the blizzard—I'd never liked that picture much. The lady looked so starchy. But there was something about the little boy, once I'd seen Annabelle, that reminded me of her. And last night, and again this morning I looked at it and thought how right I was. And of course they would be distant cousins, in a way."

"Madame d'Aubigny was related to Lady Rosaleen. I'd hazard a guess that *she* had it moved. She's never gone quite so far at my place, but then I never issued orders that she must be obeyed."

He said, imperturbable as ever, "Well, if she's to live here, she must have things to her liking."

"Is she?"

"I hope so. I plan to ask Annabelle to marry me tomorrow. It may not be according to the rules, asking a girl at the third time of meeting, but we've lost enough time."

"I asked Dilys the fifth time," I said, reckoning back.

"And it worked. You're happy."

"Oh yes, we're happy. I sincerely hope you will be."

"And all due to you. When I think . . . I can never be grateful enough. Well, shall we?" Longing to get back to the beloved.

Actually, for a couple four years and more married to be alone with a couple absolutely engrossed with each other is a bit dull. And Dilys looked tired. Again I attributed it to boredom. I thought to myself, an early move, an early night, then it will be tomorrow, and he can ask his question, they'll be engaged and there will be no need to keep up this pretence at chaperonage. Of Annabelle's answer there was never a second's doubt. After all she had been willing to marry Bowdegrave, for whom she felt nothing but gratitude. She was now head over heels in love. When Franklin and I went into the drawing room a tea tray was brought in by Dilys, as the married woman, should have wielded the teapot, but she said, "You pour, Annabelle," and Annabelle seated herself on a chair, white, garlanded with the ghosts of rosebuds and forget-me-nots, and took charge of the tray on one of those pale marble tables. She said:

"I still think I must be dreaming. I used to steal into this room and pretend that I was pouring tea for my friends." She embraced us all with an entranced look.

"You didn't know me then," John Franklin said.

"I didn't know anybody. All my friends were imaginary. Until that night. And by then even the room was a dream; I never expected to see it again. Or you. But I used to think of it, of being here, pouring tea for you—and my friends, of course."

There was a little talk about chance, accident, coincidence. Dilys looked tired-bored-sick, more so every minute and I thought: Of course, poor darling, she never saw anything romantic about me; I was just a refuge when she was distraught and miserable and frightened. All this storybook stuff must be very irksome to her.

I made some excuse about having to be up very early next morning and stood up. Annabelle jumped like somebody too suddenly wakened and said, "Mamma! I had completely forgotten her."

"I have no doubt she's happily occupied," Franklin said. "Come on, we'll go and find her."

They went out together. Dilys said, "She'll lead him a fine dance." She did not mean Annabelle.

When found, Madame d'Aubigny refused to budge. What had happened, I think, was that her mind had ceased to wander and had settled. Perhaps, living at Nethergate, looking after old Jack Franklin, she had been reasonably happy, and back in the same place she clutched at the chance to be happy again.

She had, in the course of a single evening, ensconced herself very comfortably in a room not far from the kitchen. When Annabelle came back and appealed to me—"Perhaps she might listen to you, Stephen"—and I went, she was seated at one end of a table, going through what looked to me like a lot of household books and a sheaf of bills. She'd been fed, a tray at the other end of the table bore witness to that; and I had been right about the picture; at least I assumed so; propped face against the wall, it was the right size and shape. She looked far more composed than I had ever seen her. Even that night before the tragedy at Abhurst she had been uneasy, incapable of concentration. Then, under the shock, her mind had cracked and for three months she had been picking over the pieces—this to be accepted, that to be rejected.

Now, in Nethergate, several bits of what was acceptable seemed to have coalesced. Crazy still, of course, but not shattered, not wandering.

She greeted me with a scowl. "I thought I gave orders that I was not to be disturbed," she said. "Whatever it is, it must wait. I am busy."

That she should not recognise me was understandable. Her complete repudiation of Annabelle was amazing. She made no distinction between us, Dilys and me and John Franklin and her own daughter. She said, addressing us as one, "I cannot be bothered with you now. I have too much to do. The books have not been well kept. And some of the bills are extortionate."

Annabelle cried and said she could not possibly leave Mamma here, all distraught as she was, and John Franklin said why not? She seemed happy and he'd see that no harm came to her and he said that the last time he'd seen Annabelle cry he'd offered his shoulder to cry on and she'd scorned it; how about now? So she leaned against him for a bit, and cried, and he took advantage of the situation and hugged her and said he'd be over to Ockley first thing in the morning, and please not to worry, please not to cry . . .

About halfway home Annabelle said dolefully, "It had been such a happy evening, hadn't it? And now she is there without so much as a comb . . ."

"She'll soon find one," Dilys said, rather drily.

"She seemed not to *know* me," Annabelle said. "Did you notice? It's never been like that before. However vague she was, she's always known me."

Once again Dilys's reply lacked her usual amiability:

"If she doesn't know you she won't scold you." It was true that some of Mamma's remarks to her daughter had been tinged with acerbity.

Annabelle was instantly defensive, "She only criticised me —very mildly—because she was worried about me. Nobody ever had a better mother."

This again was a relationship outside Dilys's understanding; her own mother had run away with a lover when Dilys was very young and she'd been left with her father, embittered by his loss and drinking hard in an effort to forget. Until she married me Dilys's life had been loveless, and my love had never completely satisfied her. Somehow that thought sent my mind back to what Annabelle had said about Madame d'Aubigny's hard life: "She slaved, she almost killed herself to keep me alive and at school." I thought I saw a possible explanation of Mamma's curious behaviour this evening. Without even admitting it to herself she might always have regarded her child as a burden, beloved, but a burden nevertheless. She may have sensed somehow that in future Annabelle would be safe; she could cast off all responsibility, even that of remembering.

It was all guesswork, of course, but it occupied my mind during the rest of the drive home. With Dilys in her present mood silence was best.

I thought that if Madame d'Aubigny persisted in this masquerade, and something about the way she had slipped into place assured me that she would, it would be embarrassing for Annabelle and for Franklin. But Annabelle would have the comfort of knowing that Mamma was happy, and Franklin was as well-equipped to face such a situation as any man I knew. Any malicious gossip who spoke of exploiting a half-witted relative need only to be confronted by Madame d'Aubigny. The one thing she had never lost was dignity.

"We've been extremely lucky," Dilys said. "Thank God for John Franklin."

"I was doing my best," I said. "Only yesterday . . ." Only yesterday but it seemed like the remote past. "I had a plan." Did I not deserve a word, a thought of recommendation for being willing to hack Ockley Manor about, sacrifice the little room that was my estate office in order that Mamma should have a kitchen, spend money on a partition, and a new entrance? "I couldn't have you worried any more," I said. "And the House in the Woods was very . . . damp."

Dilys unpinned her hair and shook it out.

"Then I'm doubly thankful to John Franklin! Of all the lunatic ideas! We are going to need all our space! I didn't want to raise any false hopes, but I am sure now. We're going to have a baby."

I said *God,* and *Darling* and *Dilys*. I said all the ordinary things—being an ordinary man.